Vampires in Love

VAMPIRES in LOVE

EDITED BY
ROSALIND M. GREENBERG
& MARTIN H. GREENBERG

FALL RIVER PRESS

Book design by Michele Trombley

Fall River Press
122 Fifth Avenue
New York, NY 10011

ISBN: 978-1-4351-1852-2

Printed and bound in the United States of America

1 3 5 7 9 10 8 6 4 2

CONTENTS

$\mathcal{I}$NTRODUCTION

JOHN HELFERS

The vampire, that legendary, immortal creature of the night, has served many purposes throughout history. From cautionary early folktales and legends spun by villagers as warnings against corpses that might rise from the grave with a thirst for blood, to the explorations of the erotic in poems such as "The Vampire," by Heinrich August Ossenfelder (published in 1748), the vampire has come to symbolize a variety of uninhibited behaviors and unholy appetites in numerous cultures. The most famous fictional treatment of the vampire (at least, until recently), Bram Stoker's *Dracula*, interpreted the titular bloodsucker not as a ravishing creature of darkness, so much as a stealthy assault on Victorian England ways and morals by suave, suspicious foreigners.

During the twentieth century, the vampire underwent several metamorphoses, related to the decade in which it popped up. From the fanged monstrosities that appeared during the pulp era to Chelsea Quinn-Yarbro's seminal Count Saint-Germain, one of the earliest recastings of the vampire as hero in the late 1970s; the brooding, attractive Louis, Lestat, and company that Anne Rice re-imagined in her lush, modern Gothic tales; and Nancy A. Collins's kick-ass-and-take-no-names vampire-turned-vampire hunter Sonja Blue in the early 1990s.

The most recent reinterpretations are Charlaine Harris' Sookie Stackhouse series, J.R. Ward's *Brotherhood of the Black Dagger* series, and the worldwide bestselling young-adult novels (*Twilight*, *New Moon*, *Eclipse*, and *Breaking Dawn*) by Stephenie Meyer, featuring a teenage girl in love with a 200-year-old vampire who loves her but who cannot consummate their relationship for fear of killing her.

Meyer isn't the only one to capitalize on the vampire as a figure of sensuality and longing, particularly in the young-adult arena. Tales of hot, young-looking, but ancient-minded vampires are being written by Rachel Caine (the *Morganville Vampires* series), P. C. and Kristin Cast (the *House of Night* series), and L. J. Smith (the *Vampire Diaries*).

So what is the allure of vampires in love? It could be many things—but what it all comes down to is that vampire romance stories fulfill many of the same objectives that any other kind of romance story fulfills—an often incredible story of two people overcoming whatever impediments fate or society may throw in their path to be together at the end of the novel. And what could be a more powerful obstacle than when one of the couple is a vampire? If romances are about taming the bestial, savage nature of a man, then one who could easily break his lover's neck or drain every last drop of blood from her surely qualifies. And what a sense of power can be had by imagining that this master of the night, who is stronger, faster, much more dangerous than any ordinary man—who exists on human blood—can be tamed by the charm (and sometimes wiles) of a (usually) relatively ordinary woman?

Mind you, although there are a lot stories that partner female vampires and human men (several of which are included in this anthology), the vast majority of stories of this kind are aimed squarely at the female audience. Say what you will, but the fact is that the market for romantic vampire fiction is very deep, and seems to be insatiable (pun intended).

With that in mind, we've assembled some of the very best vampire romance stories published during the last rise of the "vampire as seductor"

wave, which has yet to crest, as far as I can see. We're pleased to offer a rare short story from Gothic expert Anne Rice, wherein a young woman travels to her family's secluded country estate, Rampling Gate, despite the wishes of her deceased father, and finds out just what is so sinister about their ancestral home. Bestselling author L. A. Banks tells of a lonely female vampire who's been seeking a companion for those long, endless nights, and who just might have found one in a cop who's infiltrating the mob. Noir author Ed Gorman reveals his softer side in "Valentine from a Vampire," about a normal cab driver who risks everything to save the woman of his dreams before she is turned into one of the undead. Kristine Kathryn Rusch gives us "The Beautiful, the Damned," and reveals just how immortal vampires while away their endless nights—and what happens when one of them falls in love all over again. In "Eternity Embraced," Larissa Ione tells of the most horrible choice a vampire slayer has to make—whether or not to put a stake in the heart of the man she loves. And Norman Partridge's "Do Not Hasten to Bid Me Adieu" tells the story of what might have happened after Stoker's *Dracula*, and of a love that goes beyond life—and death.

So here you have them: twenty stories (and one poem) celebrating the living and the undead, who come together in love (and occasionally lust) as men and women, and try to win the heart of that most attractive—and amoral—of creatures—the vampire.

VAMPIRE SESTINA

NEIL GAIMAN

I wait here at the boundaries of dream,
all shadow-wrapped. The dark air tastes of night,
so cold and crisp, and I wait for my love.
The moon has bleached the colour from her stone.
She'll come, and then we'll stalk this pretty world
alive to darkness and the tang of blood.

It is a lonely game, the quest for blood,
but still, a body's got the right to dream
and I'd not give it up for all the world.
The moon has leeched the darkness from the night.
I stand in the shadows, staring at her stone:
Undead, my lover . . . O, undead my love?

I dreamt you while I slept today and love
meant more to me than life—meant more than blood.
The sunlight sought me, deep beneath my stone,
more dead than any corpse but still a-dream
until I woke as vapour into night
and sunset forced me out into the world.

For many centuries I've walked the world
dispensing something that resembled love—
a stolen kiss, then back into the night
contented by the life and by the blood.
And come the morning I was just a dream,
cold body chilling underneath a stone.
I said I would not hurt you. Am I stone
to leave you prey to time and to the world?
I offered you a truth beyond your dreams
while all you had to offer was your love.
I told you not to worry, and that blood
tastes sweeter on the wing and late at night.

Sometimes my lovers rise to walk the night . . .
Sometimes they lie, cold corpse beneath a stone,
and never know the joys of bed and blood,
of walking through the shadows of the world;
instead they rot to maggots. O my love
they whispered you had risen, in my dream.

I've waited by your stone for half the night
but you won't leave your dream to hunt for blood.
Goodnight, my love. I offered you the world.

THE MASTER OF RAMPLING GATE

ANNE RICE

SPRING 1888

*R*ampling Gate. It was so real to us in the old pictures, rising like a fairy-tale castle out of its own dark wood. A wilderness of gables and chimneys between those two immense towers, gray stone walls mantled in ivy, mullioned windows reflecting the drifting clouds.

But why had Father never taken us there? And why, on his deathbed, had he told my brother that Rampling Gate must be torn down, stone by stone? "I should have done it, Richard," he said. "But I was born in that house, as my father was, and his father before him. You must do it now, Richard. It has no claim on you. Tear it down."

Was it any wonder that not two months after Father's passing, Richard and I were on the noon train headed south for the mysterious mansion that had stood upon the rise above the village of Rampling for four hundred years? Surely Father would have understood. How could we destroy the old place when we had never seen it?

But, as the train moved slowly through the outskirts of London I can't say we were very sure of ourselves, no matter how curious and excited we were.

Richard had just finished four years at Oxford. Two whirlwind social seasons in London had proved me something of a shy success. I still preferred scribbling poems and stories in my room to dancing the night away, but I'd kept that a good secret. And though we had lost our mother when we were little, Father had given us the best of everything. Now the carefree years were ended. We had to be independent and wise.

The evening before, we had pored over at the old pictures of Rampling Gate, recalling in hushed, tentative voices the night Father had taken those pictures down from the walls.

I couldn't have been more than six and Richard eight when it happened, yet we remembered well the strange incident in Victoria Station that had precipitated Father's uncharacteristic rage. We had gone there after supper to say farewell to a school friend of Richard's, and Father had caught a glimpse, quite unexpectedly, of a young man at the lighted window of an incoming train. I could remember the young man's face clearly to this day: remarkably handsome, with a head of lustrous brown hair, his large black eyes regarding Father with the saddest expression as Father drew back. *"Unspeakable horror!"* Father had whispered. Richard and I had been too amazed to speak a word. Later that night, Father and Mother quarreled, and we crept out of our rooms to listen on the stairs.

"That he should dare to come to London!" Father said over and over. "Is it not enough for him to be the undisputed master of Rampling Gate?"

How we puzzled over it as little ones! Who was this stranger, and how could he be master of a house that belonged to our father, a house that had been left in the care of an old, blind housekeeper for years?

But now after looking at the pictures again, it was too dreadful to think of Father's exhortation. And too exhilarating to think of the house itself. I'd packed my manuscripts, for—who knew?—maybe in that melancholy and exquisite setting I'd find exactly the inspiration I needed for the story I'd been writing in my head.

Yet there was something almost illicit about the excitement I felt. I saw in my mind's eye the pale young man again, with his black greatcoat and red woolen cravat. Like bone china, his complexion had been. Strange to remember so vividly, And I realized now that in those few remarkable moments, he had created for me an ideal of masculine beauty that I had never questioned since. But Father had been so angry, I felt an unmistakable pang of guilt.

* * *

It was late afternoon when the old trap carried us up the gentle slope from the little railway station and we had our first real look at the house. The sky had paled to a deep rose hue beyond a hank of softly gilded clouds, and the last rays of the sun struck the uppermost panes of the leaded windows and filled them with solid gold.

"Oh, but it's too majestic," I whispered, "Too like a great cathedral, and to think that it belongs to us!"

Richard gave me the smallest kiss on the cheek.

I wanted with all my heart to jump down from the trap and draw near on foot, letting those towers slowly grow larger and larger above me, but our old horse was gaining speed.

When we reached the massive front door Richard and I were spirited into the great hall by the tiny figure of the blind housekeeper Mrs. Blessington, our footfalls echoing loudly on the marble tile, and our eyes dazzled by the dusty shafts of light that fell on the long oak table and its heavily carved chairs, on the somber tapestries that stirred ever so slightly against the soaring walls.

"Richard, it is an enchanted place!" I cried, unable to contain myself.

Mrs. Blessington laughed gaily, her dry hand closing tightly on mine.

We found our bedchambers well aired, with snow-white linen on the beds and fires blazing cozily on the hearths. The small, diamond-paned

windows opened on a glorious view of the lake and the oaks that enclosed it and the few scattered lights that marked the village beyond.

That night we laughed like children as we supped at the great oak table, our candles giving only a feeble light. And afterward we had a fierce battle of pocket billiards in the game room and a little too much brandy, I fear.

It was just before I went to bed that I asked Mrs. Blessington if there had been anyone in this house since my father left it, years before:

"No, my dear," she said quickly, fluffing the feather pillows. "When your father went away to Oxford, he never came back."

"There was never a young intruder after that? . . ." I pressed her, though in truth I had little appetite for anything that would disturb the happiness I felt. How I loved the Spartan cleanliness of this bedchamber, the walls bare of paper and ornament, the high luster of the walnut-paneled bed.

"A young intruder?" With an unerring certainty about her surroundings, she lifted the poker and stirred the fire. "No, dear. Whatever made you think there was?"

"Are there no ghost stories, Mrs. Blessington?" I asked suddenly, startling myself. *Unspeakable horror.* But what was I thinking—that that young man had not been real?

"Oh, no, darling," she said, smiling. "No ghost would ever dare to trouble Rampling Gate.

* * *

Nothing, in fact, troubled the serenity of the days that followed—long walks through the overgrown gardens, trips in the little skiff to and fro across the lake, tea under the hot glass of the empty conservatory. Early evening found us reading and writing by the library fire.

All our inquiries in the village met with the same answers: The villagers cherished the house. There was not a single disquieting legend or tale.

How were we going to tell them of Father's edict? How were we going
to remind ourselves?

Richard was ending a wealth of classical material on the library shelves
and I had the desk in the corner entirely to myself.

Never had I known such quiet. It seemed the atmosphere of Rampling
Gate permeated my simplest written descriptions and wove its way
richly into the plots and characters I created. The Monday after our
arrival I finished my first real short story, and after copying out a fresh
draft, I went off to the village on foot to post it boldly to the editors of
Blackwood's Magazine.

It was a warm afternoon, and I took my time as I came back. What
had disturbed our father so about this lovely corner of England?
What had so darkened his last hours that he laid his curse upon this
spot? My heart opened to this unearthly stillness, to an indisputable
magnificence that caused me utterly to forget myself. There were
times here when I felt I was a disembodied intellect drifting through
a fathomless silence, up and down garden paths and stone corridors
that had witnessed too much to take cognizance of one small and
fragile young woman who in random moments actually talked aloud
to the suits of armor around her, to the broken statues in the garden,
the fountain cherubs who had had no water to pour from their conches
for years and years.

But was there in this loveliness some malignant force that was eluding
us still, some untold story? *Unspeakable horror* . . . Even in the flood
of brilliant sunlight, those words gave me a chill.

As I came slowly up the slope I saw Richard walking lazily
along the uneven shore of the lake. Now and then he glanced up
at the distant battlements, his expression dreamy, almost blissfully
contented.

Rampling Gate had him. And I understood perfectly because it also
had me.

With a new sense of determination I went to him and placed my hand gently on his arm. For a moment he looked at me as if he did not even know me, and then he said softly:

"How will I ever do it, Julie? And one way or the other, it will be on my conscience all my life."

"It's time to seek advice, Richard," I said. "Write to our lawyers in London. Write to Father's clergyman, Dr. Matthews. Explain everything. We cannot do this alone."

* * *

It was three o'clock in the morning when I opened my eyes. But I had been awake for a long time. And I felt not fear, lying there alone, but something else—some vague and relentless agitation, some sense of emptiness and need that caused me finally to rise from my bed. What was this house, really? A place, or merely a state of mind? What was it doing to my soul?

I felt overwhelmed, yet shut out of some great and dazzling secret. Driven by an unbearable restlessness, I pulled on my woolen wrapper and my slippers and went into the hall.

The moonlight fell full on the oak stairway, and the vestibule far below . . . . Maybe I could write of the confusion I suffered now, put on paper the inexplicable longing I felt. Certainly it was worth the effort, and I made my way soundlessly down the steps.

The great hall gaped before me, the moonlight here and there touching upon a pair of crossed swords or a mounted shield. But far beyond, in the alcove just outside the library, I saw the uneven glow of the fire. So Richard was there. A sense of well-being pervaded me and quieted me. At the same time, the distance between us seemed endless and I became desperate to cross it, hurrying past the long supper table and finally into the alcove before the library doors.

The fire blazed beneath the stone mantelpiece and a figure sat in the leather chair before it, bent over a loose collection of pages that he held in his slender hands. He was reading the pages eagerly, and the fire suffused his face with a warm, golden light.

But it was not Richard. It was the same young man I had seen on the train in Victoria Station fifteen years ago. And not a single aspect of that taut young face had changed. There was the very same hair, thick and lustrous and only carelessly combed as it hung to the collar of his black coat, and those dark eyes that looked up suddenly and fixed me with a most curious expression as I almost screamed.

We stared at each other across that shadowy room, I stranded in the doorway, he visibly and undeniably shaken that I had caught him unawares. My heart stopped.

And in a split second he rose and moved toward me, closing the gap between us, reaching out with those slender white hands.

"Julie!" he whispered, in a voice so low that it seemed my own thoughts were speaking to me. But this was no dream. He was holding me and the scream had broken loose from me, deafening, uncontrollable and echoing from the four walls.

I was alone. Clutching at the door frame; I staggered forward, and then in a moment of perfect clarity I saw the young stranger again, saw him standing in the open door to the garden, looking back over his shoulder; then he was gone.

I could not stop screaming. I could not stop even as I heard Richard's voice calling me, heard his feet pound down that broad, hollow staircase and through the great hall. I could not stop even as he shook me, pleaded with me, settled me in a chair.

Finally I managed to describe what I had seen.

"But you know who it was!" I said almost hysterically. "It was he—the young man from the train!"

"Now, wait," Richard said. "He had his back to the fire, Julie. And you could not see his face clearly—"

"Richard, it was he! Don't you understand? He touched me. He called me Julie," I whispered. "Good God, Richard, look at the fire. I didn't light it—he did. He was here!"

All but pushing Richard out of the way, I went to the heap of papers that lay strewn on the carpet before the hearth. "My story," I whispered, snatching up the pages. "He's been reading my story, Richard. And—dear God—he's read your letters, the letters to Mr. Partridge and Dr. Matthews, about tearing down the house!"

"Surely you don't believe it was the same man, Julie, after all these years . . . ?"

"But he has not changed, Richard, not in the smallest detail. There is no mistake, I tell you. It was the very same man!"

* * *

The next day was the most trying since we had come. Together we commenced a search of the house. Darkness found us only half finished, frustrated everywhere by locked doors we could not open and old staircases that were not safe.

And it was also quite clear by suppertime that Richard did not believe I had seen anyone in the study at all. As for the fire—well, he had failed to put it out properly before going to bed; and the pages—well, one of us had put them there and forgotten them, of course . . .

But I knew what I had seen.

And what obsessed me more than anything else was the gentle countenance of the mysterious man I had glimpsed, the innocent eyes that had fixed on me for one moment before I screamed.

"You would be wise to do one very important thing before you retire," I said crossly. "Leave out a note to the effect that you do not intend to

tear down the house."

"Julie, you have created an impossible dilemma," Richard declared, the color rising in his face. "You insist we reassure this apparition that the house will not be destroyed, when in fact you verify the existence of the very creature that drove our father to say what he did."

"Oh, I wish I had never come here!" I burst out suddenly.

"Then we should go, and decide this matter at home."

"No—that's just it. I could never go without knowing. I could never go on living without knowing now!"

* * *

Anger must be an excellent antidote to fear, for surely something worked to alleviate my natural alarm. I did not undress that night, but rather sat in the darkened bedroom, gazing at the small square of diamond-paned window until I heard the house fall quiet. When the grandfather clock in the great hall chimed the hour of eleven, Rampling Gate was, as usual, fast asleep.

I felt a dark exultation as I imagined myself going out of the room and down the stairs. But I knew I should wait one more hour. I should let the night reach its peak. My heart was beating too fast, and dreamily I recollected the face I had seen, the voice that had said my name.

Why did it seem in retrospect so intimate, that we had known each other before, spoken together a thousand times? Was it because he had read my story, those words that came from my very soul?

"Who are you?" I believe I whispered aloud, "Where are you at this moment?" I uttered the word, "Come."

The door opened without a sound and he was standing there. He was dressed exactly as he had been the night before and his dark eyes were riveted on me with that same obvious curiosity, his mouth just a little slack, like that of a boy.

I sat forward, and he raised his finger as if to reassure me and gave a little nod.

"Ah, it is you!" I whispered.

"Yes," he said in a soft, unobtrusive voice.

"And you are not a spirit!" I looked at his mud-splattered boots, at the faintest smear of dust on that perfect white cheek.

"A spirit?" he asked almost mournfuliy, "Would that I were that."

Dazed, I watched him come toward me; the room darkened and I felt his cool, silken hands on my face. I had risen. I was standing before him, and I looked up into his eyes.

I heard my own heartbeat. I heard it as I had the night before, right at the moment I had screamed. Dear God, I was talking to him! He was in my room and I was talking to him! And then suddenly I was in his arms.

"Real, absolutely real!" I whispered, and a low, zinging sensation coursed through me so that I had to steady myself.

He was peering at me as if trying to comprehend something terribly important. His lips had a ruddy look to them, a soft look for all his handsomeness, as if he had never been kissed. A slight dizziness came over me, a slight confusion in which I was not at all sure that he was even there.

"Oh, but I am," he said, as if I had spoken my doubt. I felt his breath. against my cheek, and it was almost sweet. "I am here, and I have watched you ever since you came."

"Yes..."

My eyes were closing. In a dim flash, as of a match being struck, I saw my father, heard his voice. No, Julie . . . But that was surely a dream.

"Only a little kiss," said the voice of the one who was really here. I felt his lips against my neck. "I would never harm you. No harm ever for the children of this house. Just the little kiss, Julie, and the understanding that it imparts, that you cannot destroy Rampling Gate, Julie—that you can never, never drive me away."

The core of my being, that secret place where all desires and all commandments are nurtured, opened to him without a struggle or a sound. I would have fallen if he had not held me. My arms closed about him, my hands slipping into the soft, silken mass of his hair.

I was floating, and there was, as there had always been at Rampling Gate, an endless peace. It was Rampling Gate I felt enclosing me; it was that timeless and impenetrable secret that had opened itself at last . . . *A power within me of enormous ken . . . To see as a god sees, and take the depth of things as nimbly as the outward eyes can size and shape pervade . . .* Yes, those very words from Keats, which I had quoted in the pages of my story that he had read.

But in a violent instant he had released me. "Too innocent," he whispered.

I went reeling across the bedroom floor and caught hold of the frame of the window. I rested my forehead against the stone wall.

There was a tingling pain in my throat where his lips had touched me that was almost pleasurable; a delicious throbbing that would not stop, I knew what he was!

I turned and saw all the room clearly—the bed, the fireplace, the chair. And he stood still exactly as I'd left him and there was the most appalling anguish in his face.

"Something of menace, unspeakable menace," I whispered, backing away.

"Something ancient, something that defies understanding," he pleaded, "Something that can and will go on." But he was shaken and he would not look into my eyes.

I touched that pulsing pain with the tips of my fingers and, looking down at them, saw the blood. "Vampire!" I gasped. "And yet you suffer so, and it is as if you can love!"

"Love? I have loved you since you came. I loved you when I read your secret thoughts and had not yet seen your face."

He drew me to him ever so gently, and slipping his arm around me, guided me to the door.

I tried for one desperate moment to resist him. And as any gentleman might, he stepped back respectfully and took my hand.

Through the long upstairs corridor we passed, and through a small wooden doorway to a screw stair that I had not seen before. I soon realized we were ascending in the north tower, a ruined portion of the structure that had been sealed off years before.

Through one tiny window after another I saw the gently rolling landscape and the small cluster of dim lights that marked the village of Rampling and the pale streak of white that was the London road.

Up and up we climbed, until we reached the topmost chamber, and this he opened with an iron key. He held back the door for me to enter and I found myself in a spacious room whose high, narrow windows contained no glass. A flood of moonlight revealed the most curious mixture of furnishings and objects—a writing-table, a great shelf of books, soft leather chairs, and scores of maps and framed pictures affixed to the walls. Candles all about had dripped their wax on every surface, and in the very midst of this chaos lay my poems, my old sketches—early writings that I had brought with me and never even unpacked.

I saw a black silk top hat and a walking stick, and a bouquet of withered flowers, dry as straw, and daguerreotypes and tintypes in their little velvet cases, and London newspapers and opened books.

There was no place for sleeping in this room.

And when I thought of that, where he must lie when he went to rest, a shudder passed over me and I felt, quite palpably, his lips touching my throat again, and I had the sudden urge to cry.

But he was holding me in his arms; he was kissing my cheeks and my lips ever so softly.

"My father knew what you were!" I whispered.

"Yes," he answered, "and his father before him. And all of them in an unbroken chain over the years. Out of loneliness or rage, know not which, I always told them. I always made them acknowledge, accept."

I backed away and he didn't try to stop me. He lighted the candles about us one by one.

I was stunned by the sight of him in the light, the gleam in his large black eyes and the gloss of his hair. Not even in the railway station had I seen him so clearly as I did now, amid the radiance of the candles. He broke my heart.

And yet he looked at me as though I were a feast for his eyes, and he said my name again and I felt the blood rush to my face. But there seemed a great break suddenly in the passage of time. What had I been thinking! *Yes, never tell, never disturb . . . something ancient, something greater than good and evil . . .* But no I felt dizzy again. I heard father's voice: Tear it down, Richard, stone by stone.

He had drawn me to the window. And as the lights of Rampling were subtracted from the darkness below, a great wood stretched out in all directions, far older and denser than the forest of Rampling Gate. I was afraid suddenly, as if I were slipping into a maelstrom of visions from which I could never, of my own will, return.

There was that sense of our talking together, talking and talking in low, agitated voices, and I was saying that I should not give in.

"Bear witness—that is all I ask of you, Julie."

And there was in me some dim certainty that by these visions alone I would be fatally changed.

But the very room was losing its substance, as if a soundless wind of terrific force were blowing it apart. The vision had already begun . . .

We were riding horseback through a forest, he and I. And the trees were so high and so thick that scarcely any sun at all broke through to the fragrant, leaf-strewn ground.

Yet we had no time to linger in this magical place. We had come to the fresh-tilled earth that surrounded a village I somehow knew was called Knorwood, with its gabled roofs and its tiny, crooked streets. We saw the monastery of Knorwood and the little church with the bell chiming vespers under the lowering sky. A great, bustling life resided in Knorwood, a thousand voices rising in common prayer.

Far beyond, on the rise above the forest, stood the round tower of a truly ancient castle; and to that ruined castle—no more than a shell of itself anymore—as darkness fell in earnest we rode. Through its empty chambers we roamed, impetuous children, the horses and the road quite forgotten, and to the lord of the castle, a gaunt and white-skinned creature standing before the roaring fire of the roofless hall, we came. He turned and fixed us with his narrow and glittering eyes, A dead thing he was, I understood, but he carried within himself a priceless magic. And my companion, my innocent young man, stepped forward into the lord's arms.

I saw the kiss. I saw the young man grow pale and struggle and turn away, and the lord retreated with the wisest, saddest smile.

I understood. I knew. But the castle was dissolving as surely as anything in this dream might dissolve, and we were in some damp and close place.

The stench was unbearable to me; it was that most terrible of all stenches, the stench of death. And I heard my steps on the cobblestones and I reached out to steady myself against a wall. The tiny marketplace was deserted; the doors and windows gaped open to the vagrant wind. Up one side and down the other of the crooked street I saw the marks on the houses. And I knew what the marks meant. The Black Death had come to the village of Knorwood. The Black Death had laid it waste. And in a moment of suffocating horror I realized that no one, not a single person, was left alive.

But this was not quite true. There was a young man walking in fits and starts up the narrow alleyway. He was staggering, almost falling, as

he pushed in one door after another, and at last came to a hot, reeking place where a child screamed on the floor. Mother and father lay dead in the bed. And the sleek fat cat of the household, unharmed, played with the screaming infant, whose eyes bulged in its tiny, sunken face.

Stop it," I heard myself gasp. I was holding my head with both hands. "Stop it—stop it. Please!" I was screaming, and my screams would surely pierce the vision and this crude little dwelling would collapse around me and I would rouse the household of Rampling Gate, but I did not. The young man turned and stared at me, and in the close, stinking room I could not see his face.

But I knew it was he, my companion, and I could smell his fever and his sickness, and the stink of the dying infant, and see the gleaming body of the cat as it pawed at the child's outstretched hand.

"Stop it, you've lost control of it!" I screamed, surely with all my strength, but the infant screamed louder. "Make it stop!"

"I cannot," he whispered. "It goes on forever! It will never stop!"

And with a great shriek I kicked at the cat and sent it flying out of the filthy room, overturning the milk pail as it went.

Death in all the houses of Knorwood. Death in the cloister, death in the open fields. It seemed the Judgment of God—I was sobbing, begging to be released—it seemed the very end of Creation itself.

But as night came down over the dead village he was alive still, stumbling up the slopes, through the forest, toward that tower where the lord stood at the broken arch of the window, waiting for him to come.

"Don't go!" I begged him: I ran alongside him, crying, but he didn't hear.

The lord turned and smiled with infinite sadness as the young man on his knees begged for salvation, when it was damnation this lord offered, when it was only damnation that the lord would give.

"Yes, damned, then, but living, breathing!" the young man cried, and the lord opened his arms.

17

The kiss again, the lethal kiss, the blood drawn out of his dying body, and then the lord lifting the heavy head of the young man so the youth could take the blood back again from the body of the lord himself.

I screamed, "Do not—do not drink!" He turned, and his face was now so perfectly the visage of death that I couldn't believe there was animation left in him; yet he asked: "What would you do? Would you go back to Knorwood, would you open those doors one after another, would you ring the bell in the empty church—and if you did, who would hear?"

He didn't wait for my answer. And I had none now to give. He locked his innocent mouth to the vein that pulsed with every semblance of life beneath the lord's cold and translucent flesh. And the blood jetted into the young body, vanquishing in one great burst the fever and the sickness that had attacked it, driving it out along with the mortal life.

He stood now in the hall of the lord alone. Immortality was his, and the blood thirst he would need to sustain it, and that thirst I could feel with my whole soul.

And each and every thing was transfigured in his vision—to the exquisite essence of itself. A wordless voice spoke from the starry veil of heaven; it sang in the wind that rushed through the broken timbers; it sighed in the flames that ate at the sooted stones of the hearth. It was the eternal rhythm of the universe that played beneath every surface as the last living creature in the village—that tiny child—fell silent in the maw of time.

A soft wind sifted and scattered the soil from the newly turned furrows in the empty fields. The rain fell from the black and endless sky.

Years and years passed. And all that had been. Knorwood melted into the earth. The forest sent out its silent sentinels, and mighty trunks rose where there had been huts and houses, where there had been monastery walls. And it seemed the horror beyond all horrors that no one should know anymore of those who had lived and died in that small and

insignificant village, that not anywhere in the great archives in which all history is recorded should a mention of Knorwood exist.

Yet one remained who knew, one who had witnessed, one who had seen the Ramplings come in the years that followed, seen them raise their house upon the very slope where the ancient castle had once stood, one who saw a new village collect itself slowly upon the unmarked grave of the old.

And all through the walls of Rampling Gate were the stones of that old castle, the stones of the forgotten monastery, the stories of that little church.

We were once again back in the tower.

"It is my shrine," he whispered. "My sanctuary. It is the only thing that endures as I endure. And you love it as I love it, Julie. You have written it . . . You love its grandeur, And its gloom."

"Yes, yes . . . as it's always been . . ." I was crying, though I didn't move my lips.

He had turned to me from the window, and I could feel his endless craving with all my heart.

"What else do you want from me!" I pleaded. "What else can I give?"

A torrent of images answered me. It was beginning again. I was once again relinquishing myself, yet in a great rash of lights and noise I was enlivened and made whole as I had been when we rode together through the forest, but it was into the world of now, this hour, that we passed.

We were flying through the rural darkness along the railway toward London, where the night-time city burst like an enormous bubble in a shower of laughter and motion and glaring light. He was walking with me under the gas lamps, his face all but shimmering with that same dark innocence, that same irresistible warmth. It seemed we were holding tight to each other in the very midst of a crowd. And the crowd was a living thing, a writhing thing, and everywhere there came a dark, rich aroma from it, the aroma of fresh blood. Women in white fur and gentlemen in opera capes swept through the brightly lighted doors of the

theater; the blare of the music hall inundated us and then faded away. Only a thin soprano voice was left, singing a high, plaintive song. I was in his arms and his lips were covering mine, and there came that dull, zinging sensation again, that great, uncontrollable opening within myself. Thirst, and the promise of satiation measured only by the intensity of that thirst. Up back staircases we fled together, into high-ceilinged bedrooms papered in red damask, where the loveliest women reclined on brass beds, and the aroma was so strong now that I could not bear it and he said: "Drink, They are your victims! They will give you eternity—you must drink." And I felt the warmth filling me, charging me, blurring my vision until we broke free again, light and invisible, it seemed, as we moved over the rooftops and down again through rain-drenched streets. But the rain did not touch us; the falling snow did not chill us; we had within ourselves a great and indissoluble heat. And together in the carriage we talked to each other in low, exuberant rushes of language; we were lovers; we were constant; we were immortal. We were as enduring as Rampling Gate.

Oh, don't let it stop! I felt his arms around me and I knew we were in the tower room together, and the visions had worked their fatal alchemy.

"Do you understand what I am offering you? To your ancestors I revealed myself, yes; I subjugated them. But I would make you my bride, Julie. I would share with you my power. Come with me. I will not take you against your will, but can you turn away?"

Again I heard my own scream. My hands were on his cool white skin, and his lips were gentle yet hungry, his eyes yielding and ever young. Father's alloy countenance blazed before me as if I, too, had the power to conjure. *Unspeakable horror.* I covered my face.

He stood against the backdrop of the window, against the distant drift of pale clouds. The candlelight glimmered in his eyes. Immense and sad and wise, they seemed—and oh, yes, innocent, as I have said again and again. "You are their fairest flower, Julie. To them I gave my protection

always. To you I give my love. Come to me, dearest, and Rampling Gate will truly be yours, and it will finally, truly be mine."

* * *

Nights of argument, but finally Richard had come round. He would sign over Rampling Gate to me and I should absolutely refuse to allow the place to be torn down. There would be nothing he could do then to obey Father's command. I had given him the legal impediment he needed, and of course I told him I would leave the house to his male heirs. It should always be in Rampling hands.

A clever solution, it seemed to me, since Father had not told me to destroy the place. I had no scruples in the matter now at all.

And, what remained was for him to take me to the little railway station and see me off for London, and not worry about my going home to Mayfair on my own.

"You stay here as long as you wish and do not worry," I said. I felt more tenderly toward him than I could ever express. You knew as soon as you set foot in the place that Father was quite wrong."

The great black locomotive was chugging past us, the passenger cars slowing to a stop.

"Must go now, darling—kiss me," I said.

"But what came over you, Julie—what convinced you so quickly . . . ?"

"We've been through all that, Richard," I said. "What matters is that Rampling Gate is safe and we are both happy, my dear."

I waved until I couldn't see him any more. The flickering lamps of the town were lost in the deep lavender light of the early evening, and the dark hulk of Rampling Gate appeared for one uncertain moment like the ghost of itself on the nearby rise.

I sat back and closed my eyes. Then I opened them slowly, savoring this moment for which I had waited so long.

He was smiling, seated in the far corner of the leather seat opposite, as he had been all along, and now he rose with a swift, almost delicate movement and sat beside me and enfolded me in his arms.

"It's five hours to London," he whispered,

I can wait," I said, feeling the thirst like a fever as I held tight to him, feeling his lips against my eyelids and my hair. "I want to hunt the London streets tonight," I confessed a little shyly, but I saw only approbation in his eyes.

"Beautiful Julie, my Julie . . ." he whispered.

"You'll love the house in Mayfair," I said,

"Yes . . ." he said.

"And when Richard finally tires of Rampling Gate, we shall go home."

BLOOD GOTHIC

NANCY HOLDER

She wanted to have a vampire lover. She wanted it so badly that she kept waiting for it to happen. One night, soon, she would awaken to wings flapping against the window and then take to wearing velvet ribbons and cameo lockets around her delicate, pale neck. She knew it.

She immersed herself in the world of her vampire lover: She devoured Gothic romances, consumed late-night horror movies. Visions of satin capes and eyes of fire shielded her from the harshness of the daylight, from mortality and the vain and meaningless struggles of the world of the sun. Days as a kindergarten teacher and evenings with some overly eager, casual acquaintance could not pull her from her secret existence: always a ticking portion of her brain planned, proceeded, waited.

She spent her meager earnings on dark antiques and intricate clothes. Her wardrobe was crammed with white negligees and ruffled underthings. No crosses and no mirrors, particularly not in her bedroom. White tapered candles stood in pewter sconces, and she would read late into the night by their smoky flickerings, her scented and ruffled hair combed loosely about her shoulders. She glanced at the window often.

She resented lovers—though she took them, thrilling to the fullness of life in them, the blood and the life—who insisted upon staying all night, burning their breakfast toast and making bitter coffee. Her kitchen, of course, held nothing but fresh ingredients and copper and ironware; to her chagrin, she could not do without ovens or stoves or refrigerators. Alone, she carried candles and bathed in cool water.

She waited, prepared. And at long last, her vampire lover began to come to her in dreams. They floated across the moors, glided through the fields of heather. He carried her to his crumbling castle, undressing her, pulling off her diaphanous gown, caressing her lovely body until, in the height of passion, he bit into her arched neck, drawing the life out of her and replacing it with eternal damnation and eternal love.

She awoke from these dreams drenched in sweat and feeling exhausted. The kindergarten children would find her unusually quiet and self-absorbed, and it frightened them when she rubbed her spotless neck and smiled wistfully. *Soon and soon and soon,* her veins chanted, in prayer and anticipation. *Soon.*

The children were her only regret. She would not miss her inquisitive relatives and friends, the ones who frowned and studied her as if she were a portrait of someone they knew they were supposed to recognize. Those who urged her to drop by for an hour, to come with them to films, to accompany them to the seashore. Those who were connected to her—or thought they were—by the mere gesturing of the long and milky hands of Fate. Who sought to distract her from her one true passion; who sought to discover the secret of that passion. For, true to the sacredness of her vigil for her vampire lover, she had never spoken of him to a single earthly, earthbound soul. It would be beyond them, she knew. They would not comprehend a bond of such intentioned sacrifice.

But she would regret the children. Never would a child of theirs love, coo, and murmur in the darkness; never would his proud and noble

features soften at the sight of the mother and her child of his loins. It was her single sorrow.

Her vacation was coming. June hovered like the mist and the children squirmed in anticipation. Their own true lives would begin in June. She empathized with the shining eyes and smiling faces, knowing their wait was as agonizing as her own. Silently, as the days closed in, she bade each of them a tender farewell, holding them as they threw their little arms around her neck and pressed fervent summertime kisses on her cheeks.

She booked her passage to London on a ship. Then to Romania, Bulgaria, Transylvania. The hereditary seat of her beloved; the fierce, violent backdrop of her dreams. Her suitcases opened themselves to her long, full skirts and her brooches and lockets. She peered into her hand mirror as she packed it. "I am getting pale," she thought, and the idea both terrified and delighted her.

She became paler, thinner, more exhausted as her trip wore on. After recovering from the disappointment of the raucous, modern cruise ship, she raced across the Continent to find refuge in the creaky trains and taverns she had so yearned for. Her heart thrilled as she meandered past the black silhouettes of ruined fortresses and ancient manor houses. She sat for hours in the mists, praying for the howling wolf to find her, for the bat to come and join her.

She took to drinking wine in bed, deep, rich, blood-red burgundy that glowed in the candlelight. She melted into the landscape within days, and cringed as if from the crucifix itself when flickers of her past life, her American, false existence, invaded her serenity. She did not keep a diary; she did not count the days as her summer slipped away from her. She only rejoiced that she grew weaker.

It was when she was counting out the coins for a Gypsy shawl that she realized she had no time left. Tomorrow she must make for Frankfurt and from there fly back to New York. The shopkeeper

nudged her, inquiring if she were ill, and she left with her treasure, trembling.

She flung herself on her own rented bed. "This will not do. This will not do." She pleaded with the darkness. "You must come for me tonight. I have done everything for you, my beloved, loved you above all else. You must save me." She sobbed until she ached.

She skipped her last meal of veal and paprika and sat quietly in her room. The innkeeper brought her yet another bottle of burgundy and after she assured him that she was quite all right, just a little tired, he wished his guest a pleasant trip home.

The night wore on; though her book was open before her, her eyes were riveted to the windows, her hands clenched around the wineglass as she sipped steadily, like a creature feeding. Oh, to feel him against her veins, emptying her and filling her!

Soon and soon and soon . . .

Then, all at once, it happened. The windows rattled, flapped inward. A great shadow, a curtain of ebony, fell across the bed, and the room began to whirl, faster, faster still; and she was consumed with a bitter, deathly chill. She heard, rather than saw, the wineglass crash to the floor, and struggled to keep her eyes open as she was overwhelmed, engulfed, taken.

"Is it you?" she managed to whisper through teeth that rattled with delight and cold and terror. "Is it finally to be?"

Freezing hands touched her everywhere: her face, her breasts, the desperate offering of her arched neck. Frozen and strong and never-dying. Sinking, she smiled in a rictus of mortal dread and exultation. Eternal damnation, eternal love. Her vampire lover had come for her at last.

When her eyes opened again, she let out a howl and shrank against the searing brilliance of the sun. Hastily, they closed the curtains and quickly told her where she was: home again, where everything was

warm and pleasant and she was safe from the disease that had nearly killed her.

She had been ill before she had left the States. By the time she had reached Transylvania, her anemia had been acute. Had she never noticed her own pallor, her lassitude?

Anemia. Her smile was a secret on her white lips. So they thought, but he *had* come for her, again and again. In her dreams. And on that night, he had meant to take her finally to his castle forever, to crown her the best-beloved one, his love of the moors and the mists.

She had but to wait, and he would finish the deed.

Soon and soon and soon.

She let them fret over her, wrapping her in blankets in the last days of summer. She endured the forced cheer of her relatives, allowed them to feed her rich food and drink in hopes of restoring her.

But her stomach could no longer hold the nourishment of their kind; they wrung their hands and talked of stronger measures when it became clear that she was wasting away.

At the urging of the doctor, she took walks. Small ones at first, on painfully thin feet. Swathed in wool, cowering behind sunglasses, she took tiny steps like an old woman. As she moved through the summer hours, her neck burned with an ungovernable pain that would not cease until she rested in the shadows. Her stomach lurched at the sight of grocery-store windows. But at the butcher's, she paused, and licked her lips at the sight of the raw, bloody meat.

But she did not go to him. She grew neither worse nor better.

"I am trapped," she whispered to the night as she stared into the flames of a candle by her bed. "I am disappearing between your world and mine, my beloved. Help me. Come for me." She rubbed her neck, which ached and throbbed but showed no outward signs of his devotion. Her throat was parched, bone-dry, but water did not quench her thirst.

At long last, she dreamed again. Her vampire lover came for her as before, joyous in their reunion. They soared above the crooked trees at the foothills, streamed like black banners above the mountain crags to his castle. He could not touch her enough, worship her enough, and they were wild in their abandon as he carried her in her diaphanous gown to the gates of his fortress.

But at the entrance, he shook his head with sorrow and could not let her pass into the black realm with him. His fiery tears seared her neck, and she thrilled to the touch of the mark even as she cried out for him as he left her, fading into the vapors with a look of entreaty in his dark, flashing eyes.

Something was missing; he required a boon of her before he could bind her against his heart. A thing that she must give to him . . .

She walked in the sunlight, enfeebled, cowering. She thirsted, hungered, yearned. Still she dreamed of him, and still he could not take the last of her unto himself.

Days and nights and days. Her steps took her finally to the schoolyard, where once, only months before, she had embraced and kissed the children, thinking never to see them again. They were all there, who had kissed her cheeks so eagerly. Their silvery laughter was like the tinkling of bells as dust motes from their games and antics whirled around their feet. How free they seemed to her who was so troubled, how content and at peace.

The children.

She shambled forward, eyes widening behind the shields of smoky glass. He required something of her first.

Her one regret. Her only sorrow.

She thirsted. The burns on her neck pulsated with pain.

Tears of gratitude welled in her eyes for the revelation that had not come too late. Weeping, she pushed open the gate of the schoolyard and reached out a skeleton-limb to a child standing apart from the

rest, engrossed in a solitary game of cat's cradle. Tawny-headed, ruddy-cheeked, filled with the blood and the life.

For him, as a token of their love.

"My little one, do you remember me?" she said softly.

The boy turned. And smiled back uncertainly in innocence and trust.

Then, as she came for him, swooped down on him like a great, winged thing, with eyes that burned through the glasses, teeth that flashed, once, twice . . .

soon, soon, soon.

TWILIGHT

KELLEY ARMSTRONG

*A*nother life taken. Another year to live.

That is the bargain that rules our existence. We feed off blood, but for three hundred and sixty-four days a year, it is merely that: feeding. Yet on that last day—or sometime before the anniversary of our rebirth as vampires—we must drain the lifeblood of one person. Fail and we begin the rapid descent into death.

As I sipped white wine on the outdoor patio, I watched the steady stream of passersby. Although there was a chill in the air—late autumn coming fast and sharp—the patio was crowded, no one willing to surrender the dream of summer quite yet. Leaves fluttering onto the tables were lauded as decorations. The scent of a distant wood-fire was willfully mistaken for candles. The sun, almost gone despite the still early hour, only added romance to the meal. All embellishments to the night, not signs of impending winter.

I sipped my wine and watched night fall. At the next table, a lone businessman eyed me. That was the sort of man I often had the misfortune to attract: middle-aged and prosperous, laboring under the delusion that success and wealth were such irresistible lures that he could allow his waistband and jowls to thicken unchecked.

30

Under other circumstances, I might have returned the attention, let him lead me to some tawdry motel, then take *my* dinner. He would survive, of course, waking weakened, blaming it on too much wine. A meal without guilt. Any man who took such a chance with a stranger—particularly when he bore a wedding band—deserved an occasional bout of morning-after discomfort.

He did not, however, deserve to serve as my annual kill. I can justify many things, but not that. Yet I found myself toying with the idea more that I should have, prodded by a niggling voice that told me I was already late.

I stared at the glow over the horizon. The sun had set on the anniversary of my rebirth, and I hadn't taken a life. Yet there was no need for panic. I would hardly explode into dust at midnight. I would weaken as I began the descent into death, but I could avoid that simply by fulfilling my bargain tonight.

I measured the darkness, deemed it enough for hunting, then laid a twenty on the table and left.

A bell tolled ten. Two hours left. I chastised myself for being so dramatic. I loathe vampires given to theatrics—those who have read too many horror novels and labor under the delusion that's how they're supposed to behave. I despise any sign of it in myself and yet, under the circumstances, perhaps it could be forgiven.

In all the years that came before this, I had never reached this date without fulfilling my obligation. I had chosen this vampiric life and would not risk losing it through carelessness.

Only once had I ever neared my rebirth day, and then only due to circumstances beyond my control. It had been 1867 . . . or perhaps 1869. I'd been hunting for my annual victim when I'd found myself tossed into a Hungarian prison. I hadn't been caught at my kill—I'd never made so amateurish a mistaken even when I'd been an amateur.

31

The prison sojourn had been Aaron's fault, as such things usually were. We'd been hunting my victim when he'd come across a nobleman whipping a servant in the street. Naturally, Aaron couldn't leave well enough alone. In the ensuing confusion of the brawl, I'd been rousted with him and thrown into a pest-infested cell that wouldn't pass any modern health code.

Aaron had worked himself into a full-frothing frenzy, seeing my rebirth anniversary only days away while I languished in prison, waiting for justice that seemed unlikely to come swiftly. I hadn't been concerned. When one partakes of Aaron's company, one learns to expect such inconveniences. While he plotted, schemed and swore he'd get us out on time, I simply waited. There was time yet and no need to panic until panic was warranted.

The day before my rebirth anniversary, as I'd begun to suspect that a more strenuous course of action might be required, we'd been released. I'd compensated for the trouble and delay by taking the life of a prison guard who'd enjoyed his work far more than was necessary.

This year, my only excuse for not taking a victim yet was that I hadn't gotten around to it. As for why, I was somewhat . . . baffled. I am nothing if not conscientious about my obligations. Yet, this year, delays had arisen, and somehow I'd been content to watch the days slip past and tell myself I would get around to it, as if it was no more momentous than a missed salon appointment.

The week had passed and I'd been unable to work up any sense of urgency until today, and even now, it was only an oddly cerebral concern. No matter. I would take care of it tonight.

As I walked, an old drunkard drew my gaze. I watched him totter into the shadows of an alley and thought: "There's a possibility . . ." Perhaps I could get this chore over with sooner than expected. I could be quite finicky—refusing to feed off sleeping vagrants—yet as my annual kill, this one was a choice I could make.

Every vampire deals with our "bargain" in the way that best suits his temperament and capacity for guilt and remorse. I cull from the edges—the sick, the elderly, those already nearing their end. I do not fool myself into thinking this is a just choice. There's no way to know whether that cancer-wracked woman might have been on the brink of remission or if that elderly man had been enjoying his last days to the fullest. I make the choice because it is one I can live with.

This old drunkard would do. As I watched him, I felt the gnawing in the pit of my stomach, telling me I'd already waited too long. I should follow him into that alley, and get this over with. I *wanted* to get it over with—that there was no question of that, no possibility I was conflicted on this point. Other vampires may struggle with our bargain. I do not.

Yet even as I visualized myself following the drunk into the alley, my legs didn't follow through. I stood there, watching him disappear into the darkness. Then I moved on.

A block farther, a crowd poured from a movie theater. As it passed, its life force enveloped me. I wasn't hungry, yet I could still feel that tingle of anticipation, of hunger. I could smell their blood, hear the rush of it through their veins. The scent and sound of life.

Twenty steps later, and they were still passing, an endless stream of humanity disgorged by a packed theater. How many seats were inside? Three hundred, three fifty? As many years as had passed since my rebirth?

One life per year. It seems so moderate a price . . . until you looked back and realized you could fill a movie theater with your victims. A sobering thought, even for one not inclined to dwell on such things. No matter. There wouldn't be hundreds more. Not from this vampire.

Contrary to legend, our gift of longevity comes with an expiry date. Mine was drawing near. I'd felt the signs, the disconnect from the world, a growing disinterest in all around me. For me, that was nothing new.

I'd long since learned to keep my distance from a world that changed while I didn't.

After some struggle with denial, I'd accepted that I had begun the decline toward death. But it would be slow, and I still had years left, decades even. Or, I would, if I could get past this silly bout of ennui and make my rebirth kill.

As the crowd dwindled, I looked over my shoulder to watch them go and considered taking a life from them. A random kill. I'd done it once before, more than a century ago, during a particularly bleak time when I hadn't been able to rouse enough feeling to care. Yet later I'd regretted it, having let myself indulge my darkest inclinations simply because I'd been in a dark place myself. Unacceptable. I wouldn't do it again.

I wrenched my gaze from the dispersing crowd. This was ridiculous. I was no angst-ridden cinema vampire, bemoaning the choice she'd made in life. I was no flighty youngster, easily distracted from duty, abhorring responsibility. I was Cassandra DuCharme, senior vampire delegate to the interracial council. If any vampire had come to me with this problem—"I'm having trouble making my annual kill"—I'd have shown her the sharp side of my tongue, hauled her into the alley with that drunk and told her, as Aaron might say, to "piss or get off the pot."

I turned around and headed back to the alley.

I'd gone only a few steps when I picked up a sense of the drunkard. Excitement swept through me. I closed my eyes and smiled. That was more like it.

The quickening accelerated as I slid into the shadows. My stride smoothed out, each step taken with care, rolling toe to heel, making no sound.

That sense of my prey grew stronger with each step, telling me he was near. I could see a recessed emergency exit a dozen feet ahead. A shoe

protruded from the darkness. I crept forward until I spotted a dark form crumpled inside.

The rush of his blood vibrated through the air. My canines lengthened and I allowed myself one shudder of anticipation, then shook it off and focused on the sound of his breathing.

A gust whipped along the alley, scattering candy wrappers and leaflets, and the stink of alcohol washed over me. I caught the extra notes in his breathing—the deep, almost determined rhythm. Passed out drunk. He'd probably stumbled into the first semi-sheltered place he'd seen and collapsed.

That would make it easier.

Still, I hesitated, telling myself I needed to be sure. But the rhythm of his breathing stayed steady. He was clearly asleep and unlikely to awake even if I bounded over there and shouted in his ear.

So what was I waiting for? I should be in that doorway already, reveling in the luck of finding so easy a victim.

I shook the lead from my bones and crossed the alley.

The drunkard wore an army jacket, a real one if I was any judge. I resisted the fanciful urge to speculate, to imagine him as some shell-shocked soldier turned to drink by the horrors of war. More likely, he'd bought the jacket at a thrift shop. Or stolen it.

His hair was matted, so filthy it was impossible to tell the original color. Above the scraggly beard, though, his face was unlined. Younger than I'd first imagined. Significantly younger.

That gave me pause, but while he was not the old drunkard I'd first imagined, he was certainly no healthy young man. I could sense disease and wasting, most likely cirrhosis. Not my ideal target, but he would do.

And yet . . .

Almost before I realized it, I was striding toward the road.

He wasn't right. I was succumbing to that panic, and that was unnecessary, even dangerous. If I made the wrong choice, I'd regret it.

Better to let the pressure of this ominous date pass and find a better choice tomorrow.

I slid into the park and stepped off the path. The ground was hard, so I could walk swiftly and silently.

As I stepped from the wooded patch, my exit startled two young men huddled together. Their gazes tripped over me, eyes glittering under the shadows of their hoods, like jackals spotting easy prey. I met the stronger one's gaze. He broke first, grumbling deep in his throat. Then he shuffled back and waved his friend away as he muttered some excuse for moving on.

I watched them go, considering . . . then dismissing.

It was easy to separate one victim from a group. Not nearly so simple when the "group" consisted of only two people. As the young men disappeared into the shadows, I resumed my silent trek across the park.

My goal lay twenty paces away. Had I not sensed him, I likely would have passed by. He'd ignored a park bench under the light and instead had stretched out the top of a raised garden, hidden under the bushes and amidst the dying flowers.

He lay on his back with his eyes closed. His face was peaceful, relaxed. A handsome face, broad and tanned. He had thick blond hair and the healthy vitality of a young man in his prime. A big man, too, tall and solid, his muscular arms crossed behind his head, his slim hips and long denim-clad legs ending in work boots crossed at the ankles.

I circled north to sneak up behind his head. He lay completely motionless, even his chest still, not rising and falling with the slow rhythm of breathing. I crossed the last few feet between us and stopped just behind his head. Then I leaned over.

His eyes opened. Deep brown eyes, the color of rich earth. He snarled a yawn.

"'Bout time, Cass," he said. "Couple of punks been circling to see if I'm still conscious. Another few minutes, and I'd have had to teach them to let sleeping vamps lie."

"Shall I go away then? Let you have your fun?"

Aaron grinned. "Nah. They come back? We can both have fun." He heaved his legs over the side of the garden wall, and sat up, shaking off sleep. Then, catching a glimpse of my face, his grin dropped into a frown. "You didn't do it, did you?"

"I couldn't find anyone."

"Couldn't find—?" He pushed to his feet, towering over me. "Goddamn it, what are you playing at? First you let it go until the last minute, then you 'can't find anyone'?"

I checked my watch. "It's not the last minute. I still have ten left. I trust that if I explode at midnight, you'll be kind enough to sweep up the bits. I would like to be scattered over the Atlantic but, if you're pressed for time, the Charleston River will do."

He glowered at me. "A hundred and twenty years together, and you never got within a week of your rebirth day without making your kill."

"Hungary. 1867."

"Sixty-eight. And I don't see any bars this time. So what was your excuse?"

"Among others, I was busy researching that council matter Paige brought to my attention. I admit I let things creep up on me this year, and a century ago that would never have happened, but while we were apart, I changed—"

"Bullshit. You never change. Except to get more impervious, more pigheaded and more cranky."

"The word is 'crankier.' "

He muttered a few more descriptors under his breath. I started down the path.

"You'd better be going off to find someone," he called after me.

"No, I'm heading home to bed. I'm tired."

"Tired?" He strode up beside me. "You don't get tired. You're—"

He stopped, mouth closing so fast his teeth clicked.

"The word is 'dying,'" I said. "And, while that is true, and it is equally true that my recent inability to sleep is a symptom of that, tonight I am, indeed, tired."

"Because you're late for your kill. You can't pull this shit, Cassandra, not in your condition."

I gave an unladylike snort and kept walking.

His fingers closed around my arm. "Let's go find those punks. Have some fun." A broad, boyish grin. "I think one has a gun. Been a long time since I got shot."

"Another day."

"A hunt then."

"I'm not hungry."

"Well, I am. Maybe you couldn't find someone suitable, but I can. I know what you look for. We'll hunt together. I'll get a snack; you'll get another year. Fair enough?"

He tried to grin, but I could see a hint of panic behind his eyes. I felt an answering prickle of worry, but told myself I was being ridiculous. I'd simply had too much on my mind lately. I was tired and easily distracted. I needed to snap out of this embarrassing lethargy and make this kill, and I would do so tomorrow, once Aaron had gone back to Atlanta.

"It's not the end of the world—or *my* world—if I don't take a life tonight, Aaron. You've been late yourself, when you couldn't find someone suitable. I haven't—and perhaps I'd simply like to know what that's like." I touched his arm. "At my age, new experiences are few and far between. I take them where I can."

He hesitated, then nodded, mollified, and accompanied me from the park.

Aaron followed me home. That wasn't nearly as exciting a prospect as it sounds. These days we were simply friends. His choice. If I had my way, tired or not, I would have found the energy to accommodate him.

When I first met Aaron, less than a year after his rebirth, he'd accused me of helping him in his new life because he looked like something to "decorate my bed with." True enough.

Even as a human, I had never been able to rouse more than a passing interest in men of my own class. Too well mannered, too gently spoken, too *soft*. My tastes had run to stable boys and, later, to discreet working men.

Finding Aaron as a newly reborn vampire, a big strapping farm boy with hands as rough as his manners, I will admit that my first thought was indeed carnal. He was younger than I liked, but I'd decided I could live with that.

So I'd trained him in the life of a vampire. In return, I'd received friendship, protection . . . and endless nights alone, frustrated beyond reason. It was preposterous, of course. I'd never had any trouble leading men to my bed and there I'd been, reduced to chasing a virile young man who strung me along as if he were some coy maiden. I told myself it wasn't his fault—he was English. Thankfully, when he finally capitulated, I discovered he wasn't nearly as repressed as I'd feared.

Over a hundred years together. It was no grand romance. The word "love" never passed between us. We were partners in every sense—best friends, hunting allies and faithful lovers. Then came the morning I woke, looked over at him, and imagined *not* seeing him there, tried to picture life without him. I'd gone cold at the thought.

I had told myself I'd never allow that again. When you've lost everyone, you learn the danger of attachments. As a vampire, you must accept that every person you ever know will die, and you are the only constant in your life, the only person you can—and should—rely on. So I made a decision.

I betrayed Aaron. Not with another man. Had I done that, he'd simply have flown into a rage and, once past it, demanded to know what was really bothering me. What I did instead was a deeper betrayal, one that said, more coldly than I could ever speak the words "I don't want you anymore."

After over half a century apart, happenstance had brought us together again. We'd resisted the pull of that past bond, reminded ourselves of what had happened the last time and yet, gradually, we'd drifted back into friendship. Only friendship. Sex was not allowed—Aaron's way of keeping his distance. Given the choice between having him as a friend and not having him in my life at all, I'd gladly choose the former . . . though that didn't keep me from hoping to change his mind.

That night I slept. It was the first time I'd done more than catnapped in over a year. While I longed to seize on this as some sign that I wasn't dying, I knew Aaron's assessment was far more likely—I was tired because I'd missed my annual kill.

Was this what happened, then, when we didn't hold up our end of the bargain? An increasing lethargy that would lead to death? I shook it off. I had no intention of exploring the phenomenon further. Come sunset, I would end this foolishness and take a life.

As I entered my living room that morning, I heard a dull slapping from the open patio doors. Aaron was in the yard, building a new retaining wall for my garden.

When he'd been here in the spring, he'd commented on the crumbling wall, and said, "I could fix that for you." I'd nodded and said, "Yes, I suppose you could." Three more intervening visits. Three more hints about the wall. Yet I refused to ask for his help. I had lost that right

when I betrayed him. So yesterday, he'd shown up on my doorstep, masonry tools in one hand, suitcase in the other, and announced he was building a new wall for my rebirth day.

That meant he had a reason to stay until he'd finished it. Had he simply decided my rebirth day made a good excuse? Or was there more than that? When I'd spoken to him this week, had something in my voice told him I had yet to take my annual victim?

I watched Aaron through the patio doors. The breeze was chilly, but the sun beat down and he had his shirt off as he worked, oblivious to all around him. This was what he did for a living—masonry, the latest in a string of "careers." I chided him that, after two hundred years, one should have a healthy retirement savings plan. He only pointed the finger back at me, declaring that I too worked when I didn't need to. But I was self-employed, and selling art and antiques was certainly not in the same category as the physically demanding jobs he undertook. Yet another matter on which we disagreed—with vigor and enthusiasm.

I watched him for another minute, then headed for the kitchen to make him an iced tea.

I went out later to check a new shipment at an antique shop. When I got home, Aaron was sitting on the couch, a pile of newspapers on the table and one spread in his hands.

"I hope you didn't take those from my trash."

"I wouldn't have had to, if you'd recycle." He peered around the side of the paper. "That blue box in the garage? That's what it's for, not holding garden tools."

I waved him off. "Three hundred and fifty years and I have never been deprived of a newspaper or book by want of paper. I'm not going to start recycling now. I'm too old."

"Too stubborn." He gave a sly grin. "Or too lazy."

He earned a glare for that one. I walked over and snatched up a stray paper from the carpet before it stained.

"If you're that desperate for reading material, just tell me and I'll walk to the store and buy you a magazine."

He folded the paper and laid it on the coffee table, then patted the spot next to him. I hesitated, sensing trouble, and took a place at the opposite end, perched on the edge. He reached over, his hand going around my waist, and dragged me until I was sitting against him.

"Remember when we met, Cass?"

"Vaguely."

He laughed. "Your memory isn't *that* bad. Remember what you did for me? My first rebirth day was coming, and I'd decided I wasn't doing it. You found me a victim, a choice I could live with." With his free hand, he picked up a paper separated from the rest and dropped it onto my lap. "Found you a victim."

I sighed. "Aaron, I don't need you to—"

"Too late." He poked a calloused finger at the top article on the folded page. "Right there."

The week-old story told of a terminally ill patient fighting for the right to die. When I looked over at Aaron, he was grinning, pleased with himself.

"Perfect, isn't it?" he said. "Exactly what you look for. She wants to die. She's in pain."

"She's in a palliative care ward. How would I even get in there, let alone kill her?"

"Is that a challenge?" His arm tightened around my waist. "Because if it is, I'm up for it. You know I am."

He was still smiling, but behind it lurked a shadow of desperation. Again, his worry ignited mine. Perhaps this added incentive was exactly what I needed. It wouldn't be easy, but it could be interesting, particularly with Aaron's help.

Any other time, I'd have pounced on the idea, but now, even as I envisioned it, I felt only a spark of interest, buried under an inexplicable layer of lethargy, even antipathy, and all I could think was "Oh, but it would just be so much *work*."

My hackles rose at such indolence, but I squelched my indignation. I *was* determined to take a life tonight. I would allow nothing to stand in the way of that. Therefore, I could not enter into a plan that might prove too difficult. Better to keep this simple, so I would have no excuse for failure.

I lay the paper aside. "Are you hungry?"

A faint frown.

"Last night, you said you were hungry," I continued. "If you were telling the truth, then I presume you still need to feed, unless you slipped out last night."

"I thought we'd be hunting together later. So I waited."

"Then we'll hunt tonight. But not—" A wave at the paper. "—in a hospital."

We strolled along the sidewalk. It was almost dark now, the sun only a red-tinged memory along the horizon. As I watched a flower seller clear her outdoor stock for the night, Aaron snapped his fingers.

"Flowers. That's what's missing in your house. You always have flowers."

"The last arrangement wilted early. I was going to pick up more when I was out today, but I didn't get the chance."

He seemed to cheer at that, as if reading some hidden message in my words.

"Here then," he said. "I'll get some for you now."

I arched my brows. "And carry bouquets on a hunt?"

"Think I can't? Sounds like a challenge."

I laughed and laid my fingers on his forearm. "We'll get some tomorrow."

He took my hand and looped it through his arm as we resumed walking.

"We're going to Paris this spring," he said after a moment.

"Are we? Dare I ask what prompted that?"

"Flowers. Spring. Paris."

"Ah. A thoughtful gesture, but Paris in the spring is highly overrated. And overpriced."

"Too bad. I'm taking you. I'll book the time off when I get home, and call you with the dates."

When I didn't argue, he glanced over at me, then grinned and quickened his pace, launching into a "remember when" story of our last spring in Paris.

We bickered over the choice of victim. Aaron wanted to find one to suit my preference, but I insisted we select his type. Finally, he capitulated.

The fight dampened the evening's mood, but only temporarily. Once Aaron found a target, he forgot everything else.

In the early years, Aaron had struggled with vampiric life. He'd died rescuing a stranger from a petty thug. And his reward? After a life spent thinking of others, he'd been reborn as one who fed off them. Ironic and cruel.

Yet we'd found a way for him to justify—even relish—the harder facts of our survival. He fed from the dregs of society, punks and criminals like those youths in the park. For his annual kill, he condemned those whose crimes he deemed worthy of the harshest punishment. And so he could feel he did some good in this parasitic life.

As he said, I'd found his first victim. Now, two hundred years later, he no longer scoured newspapers or tracked down rumors, but seemed

able to locate victims by intuition alone, as I could find the dying. The predatory instinct will adapt to anything that ensures the survival of the host.

Tonight's choice was a drug dealer with feral eyes and a quick switchblade. We watched from the shadows as the man threatened a young runner. Aaron rocked on the balls at his feet, his gaze fixed on that waving knife, but I laid my hand on his arm. As the runner loped toward the street, Aaron's lips curved, happy to see him go, but even happier with what the boy's safe departure portended—not a quick intervention but a true hunt.

We tracked the man for over an hour before Aaron's hunger won out. With no small amount of regret, he stopped toying with his dinner and I lured the drug dealer into an alleyway. An easy maneuver, as such things usually were with men like this, too greedy and cocksure to feel threatened by a middle-aged woman.

As Aaron's fangs sank into the drug dealer's throat, the man's eyes bugged in horror, unable to believe what was happening. This was the most dangerous point of feeding, that split second where they felt our fangs and felt a nightmare come to life. It is but a moment, then the sedative in our saliva takes hold and they pass out, those last few seconds wiped from memory when they wake.

The man lashed out once, then slumped in Aaron's grasp. Still gripping the man's shirtfront, Aaron began to drink, gulping the blood. His eyes were closed, face rapturous, and I watched him, enjoying the sight of his pleasure, his appetite.

He'd been hungrier than he'd let on. Typical for Aaron, waiting that extra day or two, not to practice control or avoid feeding, but to drink heartily. Delayed gratification for heightened pleasure. I shivered.

"Cass?"

He licked a fallen drop from the corner of his mouth as he held the man out for me.

This was how we hunted—how Aaron liked it, not taking separate victims but sharing. He always made the disabling bite, drank some, then let me feed to satiation. If I took too much for him to continue feeding safely, he'd find a second victim. There was no sense arguing that I could find my own food—he knew that, but continued, compelled by a need to protect and provide.

"You go on," I said softly. "You're still hungry."

He thrust the man to me. "Yours."

His jaw set and I knew his insistence had nothing to do with providing sustenance.

As Aaron held the man up for me, I moved forward. My canines lengthened, throat tightening, and I allowed myself a shudder of anticipation.

I lowered my mouth to the man's throat, scraped my canines over the skin, tasting, preparing. Then, with one swift bite, my mouth filled with—

I jerked back, almost choking. I resisted the urge to spit, and forced—with effort—the mouthful down, my stomach revolting in disgust.

It tasted like . . . blood.

When I became a vampire, I thought this would be the most unbearable part: drinking blood. But the moment that first drop of blood touched my tongue, I'd realized my worries had been for naught. There was no word for the taste; no human memory that came close. I can only say that it was so perfect a food that I could never tire of it nor wish for something else.

But this tasted like *blood*, like my human memory of it. Once, before I'd completed the transition to vampire, I'd filled a goblet with cow's blood and forced it down, preparing for my new life. I could still taste

the thick, metallic fluid that had coated my mouth and tongue, then sat in my stomach for no more than a minute before returning the way it had gone down.

Now, after only a mouthful of this man's blood, I had to clamp my mouth shut to keep from gagging. Aaron dropped the man and grabbed for me. I waved him aside.

"I swallowed wrong."

I rubbed my throat, lips curving in a moue of annoyance, then looked around, and found the man at my feet. I steeled myself and bent. Aaron crouched to lift the man for me, but I motioned him back, and shielded my face, so he wouldn't see my reaction. Then I forced my mouth to the man's throat.

The bleeding had already stopped. I bit his neck again, my nails digging into my palms, eyes closed, letting the disgusting taste fill my mouth, then swallowing. Drink, swallow. Drink, swallow. My nails broke my skin, but I felt no pain. I wished I could, if only to give me something else to think about.

It wasn't only the taste. That I could struggle past. But my whole body rebelled at the very sensation of the blood filling my stomach, screaming at me to stop, as if what I was doing was unnatural, even dangerous.

I managed one last swallow. And then . . . I couldn't. I simply couldn't. I hung there, fangs still in the man's neck, willing myself to suck, to fill my mouth, to finish this, mentally screaming, raging against the preposterousness of it. I was a vampire; I drank blood. And even if I didn't want to, by God, I would force every drop down my throat—

My stomach heaved. I swallowed hard.

I could sense Aaron behind me. Hovering. Watching. Worrying.

Another heave. If I took one more sip, I'd vomit and give Aaron reason to worry, to panic, and give *myself* reason to panic.

It was the victim. God only knew what poisons this drug dealer had swimming through his veins and, while such things don't affect

vampires, I am a delicate feeder, too sensitive to anomalies in the blood. I've gone hungry rather than drink anything that tastes "off." There was no sense asking Aaron to confirm it—he could swill week-old blood and not notice.

That was it, then. The victim. Just the victim.

I sealed the wound with my tongue and stepped back.

"Cass . . ." Aaron's voice was low with warning. "You need to finish him."

"I—" The word "can't" rose to my lips, but I swallowed it back. I couldn't say that. Wouldn't. This was just another temporary hurdle. I'd rest tonight and find a victim of my own choosing tomorrow.

"He isn't right," I said, then turned and headed down the alley.

After a moment, I heard Aaron throw the unconscious man into a heap of trash bags and storm off in the opposite direction.

Any other man would have thrown up his hands and left me there. I arrived at my car to find Aaron waiting by the driver's door. I handed him the keys and got in the passenger's side.

At home, as I headed toward my room, Aaron called after me. "I hope you're not going to tell me you're tired again."

"No, I'm taking a bath to scrub off the filth of that alley. Then, if you aren't ready to retire, we could have a glass of wine, perhaps light the fire. It's getting cool."

He paused, still ready for a fight, but finding no excuse in my words.

"I'll start the fire," he said.

"Thank you."

No more than ten minutes after I got into the tub, the door banged open with such a crash that I started, sloshing bubbles over the side. Aaron barreled in and shoved a small book at me. My appointment book.

"I found this in your desk."

"Keen detective work. Practicing for your next council investigation?"

"*Our* next council investigation."

I reached for my loofah brush. "My mistake. That's what I meant."

"Is it?"

I looked up, trying to understand his meaning, but seeing only rage in his eyes. He was determined to find out what had happened in that alley, and somehow this was his route there. My stomach clenched, as if the blood was still pooled in it, curdling. I wouldn't have this conversation. I wouldn't.

Ostensibly reaching for the loofah brush, I rose, letting the bubbles slide from me. Aaron's gaze dropped from my face. I tucked my legs under, took hold of the side of the tub and started to rise. He let me get halfway up, then put his hand on my head and firmly pushed me down.

I reclined into the tub again, then leaned my head back, floating, breasts and belly peeking from the water. Aaron watched for a moment, before tearing his gaze away with a growl.

"Stop that, Cass. I'm not going to run off and I'm not going to be distracted. I want to talk to you."

I sighed. "About my appointment book, I presume."

He lifted it. "Last week. On the day marked 'birthday.' The date you must have planned to make your kill. There's nothing else scheduled."

"Of course not. I keep that day open—"

"But you said you were busy. That's why you didn't do it."

"I don't believe I said that. I said things came up."

"Such as . . . ?"

I raised a leg onto the rim and ran the loofah brush down it. Aaron's eyes followed, but after a second, he forced his gaze back to mine and repeated the question.

I sighed. "Very well. Let's see. On that particular day, it was a midnight end-of-season designer clothing sale. As I was driving out of the city to

make my kill, I saw the sign and stopped. By the time I left, it was too late to hunt."

He glowered at me. "That's not funny."

"I didn't say it was."

The glower deepened to a scowl. "You postponed your annual kill to . . . *shop*? Bullshit. Yeah, you like your fancy clothes, and you're cheap as hell. But getting distracted by a clothing sale?" He snorted. "That's like a cop stopping a high speed chase to grab donuts."

I went quiet for a moment, then said, as evenly as I could. "Perhaps. But I did."

He searched my gaze, finding the truth in my eyes. "Then something's wrong. Very wrong. And you know it."

I shuttered my gaze. "All I know is that you're making too big a deal of this, as always. You take the smallest—"

"Cassandra DuCharme skips her annual kill to go *shopping*? That's not small. That's apocalyptic."

"Oh, please, spare me the—"

He shoved the open book in my face. "Forget the sale. Explain the rest of it. You had nothing scheduled all week. You had no excuse. You didn't forget. You didn't get distracted." His voice dropped as he lowered himself to the edge of the tub. "You have no intention of taking a life."

"You . . . you think I'm trying to kill myself?" I laughed, the sound almost bitter. "Do you forget how I became what I am, Aaron? I *chose* it. I risked everything to get this life, and if you think I'd throw that away one minute before my time is up—"

"How you came into this life is exactly why you're hell-bent on leaving it like this." He snagged my gaze and held it. "You cheated death. No, you *beat* it—by sheer goddamned force of will. You said 'I won't die.' And now, when it's coming around again, you're damned well not going to sit back and let it happen. You chose once. You'll choose again."

I paused, looked away, then back at him. "Why are you here, Aaron?"

"I came to fix your wall—"

"At no prompting from me. No hints from me. You came of your own accord, correct?"

"Yeah, but—"

"Then, if I'd planned to let myself die, presumably, you wouldn't have seen me again." I met his gaze. "Do you think I would do that? Of everyone I know in this world, would I leave you without saying goodbye?"

His jaw worked, but he said nothing. After a moment, he pushed to his feet, and walked out.

I lay in bed, propped on my pillows, staring at the wall. Aaron was right. When the time came, I would leave this vampiric life as I'd come into it: by choice. But this was not that time. There was no doubt of that, no possibility that I was subconsciously trying to end my life. That was preposterous. I had no qualms about suicide. Fears . . . perhaps. Yet no different than my fear of death itself.

When the time came, yes. But I would never be so irresponsible as to end my life before my affairs were in order. My estate would need to be disposed of in advance, given to those I wished to see benefit. Of equal concern was the discovery and disposal of my body. To leave that to chance would be unforgivably irresponsible.

I would make my peace with Aaron and make amends for my betrayal or, at the very least, ensure he understood that whatever I had done to him, the reason for it, the *failing* behind it, had been mine.

Then there was the council. Aaron was already my co-delegate, but I had to ready him to take my senior position and ready the vampire community to accept that change. Moreover, as the senior overall council member, it was my duty to pass on all I knew to Paige, as the

keeper of records, something I'd been postponing, unwilling to accept that my time was ending.

Ending.

My stomach clenched at the thought. I closed my eyes and shuddered.

I had never lacked for backbone and never stood for the lack of it in others. Now I needed to face and accept this reality. I was dying. Not beginning a lengthy descent, but at the end of the slope.

I now knew how a vampire died. A rebirth date came and we discovered, without warning, that we could not fulfill our end of the bargain. Not *would* not, but *could* not.

If I could not overcome this, I would die. Not in decades, but days.

Panic surged in me, coupled with an overwhelming wave of raw rage. Of all the ways to die, could any be more humiliating in its sublime ridiculousness? Not to die suddenly, existence snuffed out as my time ended. Not to die, beheaded, at the hands of an enemy. Not to grow ill and fade away. Not even to pass in my sleep. Such deaths couldn't be helped, and while I would have raged against that, the injustice of it, such a fate was nothing compared to this—to die because I inexplicably lacked the will to do something I'd done hundreds of times before.

No, that wasn't possible. I wouldn't *let* it be possible.

I would get out of this bed, find a victim and force myself to drain his blood if I vomited up every mouthful.

I envisioned myself standing, yanking on clothing, striding from the room . . .

Yet I didn't move.

My limbs felt leaden. Inside, I was spitting mad, snarling and cursing, but my body lay as still and calm as if I'd already passed.

I pushed down the burbling panic.

Consider the matter with care and logic. I should have taken Aaron's victim, while I still had the strength, but now that I'd missed my

opportunity, I couldn't chance waiting another day. I'd rest for an hour or so, until Aaron had retired.

Better for him not to know. I wouldn't let him pity me, and coddle me simply because it was in his nature to help the sick, the weak, the needy. I would not be needy.

I'd stay awake and wait until the house grew quiet. Then I'd do this—alone.

I fixed my gaze on the light, staring at it to keep myself awake. Minutes ticked past, each feeling like an hour. My eyes burned. My body begged for sleep. I refused. It threatened to pull me under even with my eyes wide. I compromised. I'd close them for a moment's rest and then I'd leave.

I shut my eyes and all went dark.

I awoke to the smell of flowers. I usually had some in the house, so the smell came as no surprise, and I drowsily stretched, rested and refreshed.

Then I remembered I hadn't replaced my last flowers and I was seized by the sudden vision of my corpse lying on my bed, surrounded by funeral wreaths. I bolted upright and found myself staring in horror at a room of flowers . . . before realizing that the fact I was sitting upright would suggest I was not dead.

With a deep sigh, I looked around. Flowers did indeed fill my room. There were at least a dozen bouquets, each a riot of blooms, with no unifying theme of color, shape or type. I smiled. Aaron.

My feet lit on the cool hardwood as I crossed to a piece of paper propped against the nearest bouquet. An advertisement for flights to France. Beside another was a list of hotels. A picture of the Eiffel Tower adorned a third. Random images of Parisian travel littered the room, again with no obvious theme, simply pages hurriedly

printed from websites. Typically Aaron. Making his point with all the finesse of a sledgehammer wielded with equal parts enthusiasm and determination.

Should I still fail to be swayed, he'd scrawled a note with letters two inches high, the paper thrust into a bouquet of roses. Paige had called. She was still working on that case and needed my help. In smaller letters below, he informed me that today's paper carried another article on the palliative care patient who wanted to die.

I dressed, then tucked two of the pages into my pocket, and slipped out the side door.

I didn't go to the hospital Aaron had suggested. It was too late for that. If I was having difficulty making this kill, I could not compound that by choosing one that would itself be difficult.

So I returned to the alley where I'd found—and dismissed—my first choice two nights ago. The drunkard wasn't there, of course. No one was. But I traversed the maze of alleys and back roads in search of another victim. I couldn't wait for nightfall. I couldn't risk falling asleep again or I might not wake up.

When an exit door swung open, I darted into an alley to avoid detection and spotted my victim. A woman, sitting in an alcove, surrounded by grocery bags stuffed with what looked like trash but, I presumed, encompassed the sum of her worldly belongings. Behind me, whoever opened that door tossed trash into the alley, and slammed it shut again. The woman didn't move. She stared straight ahead, gaze vacant. Resting before someone told her to move on.

Even as I watched her, evaluated her, and decided she would do, something deep in me threw up excuses. Not old enough. Not sick enough. Too dangerous a location. Too dangerous a time of day. Keep looking. Find someone better, someplace safer. But if I left here, left *her*,

I would grow more tired, more distracted and more disinterested with every passing hour.

She would do. She had to. For once, not a choice I could live with, but the choice that would let me live.

There was no way to approach without the woman seeing me. Unlike Aaron, I didn't like to let my victims see the specter of death approach, but today I had no choice. So I straightened and started toward her, as if it was perfectly natural for a well-dressed middle-aged woman to cut through alleyways.

Out of the corner of my eye, I saw her look up as I passed. She tensed, then relaxed, seeing no threat. I turned, as if just noticing her. Then with a brisk nod, I took a twenty from my wallet.

A cruel ruse? Or making her last memory a pleasant one? Perhaps both. As expected, she smiled, her guard lowering even more. I reached down, but let go of the bill too soon. As it fluttered to the ground, I murmured an apology and bent, as if to retrieve it, but she was already snatching it up. I kept bending, still apologizing . . . and sank my fangs into the back of her neck.

She gave one gasp before the sedative took effect and she fell forward. I tugged her into the alcove, propped her against the wall and crouched beside her still form.

As my fangs pierced her jugular, I braced myself. The blood filled my mouth, as thick, hot and horrible at the drug dealer's the night before. My throat tried to seize up, rejecting it, but I swallowed hard. Another mouthful. Another swallow. Drink. Swallow. Drink. Swallow.

My stomach heaved. I pulled back from the woman, closed my eyes, lifted my chin and swallowed the blood. Another heave, and my mouth filled, the taste too horrible to describe. I gritted my teeth and swallowed.

With every mouthful now, some came back up. I swallowed it again. Soon my whole body was shaking, my brain screaming that this wasn't right, that I was killing myself, drowning.

My stomach gave one violent heave, my throat refilling. I clamped my hand to my mouth, eyes squeezed shut as I forced myself to swallow the regurgitated blood.

Body shaking, I crouched over her again. I opened my eyes and saw the woman lying there. I couldn't do this. I couldn't—

One hand still pressed to my mouth, I tugged the pages from my pocket. I unfolded them and forced myself to look. Paris. Aaron. Paige. The council. I wasn't done yet. Soon . . . but not yet.

I squeezed my eyes shut, then slammed my fangs into the woman's throat and drank.

Her pulse started to fade. My stomach was convulsing now, body trembling so hard I could barely keep my mouth locked on her neck. Even as I pushed on, seeing the end in sight, I knew this wasn't success. I'd won only the first round of a match I was doomed to lose.

The last drops of blood filled my mouth. Her heart beat slower, and slower, then . . . stopped.

Another life taken. Another year to live.

DO NOT HASTEN TO BID ME ADIEU

NORMAN PARTRIDGE

ONE

*H*e was done up all mysterious-like—black bandanna covering half his face, black duster, black boots and hat. Traveling incognito, just like that coachman who picked up Harker at the Borgo Pass.

Yeah. As a red man might figure it, that was many moons ago . . . at the beginning of the story. Stoker's story, anyway. But that tale of mannered woe and stiff-upper-lip bravado was as crazy as the lies Texans told about Crockett and his Alamo bunch. Harker didn't exist. Leastways, the man in black had never met him.

Nobody argued sweet-told lies, though. Nobody in England, anyhow. Especially with Stoker tying things up so neat and proper, and the count gone to dust and dirt and all.

A grin wrinkled the masked man's face as he remembered the vampire crumbling to nothing finger-snap quick, like the remnants of a cow-flop campfire worried by an unbridled prairie wind. Son of a bitch must have been *mucho* old. Count Dracula had departed this vale of tears, gone off to suckle the devil's own tit . . . though the man in

black doubted that Dracula's scientific turn of mind would allow him to believe in Old Scratch.

You could slice it fine or thick—ultimately, the fate of Count Dracula didn't make no nevermind. The man in black was one hell of a long way from Whitby, and his dealings with the count seemed about as unreal as Stoker's scribblings. Leastways, that business was behind him. This was to be *his* story. And he was just about to slap the ribbons to it.

Slap the ribbons he did, and the horses picked up the pace. The wagon bucked over ruts, creaking like an arthritic dinosaur. Big black box jostling in the back. Tired horses sweating steam up front. West Texas sky a quilt for the night, patched blood red and bruise purple and shot through with blue-pink streaks, same color as the meat that lines a woman's heart.

And black. Thick black squares in that quilt, too. More coming every second. Awful soon, there'd be nothing but those black squares and a round white moon.

Not yet, though. The man could still see the faint outline of a town on the horizon. There was Morrisville, up ahead, waiting in the red and purple and blue-pink shadows.

He wondered what she'd make of Morrisville. It was about as far from the stone manors of Whitby as one could possibly get. No vine-covered mysteries here. No cool salt breezes whispering from the green sea, blanketing emerald lawns, traveling lush garden paths. Not much of anything green at all. No crumbling Carfax estate, either. And no swirling fog to mask the night—everything right out in the open, just as plain as the nose on your face. A West Texas shit-splat. Cattle business, mostly. A matchstick kind of town. Wooden buildings—wind-dried, sun-bleached—that weren't much more than tinder dreading the match.

The people who lived there were the same way.

But it wasn't the town that made this place. He'd told her that. It was that big blanket of a sky, an eternal wave threatening to break over the

dead dry husk of the prairie, fading darker with each turn of the wagon wheels—cresting, cresting—ready to smother the earth like a hungry thing.

Not a bigger, blacker night anywhere on the planet. When that nightwave broke, as it did all too rarely—wide and mean and full-up with mad lightning and thunder—it was something to see.

He'd promised her that. He'd promised to show her the heart of a wild Texas night, the way she'd shown him the shadows of Whitby.

Not that he always kept his promises. But this one was a promise to himself as much as it was a promise to her.

He'd hidden from it for a while. Sure. In the wake of all that horror, he'd run. But finally he'd returned to Whitby, and to her. He'd returned to keep his promise.

And now he was coming home.

* * *

"Not another place like it anywhere, Miss Lucy. Damn sure not on this side of the pond, anyhow."

She didn't fake a blush or get all offended by his language, like so many of the English missies did, and he liked that. She played right with him, like she knew the game. Not just knew it, but thrived on it. "No," she said. "Nothing here could possibly resemble your Texas, Quincey P. Morris. Because no one here resembles you."

She took him by the lapels and kissed him like she was so hungry for it, like she couldn't wait another moment, and then he had her in his arms and they were moving together, off the terrace, away from the house and the party and the dry rattle of polite conversation. He was pulling her and she was pushing him and together they were going back, back into the shadows of Whitby, deep into the garden where fog settled like velvet and the air carried what for him would always be the green scent of England.

And then they were alone. The party sounds were a world away. But those sounds were nothing worth hearing—they were dead sounds compared to the music secret lovers could make. Matched with the rustle of her skirts, and the whisper of his fingers on her tender thighs, and the sweet duet of hungry lips, the sounds locked up in the big stone house were as sad and empty as the cries of the damned souls in Dr. Seward's loony bin, and he drew her away from them, and she pushed him away from them, and together they entered another world where strange shadows met, cloaking them like fringed buckskin, like gathered satin.

Buckskin and satin. It wasn't what you'd call a likely match. They'd been dancing around it for months. But now the dancing was over.

"God, I want you," he said.

She didn't say anything. There was really nothing more to say. She gave. She took. And he did the same.

* * *

He reined in the horses just short of town. Everything was black but that one circle of white hanging high in the sky.

He stepped down from the driver's box and stretched. He drew the night air deep into his lungs. The air was dry and dusty, and there wasn't anything in it that was pleasant.

He was tired. He lay down on top of the big black box in the back of the wagon and thought of her. His fingers traveled wood warped in the leaky cargo hold of a British ship. Splinters fought his callused hands, lost the battle. But he lost the war, because the dissonant rasp of rough fingers on warped wood was nothing like the music the same rough fingers could make when exploring a young woman's thighs.

He didn't give up easy, though. He searched for the memory of the green scent of England, and the music he'd made there, and shadows

of satin and buckskin. He-searched for the perfume of her hair, and her skin. The ready, eager perfume of her sex.

His hands traveled the wood. Scurrying like scorpions. Damn things just wouldn't give up, and he couldn't help laughing.

Raindrops beaded on the box. The nightwave was breaking.

No. Not raindrops at all. Only his tears.

The sky was empty. No clouds No rain.

No lightning.

But there was lightning in his eyes.

TWO

The morning sunlight couldn't penetrate the filthy jailhouse window. That didn't bother the man in black. He had grown to appreciate the darkness.

Sheriff Josh Muller scratched his head. "This is the damnednest thing, Quincey. You got to admit that that Stoker fella made it pretty plain in his book."

Quincey smiled. "You believe the lies that Buntline wrote about Buffalo Bill, too?"

"Shit no. Quince. But hell, that Stoker is an Englishman. I thought they was different and all—"

"I used to think that. Until I got to know a few of the bastards, that is."

"Well," the sheriff said, "that may be . . . but the way it was, was . . . we all thought that you had been killed by them Transylvanian gypsies, like you was in the book."

"I've been some places, before and since. But we never got to Transylvania. Not one of us. And I ain't even feelin' poorly."

"But in the book—"

"Just how stupid are you, Josh? You believe in vampires, too? Your bowels get loose thinkin' about Count Dracula?"

"Hell, no, of course not, but—"

"Shit, Josh, I didn't mean that like a question you were supposed to answer."

"Huh?"

Quincey sighed. "Let's toss this on the fire and watch it sizzle. It's real simple—I *ain't* dead. I'm *back*. Things are gonna be just like they used to be. We can start with this here window."

Quincey Morris shot a thumb over his shoulder. The sheriff looked up and saw how dirty the window was. He grabbed a rag from his desk. "I'll take care of it, Quince."

"You don't get it," the man in black said.

"Huh?"

Again, Quincey sighed. "I *ain't* dead. I'm *back*. Things are gonna be just like they used to be. And this *is* Morrisville, right?"

The sheriff squinted at the words painted on the window. He wasn't a particularly fast reader—he'd been four months reading the Stoker book, and that was with his son doing most of the reading out loud. On top of that, he had to read this backwards. He started in, reading right to left: O-W-E-N-S-V-I-L-L . . .

That was as far as he got. Quincey Morris picked up a chair and sent it flying through the glass, and then the word wasn't there anymore.

Morris stepped through the opening and started toward his wagon. He stopped in the street, which was like a river of sunlight, turned, and squinted at the sheriff "Get that window fixed," he said. "Before I come back."

"Where are you headed?" The words were out of Josh Muller's mouth before he could stop himself, and he flinched at the grin Morris gave him in return.

"I'm goin' home," was all he said

* * *

There in the shadows, none of it mattered, because it was only the two of them. Two creatures from different worlds, but with hearts that were the same.

He'd come one hell of a long way to find this. Searched the world over. He'd known that he'd find it, once he went looking, same as he'd known that it was something he had to go out and find if he wanted to keep on living. His gut told him, *Find it, or put a bullet in your brainpan.* But he hadn't known it would feel like this. It never had before. But this time, with this person…she filled him up like no one else. And he figured it was the same with her.

"I want you."

"I think you just had me, Mr. Morris."

Her laughter tickled his neck, warm breath washing a cool patch traced by her tongue, drawn by her lips. Just a bruise, but as sure and real as a brand. He belonged to her. He knew that. But he didn't know—

The words slipped out before he could think them through. "I want you, forever."

That about said it, all right.

He felt her shiver, and then her lips found his.

"Forever is a long time," she said.

They laughed about that, embracing in the shadows.

They actually laughed.

* * *

She came running out of the big house as soon as he turned in from the road. Seeing her, he didn't feel a thing. That made him happy, because in England, in the midst of everything else, he'd thought about her a lot. He'd wondered just what kind of fuel made her belly burn, and why she wasn't more honest about it, in the way of the count. He wondered why she'd never gone ahead and torn open

his jugular, the way a vampire would, because she sure as hell had torn open his heart.

Leonora ran through the blowing dust, her hair a blond tangle, and she was up on the driver's box sitting next to him before he could slow the horses—her arms around him, her lips on his cheek, her little flute of a voice all happy. "Quince! Oh, Quince! It *is* you! We thought you were dead!"

He shook his head. His eyes were on the big house. It hadn't changed. Not in the looks department, anyway. The occupants . . . now that was a different story.

"Miss me?" he asked, and his tone of voice was not a pleasant thing.

"I'm sorry." She said it like she'd done something silly, like maybe she'd spilled some salt at the supper table or something. "I'm glad you came back." She hugged him. "It'll be different now. We've both had a chance to grow up."

He chuckled at that one, and she got it crossed up. "Oh, Quince, we'll work it out, you'll see. We both made mistakes But it's not too late to straighten them out." She leaned over and kissed his neck, her tongue working between her lips.

Quincey flushed with anger and embarrassment. The bitch. And with the box right there, behind them, in plain view. With him dressed head to toe in black. God, Leonora had the perceptive abilities of a blind armadillo.

He shoved her, hard. She tumbled off the driver's box. Her skirts caught on the seat, tearing as she fell. She landed in the dirt, petticoats bunched up around her waist.

She cussed him real good. But he didn't hear her at all, because suddenly he could see everything so clearly. The golden wedding band on her finger didn't mean much. Not to her it didn't, so it didn't mean anything to him. But the fist-sized bruises on her legs did.

He'd seen enough. He'd drawn a couple conclusions. Hal Owens hadn't changed. Looking at those bruises, that was for damn sure. And it was

misery that filled up Leonora's belly—that had to be the answer which had eluded him for so long—and at present it seemed that she was having to make do with her own. Knowing Leonora as he did, he figured that she was probably about ready for a change of menu, and he wanted to make it real clear that he wasn't going to be the next course.

"You bastard," she yelled. "You're finished around here! You can't just come walkin' back into town, big as you please! This ain't Morrisville, anymore, Quincey! It's Owensville! And Hal's gonna kill you! I'm his wife, dammit! And when I tell him what you did to me, he's gonna flat-out kill you!" She scooped up fistfuls of dirt and threw them at him. "You don't belong here anymore, you bastard!"

She was right about that. He didn't belong here anymore. This wasn't his world. His world was contained in a big black box. That was the only place for him anymore. Anywhere else there was only trouble.

Didn't matter where he went these days, folks were always threatening him. Threats seemed to be his lot in life.

* * *

Take Arthur Holmwood, for instance. He was a big one for threats. The morning after the Westenras' party, he'd visited Quincey's lodgings, bringing with him Dr. Seward and a varnished box with brass hinges.

"I demand satisfaction." he'd said, opening the box and setting it on the table.

Quincey stared down at the pistols. Flintlocks. Real pioneer stuff. "Hell, Art," he said, snatching his Peacemaker from beneath his breakfast napkin (Texas habits died hard, after all), "let's you and me get real satisfied, then."

The doctor went ahead and pissed in the pot. "Look here, Morris. You're in England now. A man does things in a certain way here. A gentleman, I should say."

Quincey was sufficiently cowed to table his Peacemaker. "Maybe I am a fish out of water, like you say, Doc." He examined one of the dueling pistols. "But ain't these a little old-fashioned, even for England? I thought this kind of thing went out with powdered wigs and such."

"A concession to you." Holmwood sneered. "We understand that in your Texas, men duel in the streets quite regularly."

Quincey grinned. "That's kind of an exaggeration."

"The fact remains that you compromised Miss Lucy's honor."

"Who says?"

Seward straightened. "I myself observed the way you thrust yourself upon her last night, on the terrace. And I saw Miss Lucy leave the party in your charge."

"You get a real good look, Doc?" Quincey's eyes narrowed. "You get a right proper fly-on-a-dung-pile-close-up view, or are you just telling tales out of school."

Holmwood's hand darted out. Fisted, but he did his business with a pair of kid gloves knotted in his grip. The gloves slapped the Texan's left cheek and came back for his right, at which time Quincey Morris exploded from his chair and kneed Arthur Holmwood in the balls.

Holmwood was a tall man. He seemed to go down in sections. Dr Seward trembled as Quincey retrieved his Peacemaker, and he didn't calm down at all when the Texan bolstered the weapon.

Quincey didn't see any point to stretching things out, not when there was serious fence-mending to do at the Westenras' house. "I hope you boys will think on this real seriously," he said as he stepped over Holmwood and made for the door.

* * *

There was a Mexican kid pretending to do some work behind the big house. Quincey gave him a nickel and took him around front.

The kid wasn't happy to see the box. He crossed himself several times. Then he spit on his palms and took one end, delighted to find that the box wasn't as heavy as it looked.

They set it in the parlor. Quincey had to take a chair and catch his breath. After all that time on the ship, and then more time sitting on his butt slapping reins to a pair of swaybacks, he wasn't much good. Of course, this wasn't as tough as when he'd had to haul the box from the Westenra family tomb, all by his lonesome, but it was bad enough. By the time he remembered to thank the kid, the kid had already gone.

Nothing for it, then.

Nothing, but to do it.

The words came back to him, echoing in his head. And it wasn't the voice of some European doctor, like in Stoker's book. It was Seward's voice. *"One moment's courage, and it is done."*

He shook those words away. He was alone here. The parlor hadn't changed much since the day he'd left to tour the world. The curtains were heavy and dark, and the deep shadows seemed to brush his cheek, one moment buckskin-rough, next moment satin-smooth.

Like the shadows in the Westenras' garden. The shadows where he'd held Lucy to him. Held her so close.

No. He wouldn't think of that. Not now. He had work to do. He couldn't start thinking about how it had been, because then he'd certainly start thinking about how it might be, again . . .

One moment's courage, and it is done.

God, how he wanted to laugh, but he kept it inside.

His big bowie knife was in his hand. He didn't know quite how it had gotten there. He went to work on the lid of the box, first removing brass screws, then removing the hinges.

One moment's courage . . .

The lid crashed heavily to the floor, but he never heard it. His horror was too great for that. After all this time, the stink of garlic burned his nostrils, scorched his lungs. But that wasn't the hell of it.

The hell of it was that she had moved. Oh, *she* hadn't moved. He knew that. He could see the stake spearing her poor breast, the breast that he had teased between his own lips. She couldn't move. Not with the stake there.

But the churning Atlantic had rocked a sailing ship, and that had moved her. And a bucking wagon had jostled over the rutted roads of Texas, and that had moved her. And now her poor head, her poor severed head with all that dark and beautiful hair, was trapped between her own sweet legs, nestled between her own tender thighs, just as his head had been.

Once. A long time ago. Maybe, once again . . . No. He wouldn't start thinking like that. He stared at her head, knowing he'd have to touch it. There was no sign of decay, no stink of corruption. But he could see the buds of garlic jammed into the open hole of her throat, the ragged gashes and severed muscles, the dangling ropes of flesh.

In his mind's eye, he saw Seward standing stiff and straight with a scalpel in his bloodstained grip.

And that bastard called himself a doctor.

* * *

There were shadows, of course, in their secret place in the Westenra garden. And he held her, as he had before. But now she never stopped shaking.

"You shouldn't have done it." she said. "Arthur is behaving like one of Seward's lunatics. You must be careful."

"You're the one has to be careful, Lucy," he said.

"No." She laughed. "Mother has disregarded the entire episode. Well,

nearly so. She's convinced that I behaved quite recklessly—and this judging from one kiss on the terrace. I had to assure her that we did nothing more than tour the garden in search of a better view of the moon. I said that was the custom in Texas. I'm not certain that she accepted my story, but. . ." She kissed him, very quickly. "I've feigned illness for her benefit, and she believes that I am in the grip of a rare and exotic fever. Seward has convinced her of this, I think. Once I'm pronounced fit, I'm certain that she will forgive your imagined indiscretion."

"Now, Miss Lucy, I don't think that was my *imagination*," he joked.

She laughed, trembling laughter there in his arms. "Seward has consulted a specialist. A European fellow. He's said to be an expert in fevers of the blood. I'm to see him tomorrow. That ought to put an end to the charade."

He wanted to say it. More than anything, he wanted to say, *Forget tomorrow. Let's leave here, tonight.* But he didn't say it, because she was trembling so.

"You English." he said. "You do love your charades." Moonlight washed the shadows. He caught the wild look in her eye. A twin to the fearful look a colt gets just before it's broken.

He kept his silence. He *was* imagining things. He held her. It was the last time he would hold her, alive.

THREE

Quincey pushed through the double doors of the salon and was surprised to find it deserted except for a sleepy-eyed man who was polishing the piano.

"You the piano player?" Quincey asked.

"Sure," the fellow said.

Quincey brought out the Peacemaker. "Can you play 'Red River Valley'?"

"S-sure." The man sat down, rolled up his sleeves.

'Not here." Quincey said.

"H-huh?"

"I got a big house on the edge of town."

The man swallowed hard. "You mean Mr. Owens's place?"

"No. I mean my place."

"H-huh?"

"Anyway, you go on up there, and you wait for me."

The man rose from the piano stool, both eyes on the Peacemaker, and started toward the double doors.

"Wait a minute." Quincey said. 'You're forgetting something."

"W-what?"

"Well, I don't have a piano up at the house."

"Y-you don't?"

"Nope."

"Well. . . Hell, mister, what do you want me to do?"

Quincey cocked the Peacemaker. "I guess you'd better start pushing."

"You mean . . . you want me to take the piano with me?"

Quincey nodded. "Now, I'll be home in a couple hours or so. You put the piano in the parlor, then you help yourself to a glass of whiskey. But don't linger in the parlor, hear?"

The man nodded. He seemed to catch on pretty quick. Had to be that he was a stranger in these parts.

Quincey moved on. He stopped off at Murphy's laundry, asked a few questions about garlic, received a few expansive answers detailing the amazing restorative power of Mrs. Murphy's soap, after which he set a gunnysack on the counter. He set it down real gentle-like, and the rough material settled over something kind of round, and, seeing this, Mr. Murphy excused himself and made a beeline for the saloon.

Next Quincey stopped off at the church with a bottle of whiskey for the preacher. They chatted a bit, and Quincey had a snort before moving on, just to be sociable.

He had just stepped into the home of Mrs. Danvers, the best seamstress in town, when he glanced through the window and spotted Hal Owens coming his way, two men in tow, one of them being the sheriff.

* * *

Things were never quite so plain in England. Oh, they were just as dangerous, that was for sure. But, with the exception of lunatics like Arthur Holmwood, the upper crust of Whitby cloaked their confrontational behavior in a veil of politeness.

Three nights running, Quincey stood alone in the garden, just waiting. Finally, he went to Lucy's mother in the light of day, hat literally in hand. He inquired as to Lucy's health. Mrs Westenra said that Lucy was convalescing. Three similar visits, and his testiness began to show through.

So did Mrs. Westenra's. She blamed Quincey for her daughter's poor health. He wanted to tell her that the whole thing was melodrama, and for her benefit, too, but he held off.

And that was when the old woman slipped up. Or maybe she didn't, because her voice was as sharp as his Bowie, and it was plain that she intended to do damage with it. "Lucy's condition is quite serious," she said. "Her behavior of late, which Dr. Seward has described in no small detail . . . Well, I mean to tell you that Lucy has shown little consideration for her family or her station, and there is no doubt that she is quite ill. We have placed her in hospital, under the care of Dr. Seward and his associates."

Mrs. Westenra had torn away the veil. He would not keep silent now. He made it as plain as plain could be. "You want to break her. You want to pocket her, heart and soul."

She seemed to consider her answer very carefully. Finally, she said, "We only do what we must."

* * *

"Nobody wants you here," Owens said.

Quincey grinned. Funny that Owens should say that. Those were the same words that had spilled from Seward's lips when Quincey confronted him at the asylum.

Of course, that had happened an ocean away, and Dr. Seward hadn't had a gun. But he'd had a needle, and that had done the job for him right proper.

Quincey stared down at Mrs. Danvers's sewing table. There were needles here, too. Sharp ones, little slivers of metal. But these needles weren't attached to syringes. They weren't like Dr. Seward's needles at all.

Something pressed against Quincey's stomach. He blinked several times, but he couldn't decide who was standing in front of him. Owens, or Seward, or . . .

Someone said, "Get out of town, or I'll make you wish you was dead." There was a sharp click. The pressure on Quincey's belly increased, and a heavy hand dropped onto his shoulder.

The hand of Count Dracula. A European nobleman and scientist. Stoker had split him into two characters—a kindly doctor and a hellborn monster. But Quincey knew that the truth was somewhere in between.

"Start movin', Quince. Otherwise, I'll spill your innards all over the floor."

The Count had only held him. He didn't make idle threats. He didn't use his teeth. He didn't spill a single drop of Quincey's blood. He let Seward do all the work, jabbing Quincey's arm with the needle, day after day, week after week.

That wasn't how the count handled Lucy, though. He had a special way with Dr. Seward's most combative patient, a method that brought real results. He emptied her bit by bit, draining her blood, and with it the strength that so disturbed Lucy's mother and the independent spirit that so troubled unsuccessful suitors such as Seward and Holmwood. The blind fools had been so happy at first, until they realized that they'd been

suckered by another outsider, a Transylvanian bastard with good manners who was much worse than anything that had ever come out of Texas.

They'd come to him, of course. The stranger with the wild gleam in his eyes. Told him the whole awful tale. Cut him out of the straitjacket with his own Bowie, placed the Peacemaker in one hand. A silver crucifix and an iron stake jammed in a cricketing bag filled the other.

"You make your play, Quince." Owens said. "I'm not goin' to give you forever."

"Forever is a long time."

"You ain't listenin' to me, Quince."

"One moment's courage, and it is done."

Count Dracula, waiting for him in the ruins of the chapel at Carfax. His fangs gleaming in the dark . . . fangs that could take everything . . .

The pistol bucked against Quincey's belly. The slug ripped straight through him, shattered the window behind. Blood spilled out of him, running down his leg. Lucy's blood on the Count's lips, spilling from her neck as he took and took and took some more. Quincey could see it from the depths of Seward's hell, he could see the garden and the shadows and their love flowing in Lucy's blood. Her strength, her dreams, her spirit . . .

"This is my town," Owens said, his hand still heavy on Quincey's shoulder. "I took it, and I mean to keep it."

Quincey opened his mouth. A gout of blood bubbled over his lips. He couldn't find words. Only blood, rushing away, running down his leg, spilling over his lips. It seemed his blood was everywhere, rushing wild, like once-still waters escaping the rubble of a collapsed dam.

He sagged against Owens. The big man laughed.

And then the big man screamed.

Quincey's teeth were at Owens's neck. He ripped through flesh, tore muscle and artery. Blood filled his mouth, and the Peacemaker thundered again and again in his hand, and then Owens was nothing

73

but a leaking mess there in his arms, a husk of a man puddling red, washing away to nothing so fast, spurting red rich blood one second, then stagnant-pool dead the next.

Quincey's gun was empty He fumbled for his bowie, arming himself against Owens's compadres.

There was no need.

Mrs. Danvers stood over them, a smoking shotgun in her hands.

Quincey released Owens's corpse. Watched it drop to the floor.

"Let me get a look at you," Mrs. Danvers said.

"There ain't no time for that," he said.

* * *

Dracula chuckled. "I can't believe it is you they sent. The American cowboy. The romantic."

Quincey studied the count's amused grin. Unnatural canines gleamed in the moonlight. In the ruined wasteland of Carfax, Dracula seemed strangely alive.

"Make your play," Quincey offered.

Icy laughter rode the shadows. "There is no need for such melodrama, Mr. Morris. I only wanted the blood. Nothing else. And I have taken that."

"That ain't what Seward says." Quincey squinted, his eyes adjusting to the darkness. "He claims you're after Miss Lucy's soul."

Again, the laughter. "I am a man of science, Mr. Morris. I accept my condition, and my biological need. Disease, and the transmission of disease, make for interesting study. I am more skeptical concerning the mythology of my kind. Fairy stories bore me. Certainly, powers exist which I cannot explain. But I cannot explain the moon and the stars, yet I know that these things exist because I see them in the night sky. It is the same with my special abilities—they exist, I use them, hence

I believe in them. As for the human soul, I cannot see any evidence of such a thing. What I cannot see, I refuse to believe."

But Quincey could see. He could see Dracula, clearer every second. The narrow outline of his jaw. The eyes burning beneath his heavy brow. The long, thin line of his lips hiding jaws that could gape so wide.

"You don't want her," Quincey said. "That's what you're saying."

"I only want a full belly, Mr. Morris. That is the way of it." He stepped forward, his eyes like coals. "I only take the blood. Your kind is different. You want everything. The flesh, the heart, the . . . soul, which of course has a certain tangibility fueled by *your* belief. You take it all. In comparison, I demand very little—"

"We take. But we give, too."

"That is what your kind would have me believe. I have seen little evidence that this is the truth." Red eyes swam in the darkness. "Think about it, Mr. Morris. They have sent you here to kill me. They have told you how evil I am. But who are they—these men who brought me to your Miss Lucy? What do they want?' He did not blink; he only advanced. "Think on it, Mr. Morris. Examine the needs of these men, Seward and Holmwood. Look into your own heart. Examine your needs."

And now Quincey smiled. "Maybe I ain't as smart as you, Count." He stepped forward. "Maybe you could take a look for me . . . let me know just what you see."

Their eyes met.

The vampire stumbled backward. He had looked into Quincey Morris's eyes. Seen a pair of empty green wells. Bottomless green pits. Something was alive there, undying, something that had known pain and hurt, and, very briefly, ecstasy.

Very suddenly, the vampire realized that he had never known real hunger at all.

The vampire tried to steady himself, but his voice trembled. "What I can see . . . I believe."

Quincey Morris did not blink.

He took the stake from Seward's bag.

"I want you to know that this ain't something I take lightly," he said.

FOUR

He'd drawn a sash around his belly, but it hadn't done much good. His jeans were stiff with blood, and his left boot seemed to be swimming with the stuff. That was his guess, anyway—there wasn't much more than a tingle of feeling in his left foot, and he wasn't going to stoop low and investigate.

Seeing himself in the mirror was bad enough. His face was so white. Almost like the count's.

Almost like her face, in death.

Mrs. Danvers stepped away from the coffin, tucking a pair of scissors into a carpetbag. "I did the best I could," she said.

"I'm much obliged, ma'am." Quincey leaned against the lip of the box, numb fingers brushing the yellow ribbon that circled Lucy's neck.

"You can't see them stitches at all," the whiskey-breathed preacher said, and the seamstress cut him off with a glance.

"You did a fine job, Mrs. Danvers." Quincey tried to smile. "You can go on home now."

"If you don't mind, I think I'd like to stay."

"That'll be fine." Quincey said.

He turned to the preacher, but he didn't look at him. Instead, he stared through the parlor window. Outside, the sky was going to blood red and bruise purple.

He reached into the box. His fingers were cold, clumsy. Lucy's delicate hand almost seemed warm by comparison.

Quincey nodded at the preacher. "Let's get on with it."

The preacher started in. Quincey had heard the words many times. He'd

seen people stand up to them, and he'd seen people totter under their weight, and he'd seen plenty who didn't care a damn for them at all.

But this time it was him hearing those words. Him answering them. And when the preacher got to the part about taking . . . *do you take this woman* . . . Quincey said, "Right now I just want to give."

That's what the count couldn't understand, him with all the emotion of a tick. Seward and Holmwood, even Lucy's mother, they weren't much better. But Quincey understood. Now more than ever. He held tight to Lucy's hand.

"If you've a mind to, you can go ahead and kiss her now," the preacher said.

Quincey bent low. His lips brushed hers, ever so gently. He caught a faint whiff of Mrs. Murphy's soap, no trace of garlic at all.

With some effort, he straightened. It seemed some time had passed, because the preacher was gone, and the evening sky was veined with blue-pink streaks.

The piano player just sat there, his eyes closed tight, his hands fisted in his lap. "You can play it now," Quincey said, and the man got right to it, fingers light and shaky on the keys, voice no more than a whisper:

> *"Come and sit by my side if you love me,*
> *Do not hasten to bid me adieu.*
> *But remember the Red River Valley,*
> *And the cowboy who loved you so true."*

Quincey listened to the words, holding Lucy's hand, watching the night. The sky was going black now, blacker every second. There was no blood left in it at all.

Just like you, you damn fool, he thought.

He pulled his Bowie from its sheath. Seward's words rang in his ears: *"One moment's courage, and it is done."*

But Seward hadn't been talking to Quincey when he'd said those words. Those words were for Holmwood. And Quincey had heard them, but he'd been about ten steps short of doing something about them. If he hadn't taken the time to discuss philosophy with Count Dracula, that might have been different. As it was, Holmwood had had plenty of time to use the stake, while Seward had done his business with a scalpel.

For too many moments, Quincey had watched them, too stunned to move. But when he did move, there was no stopping him.

He used the Bowie, and he left Whitby that night.

He ran out. He wasn't proud of that. And all the time he was running, he'd thought. *So much blood, all spilled for no good reason. Dracula, with the needs of a tick. Holmwood and Seward, who wanted to be masters or nothing at all.*

He ran out. Sure. But he came back. Because he knew that there was more to the blood, more than just the taking.

One moment's courage . . .

Quincey stared down at the stake jammed through his beloved's heart, the cold shaft spearing the blue-pink muscle that had thundered at the touch of his fingers. The Bowie shook in his hand. The piano man sang:

> *"There never could be such a longing,*
> *In the heart of a poor cowboy's breast,*
> *As dwells in this heart you are breaking,*
> *While I wait in my home in the West."*

Outside, the sky was black. Every square in the quilt. No moon tonight. Thunder rumbled, rattling the windows.

Quincey put the Bowie to his neck. Lightning flashed, and white spiderwebs of brightness danced on Lucy's flesh. The shadows receded for the briefest moment, then flooded the parlor once more, and Quincey was lost in them. Lost in shadows he'd brought home from Whitby.

One moment's courage . . .

He sliced his neck, praying that there was some red left in him. A thin line of blood welled from the wound, overflowing the spot where Lucy had branded him with eager kisses.

He sagged against the box. Pressed his neck to her lips.

He dropped the Bowie. His hand closed around the stake.

One moment's courage . . .

He tore the wooden shaft from her heart, and waited.

Minutes passed. He closed his eyes. Buried his face in her dark hair. His hands were scorpions, scurrying every where dancing to the music of her tender thighs.

Her breast did not rise, did not fall. She did not breathe.

She would never breathe again.

But her lips parted. Her fangs gleamed. And she drank.

Together, they welcomed the night.

THE SILVER COLLAR

GARRY KILWORTH

The remote Scottish island came into view just as the sun was setting. Outside the natural harbor, the sea was kicking a little in its traces and tossing its white manes in the dying light. My small outboard motor struggled against the ebbing tide, sometimes whining as it raced in the air as a particularly low trough left it without water to push against the blades of its propeller. By the time I reached the jetty, the moon was up and casting its chill light upon the shore and purple-heather hills beyond. There was a smothered atmosphere to this lonely place of rock and thin soil, as if the coarse grass and hardy plants had descended as a complete layer to wrap the ruggedness in a faded cover, hiding the nakedness from mean, inquisitive eyes.

As the agents had promised, he was waiting on the quay, his tall, emaciated figure stark against the gentle upward slope of the hinterland: a splinter of granite from the rock on which he made his home.

"I've brought the provisions," I called, as he took the line and secured it.

"Good. Will you come up to the croft? There's a peat fire going—it's warm, and I have some scotch. Nothing like a dram before an open fire, with the smell of burning peat filling the room."

"I could just make it out with the tide," I said. "Perhaps I should go now." It was not that I was reluctant to accept the invitation from this eremite, this strange recluse—on the contrary, he interested me—but I had to be sure to get back to the mainland that night, since I was to crew a fishing vessel the next day.

"You have time for a dram," his voice drifted away on the cold wind that had sprung up within minutes, like a breath from the mouth of the icy north. I had to admit to myself that a whisky, by the fire, would set me on my toes for the return trip, and his tone had a faintly insistent quality about it which made the offer difficult to refuse.

"Just a minute then—and thanks. You lead the way."

I followed his lean, lithe figure up through the heather, which scratched at my ankles through my seasocks. The path was obviously not well used and I imagined he spent his time in and around his croft, for even in the moonlight I could discern no other tracks incising the soft shape of the hill.

We reached his dwelling and he opened the wooden door, allowing me to enter first. Then, seating me in front of the fire, he poured me a generous whiskey before sitting down himself. I listened to the wind, locked outside the timber and turf croft, and waited for him to speak.

He said, "John, isn't it? They told me on the radio."

"Yes—and you're Samual."

"Sam. You must call me Sam."

I told him I would and there was a period of silence while we regarded each other. Peat is not a consistent fuel, and tends to spurt and spit colorful plumes of flame as the gases escape, having been held prisoner from the seasons for God knows how long. Nevertheless, I was able to study my host in the brief periods of illumination that the fire

afforded. He could have been any age, but I knew he was my senior by a great many years. The same thoughts must have been passing through his own head, for he remarked, "John, how old are you? I would guess at twenty."

"Nearer thirty, Sam. I was twenty-six last birthday." He nodded, saying that those who live a solitary life, away from others, have great difficulty in assessing the ages of people they do meet. Recent events slipped from his memory quite quickly, while the past seemed so close.

He leaned forward, into the hissing fire, as if drawing a breath from the ancient atmospheres it released into the room. Behind him, the earthen walls of the croft, held together by rough timbers and unhewn stones, seemed to move closer to his shoulder, as if ready to support his words with confirmation. I sensed a story coming. I recognized the pose from being in the company of sailors on long voyages and hoped he would finish before I had to leave.

"You're a good-looking boy," he said. "So was I, once upon a time." He paused to stir the flames and a blue-green cough from the peat illuminated his face. The skin was taut over the high cheekbones and there was a wanness to it, no doubt brought about by the inclement weather of the isles—the lack of sunshine and the constant misty rain that comes in as white veils from the north. Yes, he had been handsome—still was. I was surprised by his youthful features and suspected that he was not as old as he implied.

"A long time ago," he began, "when we had horse-drawn vehicles and things were different, in more ways than one . . ."

A sharp whistling note—the wind squeezing through two tightly packed logs in the croft—distracted me. Horse-drawn vehicles? What was this? A second-hand tale, surely? Yet he continued in the first person.

" . . . gas lighting in the streets. A different set of values. A different set of beliefs. We were more pagan then. Still had our roots buried in dark

thoughts. Machines have changed all that. Those sort of pagan, mystical ideas can't share a world with machines. Unnatural beings can only exist close to the natural world and nature's been displaced.

* * *

Yes, a different world—different things to fear. I was afraid as a young man—the reasons may seem trivial to you, now, in your time. I was afraid of, well, getting into something I couldn't get out of. Woman trouble, for instance—especially one not of my class. You understand?

I got involved once. Must have been about your age, or maybe a bit younger since I'd only just finished my apprenticeship and was a journeyman at the time. Silversmith. You knew that? No, of course you didn't. A silversmith, and a good one too. My master trusted me with one of his three shops, which puffed my pride a bit, I don't mind telling you. Anyway, it happened that I was working late one evening, when I heard the basement doorbell jangle.

I had just finished lighting the gas lamps in the workshop at the back, so I hurried to the counter where a customer was waiting. She had left the door open and the sounds from the street were distracting, the basement of course being on a level with the cobbled road. Coaches were rumbling by and the noise of street urchins and flower sellers was fighting for attention with the foghorns from the river. As politely as I could, I went behind the customer and closed the door. Then I turned to her and said, 'Yes madam? Can I be of service?'

She was wearing one of those large satin cloaks that only ladies of quality could afford and she threw back the hood to reveal one of the most beautiful faces I have ever seen in my life. There was a purity to her complexion that went deeper than her flawless skin, much deeper. And her eyes—how can I describe her eyes?—they were like black mirrors and you felt you could see the reflection of your own soul in

them. Her hair was dark—coiled on her head—and it contrasted sharply with that complexion, pale as a winter moon, and soft, soft as the velvet I used for polishing the silver.

'Yes,' she replied. 'You may be of service. You are the silversmith, are you not?'

'The journeyman, madam. I'm in charge of this shop.'

She seemed a little agitated, her fingers playing nervously with her reticule.

'I . . .' she faltered, then continued. 'I have a rather unusual request. Are you able to keep a secret, silversmith?'

'My work is confidential, if the customer wishes it so. Is it some special design you require? Something to surprise a loved one with? I have some very fine filigree work here.' I removed a tray from beneath the counter. 'There's something for both the lady and the gentleman. A cigar case, perhaps? This one has a crest wrought into the case in fine silver wire—an eagle, as you can see. It has been fashioned especially for a particular customer, but I can do something similar if you require . . .'

I stopped talking because she was shaking her head and seemed to be getting impatient with me.

'Nothing like that. Something very personal. I want you to make me a collar—a silver collar. Is that possible?'

'All things are possible.' I smiled. 'Given the time of course. A tort of some kind?'

'No, you misunderstand me.' A small frown marred the ivory forehead and she glanced anxiously towards the shop door. 'Perhaps I made a mistake . . . ?'

Worried, in case I lost her custom, I assured her that whatever was her request I should do my utmost to fulfill it. At the same time I told her that I could be trusted to keep the nature of the work to myself.

'No one shall know about this but the craftsman and the customer—you and I.'

She smiled at me then: a bewitching, spellbinding smile, and my heart melted within me. I would have done anything for her at that moment—I would have robbed my master—and I think she knew it.

'I'm sorry,' she said. 'I should have realized I could trust you. You have a kind face. A gentle face. One should learn to trust in faces.

'I want you—I want you to make me a collar which will cover my whole neck, especially the throat. I have a picture here, of some savages in Africa. The women have metal bands around their necks which envelop them from shoulder to chin. I want you to encase me in a similar fashion, except with one single piece of silver, do you understand? And I want it to fit tightly, so that not even your . . .' She took my hand in her own small gloved fingers. 'So that not even your little finger will be able to find its way beneath.'

I was, of course, extremely perturbed at such a request. I tried to explain to her that she would have to take the collar off quite frequently, or the skin beneath would become diseased. Her neck would certainly become very ugly.

'In any case, it will chafe and become quite sore. There will be constant irritation . . .'

She dropped my hand and said, no, I still misunderstood. The collar was to be worn permanently. She had no desire to remove it, once I had fashioned it around her neck. There was to be no locking device or anything of that sort. She wanted me to seal the metal.

'But?' I began, but she interrupted me in a firm voice.

'Silversmith, I have stated my request, my requirements. Will you carry out my wishes, or do I find another craftsman? I should be loath to do so, for I feel we have reached a level of understanding which might be difficult elsewhere. I'm going to be frank with you. This device, well—its purpose is protective. My husband-to-be is not—not like other men, but I love him just the same. I don't wish to embarrass you with talk that's not proper between strangers, and personal to

my situation, but the collar is necessary to ensure my marriage is happy—a limited happiness. Limited to a lifetime. I'm sure you *must* understand now. If you want me to leave your shop, I shall do so, but I am appealing to you because you are young and must know the pain of love—unfulfilled love. You are a handsome man and I don't doubt you have a young lady whom you adore. If she were suffering under some terrible affliction, a disease which you might contract from her, I'm sure it would make no difference to your feelings. You would strive to find a way in which you could live together, yet remain uncontaminated yourself. Am I right?'

I managed to breathe the word 'Yes,' but at the time I was filled with visions of horror. Visions of this beautiful young woman being wooed by some foul creature of the night—a supernatural beast that had no right to be treading on the same earth, let alone touching that sacred skin, kissing—my mind reeled—kissing those soft, moist lips with his monstrous mouth. How could she? Even the thought of it made me shudder in revulsion.

'Ah,' she smiled, knowingly. 'You want to save me from him. You think he is ugly and that I've been hypnotized, somehow, into believing otherwise? You're quite wrong. He's handsome in a way that you'd surely understand—and sensitive, kind, gentle—those things a woman finds important. He's also very cultured. His blood . . .

I winced and took a step backward, but she was lost in some kind of reverie as she listed his attributes and I'm sure was unaware of my presence for some time.

'. . . his blood is unimpeachable, reaching back through a royal lineage to the most notable of European families. I love him, yet I do not want to become one of his kind, for that would destroy my love . . .'

'And—he loves you of course,' I said, daringly.

For a moment those bright eyes clouded over, but she replied, 'In his way. It's not important that we both feel the same *kind* of love. We want

to be together, to share our lives. I prefer him to any man I have ever met and I will not be deterred by an obstacle that's neither his fault, nor mine. A barrier that's been placed in our way by the injustice of nature. He can't help the way he is—and I want to go to him. That's all there is to it.'

For a long time neither of us said anything. My throat felt too dry and constricted for words, and deep inside me I could feel something struggling, like a small creature fighting the folds of a net. The situation was beyond my comprehension: that is, I did not wish to allow it to enter my full understanding or I would have run screaming from the shop and made myself look foolish to my neighbors.

'Will you do it, silversmith?'

'But,' I said, 'a collar covers only the throat . . .' I left the rest unsaid, but I was concerned that she was not protecting herself fully: the other parts of her anatomy—the wrists, the thighs.

She became very angry. 'He isn't an animal. He's a gentleman. I'm merely guarding against—against moments of high passion. It's not just a matter of survival with him. The act is sensual and spiritual, as well as—as well as—what you're suggesting,' there was a note of loathing in her tone, 'is tantamount to rape.'

She was so incensed that I did not dare say that her lover must have satisfied his need *somewhere*, and therefore had compromised the manners and morals of a gentleman many times.

'Will you help me?' The eyes were pleading now. I tried to look out of the small, half-moon window, at the yellow-lighted streets, at the feet moving by on the pavement above, in an attempt to distract myself, but they were magnetic, those eyes, and they drew me back in less than a moment. I felt helpless—a trapped bird—in their unremitting gaze of anguish, and of course, I submitted.

I agreed. I just heard myself saying, 'Yes,' and led her into the back of the shop where I began the work. It was not a difficult task to actually fashion the collar, though the sealing of it was somewhat painful to her

and had to be carried out in stages, which took us well into the night hours. I must have, subconsciously perhaps, continued to glance through the workshop door at the window, for she said once, very quietly, 'He will not come here.'

Such a beautiful throat she had too. Very long, and elegant. It seemed a sacrilege to encase such beauty in metal, though I made the collar as attractive as I made any silver ornament which might adorn a pretty woman. On the outside of the metal I engraved centripetal designs and at her request, some representational forms: Christ on the cross, immediately over her jugular vein, but also Zeus and Europa, and Zeus and Leda, with the Greek god in his bestial forms of the bull and the swan. I think she had been seduced by the thought that she was marrying some kind of deity.

When I had finished, she paid me and left. I watched her walk out, into the early morning mists, with a heavy guilt in my heart. What could I have done? I was just a common craftsman and had no right interfering in the lives of others. Perhaps I should have tried harder to dissuade her, but I doubt she would have listened to my impertinence for more than a few moments. Besides, I had, during those few short hours, fallen in love with her—utterly—and when she realized she had made a mistake, she would have to come back to me again, to have the collar removed.

I wanted desperately to see her again, though I knew that any chance of romance was impossible, hopeless. She was not of my class—or rather, I was not of hers, and her beauty was more than I could ever aspire to, though I knew myself to be a good-looking young man. Some had called me beautiful—it was that kind of handsomeness that I had been blessed with, rather than the rugged sort.

But despite my physical advantages, I had nothing which would attract a lady of quality from her own kind. The most I could ever hope for—the very most—was perhaps to serve her in some way.

Three weeks later she was back, looking somewhat distraught. 'I want it to come off,' she said. 'It must be removed.'

My fingers trembled as I worked at cutting her free—a much simpler task than the previous one.

'You've left him,' I said. 'Won't he follow?'

'No, you're quite wrong.' There was a haunted look to her eyes which chilled me to the bone. 'It's not that. I was too mistrustful. I love him too much to withhold from him the very thing he desires. I must give myself to him—wholly and completely. I need him, you see. And he needs me—yet like this I cannot give him the kind of love he has to have. I've been selfish. Very selfish. I must go to him . . .'

'Are you mad?' I cried, forgetting my position. 'You'll become like him—you'll become—'

'How *dare* you! How dare you preach to *me*? Just do your work, silversmith. Remove the collar!'

I was weak of course, as most of us are when confronted by a superior being. I cut the collar loose and put it aside. She rubbed her neck and complained loudly that flakes of skin were coming away in her hands.

'It's ugly,' she said. 'Scrawny. He'll never want me like this.'

'No—thank God!' I cried, gathering my courage.

At that moment she looked me full in the eyes and a strange expression came over her face.

'You're in love with me, aren't you? That's why you're so concerned, silversmith. Oh dear, I am so dreadfully sorry. I thought you were just being meddlesome. It was genuine concern for my welfare and I didn't recognize it at first. Dear man,' she touched my cheek. 'Don't look so sad. It cannot be, you know. You should find some nice girl and try to forget, because you'll never see me again after tonight. And don't worry about me. I know what I'm doing.'

With that, she gathered up her skirts and was gone again, down toward the river. The sun was just coming up, since she had arrived not

long before the dawn, and I thought: At least she will have a few hours more of natural life.

After that I tried to follow her advice and put her out of my mind. I did my work, something I had always enjoyed, and rarely left the shop. I felt that if I could get over a few months without a change in my normal pattern of existence, I should be safe. There were nightmares of course, to be gone through after sunsets, but those I was able to cope with. I have always managed to keep my dreams at a respectable distance and not let them interfere with my normal activities.

Then, one day, as I was working on a pendant—a butterfly requested by a banker for his wife—a small boy brought me a message. Though it was unsigned, I knew it was from her and my hands trembled as I read the words.

They simply said, *'Come. I need you.'*

Underneath this request was scrawled an address, which I knew to be located down by one of the wharves, south of the river.

She needed me—and I knew exactly what for. I touched my throat. I wanted her too, but for different reasons. I did not have the courage that she had—the kind of sacrificial courage that's produced by an overwhelming love. But I was not without strength. If there was a chance, just a chance, that I could meet with her and come away unscathed, then I was prepared to accept the risk.

But I didn't see how that was possible. Her kind, as she had become, possessed a physical strength which would make any escape fraught with difficulty.

I had no illusions about her being in love with me—or even fond of me.

She wanted to use me for her own purposes, which were as far away from love as earth is from the stars. I remembered seeing deep gouges in the silver collar, the time she had come to have it removed. They were like the claw marks of some beast, incised into the trunk of a tree. No wonder she had asked to have it sealed. Whoever, whatever, had made

those marks would have had the strength to tear away any hinges or lock. The frenzy to get at what lay beneath the silver must have been appalling to witness—experience—yet she had gone back to him, without the collar's protection.

I wanted her. I dreamed about having her, warm and close to me. That she had become something other than the beautiful woman who had entered my shop was no deterrent. I knew she would be just as lovely in her new form and I desired her above all things. For nights I lay awake, running different schemes over in my mind, trying to find a path which would allow us to make love together, just once, and yet let me walk away safely afterward. Even as I schemed, I saw her beauty laid before me, willingly, and my body and soul ached for her presence.

One chance. I had this one chance of loving a woman a dozen places above my station: a woman whose refined ways and manner of speech had captivated me from the moment I met her. A woman whose dignity, elegance, and gracefulness were without parallel. Whose form surpassed that of the finest silverwork figurine I had ever known.

I had to find a way.

Finally, I came up with a plan which seemed to suit my purposes, and taking my courage in both hands I wrote her a note which said, *'I'm waiting for you. You must come to me.'* I found an urchin to carry it for me and told him to put it through the letter box of the address she had given me.

That afternoon I visited the church and a purveyor of medical instruments.

That evening I spent wandering the streets, alternately praising myself for dreaming up such a clever plan and cursing myself for my foolhardiness in carrying it through. As I strolled through the backstreets, stepping around the gin-soaked drunks and tipping my hat to the factory girls as they hurried home from a sixteen-hour day

in some garment manufacturer's sweatshop, or a hosiery, I realized that
for once I had allowed my emotions to overrule my intellect. I'm not
saying I was an intelligent young man—not above the average—but
I was wise enough to know that there was great danger in what I
proposed to do, yet the force of my feelings was more powerful than
fear. I could not deny them their expression. The heart has no reason,
but its drive is stronger than sense dictates.

The barges on the river ploughed slowly against the current as I
leaned on the wrought-iron balustrade overlooking the water. I could
see the gas lamps reflected on the dark surface and thought about
the shadow world that lived alongside our own, where nothing was
rigid, set, but could be warped and twisted, like those lights in the
water when the ripples from the barges passed through them. Would
it take me and twist me into something, not ugly, but insubstantial?
Into something that has the appearance of the real thing, but which is
evanescent in the daylight and can only make its appearance at night,
when vacuous shapes and phantasms take on a semblance of life and
mock it with their unreal forms?

When the smell of the mud below me began to waft upward, as the
tide retreated and the river diminished, I made my way homeward. There
was a sharpness to the air which cut into my confidence and I was glad
to be leaving it behind for the warmth and security of my rooms. Security?
I laughed at myself, having voluntarily exposed my vulnerability.

She came.

There was a scratching at the casement windowpane in the early hours
of the morning and I opened it and let her in. She had not changed. If
anything, she was more beautiful than ever, with a paler color to her
cheeks and a fuller red to her lips.

No words were exchanged between us. I lay on the bed naked and
she joined me after removing her garments. She stroked my hair and the
nape of my neck as I sank into her soft young body. I cannot describe

the ecstasy. It was—*unearthly*. She allowed me—encouraged me—and the happiness of those moments was worth all the risks of entering Hell for a taste of Heaven.

Of course, the moment came when she lowered her head to the base of my throat. I felt the black coils of her hair against my cheek: smelled their sweet fragrance. I could sense the pulse in my neck, throbbing with blood. Her body was warm against mine—deliciously warm. I wanted her to stay there forever. There was just a hint of pain in my throat—a needleprick, no more, and then a feeling of drifting, floating on warm water, as if I had suddenly been transported to tropic seas and lay in the shallows of some sunbleached island's beaches. I felt no fear—only, bliss.

Then, suddenly, she snorted, springing to her feet like no athlete I have ever seen. Her eyes were blazing and she spat and hissed into my face.

'What have you done?' she shrieked.

Then the fear came, rushing to my heart. I cowered at the bedhead, pulling my legs up to my chest in an effort to get as far away from her as possible.

Again she cried, 'What have you done?'

'Holy water,' I said. 'I've injected holy water into my veins.'

She let out another wail which made my ears sing. Her hands reached for me and I saw those long nails, like talons, ready to slash at an artery, but the fear was gone from me. I just wanted her back in bed with me. I no longer cared for the consequences.

'Please?' I said, reaching for her. 'Help me? I want you to help me.'

She withdrew from me then and sprang to the window. It was getting close to dawn: The first rays of the sun were sliding over the horizon.

'You fool,' she said, and then she was gone, out into the murk. I jumped up and looked for her through the window, but all I could see was the mist on the river, curling its way around the rotten stumps of an old jetty.

Once I had recovered my common sense and was out of her influence, I remember thinking to myself that I would have to make a collar—a silver collar . . .

* * *

The fire spat in the grate and I jerked upright. I had no idea how long Sam had been talking but the peat was almost all ashes.

"The tide," I said, alarmed. "I must leave."

"I haven't finished," he complained, but I was already on my feet. I opened the door and began to walk quickly down the narrow path we had made through the heather, to where my boat lay, but even as I approached it, I could see that it was lying on its side in the slick, glinting mud.

Angry, I looked back at the croft on the hillside. He must have known. He must have known. I was about to march back and take Sam to task, when I suddenly saw the croft in a new perspective. It was like most dwellings of its kind—timber framed, with sods of earth filling the cracks, and stones holding down the turf on the roof. But it was a peculiar shape—more of a mound than the normal four walls and a roof—and was without windows.

My mind suddenly ran wild with frightening images of wood, earth, and rocks. The wooden coffin goes inside the earth and the headstone weights it down. A mound—a burial mound. *He hadn't been able to stay away from her. The same trap that had caught her . . .*

I turned back to the boat and tried dragging it across the moonlit mud, toward the distant water, but it was too heavy. I could only inch it along, and rapidly became tired. The muscles in my arms and legs screamed at me. All the time I labored, one side of my mind kept telling me not to be so foolish, while the other was equally insistent regarding the need to get away. I could hear myself repeating the words. *"He couldn't stay away from her. He couldn't stay away."*

I had covered about six yards when I heard a voice at my shoulder—a soft, dry voice, full of concern.

"Here, John, let me help you . . ."

* * *

Sam did help me that day, more than I wished him to. I don't hate him for that, especially now that so many years have passed. Since then I have obtained this job, of night ferryman on the loch, helping young ladies like the one I have in the skiff with me now—a runaway, off to join her lover.

"Don't worry," I try to reassure her, after telling her my story, "we sailors are fond of our tales. Come and join me by the tiller. I'll show you how to manage the boat. Do I frighten you? I don't mean to. I only want to help you . . ."

FINDERS KEEPERS

L. A. BANKS

ATLANTIC CITY, NEW JERSEY

She kissed his forehead, tasting the thin sheen of salty moisture that still lingered on his skin, considering him before she gently closed his eyes. He had a handsome face, that of a Roman; dark lashes that rested against his now porcelain-pale skin; a strong, aristocratic nose; rugged square jaw. But he wasn't a keeper.

Slightly forlorn, she peeled herself away from his nude, lifeless body with a sigh, studying the tall, athletic form in repose on the bed as she took her time to dress. A thread-width finger of crimson seeped from his wound, the scarlet beacon drawing her back to his side to taste the last of him. His body twitched from the invasion; she kissed his lips as a goodbye and a thank you, leaving a red print of his essence against his mouth. But he wasn't a keeper.

Death was like delicious prose when delivered with elegance and style. It had a prologue, a body, and then an epilogue, no less than fine dining replete with an appetizer, entrée, followed by dessert. The composition of it all was quiet, pleasurable, and perfect. She felt no guilt as she

turned toward the terrace doors and faced the moon. She would shower later, back at her lair. This man's death was an elegant kill, as always. Society was the better for it, she was the better for it, and if there was an Ultimate Maker, then the drained man on the bed could hash out the particulars with the judge of creation regarding whether or not his life had been lived in vain.

It was always a philosophical question that niggled her—would a so-called victim dare ask the Divine for recompense, after having killed so many men himself for blood money? One less mob enforcer lost at a casino would not imperil the world. Perhaps she provided a true service to mankind. The man her feed would have killed tonight had been given a night of reprieve . . . an honest man would therefore get one more night to live—she just hoped he'd made the most of the time.

A slight smile graced her lips, exposing a hint of fang as she retracted them. Her logic was sound in her own mind as she leaped up on the terrace railing, balancing on it for a moment before allowing the night to pull her into its dark folds of freedom.

Wind rushed through her hair and buffeted her face. Plummeting helped her remember being alive, the joy, the fear, the pain.

But after a few moments, she finally allowed the fierceness of the wind to abate so she could hover on the gentleness of the evening breeze. Floating high above the Atlantic City boardwalk, her thoughts drifted to her human days. Back then, it was the humans who were beasts. Things were not so different now, she reasoned, spying the antlike creatures that dotted the boardwalk and streets below. Humans killed more of their own than her kind did, and for much more senseless reasons. Men who'd wanted her called her a witch—when she denied their advances; women who'd envied her beauty joined in their persecution. Murderous group thinking prevailed over logic, as was the human way.

The verdict was simple and heartless. It was in everyone's best interest that she be exterminated, everyone's best interest but hers. Mysterious

deaths had been blamed on her sorcery, when all she'd had was the gift, or curse, of second sight. No one had given a single thought to the nobleman stranger that had recently come ashore with his ship and largess. He was above the law and above their suspicion or contempt. They had been elegantly glamoured.

People. She hated that she even needed them for blood.

The midnight blue horizon drew her attention. Moonlight sent shards of opalescence to ripple against the blue-black water. It was so beautiful. If she could stay airborne all night, she would.

Memories rolled across her mind in unrelenting waves. Haiti was a small lush place then . . . too small to hide in. Who would risk their life to give sanctuary to a motherless child? No one was that brave when a mob came calling. They'd easily found her, had mercilessly beaten and violated her, and then dragged her to a pyre to cover their shame. Already half-dead from the abuse and hemorrhaging badly, they'd lit tinder around her. Flames quickly caught the hem of her ragged dress. Heat raced up her legs, but she was too weak to move and could barely scream. Her protest came out as a deep, resounding moan of agony. She would have been their bonfire that night, had a man with honor not shown up. Maybe that's why she loved the weightlessness of vapor so.

That was how Alfonse had come to her, as vapor.

Searing heat had given way to cool relief. The jeers and curses all around her had turned into screams of terror. Something that no human mind could fathom had rescued her from the flames, and now the townspeople knew beyond a shadow of a doubt that there was more on the island to fear than her. The least likely person, the nobleman of means, wielded the wrath and destructive power of an entity that they were horrified to name.

Humans fled. The beach had returned to a place of peace beneath the moon. A gentle hand had cradled her skull, lifting her throat to his

mouth. A gentle whisper offered her a choice with a promise, "I will not hurt you; do you want to live?"

Something human within her recoiled as she swallowed her own blood, but that feral, primal animus within knew she was dying, and it fought with all its might to survive. Blood choked her words; all she could do was nod. But her mind screamed a thousand questions as his beautiful lips parted and the moonlight glinted off his fangs.

Yet, his murmur was so serene. "Relax. I must do this now before your heart stops beating or it will be too late, *cherie.*"

She remembered her *making* as though it were only moments ago. More than two hundred years still could not eclipse the horror of what people had done to her, nor could she ever forget what Alfonse had given her.

Through his sanguine kiss, her broken bones and violated flesh had begun to knit as her muscles relaxed. Raw nail beds from fighting rapists and aggressors began to heal. Pain literally ceased with his kiss, and then there was only sweet pressure at her neck. Life was draining out of her with each suckle; the world slowed down, her hearing dulled, her eyes closed against the moon. The burns that had engulfed her legs cooled, the puffiness of her swollen face eased. For a moment, there was a velvet cloak of dark peace that enveloped her, a totality of nothingness so peaceful that if she could have, she would have wept. Initially, she could feel him, then see him within her mind's eye as he threw his head back with his eyes closed, ecstasy staining his expression, chest heaving from the exertion, moonlight casting crimson prisms in saliva and blood against porcelain canines. He was horrifying and gorgeous, this nobleman that had claimed her.

"Breathe," he'd commanded.

A gasp shuddered through her and relief made him hug her.

Tears stung her eyes as she searched for a place to discreetly land amongst the modern day humans that strolled the Atlantic City

boardwalk so carefree at night. It was time to return her thoughts to the present. Without Alfonse, the past was a place of pain.

But the memories had a stranglehold on her. Her first question upon her awakening in Alfonse's arms had been so naïve.

"I will live?"

His dark eyes had flashed with both triumph and remorse. "*Non*. You will exist." He'd then touched her disheveled hair with reverence. "I'm sorry, it was the only way."

Even then she hadn't fully understood. All she was sure of was that a strange nobleman had found her and had saved her at her darkest hour. His handsome face still haunted her . . . deeply intense, dark eyes . . . thick brows furrowed in a frown of concern. Square jaw owning a slight cleft. Strong, Romanesque nose. A shock of glistening brunette hair spilling across his shoulders when the wind tired of it. His mouth lush and ruby-stained, punished by the suckle.

"Why didn't you just let me die?" It had seemed fair enough a question then.

"Because you'd fought so hard to live, and what they'd accused you of was a lie. I am a man of principle. Without principles, we are all just animals."

His admission became a sensual murmur that bonded them forever. "I have watched you since I came to this island . . . you are an exquisite beauty that I could never allow to endure the sentence for my sins. Even being what I am, there is a code of ethics. Never take more than you need, never take from those who are innocent, *ma cherie*. Break no hearts; cull the herd of its own beasts. Feed from the damned and don't allow them to wake up. They'd blamed you for my feeds, a convenient scapegoat to give them license to act out their lusts and anger. Fools, the lot of them. How could they think a woman who walks in the sunlight amongst them could be capable of such crimes?"

Still, she wasn't sure of what he'd admitted, but she did understand how a woman of no pedigree, no social standing, born at the wrong time to the wrong majority could be blamed. Her response had pained him as she'd taken up his hand within hers.

"Look at my hand, look at yours. What do you see? Look at your clothes, look at mine. That is enough of a reason for them to excuse you and to lynch me."

She'd expected him to snatch his hand away in offense, but her simple truth had gentled his expression from outrage at the mob that had violated her humanity to something else that she, even now, couldn't describe. His words had become tender like his touch, his fingers dappling the pleasure of a caress against her cheek as he'd spoken in a gentle timbre.

"I see beautiful, cinnamon-hued skin perfumed by oils and flavors of the earth. I see deep, amber-brown, expressive eyes, so gorgeous and with depth so vast that they rival the jewel-blue sea. I see thick, lush tendrils of mahogany hair that appears to be as velvet under the night sky. I see a face of an angel, a mouth so inviting I tremble."

He looked away out toward the surf, his voice becoming distant as he spoke a truth that was hard to bear. "I've also sadly witnessed a soul that was pure have to flee its earthly housing well before its time, heard a heart that was loving stop beating while you were in my arms . . . then, as now, I see a body created in majesty that is still yearning for affection beyond lust. I see a brilliant mind trapped in an era of ignorance, straining for recognition and release. I see a woman held captive by circumstance and accident of birth, a hostage of men who have no right to own another living soul. The small attention I gave you upon arriving here at night caused them to hate you more . . . jealousy is a tireless monster that no one can understand."

It was her turn to look away then. Tears mixed with rage as she remembered the respectful attention the new nobleman had given her,

and the way men with lesser wealth had resented her reciprocated charm. Women on the island, black and white, hated her because of the attention she'd garnered from the wealthy stranger. Men on the island seethed with outrage, those of all hues taking offense that she would be so enamored with a stranger that she'd deny their advances.

She hadn't thought she was better, or that they were lesser; Alfonse duBenet had given her a jewel that no man had offered. Respect set in kindness. He didn't presume to own her, hadn't presumed that due to her station versus his that he could simply take her. He'd actually tried to begin the slow process of courting her. That is what had been viewed as scandalous. That was where the true crime had been committed, according to the locals. And she'd blossomed under Alfonse's gifts of emotional tenderness. She'd seen that as his difference, the respect and tenderness he'd offered. Not until the night he'd rescued her had she realized that he was something beyond human. But, then again, so were they.

It was humans that had ultimately abused her, had tried to murder her. A vampire had killed her, but in so doing had saved her. The simplicity of it was both profound and perverse.

Alfonse had released a sigh of frustration when he saw her thinking too hard and had then given her his hand. "Be my bride and let us seek our revenge by outliving them all. We will have to go to the mainland. They now know what I am, as well as will correctly assume you are that, too. If we stay on this small island, they will find us by daylight . . . we must leave tonight, *cherie*."

His human crew was already waiting. The ship had been loaded, the hull of it prepared. Protection sealed it. That was the first time she'd crossed the sea. New Orleans eventually became her home, but not before he'd shown her the world. She missed Alfonse so terribly that her heart still contracted with phantom pains when she thought about him.

Shaking the memory, she alighted on a deserted section of boardwalk. The night was still young as she considered the moon. Only a little

after midnight. Normally she didn't hunt so early and preferred being out in the ocean breeze as long as possible. But the man she'd fed on so reminded her of Alfonse. Yet his physical attributes were where the similarity had begun and ended. The man's mind was repugnant. His thoughts pedestrian . . . common. She had done a good deed—freeing a beautiful body of a stagnant soul. At least the physical work of art could decompose in peace and not be mocked by adulterous misuse from the banal mind that had controlled it. He wasn't even a good lover, thus not worthy of being a vampire.

The shadow of a building provided her reentry into solid form near humans. A quick autumn breeze took up the edges of her little black dress as she stepped into the light, giving passerby men a glimpse of her long, sleek legs and a flash of red thong. Brief curiosity and lust filled their eyes. She dismissed them mentally while she listened to their life stories in her head as she walked toward the boardwalk rails to stare out at the ocean. All average Joes; none worth pursuing, and she'd just eaten. Never take more than you need. The casinos here were just not like those in Monaco. The beaches here so unlike the Caribbean or the Mediterranean. Losing Alfonse was a tragedy.

Tears rose in her eyes and then burned away. Time had bled out the tears, but not the pain or the memory. Nightly survival was a game of chance; the casinos were that as well. The baccarat tables and high rollers' dens were filled with men who thrived on risk and survived. That was the energy that drew her and ignited her. That was the energy that disappointed her.

Bored insane she wondered if she might try a new milieu this century . . . politicians, perhaps. Most were duplicitous, foul creatures that were predatory in nature, so why not? It would be no different than hand-picking criminals to feed from.

However, hiding their deaths would be more problematic. Siphoning a hit-man dry would not create a full-scale investigation. It would go into

a cold-case homicide file; police wouldn't expend too much manpower on it. The organization her feed hailed from would retaliate, if necessary, against their assumed enemies, which would allow her to feed off the opposing side for a while until they retaliated—and the authorities would be none the wiser. A beautiful cycle until she moved on. It would all remain in the province of organized crime. Simple, elegant. Going after white-collar political criminals with high-profile posts would be messy, even if more satisfying. Maybe one day.

For now she was stuck in North America until she could develop a foolproof plan to cross the forbidding sea. Daylight was the barrier. One could travel as vapor only so far before depleting one's energy. The specter of being lost at sea at sunrise, decomposing and burning in the water, was compelling enough of a reason to stay on shore. Alfonse had taught her that, too, had taught her how to glamour human helpers to keep their coffins closed in the cargo hull until night. But with new technology and Homeland Security, new maritime laws, as well as the ineptness of this era's baggage handlers were she to dare a plane flight, would mean she'd surely fry in their care. She allowed her shoulders to slump. For now she was not just stuck, but trapped on this continent since Alfonse's demise.

Pushing away from the rail with renewed annoyance, she headed toward the bright lights, not caring which casino she entered. They were all the same; just like the feeds had been. Vegas was a notch up from where she was now, but it lacked a beach, and being a spawn of the Caribbean, the night air for her required surf. Down in the delta the feeds that came into the casinos were so po'boy-southern fried that they threatened to make her kill sloppily in outrage. She'd had to move from there, and her beloved New Orleans just wasn't the same since the flood.

Miami had potential, but there was so much competition to feed on the drug lords that often territorial plunder wars broke out amongst her kind, and she didn't need the hassle. Each coven was so protective

of its land rights. Same with LA; California was another world. The northeastern seaboard held the greatest potential at the moment, as did the Connecticut tract, or going up into Michigan and over into Canada. Still, one had to be careful of regional vampire politics.

She was older than most, but was also made by Alfonse—whom many had ill feelings about because he'd been merciless in enforcing his code of ethics: *Never the innocent, never take more than you need.* Gorging orgies had been put to a stop in his region. Making children was considered heresy in Alfonse's book.

He had garnered formidable enemies because of his extreme views . . . because of his extreme mercy toward humans. For that mercy, they had colluded to mercilessly expose him to sunlight in a devastating coup. The only thing that had saved her was another male wanted her for himself. Her face became tight as thoughts of vengeance tainted her mood. Yes, she'd played along until she could return the favor of sunlight exposure, but that had left her alone, an outcast from polite vampire society. That was the main reason she couldn't trust a cargo ship or flight abroad.

However, Montreal was beautiful and Quebec was her refuge when she needed a taste of Europe, albeit neither was a seaside town. But up there, any death of a local human was a big deal in that pristine environment and created too much attention. So, until circumstances changed, or her code of feeding off those who'd been predators changed, she was stuck.

How did one stop missing a man that she'd loved for more than two hundred years?

She kept walking until the click of her high heels against the marble pierced her senses. Sometimes she lived so deeply inside her own head that she had to remember where she was and had to remember to keep up the tedious facade of being engaged in the moment, caring about the mundane goings on of human existence. Had to fit in, be unobtrusive in their world. Had to stay away from the mirrors and reflective surfaces that were all the rage in the chic hotels. Wanted a vodka martini and

hated that she had to find a feed who was drinking one and then had to entice him somewhere for just a sip from his veins. All this waiting, when she was a woman of action. Tonight, she wanted to be anywhere but here, but Atlantic City would just have to do.

Frustrated, she found a blackjack table and sat with a flop.

"Bad night?" the dealer asked with a smile.

She stared at his warm hazel eyes and dark brown skin, enjoying the way his mouth moved for a moment before she materialized a stack of chips in her clutch bag and then withdrew them to slide them onto the table. "Just a slow start, but the night is young."

He nodded, appraising her physique for a second and then dealt her cards. She studied him before looking down at her cards; he couldn't have been more than twenty-five, with his sexy chocolate self.

"Blackjack," she said quietly, and then pushed the five thousand dollars worth of chip winnings back in his direction as a tip. He was cute. Too young with too much of a future to dine on. She stood as he gaped.

"You sure, Miss?" He looked from the stack to her and then over to his pit boss.

"As ever," she murmured, blowing him a sexy kiss. "Do something positive with it. A mind is a terrible thing to waste." She made eye contact with the older pit boss to be sure the young dealer wouldn't get in trouble—he hadn't stolen the chips, it was her tip, her choice. The pit boss nodded. Now she could leave. This is what acute boredom did, made one find little stupid things to engage in to give one's life meaning.

She turned to leave but the young dealer's energy reached out to try to hold her. She could feel him summoning the nerve to ask a simple question, curiosity about to cost him dearly. Curiosity always killed the cat, and sometimes satisfaction brought it back. He was a handsome cat, even if curiosity had the potential to kill him. But he wasn't a keeper, not likely to get brought back.

"What's your name?"

She half turned and offered him a half-smile. "Not important. And . . . no . . . I don't want to meet you later when you get off your shift. Just enjoy the cash and stay healthy, baby?'

"Okay, I can do that," he said, seeming disappointed as she strode away.

She shook her head and chuckled softly to herself. Men. They always wanted more than the bargain. Five grand wasn't enough; he wanted sex, too? Maybe she would just head toward the poker tables . . . or just go out to sit under the stars to allow the night to pass without incident.

* * *

He stared at the security monitors, running back the images that didn't make sense. A chair had moved away from the table by itself. Chips had appeared on the table and the dealer looked as though he was talking to himself. He'd dealt, and cards flipped where no one was seated. Then what looked like five thousand in winnings had gotten pushed back to the dealer. The kid had even checked with the pit boss, who nodded. Chips slid toward him as he spoke to the nothingness.

It was time to take a break.

Obviously his head was all screwed up. Either someone had slipped him a mickey or he was finally having that nervous breakdown that he should have had five years ago. But he was so fuckin' close! No one else had seemed to notice; it had gone by in a flash.

"Yo, Tony, you okay?" A burly member of the security team stared at him seeming worried. "All of a sudden you don't look so good. Like you seen a ghost, or somethin'."

He dabbed at the sweat beading his brow. "I'm cool, man, just need a few. Cover for me? I need to go take a walk."

Several pairs of eyes regarded him, eyes he knew he could never fully trust. He wasn't one of them, but had worked his way inside their

organization through years of deception. And still, he was only in the outer layers of their hierarchy.

"Sure thing, man. Take ten."

He nodded, studying their predatory eyes before slipping out of the casino floor monitoring room. Maybe he was losing it, if they could see it so clearly. Sharks could always sense blood in the water from miles away, and from what Fat Joe had said and the expression on his face, it was obvious he was bleeding to death. But the big question was, had his cover been blown somehow? And ultimately, did that matter? If he was a traitor, he was dead; if he was perceived as a liability, he was dead. Sharks would eat their own if one of them was weak or injured.

Right now he seemed weak, seemed injured. He knew his eyes had given him away. His sweat in a cool, air-conditioned room had telegraphed to them that something out of the blue had made him freak. He could have replayed the images, but what if what he saw was all in his head? Then there'd be questions, deeper digging into his background. He couldn't fully trust his own, either. There had been a leak back at the Federal Task Force on Organized Crime, Jersey Division.

After what they'd done to his Meghan, his partner, and his partner's wife, there was no time for so-called healing. He kept walking. If they snuffed him in the men's room, then he'd take several of them with him.

Checking the stalls briefly, he walked past the urinals and went to the sinks, splashing water on his face quickly so that his senses remained alert. He grabbed a paper towel and stared in the mirror as he wiped away the water, not seeing himself, but the fire before he turned away.

His partner, Nate, was the inside man, he'd worked the logistics in the office. Their wives were dear friends. That day, Meghan had gone over to personally tell Carol the good news . . . she was pregnant. Tony briefly closed his eyes. The kids, thank God, were in the yard when Carol turned on the burner under a tea kettle. Both women were at ground zero when the blast rocked the kitchen. Nate heard it on the police band.

Evidence of the charred radio told them that. He'd never made it home to collect his devastated children or to bury his wife. They'd duct-taped explosives to Nate's chair, and then allowed the warehouse to go up like a Fourth of July display.

He needed a drink, even though that was thoroughly against casino policy. Fuck it. No wonder he was seeing things. Following the rules had never been his forte, at least not after what went down had gone down.

Heading toward the elevators, he kept his gaze scanning.

He'd known all along that there had to be a leak, no matter what the internal investigation revealed. His own personal investigation told him otherwise. Some people even suggested that he rest, stop asking questions, take a vacation, take time off to grieve for Meghan. There were a lot of people who didn't want the Gambiotti family to have any legal problems. Political incorrectness was entrenched in the system, as was payola. He took their advice for three months, took time off to do what he had to do. So when bodies within the department started dropping, they never suspected it was one of their own making a surgical strike. It wasn't murder, in his mind; it was a matter of principle.

Chaos bred panic. Those within the department left in the chain of command wanted the loose ends tied up quickly before death came to their door. They wanted him back on the job, back in play; suddenly, they didn't care about his healing or his loss. Survival instinct was a motherfucker. They knew that a man with nothing to lose was a dangerous thing, so they set him on the other side like a rabid dog—never the wiser about who was hitting dirty feds—and they sicced him on the side that had given the hit order. He could go after the Gambiottis with impunity, as long as he yielded results . . . but if he was caught doing anything outside the scope of the law, he was on his own, a rogue that they would necessarily disavow.

The bell sounding the elevator arrival gave him a start. He stepped inside, glad it was empty, and went down to the casino floor. He had to

talk to that blackjack dealer and pit boss before he left to go out for a smoke. A small dive bar around the corner was calling his name, but so was the need to know.

He approached the table carefully, watching the patrons and the dealer until the young man noticed him. After the hand, he shut the table down.

"Yo, man, I knew y'all was coming—ask Stan, the chick said it was my tip. Y'all ain't breaking my legs for no bullshit. I don't steal from the house, never have."

"The kid is clean, Tony," Stan said, his voice low as he entered the quiet but intense conversation.

"I haven't said a word and you all have jumped to a defense," Tony said coolly, regarding both men.

"C'mon, Tony. What are we supposed to think? One of you guys comes down here from the monitoring booth, shuts down the table, and whatever, right after the kid gets a big tip." The old man lifted his chin. "It ain't right."

"What did the woman look like?" Tony waited, knowing the cameras were now on him. If there was something shaky going on, then he had to solidify the family's trust in him by going to handle it directly. Maybe he would run back those digital images. He could show the boys in the room the thing that had triggered his reaction, and they would see him now down on the floor.

But both men looked puzzled for a moment.

"You saw the broad from the monitors," old Stan challenged, running his thick fingers through his snow-white hair.

"She was fine," the dealer said, keeping his voice low and his eyes darting around like a trapped rabbit's. "You know, man, the money type. Five ten, skin flawless. Designer black dress on. Diamond earrings, the real shit, not no CZs. Single gold bangle with some real weight. Legs that go on for miles, stilettos making her ass even hotter when she walks. Beautiful set of tits, V-neck serving it all up, but not in a hoochie type of

way. But she didn't remind me of a pro, at least not the ones around here I've seen. She had a real classy vibe, man, like she wasn't from around here—belonged in fucking Vegas or Monaco, or off some runway in Paris, but not down at the damned Jersey shore . . . like she had money to play with. Seemed like she was bored as hell, too, if you feel me. Hey, if she stole it, y'all can have it back—but I didn't steal it."

"The kid is only twenty-six, Tony. He didn't steal from the drawer; that I witnessed with my own eyes. He's not lying, the broad was old money."

The desperation in the young man's voice and fear in his eyes told him what he needed to know. One—there hadn't been a theft. Two—there was a woman at that table. But then why hadn't she shown up on the monitors? That was the part that made him question his sanity. Unnerved, he let the two men waiting on his judgment off the hook.

"All right. Keep the chips, but point out which way she went. I have some questions for her."

"Shit, you shut my table down and I'll walk you to her over by the poker tables." The young dealer seemed unconvinced that his life was no longer in jeopardy. Stan nodded and he quickly came around the edge of his table. "I don't want no problems, man, no bullshit whatsoever. Aw'ight. So, I'ma take you to her, you can ask her yourself whether or not she gave me the tip. Cool? Then you guys will have that on tape and I don't have to worry about getting into my car in the parking lot, right?"

"That'll work," Tony said calmly as the young dealer came to his side, looked around, and then shook his hand.

"There she go," he said, beginning to walk. "Can't miss her . . . ain't nothing like her in this joint."

Tony stared behind the kid for a moment before he began walking. Again, he hadn't lied. Sensuality personified oozed from her very being. The way her graceful hand took up a card and added it to her fan, the way her mesmerizing eyes studied them and the dealer, sent the temperature of the entire casino up a notch. Her face was gorgeous,

and that added to the unbelievable curves she owned made her a knockout, drop-dead, to-die-for beauty. Not since Meghan had he been so drawn to a woman. A roll in the hay with a pro was one thing, simply a matter of releasing the primal—something he'd indulged in when he had more drinks than advisable. But this woman . . .

Then, as though sensing his approach, she looked up and stared at him. There was no question she was staring at him—it was more than a visual recognition, *he felt it.* He watched her fold her hand, rake in the winnings, and stand, leaving the game.

* * *

She'd sensed someone staring at her, but until the crowd parted a bit, she wasn't sure of where the energy pull was coming from. She spotted the young dealer, whose entire aura radiated stress and flight-or-fight hormone that was palpable. Yes, he'd been the one staring at her, but there was a darker presence, a more sensual, mysterious creature behind the kid. The moment she saw the source, she froze.

His dark brown hair was pulled back in a ponytail; she wondered if it was held by a dark leather thong or a simple rubber band. She briefly closed her eyes, no longer than a slow blink, perceiving as much as she could about him in seconds. Leather held his hair. Broad shoulders filled out his black leather jacket and concealed a gun. She could taste the metallic change in the air and smell the gunpowder in the clip. He wore a black T-shirt beneath the butter soft leather, black slacks, black slip-on Cole Haans. No jewelry, just a fine gold watch made by Rolex. A pair of intense, dark eyes pierced her, asking questions in a thunder of human thoughts. A strong jaw was set hard, but his mouth was still beautiful, not a tight line of anger. His athletic body moved through the crowd with the stealth of a cat . . . he was hunting her . . . interesting. Yet there was no guile aimed at her to be found in his presence, but this was a man of mysteries.

As he neared her, it all became so clear—he was the honest man she'd saved earlier by feeding on the assassin. The irony made her smile.

"Excuse me, Miss, may I have a word with you?"

She turned and regarded the near breathless dealer and then the man that stood behind him.

She nodded, already knowing what the problem was. "I had hoped it wouldn't come to this," she said, looking past the dealer into the eyes of pure intrigue. "I was bored, gave him a large tip of my own volition. He didn't steal anything from your casino." She flashed a purse full of chips worth close to fifty thousand dollars. "Look, I have more." She pulled out another five grand and handed it to the dealer. "Just so you gentlemen who watch transactions can be clear that I did tip the man."

"See, see what I mean, Tony!" The dealer held the chips out to Tony to take, still nervous.

"You're straight, you can go back to your table and open up," Tony said quietly, not looking at the dealer, his eyes transfixed on her. "Buy you a drink?"

She gave him a half-smile. "Mind if we get out of here and go somewhere less frenetic? This place is giving me a headache."

"Great minds think alike. I'm Tony."

"Pleased to meet you, Antonio. I am Odette."

"How did you know my full name was Antonio and not just plain Anthony?"

"Because you are a complicated man and Anthony is way too simplistic for you."

"How about that drink . . . somewhere out of here?"

"I would adore a vodka martini."

He nodded. "My favorite."

"Good," she murmured. "*Tres bon.*"

* * *

113

Fat Joe took the phone away from his ear slowly, every man in the booth watching Tony leave the casino alone after money had again changed hands. "They just found Donny all fucked up in his room over at the Trump. Can't figure out what the fuck happened to him. Wasn't an ounce of blood in 'im."

"That shit is crazy," Lou said, standing. "Tony had to know Donny was gonna do 'im tonight . . . 'cuz look at the segment of floor activity he was checking out before he got all weird on us."

Fat Joe came around the desks, moving his heft swiftly to lean in and see where Lou pointed. Other henchmen in the room joined in.

"Look at that shit. I don't understand it, but somehow he must have either erased the person's image or somethin'. The dealer looks nervous, five large goes across the table. The dealer asks old Stan something, and then our boy shuts down his monitors, goes downstairs, right. He has a little talk, the dealer walks with him away from the blackjack area over toward poker, they put more cash in the dealer's hand and he leaves."

"So, the black kid is working undercover with him and they got old Stan to turn a blind eye, you think?" Fat Joe stood up straight, outrage making his face turn red.

"Yeah, and helping himself to a little pocket lining just like the other feds . . . but how he got to Donny, that's what I wanna know."

Fat Joe looked at Lou. "Does that matter how they did it? They tried to infiltrate us, are stealing money from us—even if it is a punk ass amount, and they killed a good man. The boss said to be sure that crazy bastard Tony got put down hard tonight. We can't have undercover cops thinking they can violate us like that. So, it's good he's off the premises. Saves us the trouble of having to ask him to go for a little ride."

"I'll round up the fellas," Lou said with a slight smile.

* * *

The place where he'd taken her was a dive, but it was quiet. The short walk away from the casino district had allowed her thoughts to gather along with her impressions of him. Pain so deep and so profound cloaked him and she'd almost reached out to touch him to try to dispel it.

"You're an honest man," she said, once the bartender had taken their drink orders. "Noble."

"No man is without sin," he replied, staring into her eyes. "Sin stains nobility."

"I didn't say you were without sin, I said you were an honest man. To kill those who have brutalized those you love is an honest emotion."

Her words made him draw back and a frown replaced his once serene expression. "You need to talk to me—quickly."

She smiled. "I am not your nemesis, nor your enemy." She released a sigh as their drinks came, knowing she'd never be able to sip hers without a bit of blood mixer. "There was a man in the hotel, over at the Trump Taj Mahal . . . Donny, I think his name was."

"Was?" Tony leaned in to her and grabbed her arm.

"Was," she said flatly. "He knew who you were; they all do, I suppose, if they sent him to kill you."

"He's dead?" Tony slowly let go of her arm and then cautiously downed half his martini. "How do you know all of this?"

"Because I eliminated him."

Incredulous, he simply stared at her for a moment. "You work for them and you've now set me up?"

She shook her head no "Have the rest of your martini. I don't work for anyone, haven't in *years*. He was an asshole, a very bad man, the type I despise, so . . ."

"Then how do you know all of this—like how you knew my name?" Tony's voice was a low, threatening rumble.

"If I told you, you'd never believe me."

"Try me. You just told me you killed a man and know way too much about me for comfort."

She searched his face, seeing kind eyes behind their angry veneer, seeing where the pain began and what had chased him into the arms of fate.

"They took your wife's life," she murmured. "Your partner's and his wife. The baby." Odette shook her head and then shivered. "Beasts. Humans can be animals—I've died at their hands, had that which was precious taken from me. You and I are not so different."

"Lady, stop talking in riddles," he said, now grabbing her arm again as he roughly set down his glass.

"You aren't ready for the truth . . . ask yourself, didn't you find it strange that you couldn't see me on the monitors? The moment I saw you pushing the young dealer in my direction, with you dressed in security staff black, I figured that the technology had betrayed me."

"What *the fuck* is going on, lady?"

She inclined her head toward the mirror behind the bar, motioning toward it with her chin. "I don't show up in reflections, mirrored surfaces, or even in photographs. I don't exist, but I do exist. I don't appear dangerous, but I'm deadly. And I'm so much older than you think. But I'm not evil, although everything you've been taught says that I am . . . even though some like me definitely are. You and I are the same, rogues, an enigma, cloaked in pain and invisible to most others. We cull the herds, you and I, in our own way; we keep the beasts away from the innocent. Be careful tonight—it's getting late, I need to go."

His hand had fallen away from her arm as his jaw went slack. He didn't offer protest as he stared in the mirror and she stood and walked away, too stunned to immediately gather himself. By the time his body and mind caught up to each other, allowing him to toss a twenty on the bar and dash out the door to find her, she was gone.

But a black Escalade careened over the curb, its door opened before he could draw his weapon, and beefy hands had him. Duct tape went

over his mouth; nylon cuffed his wrists as the vehicle sped to a deserted section of beach. Hardened eyes told him Odette hadn't lied. How could he have been so stupid!

His shoulder collided with the ground, the searing pain racing through his skeleton. A pair of dead, young eyes stared at him, open, glassy . . . the kid was only twenty-six. Hell, he was only thirty-seven. Struggling just made the men around him laugh. Trying to speak made them draw their weapons.

"Take the tape off and lemme hear what this sonofabitch has to say," Lou growled, leveling a nine millimeter toward Tony's face. "We've known you were a cop for months."

Another henchman ripped off the tape. Tony took a huge inhale, and then began shouting, spittle flying.

"Fuck you!" he yelled out, trying to sit up. "You kill my pregnant wife and think I'm not coming for you? You kill my partner and think there'd be no retribution?" Chest heaving, death eminent, he refused to beg them, wanted them to know that he'd take this grudge with him to hell and back. "I'll haunt you motherfuckers! This ain't over!"

The men around him laughed and shook their heads.

"Sorry, I ain't superstitious," one said.

"Yeah, me neither," Lou said, shrugging his shoulders and poking out his barrel chest. "But sorry about the wife, little bitch wasn't supposed to be at the house when it blew. Our bad."

"I'll kill you!" Tony shouted.

"Yeah, we're so scared," Lou said, and then squeezed the trigger twice.

The back of his head exploded in pain and colors for a second and then everything went dark. There was no light, no sound; he could no longer feel the sand or the wind. The chill of the night air was gone. He'd failed. It was so quick, a blink of time. He was floating and weeping inside his shattered mind. Pressure at his throat made his muscles twitch. Something tightened around him and then became light,

making him feel like he was flying away. Time stood still and yet he could feel its passage. Water now pelted his body, his forehead rested against something soft. He opened his eyes slowly to a dark angel, the shower spray blurring his vision.

Butter-cream-soft hands traced his back; cinnamon-hued breasts cushioned his chest as his knees buckled. A warm mouth sought his in a tender kiss. He had to be in heaven, because he'd just left hell on the beach. Everything was now surreal. His stomach churned and then pain soon gripped him, making him stagger backward to claw the wall, his wail an agonized echo that bounced off the tiles.

"I tried but got there too late to save the boy, that young dealer. They are animals," a familiar voice murmured. "You must eat to regain your strength, and then heal today . . . tonight we will work together."

Frantic, he looked around at the exquisite marble and gold fixtures, and then his gaze settled on Odette. "Where am I?"

"At my home, far away from them."

"You saved me?" he panted. "The last thing I remember is Lou unloaded two slugs into the back of my head." Tony's hand gingerly touched his skull and then when he felt no wound, panicked.

"I perceived that you wanted to live more than anything else, in order to avenge this travesty of justice."

"I did, but . . . but how?" He stepped out of the walk-in shower, bumping into the glass and staggering to the far side of the spacious bathroom. "I heard the shots, felt the impact, passed out. How in the fuck don't I have a huge hole in my head!" He looked around, noticing something was missing. "Where's the mirror? Where's the goddamned mirror, Odette!"

"I don't have any in the mansion," she said calmly, turning off the water and covering her nudity with a large, white Turkish towel. "They upset me."

"Why! What's going on?"

She tossed him a towel and watched him grab it swiftly. "I'm sorry, it was the only way to save you. But once you eat, you'll understand all."

"Eat? Eat! Are you insane?" He wound the towel around his waist and struggled to stand without the aid of the double sink. "I'm not hungry, I'm about to lose my mind. My brains just got blown out, but I'm not dead, this ain't a hospital, and I don't know why I'm even alive." Pain doubled him over again.

"You're not. Eat," she whispered, offering him her wrist.

He seemed confused, and then became horrified as her French manicured finger broke the skin and fangs filled his mouth at the first sight of her blood.

Tears stung his eyes but the scent of blood saturated the bathroom, drawing him to her beyond his control. He closed his eyes as he took her arm and brought it to his lips, her fingers threading through his hair, petting him as he greedily suckled, colors staining the inside of his lids, pleasure careening through his system until he could stand it no more. He threw his head back and released a moan. Her embrace opened the floodgate on years of hurt along with a torrent of tears.

Sobs of remorse choked him, a tender mouth swallowed them away. Velvet tresses were in his fist, his fingers wending their way through dripping curls. Hands so graceful, so soft removed pain from his aura with each gentle caress until towels fell away and skin burned against skin. This woman had saved him, had pulled his essence of existence away from the blackness. He had another chance to complete the mission he'd begun. Her story exploded inside his mind and he wept for her as his story entered her and she wept for him, their honesty becoming raw passion that slammed against the walls and melted down to body-slicked heat on the towel-strewn floor.

The storm of emotions and pleasure was so swift that it left them both breathless. He stared down at her, tracing the edge of her beautiful brows and then cradled her cheek.

"Why did you come back for me?" he murmured, still out of breath.

"Because you were a keeper. I found you after a very long search. A nobleman . . . and it has been centuries since I'd found someone worth saving." A gentle smile eased out of hiding on her face. "Plus, I so badly wanted a vodka martini."

He paused to catch his breath, his mind laboring under the new knowledge it had just received. "What they did to you was unforgivable."

"I became what I am, much like you did tonight," she murmured, touching his cheek, her smile fading. "Someone cared enough about me to give me another chance and I loved him for that . . . and for whom he was."

He understood what Odette was telling him, he'd loved Meghan that way. But it was becoming so difficult to hold onto the memory or to nurse it to life.

"Imagine after more than two hundred years . . . the memories fade and all you have left is the pain." Her stare was so hypnotic, so open, and for all that she was and all that she had done, she possessed serenity.

"I have to finish this, tomorrow night, then I can move on."

"I know you have to redress what happened to you," she said quietly, briefly closing her eyes. "Just as one day I'll route out the rest of those in the coven that participated in the coup against Alfonse."

"I know," he murmured, moving against her slowly and now appreciating the unhurried pleasure of their union. She was a beautiful woman, but there was something beyond that, something still so genuine inside her very being. It had been so long since he'd witnessed that or had allowed himself to experience the possibility it existed beyond Meghan. The fact that he felt the way he did almost seemed like a betrayal.

"It's not a betrayal," Odette murmured, brushing his mouth with hers. "They would have wanted us to go on, to thrive, and not merely survive. If we exist tortured, then the others have also won."

A gasp escaped him as Odette's slick sheath tightened around him. He studied her face as he loved her slowly, kissing her throat, then her breasts, paying delicate homage to her erect Hershey nipples with tiny suckles until she moaned. Satiny legs encircled his waist as she arched and offered him her throat. The strike into her jugular was swift but tender, her gasp sending a shudder through him that made him cry out.

The night wore on, their lovemaking an anthem, to survival, to renewal, that took them from the floor of the vast bathroom to the sprawl of her king-sized bed. He watched semi-dazed as the steel door to the basement sanctuary closed and pure darkness surrounded them, but yet he could still see.

"Rest," she whispered. "Later tonight will be ours. We have the benefit now of time, power, and stealth."

He pulled her against his chest in the darkness, finding it new that no heartbeats meshed and only cool skin now touched. The heat was gone, but not his loyalty to the one who'd saved him. The seeds of a long-time love had been planted. One that wouldn't grow old, one that understood him more than the former love of his life ever had, one that shared his altruism and even his dark side.

"I'm glad you found me," he said quietly. "I didn't want to die."

She nodded and kissed his chest. "I am glad, too. This is rare . . . it is magic."

"Finders keepers." For the first time in years, he closed his eyes with a smile.

* * *

They entered the casino just as they had left, but no monitors could perceive them. Old Stan looked at Tony and then glanced away.

"Wait here," he said to Odette. "I have to clear this up."

She nodded and perused the floor watching as her lover tried to make an old man understand. But that was pointless, people believed what they wanted to. Finally, she saw Tony hail her with a slight lift of his jaw.

"Ask Odette," he said calmly, placing a hand on Stan's shoulder.

She already knew the direction of the conversation. "He didn't kill the young dealer, they did. Tony used to work for the feds."

Stan straightened. "Then get the fuck away from me, would ya!" He spoke through his teeth. "I don't wanna wind up like that kid, and I don't wanna know what's going on—but I don't want them to see me ever talking to you."

Tony nodded. "No problem, you live well."

Odette took his arm. "There is much I have to teach you about the use of your power."

"Just get me up into the security area without them seeing me."

"Vapor?" she said with a wide grin. "Follow me to the shadows. You just don't do that on an open casino floor in polite company."

She took his hand and then pulled him into an alcove, kissing him passionately as passersby glanced at them once, and then they were gone.

Drifting replaced body weight, and then vents became passageways. Silence echoed all around him until Odette's voice entered his head.

Bullets will hurt but not kill you. However, the rage is controlling you right now, you must control the rage. Decide before you go in there whether or not you want to rip them to shreds with your bare hands and start an entirely crazy investigation, or if you want to just shoot them all so that it looks like a human-on-human crime.

Before he could answer her, he was standing inside the room and could feel her presence invisibly monitoring his first foray as a vampire.

They were eating take-out from the restaurants below. Laughter filled the room, total entitlement to joy surrounded them like his life and death and that of an innocent kid's never matter, never happened. They didn't even see him.

"I told you I would haunt you," Tony said in a low growl.

"Oh, shit!" Lou jumped up and grabbed his gun.

Four henchmen cursed and scrambled for weapons.

"I thought you whacked this bastard!" Fat Joe shouted.

In that moment, Tony decided. He didn't want to shoot them. Hand-to-hand combat just felt too good. Ripping Lou's arm out of its socket and then shooting him in the head, just felt like the right thing to do. But wisdom and vampire speed prevailed, as he unloaded his clip.

"Feed before you leave"; Odette said, materializing behind him. "Or else it's a waste."

* * *

They sat hand in hand under the stars on a bench watching the surf. A thousand questions pummeled his mind but he was grateful he didn't have to verbalize any of them for her to understand.

"It is a sexy, glorious emotion, revenge, but just like sex with a lover you don't love, once you climax, it all feels so hollow."

He nodded. Leave it to a woman to so eloquently define what was raging within him. "Now what?" he whispered. "There are so many more of them, so many I could go after, and but it all seems so pointless."

She laid her head on his shoulder. "This is why I haven't destabilized the coven. After I repaid Gustav for what he'd done to Alfonse, I sadly realized, it would never bring him back." Her soft palm stroked his chest as she looked out to the moon. "Alfonse and I decimated the town back in Haiti before we left that fateful night of my *making*. We settled all old debts, but in the end, none of that made us feel better beyond the moment of the blood-letting."

"Sorta like a crack high . . . for the moment it's an adrenaline rush like you cannot believe, and then . . . "

"And then you crash."

He stared at her. "So how do you go on living now?"

"As time passes you'll realize that the greatest thing you have is someone to share that passage of time with . . . for what felt like eons I focused on the ugliness so much that I could never see the beauty of life. Once I died I forgot how to do that."

"I had forgotten that while I was still living," he said in a sad murmur.

"I have seen the dawn of so much, though . . . cars, telephones, airplanes; I could go on and on. But also wars."

He smiled, and then chuckled sadly. "So, what do we do, become philanthropists?"

She smiled and shrugged. "Why not? We can be whatever we want to be, can right wrongs, can help or hurt. What do you want to be?"

"I don't want to hurt people," he said quietly, his voice so sad that it drew her.

She stared into his eyes and nodded, touching his lips with one finger. "Enough lessons for one night. Enough vengeance for one era. Let us focus on beauty."

He took her mouth in a slow dissolve of pleasure. He was her greatest find, something precious that she would vow to keep, and she knew that she was that for him. The irony of that truth not lost on either of them.

*F*IREFLIES

BRADLEY H. SINOR

F　*ireflies.*

　　Yes, fireflies. That was what the lights of Manhattan reminded
Miranda of, the fireflies in the bushes outside her father's house so very
long ago.

She had watched them from her bedroom window on summer evenings
from the time she was a little girl. They drifted in clouds across the lawn,
flanked by single outsiders cutting through the darkness. So far away
and yet so tantalizingly close.

You thought you could touch them, but when you reached out they
were gone. If you caught one, it was gone in a moment, as well, leaving
only a tiny dark husk on the palm of your hand.

Standing in Washington Square Park it felt like they were just a
heartbeat away from starting their nightly dance, yet seemingly impossible
to capture or even touch.

So very long ago.

Miranda drew a long drag off her unfiltered cigarette, savoring the
taste of the smoke deep in her lungs. A moment later she snuffed it out
in the dirt and loose pieces of wood that covered the rough surface of

the waist-high brick wall where she had been standing for a half hour. The dead stub disintegrated into ashes and paper in her hand.

She had arrived half an hour early, just so she could watch the people, watch the fireflies begin their dance. Around her, people gathered in twos and threes, music and conversation mixing together as lights of the Manhattan skyline grew brighter with the vanishing sun.

Fireflies . . .

For perhaps the hundredth time Miranda found herself questioning her own judgment. The day she had placed the ad in the Personals column of the East Village weekly, this moment had been the farthest thing from her mind. Miranda had stared at the small personal ad form for only a moment before beginning to write.

No, that day it had been anger, anger at her family in general and The Elders in specific. The day before, and the day after, the whole idea of the ad seemed silly and even a bit pathetic. Even more so when the recorded sounds in the voice mail box supplied by the newspaper began to accumulate.

Then there had been his voice.

Kyle.

Her original plan in dating a human was to do something to enrage the sanctimonious Elders of The Pack. *"Humans are Prey, nothing more, nothing less!"*

Not that she really disagreed; it was more their attitude, their demands of controlling every single aspect of her life.

She looked around her, at the street performers, the singers, the punks, the lovers, all the figures that filled the night in Washington Square. It was a scene she was quite familiar with. Even so her stomach was churning with uncertainty.

In full lupine form she could prowl in any of the five boroughs, easily taking her prey from the most deserted sections of the city. The Elders had

long preached that the Pack should hunt only along the edges of humanity, through broken buildings and into the shadows of forgotten lives.

That was no challenge, no fun, and Miranda enjoyed a challenge. So, taking partially human, partially wolf form, *she* sought out *her* Prey in places like Times Square, or even on Broadway itself. During The Hunt was when Miranda felt fully alive.

The tales told by the occasional survivor, the ones she *allowed* to get away, were too fantastic for even the most lurid of tabloids to print, although some had. Miranda had kept a few clippings, headlines blazing out in 18 point bold letters:

MONSTER PREYS ON MANHATTAN
KILLER RIPS THROATS FROM VICTIMS
12-FOOT TALL BEAST PROWLS CENTRAL PARK

The last one amused Miranda, considering the fact that even in her highest heels she stood only five foot three. Besides, she rarely went anywhere near Central Park. Someone else was responsible for that little rumor.

No, it was not fear that set her stomach churning. It dawned on her that ever since she had made the date to meet Kyle she had been worried whether she would actually like him, and vice versa "How . . . human," she said softly.

The big clock on the bank switched its display over to read 9:00. Miranda felt *his* presence, a gentle shifting in the air, a change in the lights around her.

Kyle.

A tall, thin figure, dressed in dark grays that seemed to flow out of light and darkness at the same time, his straw colored hair seeming to glow in the reflected lamplight that filled the park. As he passed them people stepped away, like fireflies darting away from the light.

127

"Good evening, Miranda, I'm Kyle," he said.

Miranda straightened her leather jacket, pushing it open to reveal her purple blouse and the silver wave-shaped belt buckle at her waist.

"And how can you be sure that I'm this Miranda you're looking for?" she said.

Kyle reached out and took her hand.

"The same way you know I am who you were waiting for," he said.

The funny thing was, if one of her cousins had described this situation to her, Miranda would have been certain they had OD'd on too many designer drugs and far too many romance novels.

Miranda had the sudden feeling that this was going to be a very interesting evening. Okay, he wasn't exactly what she had expected when she placed the ad, and they had talked. He was better. Showing up with him at Pack functions would be sure to enrage the Elders; she could almost hear most of the females in the Pack drooling over him now. All this was going to really help twisting the knife in the Elders' collective craw.

But there was something *different* about him. Different, but familiar. Miranda couldn't quite put her finger on just what it was, but there was something. Deep inside her The Beast recognized that difference in Kyle, and was howling in agitation. It would be so simple to let herself go, let the Beast have its freedom. But no, not now, not now!

"You can still walk away," he said, as if sensing her uncertainty.

"True. But so can you. And given the circumstances, I wouldn't blame you in the slightest," she said.

"I wouldn't dream of it." he said.

"Neither would I."

* * *

From beyond the borders of light formed by the flickering tiki torches that marked the edge of Kyle's rooftop balcony she could hear the screeching of police sirens. Rescue trucks and ambulances filled the night, all seemingly headed in the same direction. She wondered what was going on. First one sound, then two, then three, until there were too many to pick out individual ones. Miranda foliowed the sounds, listening to them merge, separate and then fade away.

Disappearing, like fireflies with the coming of light.

Fireflies.

"Here we are," said Kyle.

The sound of his voice gave Miranda a start. He moved quietly toward her, carrying two brandy glasses. It bothered her that she had not heard him approach. There was that dammed feeling again, *something* that she could almost put her finger on, but not quite. If it were something Kyle was deliberately hiding, she had to admit he was good.

She savored the aroma of the amber liquid for a long moment before letting a tiny amount slip across her lips. The taste was a thick, heady one that both burned and exhilarated as it rolled down her throat.

"This is old and very good," she said. "I'd say it was not from this century."

"And I would say that you are quite right," said Kyle. "You have an exceptional palate for one so young. It was laid down for one of Napoleon's Marshalls."

"Marshal Davout, or perhaps Soulet? I doubt it was Massena, he was too much of a teetotaler."

Kyle arched an eyebrow at her. He was startled and that was exactly what Miranda wanted. After all, you don't expect a blind date to be able to spout off the names of some of the Marshalls of France under Napoleon Bonaparte.

"So, did you slip an aphrodisiac in it?"

"Do I need one?"

Miranda laughed.

This evening had definitely *not* been the sort of thing she had expected. For a few hours she had been able to relax, to forget who she was, and to be just Miranda. She realized that it had been a long, long time since she had been able to do that. Just be Miranda. Not Miranda du Shane, daughter of Conrad and Esther du Shane; not Miranda, a daughter of the Pack; not Miranda, a were who stood outside of humanity. Just Miranda.

They had walked and talked for what seemed like hours. Eventually Kyle had led them to a small club in the East Village, Greely's Pub.

"I think you are going to like this place," said Kyle. It was decorated in the style of any number of pubs that Miranda had seen in Ireland and Scotland, but without the veneer of faux-Celtic that far too many of these places in New York had.

They had laughed and drank and danced. At one point, Miranda was pulled on stage with the band and handed an Irish drum to join in their rendition of "Gypsy Rover." The musicians seemed pleased with the result, as was Miranda.

"Is there anything you aren't good at?" Kyle asked.

"Many things."

"Perhaps we can discuss this over brandy somewhere else?"

"And where would that be?"

"At my apartment."

They sat and sipped their drinks, listening to the sounds of the city around them, feeling the breeze as it moved the across the patio. Their eyes locked and everything around them faded away. Then, between one heartbeat and the next, lips, tongues and hands began to probe every inch of their bodies, moving faster and faster across clothing and then bare skin.

Kyle lifted Miranda, holding her in the air, her long legs wrapped around him. Miranda's nails shifted to claws, carving deep paths across Kyle's back, trails of blood marking the places she had touched.

* * *

"Oh, don't they just look so purrrrty!"

"Yes, its just pure dee romantic like, like one of those movies with Tommy Hanks playing him, and she'll be played by little Meggie Ryan."

"Yeah, the gigolo and the bitch!"

Miranda had come awake a moment before the first one spoke. She and Kyle had fallen asleep on the futon. It was just after 2:00 and they were no longer alone.

Three figures stood near them, relaxed and watching. She didn't even have to see them clearly to know they were there and who they were, their scents were quite familiar. *Pack!* Gregory, Dean and Michael Ray; her cousins.

She opened her eyes, muscles tense and ready to react, and slowly rose on one elbow. Her relatives had not chosen to come in full wolf form, instead they wore the part human, part lupine appearance that had occasionally graced the covers of such intellectual publications as the *Weekly World News*.

Deep inside her the Beast screeched, demanding to challenge them. Miranda smiled. This wouldn't be the first time that she had had to put them in their places. It wouldn't be the last, she knew that much.

"Should I ask something stupid, like 'What do you want?'" said Kyle.

Miranda looked down at her lover. He had not moved a muscle, his breathing hadn't changed, nothing to alert her to the fact that he was awake.

His voice was calm and unemotional. "I suppose you could," said Gregory. His small narrow figure was half hidden behind a large container-grown tree.

"If it makes you feel better," said Dean. "You can say any damn thing that you want and I certainly won't stop you."

"Of course," said Miranda's other cousin, "That doesn't mean we might not do something after you've had your say."

"Thank you. I wondered when you three idiots were going to show yourselves. I've known you were following us since just outside of Washington Square. You might as well have been carrying signs."

Before the last word was completely said, Kyle was on his feet. He moved with a speed that surprised Miranda, grabbing Dean and throwing him hard against the balcony wall. He stood there, stunned, a moment and then slid to his knees, surprised and disoriented, the breath knocked out of him, but otherwise unharmed.

Kyle turned on one foot to face the nearest one, Dean. Then, suddenly Kyle was gone. He had leaped ten feet straight into the air and came smashing down into the other man's back and sending him into a heap on the floor.

"Good, you're good!" said Michael Ray. "But I'm better!"

"Fight, don't talk, puppy," said Kyle.

That was when Miranda caught sight of Kyle's fangs. The incisors had shifted down into place, weapons as deadly as Kyle's hands. She realized now what that *something* she had sensed about him had been. He was Family, vampiri.

"Stop this! Stop it now!" said Miranda.

The Beast flowed over her, seizing her and beginning the change with a speed that startled even Miranda. Like her cousins, she did not take full wolf form. A fine reddish-blonde fur covering her bare skin in only seconds; the Beast voice echoing from her lips.

"I said stop it, before I tear you all apart!"

Kyle and Michael Ray did not break eye contact for nearly a minute. The other two were getting stiffly to their feet, uncertain of what to do now.

"Pack?" Kyle said, politely to Miranda. Though from the tone of his voice and look of amusement on his face, she knew he had known her for what she was from the beginning.

"Well, duh! You were expecting maybe Martha Stewart? Now, all four of you back off. I'm never one to stop a fight, but this is ridiculous nonsense!"

"It's 'is fault," said Gregory' 'e started it!"

"Gregory," said Miranda. "We'll have none of that phony British accent of yours. Everybody knows you were born in Talequah, Oklahoma."

"Look, man," said Dean. "We just wanted to put a scare into you and our little cousin. Anything else she had planned was all her idea."

"We didn't know you were Family," said Gregory.

"Look, puppy, you invaded my aerie, my home. I have every right to beat the daylights out of all three of you and tack your worthless hides up over the mantle," said Kyle.

His voice was cold and as menacing as anything that Miranda had ever heard. Far different than the man she had met a few hours ago in Washington Square. That man seemed gone now, like a firefly vanishing in the darkness.

Fireflies.

"Anytime, anyplace," said Gregory.

"No! If you try anything, he won't have to do any more than watch," said Miranda. "I will kick your collective keesters from here to Crabapple Cove, Maine! And you know I can do it. Just remember last July 4th, if you don't think so!"

Miranda's three cousins looked at each other, then at her. One at a time they shifted back to human form.

"All right," said Dean. "Will you be coming with us, Miranda?"

"No," she said.

A look of confusion crossed Gregory's face. "You aren't thinking of . . . I don't think a member of the Family qualifies as proper Prey."

"No, he doesn't. But I'll be staying here for awhile, anyway," she said.

"You know The Law. Pack and Family do not mix. The Elders will not be happy," said Gregory.

"I don't care. I've never cared what The Elders had to say," she said. "I'll be staying. That is, if Kyle wants me to."

Kyle answered by taking her hand in his.

* * *

"You know that the Elders, both of Pack and Family, are not going to approve," said Kyle.

Miranda nodded. "That's what I had in mind from the beginning, gaining their disapproval. I hardly intended to involve you or The Family in my little strategy," she said.

Kyle smiled, then said in a high nasal voice, with just a touch of faux-Bostonian accent. *"A vampire and a werewolf. Oh no! Simply will not do! Not at all, at all! After all, what would the other Families say?"*

That about summed things up, although her parents and cousins of The Pack would, no doubt, be a lot more vitriolic about the idea of a relationship with Kyle. It was as serious as if he were a human, a.k.a. Prey, but a different type of serious. She could hear her father's voice quoting the Law: *"Pack and Family do not mix, save under the most extraordinary of circumstances. They go their way, we go ours, and these are not extraordinary circumstances."*

"You realize that we could be Outcast."

Being Outcast was a threat as dire as any that could be made to vampire or were, short of a *Dark Hunt*, where one of their own was Prey, and which could only end in the Final Death. The Pack was the center of the universe to a were. The Pack took care of its own, as did The Family. If you were Outcast, no longer part of The Pack or The Family, then you were Prey, as surely as if you were a mortal born.

Miranda had never seen it happen. She had heard tales of The Dark Hunt. But there had never been one in her lifetime. They were things told around campfires in the depths of the night. The very idea of being cut off was nearly impossible to conceive.

"I know, and I don't care," she said. "Do you?"

"Not particularly," he said. "Uncle Xavier has always said that I would come to a bad end."

"A bad end! That's a nice thing to say to a girl!" Miranda threw her head back in mock indignation. Out of the corner of her eye Miranda thought she spied a firefly, but when she turned toward the insect, she found an owl perched on the wall, watching the whole tableau.

Without a word, she angled her head toward Kyle, offering her bare neck.

Kyle's fangs touched her like a whisper, leaving a sensation in their wake as intense as their lovemaking had been. He barely took a spoonful of blood, but she would not have begrudged him more. Freely given, there was a strength in it that did not come otherwise.

"I hope we're not interrupted by anymore of your gate-crashing relatives, said Kyle.

Miranda let out a long sigh. This was a moment that she knew would come, it was time to lay her cards on the table. "I'm afraid that that was my fault. I sort of wanted someone to find out that I was dating outside of . . ."

"The Pack? Your species?" he said.

"Ah . . . yeah. I knew it would drive The Elders crazy. So after we made our date for tonight, I made sure I let it slip to one of my blabbermouth sisters, Linda, what I had in mind. You should have seen the look on her face when I said you weren't to be Prey," she said.

"So when did you pick up on the Rover Boys?"

"Practically from the time I got to Washington Square. You may have noticed they are about as subtle as a train wreck. I figured they would follow us and report back, not try to stage a rumble on your balcony. By now the Elders know about us. I would say they will be furious, which is exactly the way I wanted them."

"Does it matter to you, how they feel?" asked Kyle.

"Yes, but not nearly as much as it did before I placed that ad, before I came to the park."

"So what are you going to say to them, now, about us."

"Probably the same thing you'll be saying to your Uncle Xavier and the rest."

"Deal with it?"

"Exactly. I like the way you think, mister."

"Oh, really. Do you just want me for my mind?"

"No, your body as well," Miranda said as she padded back to the futon, motioning for Kyle to join her. He moved soundlessly to her side, cupping her face in his hands and bending his head down to kiss her. The thrill his touch sent through her body was indescribable. Although she knew there would be trouble ahead, all of her concerns and worries melted away in Kyle's presence. *Our affair may be brief,* she thought as her lips met his, *but like the fireflies, it will burn just as bright.*

DANCING WITH THE STAR

SUSAN SIZEMORE

*T*here are plenty of people who come into the Alhambra Club for the things we regulars can offer. It's a nice place, not flashy on the inside, hard to spot from the outside. You have to want to find the place and search for it through friends of friends of friends. If you're a mortal, that is. The rest of us have used it as a hangout for the better part of a century.

There's a television set over the bar, a big, flat-panel model, always playing with the sound off. I wasn't paying attention to it because I was engaged in seducing a handsome young man with far too many body piercings for my usual taste. I mean, if you want piercings, I'm perfectly capable of providing them for you. But, he had nice eyes and a lovely voice, and the place wasn't all that full of human patrons this evening. A girl goes with what she can sometimes. I wasn't all that hungry, so I wasn't trying too hard. I wasn't paying attention to the TV, but my friend Tiana was. I was surprised when she came up and put her cold hand on my shoulder, because she isn't normally rude enough to interrupt me when I'm working a fresh feed.

"Did you hear? There's been a twelve-car pile up on Mulholland."

This isn't the sort of thing that would normally interest me, but her excitement got my attention. I shifted my gaze to the television. It showed a scene of fire and carnage spotlighted in beams of white light shooting down from circling helicopters. A crawl on the bottom of the screen was showing statistics about the dead and injured and the amount of emergency rescue equipment called to the scene. A blonde, windblown girl reporter was excitedly talking about the same things.

Beside me, Tiana was starting to breathe heavily. I wasn't sure who was getting off on the disaster more, my friend or the reporter.

I looked back at Tiana. "So?"

Her eyes were glowing, not quite the death-eating electric blue she gets when she's feeding, but her pupils held pinprick sparks of anticipation. "You want to go have a look, Serephena?" she asked.

Normally I wouldn't have been interested, but the pleading in her voice got to me. Tiana's been my best friend for a very long time. If you know what we are you wouldn't think she and I would have that much in common. I'm a vampire and she's—well, all right—she's my ghoul friend. I feed on the living, she feeds on the energy of the dying. But we both like to shop.

"Maybe there's a dying movie star out there I can latch on to," she said. She rubbed her hands together. "A producer would be even better."

I know what that sounds like, but it really had more to do with psychic power levels than celebrity stalking. There are a lot of high-energy types in show business, a lot of people who are psychic and don't even know it.

I got up and telepathically told the pierced boy that we'd never met. "Sure," I said to Tiana. "It's been a slow night. Let's go have a look."

* * *

It was gruesome up on Mulholland Drive. Tiana ate it up—literally soaking the energy of fear and pain in through her pores. It was the scent of blood that got to me, but not in a good way. There's no fun in spilled blood. I need to take blood from the living, breathing source, to taste it fresh and hot, with the heartbeat still pulsing through it. And preferably from a volunteer, because we live in modern, humane times. Unlike some of my notorious forebears I do not get off on pain. The blood on the crash victims gave off a sick scent that roiled my stomach, but I did find hiding in the shadows and watching the emergency crews work exciting. Hey, I'm as interested in all that forensics and rescue stuff as anyone else who watches the geek TV channels, but this was "live and direct" like Max Headroom used to say on the television show nobody but me probably remembers.

It was interesting, but after a while I glanced at the sky and sighed. The night was getting on. "Had enough yet?" I asked. "You'll outgrow your size-two clothes if you feed much longer. Besides, it's an hour to sunrise."

Tiana came out of her happy trance and turned glowing blue eyes on me. "Oh, sorry, I lost track of the time."

"No problem," I said, and took her arm to help her walk away, knowing from experience that she was drunk and dizzy from feeding.

Help me! Where are you?

Here! I shouted to the voice in my head. *Where—*

"Serephena!"

I looked up into pinpoints of blue light. Tiana. I was on my knees and she was standing over me. The fierce pain in my head blocked out most thought, but I knew that our positions were all wrong. I was supposed to be helping *her.*

I wanted to run into the wreckage behind us. But when I stood my legs were too shaky. I glanced back. "I—"

Tiana shook my shoulders. "We have to go. Sunrise," she said.

That was one word I understood in all of its myriad implications of
pain, suffering, death. I had to go. Now. Whatever had just happened,
I had to get home. I took Tiana's hand and we ran together.

* * *

I have a nice studio apartment, where I sleep on a daybed in the huge
windowless bathroom. The bathroom door is reinforced and has a strong
lock, panic-room style, and the building, which I own and rent mostly
to my sort of people, has state-of–the-art security. So normally I have
no reason not to sleep very well. Normally I don't dream, either. I go to
sleep. I wake up. It all happens so quickly . . . normally . . .

* * *

*The path was made of brick, laid out in a chevron pattern. It was lined
with rose bushes and night-blooming jasmine. The air was so fragrant I
could taste it. The stars overhead formed a thick blanket of light brighter
than I'd seen them for a very long time.*

*"I need to get out of the city more," I said, and continued walking
towards the music in the distance.*

*I was wearing a dress, the skirt long and floaty and pale blue,
sprinkled with a pattern of glittering crystals that mirrored the sky.
This was not the slinky, black sort of garment I favored, but it felt right,
feminine, beautiful.*

*I was wearing, honest to God, glass slippers. Cinderella? Me? Well, it
was a dream.*

And my feet—my whole body—wanted nothing more than to dance.

*When the gazebo came into sight, as pretty as a white confection on
top of a wedding cake, I ran towards it. Something more than wonderful
waited for me there.*

"You!" I said, skidding to a halt at the entrance as I spied the man leaning with his arms crossed against a pillar.

"Me," he replied, a stranger with a familiar voice.

"But—you're a movie star!"

It was an accusation. I didn't expect my very rare dreams to go off on such grandiose tangents.

"And I worked very hard to become a genuine movie star," he answered, totally unashamed for showing up in my fantasy. "Would you prefer meeting a celebrity?" His gesture took in the small building. "Here? In our space?"

Our space? Yeah, it was, wasn't it?

I turned around, my skirts belling out around my legs. I could see my reflection in the highly polished, white marble floor. And his reflection as he came to join me. He moved with the grace of Fred Astaire. (I've been around long enough to have seen Fred and his sister Adele dance on the stage. I know what I'm talking about.)

His hands touched me, one at my waist, one gently gripping my fingers. His warmth against my coolness. The next thing I knew we were circling the room, caught up in the music.

"We're waltzing," I said. "I don't know how to waltz."

"I learned it when I auditioned for Mr. Darcy. Didn't get the role, though."

"But you learned how to dance."

"Silver linings," he said.

I studied his face. There was a sweep of dark hair across his brow, high-arching eyebrows over penetrating green eyes, severe high cheekbones softened by a lush, full mouth. "You would have made a great Darcy," I told him.

Of course he had the body of a god—or at least of a man who spent a fortune working long hours with a personal trainer—and now that body was pressed to mine. I liked it. A lot. The longer we danced the more I liked it.

My skin wasn't cool any more.

"This is—nice," he said.

"In a strange way," I answered.

"You've noticed that, have you?"

I nodded. His green eyes twinkled at me. We danced around in circles for a long, long time, caught up in the music and the flow of energy between us. That's what it was all about for me—flow and energy, give and take. For once I knew that I was giving as much as I was taking, and it felt good.

"What are you—we—doing here?" I asked.

"Dreaming about dancing," he answered. His smile devastated me. "I'm as surprised by this as you are. One moment I was floating in grey clouds—I think I was screaming, but there was no one to hear me, not even me—and the next I was here with you."

"I was in blackness," I said. "That's normal for me."

"The grey was terrifying," he said. He whirled me around faster, until we both laughed. "This is much better," he said. He pulled me closer. We weren't dancing any more, but the music played on and the world continued to spin.

"No one should be in darkness," he said. "Grey or black or any other kind, especially not alone."

I started to say that I didn't mind being alone, but being with him made me realize that I did mind. "I've been lonely and didn't know it." Though I was looking into his eyes, I was talking more to myself.

Neither of us spoke for an unknowable time after that but we continued to look into each other's eyes and shared—what? Our emotions, our souls, the essences of our beings? All of the above, I guess.

"This is such bullshit," I finally said.

"But you like it."

My gaze flicked away from his, but I couldn't stand the loss of contact for long. "If I could blush, I'd be blushing," I told him when our gazes locked again.

"We live in a time and place that's cynical about love."

"Darlin', I come from New York. People in LA are amateurs about cynicism."

He shook his head. "I used to live in New York," he said. "I tended bar while I went to drama school. I saw plenty of broken hearts there."

"Broke a few, too, I bet."

"Too bad I didn't meet you there."

I laughed. "I left long before you were born."

"Really? When were you there? How did you get to be—" He looked puzzled for a moment, then said it: "—a vampire."

Those in the know generally don't ask. Maybe they think it's rude, or that mystery is part of my mystique, or they are afraid of getting their throats ripped out. I hadn't told this story for a long time. "I worked at the Plaza back in the 1930s."

"The hotel?"

I nodded. "I was a telephone operator. There was a Mob boss that lived there."

"Lucky Luciano?"

"You've heard of him?"

"I've been doing research to play him in a film."

"Too bad. I hate seeing that bastard glamorized."

"He did bad things to you," he guessed.

"He had me killed. He wrongfully thought I'd overheard some conversations and might testify about them in court. A hit man was sent after me. It turned out that the killer was a hungry vampire. He drained me and left me for dead."

"But—"

"But the vampire didn't realize I was one of his bloodline."

"You were already a vampire?"

"No! My family came from Wallachia. There's some sort of genetic mutation that kicks in when a vampire bites us. Old Vlad the Impaler

really is Dracula, and the king of us all."

"That's amazing. I'm part Hungarian. Could I be a vampire?"

*"Depends if your grandmas got raped by the right sort of invaders,
I guess. Do you want to be a vampire?"*

He shrugged. "I want to hear more about you."

*"Nice answer. The gist of it is I woke up dead and had to start over
from there."*

"Did you go after the one who turned you?"

"You've been watching vampire movies."

"Been in one."

"I saw it, had nothing to do with my world. But you were good," I added.

*"You're lovely when you're bullshitting. What happened to the evil one
who turned you?"*

"I don't know if he was evil."

"He was a Mob hit man."

His indignation was adorable. "I'll concede his profession was evil."

"You've never done anything like that."

*His certainty of my goodness was even more adorable. "No, I haven't,"
I assured him. "But after a while of wrestling with all the implications
of immortality you get some perspective on good, evil, expediency,
stuff like that. And no, I haven't seen him again. At least, not that
I know of. I didn't get a good look at him while he was sucking the
lifeblood out of me."*

*"But how did you survive? Didn't you have to have a teacher, a mentor?
Didn't another vampire bring you into the dark world?"*

*I laughed and stroked his cheek. "I suppose there's melodrama
somewhere, but I've never been involved in any—other than being rubbed
out by a mobster, which I did find pretty melodramatic at the time."*

*He traced his hand up and down my back, sending tingling shivers all
through me. His sympathy warmed me even more than his touch. "I'm
sorry you went through such trauma. How did you survive?"*

"I found the right bar and ordered a beer. Getting all the blood drained out of you makes you thirsty."

"It was a vampire bar?"

I nodded.

"Did some instinct kick in that drew you to your own kind and they taught you how to survive?"

I nodded again. He was smart and quick on the uptake. The man had many great qualities. And he could dance in a way that made me feel like I was having sex standing up, fully clothed, without ruffling a hair or breaking a sweat. Not that vampires sweat. "I've explained me," I said. "How about you? How did you get here? Wherever here is."

"That is the problem isn't it? We seem to be dancing in limbo. Though I like being here with you."

From anyone else, any other time, I would have considered that a line. But his eyes held genuine pleasure, genuine sincerity.

"I'm falling like a rock, you know," I told him.

"Me, too. Is that a bad thing?"

We both shrugged, and that became part of the dance. We laughed together, and that was part of the music.

"As for me," he went on. "I remember being with friends at their house. We played Scrabble."

I love word games. "Scrabble? Is that any way for a movie star to spend an evening?"

"Now you know why the paparazzi hate me. I lead a quiet life."

"Me too. But how did you get here?"

We danced in silence for a while. I watched as every possible emotion crossed his face.

He finally said, "It has something to do with ice cream." He looked deep into my eyes. "Is that crazy?"

"Probably," I told him. "But much of life makes no sense."

"Life and death? Am I dead?"

I pulled him close and we stood still in the centre of the gazebo for a
long time, holding each other tight, giving comfort amidst the frightening
questions that had no answers.

"You're so good for me," he said at last. "I don't even know your name."

"Everyone knows yours." I gave a faint, sad laugh. "No one really knows
mine anymore. I—became—Serephena back in my hippie phase."

It was his turn to laugh, at me, but not mockingly. "Oh, no, that won't
do. That name isn't you. It's a flighty name. You're solid and strong and
grounded."

It was like he was giving me back myself. "Stella," I admitted. "My name
is Stella."

His smile was a blessing. It was sunshine. It was . . .

* * *

I awoke as I always did, at the moment the sun went down. It was
normally the most pleasant moment of the night. This time I woke
with an anguished shout. I lay on my back with my eyes squeezed shut
and tried to will myself back to sleep. That didn't work, of course. All
I ended up doing was crying, and the tears that rolled down onto the
pillowcase made a disgusting mess—vampire tears having blood mixed
in with the saltwater.

I stripped the bed, threw the sheets in the laundry and paced around
restlessly for a while wondering what the hell was going on in my head.
Was I going senile? Worst of all, loneliness welled up in me and grief
shook me and the heartache . . .

The heartache was a very real sensation. Physical pain radiated out
of the core of my being where my shattered soul ached for the loss of
half my being.

Or something like that.

I hurt. I really emotionally and physically hurt from what I knew had

only been a dream. It took a couple of hours before I could get myself together enough to head off to the Alhambra in the hope of staving off the painful loneliness.

There wasn't a huge crowd at the club, but the place was jumping when I showed up. Everybody was gathered around the bar, abuzz with conversation.

I spotted Tiana and went up to her. "What happened?"

"Anton went up in flames this morning," she answered.

"Why'd he do a thing like that without having a goodbye party first?" I asked. Anton was the bartender. He lived on the second floor. Used to.

"He didn't want to make a fuss."

"How'd it happen?"

"Usual way. He walked outside to see the dawn."

It happens. Every few decades the urge to end eternity gets hold of a vampire. I hadn't succumbed to the depression yet, but the way I was feeling tonight I sympathized with Anton's choice. I wasn't sure my usual panacea of shoe shopping was going to be enough.

"Did anybody sweep up his ashes?"

"Oh, yes," Tiana answered. "He's already in a nice urn over the bar with a sticky-note reminder to sprinkle some blood on him in a year or two. The problem is what are we going to do for a bartender now?"

Blood brings us back and we are usually ready to carry on after an ash vacation. I wasn't in the mood to join in the "what are we going to do to replace Anton?" discussion occupying everyone else's attention, but I did manage to elbow my way to a seat at the bar. I found myself looking up at the television overhead.

The local news was still dwelling on last night's multi-car crash. Slow news night, I supposed. "Isn't there a gang war or a car chase you could cover?" I complained to the television. "I'm bored."

"You don't feel bored," 'Tiana said, coming up beside me. "You're unhappy. I don't mean to snack on your emotions," she added when I

glared at her. "You know I can't help it. Why are you unhappy? Anton?"

I snorted. "May he rest in peace, but I don't give a damn about Anton." I turned my glare back on the TV screen. "What's so important about last night's car crash?"

"Four people died on scene," she said, "Everybody else is hospitalized, most of them in critical condition. But the real reason the networks are still covering it is—"

Her timing was perfect, because at that moment his picture appeared on the screen.

"Oh, good God!" My heart felt like a knife had been plunged into it.

Tiana's hand touched my shoulder. "I know you're a fan, but—"

"He's not dead! Tell me he isn't dead?"

I only realized I was shaking her when she shouted, "Stop it! Let go of me!"

I did. I pointed at the television. "That's the man in my dream."

"The man of your dreams? He's an actor you've got a crush on."

"I do not get crushes. And I mean he's the man that was in my dream last day. We were dancing."

"Vampires don't dream. And he was in intensive care while you were sleeping."

The relief might have killed me if that were possible. As it was, it felt like I was having a heart attack. "Intensive care? So he isn't dead?"

"Not yet, but it's only a matter of time." She glanced at the face of the reporter now on the screen. "His deathwatch is what all the media fuss is about. They're worse ghouls than I am."

I automatically patted her shoulder, knowing that this admission hurt her pride, but my mind was racing on another matter. It hadn't been a dream. Somehow, it hadn't been a dream. He'd been there and I'd been there, only where the hell was there? "How did it happen?"

"He and some friends were going out for ice cream when they ended up in the pile-up and the car went off the side of the mountain. He was

the only survivor, but he's on life support and he's been declared brain dead."

"His brain isn't dead," I said. "It's been out dancing." I was sure this was true. We'd been in telepathic contact. But how?

I heard the voice in my head again that had speared into my brain back at the crash site. *Help me! Where are you?*

"Of course! He's psychic. He called out for help when we were up at the crash, and I answered him! That's how we met!" I grabbed Tiana's cold, grey hand. "Come on, ghoul-friend!"

"Where are we going?" she asked as I pulled her towards the door.

I laughed, all my depression blown away by exaltation. "To the rescue, of course!"

* * *

"We're here. Now what?" Tiana asked as we moved across the ER waiting room.

"Go up to the ICU," I answered. "And take him home."

"He's on life support. There's probably cops and private security in the halls."

"I'll take care of them. All you have to do is create a diversion."

She licked her lips and nodded. Her skin was flushed to an almost-normal human color. This was one of her feeding grounds and she'd shown me where to sneak in. It had been easy, even with the circus in the streets.

Outside the media and fan frenzy was as thick and chaotic as I'd ever seen it in all my decades of dwelling in this town. There were news vans sprouting satellite and lighting equipment and chuffing power generators. Reporters looked solemnly into cameras as they spoke. Paparazzi were as thick as roaches in a tenement. Helicopters circled. Cops held a crowd back beyond a cordon surrounding the hospital.

People held signs and candles and flowers. Some were singing the theme song from one of his movies.

I wondered if what I was doing was any less ridiculous than the behavior of his grieving fans.

In the ER people were bleeding and screaming and crying through their own problems. It was quiet and peaceful compared to what was going on outside. No one paid any attention as we made our way through a wide doorway, down a hallway and to a door past a row of elevators. You learn to take the stairs when you want to live an under-the-radar life.

"There are three people ready to die here," Tiana said after we reached the critical-care floor and slipped into an empty room. She looked sad. Hey, she's a ghoul, but that doesn't mean she isn't a kind person.

"Can you work with that?" I asked. Hey, I'm a vampire, remember? She nodded. She prefers living off residual death energy instead of any direct involvement.

"I hate doing the soul-sucking thing, but, yeah, there's nothing that can be done for any of them."

"Is my guy one of the three?" I asked worriedly.

She looked thoughtful, then shook her head. "Low energy, but stable. Now let me get to work."

I backed out of the room as she opened her mouth for one of those screams that only the dying could hear. The dying would give up their energy to the ghoul when they heard that sound.

Pretty soon there was almost as much activity on this floor of the hospital at there was outside. Alarms went off at the nursing station, crash carts were hurried into rooms. There was running and shouting, and I moved unnoticed to the room with the guard outside the door.

The guard wasn't a problem. I made him look into my eyes and he was instantly stunned.

"Is there a security camera in there?" I asked.

"No. There's a nurse," he volunteered.

"Tell the nurse to respond to the code blues. Follow the nurse and volunteer to help." I hoped that was enough of an excuse to keep the guard from getting into too much trouble when I kidnapped his charge. I rushed into his room at once.

Inside the door I stopped with my mouth hanging open. The man on the bed was hooked up to so many tubes and gadgets I didn't know how to start freeing him. I didn't have much time, so I whispered an apology for any pain I caused him and started ripping and pulling the life-support equipment off him. Trails of his blood stained my clothes when I picked him up. The scent and warmth of it was intoxicating, but I fought off the sudden bloodlust. My fangs ached like a virgin's on her first hunt as I carried him away with me.

His weight was no problem, but I'm a small woman and he's a very tall man. Carrying him was awkward, but you manage what you have to.

I took him downstairs, through the closed cafeteria and to a courtyard garden beyond it where I set him down gently beneath a squat palm tree. I sat beside him and settled his head in my lap. My fingers touched his temples.

Are you there?

You came for me! His voice called from so far away I barely sensed it.

Do you want to live? I asked. *You know I'm a vampire. I will try to change you if you want me to. Think carefully before you choose.*

In the long silence that followed I had to fight very hard to keep my fangs from sinking into his flesh. I'd never been so aroused by the scent of blood before, but I wasn't going to taste a drop without his permission. He had to make the choice.

I thought I'd have to be Wallachian, his thought came at last.

You're part Hungarian. There's a chance you'll change.

It depends on if my grandmas got raped by the right sort of invaders?

Pretty much.

I'll die otherwise, won't I?

Yes. But that shouldn't be why you choose to become a blood drinker, a nightwalker, an exile from every part of the daylight world.

It really isn't all that bad being a vampire, but there are difficulties and the lifestyle should not be glamorized for potential newbies. No matter how much you want to share a coffin with them.

Can I stay with you if I change?

My heart sang at his question. And, oh, how my fangs ached! *Yes*, I told him. *For as long as you want. For ever if you want. For ever sounds good to me.*

Do it.

Remember that it might not take. That—

Shut up and bite me.

I couldn't argue with that. So I did.

And I'd never had a rush like it in all my years of sucking the good stuff! I couldn't count the orgasms that shook me before every drop of him was flowing inside me.

I didn't have to share my blood with him. Some sort of enzyme in my saliva was transferred to him from the bite and the enzyme would trigger the change if it were going to happen. But, just in case, I bit my wrist and poured a few drops of my blood into his mouth. Not that he was capable of swallowing. At this point he was essentially dead. He'd either get better or I'd have to dispose of his body in a way that the marks on his throat would never be seen.

I didn't want to think about disposal. I didn't want to think of him ever being dead. I held his limp body and felt it grow heavier and colder, and I worried and cried those disgusting blood-drenched vampire tears. I don't know for how long. Long enough for my mood to turn bleak and heartbroken.

Long enough for me to be aware that the sun would be up in an hour or so.

There's an almost physical pressure on the skin the closer daylight comes. Normally I'd be starting to think about getting to cover. Instead, I vowed I'd stay here and let the sun take me if he didn't come around before the end of the night. I didn't care if my ashes blew away so far there wouldn't be anything left of me. Perhaps the fire that took would burn him as well and our ashes would blend together.

Sentimental, aren't you?

I heard the thought but it took a long time before I came out of my grief enough to realize that the voice wasn't my imagination.

"You're alive!"

Don't shout. I have a hangover. That's not right. My throat hurts. I'm thirsty. My mouth tastes like sweet copper.

"That's my blood. You're alive," I repeated, the words whispered in his ear as I helped him sit up. "You're a vampire."

"I guess the right Cossacks raped my grandmas."

His voice was a rough croak, but the most delicious sound I'd ever heard. He struggled to his feet and insisted on giving me his hand to help me up. Living or dead, he was always a gentleman. When I was on my feet his arms came around me. He was weak enough that I ended up holding him up as we embraced.

"We could dance like this for ever," he said.

I sighed romantically. "We could." I looked around. "We could if the sun wasn't coming up soon. We need to get out of here."

He cupped my cheek and looked at me with his new night vision. "You're as beautiful as I dreamed you were, my Stella. Thank you for saving me, thank you for being with me now and forever."

There's no way a girl can't respond to that. I kissed him, and he kissed back and it was real and deep and better than any dream.

After a while he lifted his head and gave a dry, hacking cough. "Sorry. Thirsty."

I put my arm around his waist and helped him towards the garden door. "I know just the place where we can get a beer. Now that you've changed you can find it on your own."

"I'd rather go with you."

You have no idea how much that meant to me.

Tiana met us outside the cafeteria and guided us along her secret route out of the hospital and away from the crowd. He noticed all the fuss as we drove away, he and I squeezed into the trunk of Tiana's car.

"You have no idea how happy I am to leave the celebrity era of my life behind," he told me.

"You'll miss acting."

"I'll think of a way to get back to it. Do vampires work? Do I need a job?"

"I'm a real-estate mogul. You can live off me. Wait—" I'd remembered Anton. "The place we're heading, the Alhambra Club, needs a bartender. I know the owner. That would be me. If you're interested."

We were squeezed in pretty tightly, but he managed to pull me closer. "Does this place have a dance floor?"

I laughed, happier than I'd ever imagined I could be. "It will when we're done with it, if that's what you want," I promised. "I think dancing—being—with you is all I ever wanted."

"Me too." I couldn't stop the girlish giggle from escaping. "I guess this, is a real—"

"Hollywood ending," he finished, not having to be psychic to know what I was thinking.

VALENTINE FROM A VAMPIRE

ED GORMAN

ONE

*T*here was only one way to do it, twenty-six-year-old Sam McBride
told himself that gray February afternoon, and that was to plain
and simple do it:

Pick her up in his Checker cab as he usually did at six o'clock and
then, after she'd been riding a few blocks, say casually as possible, "You
know, Ms. Ames, there's something I think you should know about the
man you're going out with. He's a vampire."

So all afternoon, transporting fat old ladies and skinny old men and
rude businessmen and fickle suburban housewives, Sam rehearsed
his lines pretty much the way he'd memorized his part in the eighth
grade play nearly fourteen years earlier (he'd played a Pilgrim)—by
saying them over and over again until they'd lost all meaning. He tried
variations on them, of course, trying to minimize the shock they would
have on her—"Say, have you noticed your boyfriend's teeth?" or "Is
this the first vampire you've ever gone out with?" or "Was that catsup
all over your friend's mouth last night?"—so she wouldn't hate him

for saying it. (Because hating him was the exact opposite of what he wanted her to do.)

But really, when you came right down to it, there wasn't any graceful way to say it. Because when you came right down to it, calling somebody a vampire was a pretty serious accusation.

Sam sighed and kept driving, thinking over his lonely, womanless life and what an odd business life was, the older you got. Sam, six foot, slender, still gangly despite a deep voice and a need to shave twice a day, had come to the city five years ago after finishing junior college with an associate degree in retail. Unfortunately, his arrival coincided with the recession and so he'd drifted into hacking, working for a man who'd had his larynx removed and who now had to talk through one of those buzzer jobbies that sounded like bad sci-fi sound effects. The hack owner spoke just clearly enough for Sam to know he was a cheapskate.

The vampire, a man handsome as a screen star of the forties (complete with hair sleek as black ice), was named Karl Richards. Sam had met him four years ago while hauling a young woman named Debbie out to Richards's Dracula-like estate. He'd seen the way Debbie had gone into the place—a real live American girl given to lots of chitchat and some flirtiness—and how she'd come out. Debbie, pale, soft-spoken now, was never the same again. He took her out there several times afterward and then one day she stayed permanently, or at least she didn't call in for a ride back to the city. He had no idea what had happened to her. Not then, anyway. All he knew for sure was that on Valentine's Day of that year her personality underwent a most curious transformation.

Then came the next two Valentine's Days and two more women—one named Janice, who had eyes soft as a young animal's, and one named Stacey, who had remarkable legs—went in one way and came out the other.

But even then Sam hadn't allowed himself to use the word. He just said to himself that there were some weird doings involving drugs or

hypnotism or maybe even UFOs going on inside the vast walled estate. Because even alien creatures with pop-eyes and no voice boxes were easier to believe than—

—than vampires.

Then one night, cruising past the estate late with a drunken fare, Sam had glimpsed something truly eerie at the gate of the place.

One moment Karl Richards had been standing there and the next moment . . . Karl Richards was gone.

Sam didn't know if he'd turned into a bat or a slug or an Avon lady, but he sure went somewhere and there was only one semihuman creature who could do anything like that and that was—

—a vampire.

Sam spent the next month sitting up nights recording all this material on his Sony recorder. He had vague notions of maybe going to the police but every morning that he got up with that thought on his mind, he started thinking of the cops he'd met through hacking and what hard cynical bastards they were and how they'd respond to somebody who told them there was a vampire living in the mansion on the southeastern edge of this Midwestern city.

Right.

Then this year, three weeks before Valentine's, Felicia Ames got in his cab and asked to be taken to the mansion, and just like that, Sam fell in love. She was a glowing blond model given to deep (and, he imagined, poetic) sighing and long blue gazes out the cab window at wintry trees and snow-capped waves slamming the concrete piers.

Every twenty minutes since meeting her he had mentally proposed. Every thirty minutes he thought about their having a child (he wanted a kid even if he wasn't quite sure what the hell he was going to do with the little bugger).

And every forty minutes he faced up to the terrible fact that on this Valentine's Day, tonight, sleazy Karl Richards was going to convert one

more unwitting American girl into a creature of eternal darkness (or whatever they always said on those great Hammer films WTBS always ran at 2:00 A.M. every Friday night).

He was going to turn Felicia Ames into a vampire.

Or he thought he was, anyway.

But a hack driver named Sam McBride had different ideas.

TWO

"Hi, Sam."

"Hi, Ms. Ames."

"Gosh."

"What?"

"You think you'll ever stop?"

"Stop what?"

"Calling me 'Ms. Ames.' "

He flushed. "Oh. Right. I forgot. Felicia. I'm supposed to call you 'Felicia.' "

"Please."

So she sat back and he aimed the Checker into traffic, making the ride smooth as he could for her.

"Boy."

"What?" he asked.

"Long day. Whoever says modeling is a glamorous profession just doesn't know."

"Tired, huh?"

"Exhausted."

"Great."

"What?"

"I said, 'Late.' "

"Late?"

"I meant—after a long day, it's late. Maybe you shouldn't go to the mansion tonight. Maybe I should turn the cab around and take you to your apartment house. Maybe you're coming down with something, Felicia, and should go straight to bed." He said all this in a rush. He was hopeful she'd agree and he'd flip the cab around and race to her apartment and then stand guard all night to make sure that Richards didn't get in.

But now she laughed. "Oh, no. I'd never be too tired for tonight."

"Tonight?"

"Valentine's Day. Karl has promised me a very special gift."

Sam gulped. "You have any idea what it is?"

She laughed again, more softly this time. "No, but you can bet when Karl Richards says a gift is going to be special, it's going to be *very* special."

He watched her in the rearview. Outside, gray night had fallen, the only lights red and blue and green neon reflected in dirty city snow. But in the rearview her face positively radiated. For a moment he did a dangerous thing—closed his eyes to say a silent prayer for courage.

The time had come.

She'd left him no choice.

He had to tell her the truth about Karl Richards.

"Gosh, Sam, look out!"

Snapping his eyes open, he saw that he was about to sideswipe a city bus that moved through the gloom like a giant electric caterpillar. "Sam, are you all right?"

"Yes," he said. "But you're not."

"What?"

"I said you're not all right."

"Well, that's not a very nice thing to say."

"Oh, I didn't mean you're not all right OK. I meant you're not all right—you're in danger."

"Danger?"

"Felicia, would you let me buy you a cup of coffee?"

"But, Sam, I told Karl—"

He turned around and said, "Felicia, there's something you should know about Karl."

"Oh, Sam, I know what you're going to say." She sounded young and disappointed. "That he's a playboy. That he'll drop me as soon as he's bored and it won't be long before that happens." She touched him on the shoulder and a wonderful warmth spread through his entire body. She'd never touched him this way before. "It's just a storybook fling, the only one I've ever allowed myself. Really. In high school I didn't have time because I was always a cheerleader and trotting off to games. In college I didn't have time because my parents were poor and I had to work my way through. And during my first five years of modeling I didn't have time because I had to take every job that was offered me. Don't you see, Sam, this is my one chance at really having a good time. That's all."

Sam pulled into the parking lot of a McDonald's. Against the gray night it looked like a big colorful toy box filled with tiny people walking around inside.

"Felicia, there's something I've got to tell you and I guess I have to do it right here, without even waiting to go inside, right in front of Ronald McDonald and everything."

"Gosh, Sam, what's so urgent?"

"Karl."

"Karl's urgent?"

"No," Sam said, "Karl's a vampire."

THREE

They got Cokes and Sam got french fries and they took the most isolated table they could find, right on a plastic outsize Egg McMuffin who had two red eyes and kept winking at Sam.

"Vampire," Felicia said. "Gosh, Sam, that's really the most original one I've heard yet."

"Original what?"

"Oh," she said, "line, I guess you'd call it. I mean, I'm flattered." She startled him by putting her hand over his and gazing blue into his eyes. "You're a very nice guy, Sam, and over the past few weeks, we've really gotten to know each other in a strange way. And if Karl wasn't in the picture—" She withdrew her hand and shook her wonderful blond head and laughed. "But to be honest, Sam, calling him a vampire is going overboard, don't you think? How about a drug dealer? Or Communist spy? Or even a pornographer? But a vampire?" Then the smile faded from her eyes. "Sam, you don't really believe in vampires, do you?"

"I didn't."

"Didn't?"

"Till I took Debbie and Janice and Stacey out to his mansion on Valentine's Day and they changed."

"Changed?"

"Yes," Sam said, "changed."

So he told her, in detail, how they'd changed. The chalky skin. The dead eyes. The sullen silence. "Vampires," Sam said.

She took one of his french fries and nibbled at it. She'd explained to him once that she always nibbled at food. To keep her weight for the camera, that was the most pleasure she could allow herself—nibbling.

"Have you ever been heartbroken, Sam? Wanted somebody you couldn't have?"

He stared at her. "Uh, yes."

"Do you remember how you acted?"

"Acted?"

"The depression, the weight loss, the long silences? That's what you're describing here, Sam, nothing more. Karl decided it was time to get rid

of these women and move on to new ones, so he dropped them and that was how they reacted."

"Then why would they keep going back to the mansion?"

"Why, to plead their cases. Beg him to reconsider." She had another french fry. "You've been heartbroken before, haven't you, Sam? You do know what I'm talking about?"

Without hesitation, he said it, "Felicia, I'm heartbroken right now."

"You are?"

"Yes. Over you."

She blushed. For all her beauty and sophistication, Sam had found Felicia to be not only modest about her looks but just as socially vulnerable as he was himself. "Oh, Sam." She put her hand back on his. "That's really sweet and I really appreciate it but—right now there's Karl."

"Please let me take you back to your apartment tonight, Felicia. Just till after Valentine's Day passes. He's got something about Valentine's Day."

"Sam, listen, please" She sat hack in the seat "As I've tried to explain, I know this is just a fling and nothing more. But I'm enjoying it. I like being in a grand house where there are servants out of the nineteenth century and where classical music is always playing and where you sit on Louis XVI furniture and where you sip French wine from huge goblets in front of a roaring fireplace and where your tall, dark, handsome lover wears a red silk dinner jacket and speaks to you in a voice that gives you goose bumps." She laughed. "For a girl whose father ran a corner grocery store, Sam, that's pretty heady stuff."

So Sam, seeing the odds he had to overcome, said it: "He disappeared."

"What?"

"Vanished. Did you ever see the original *Dracula?*"

She sighed. "Oh, Sam, please. It isn't fun anymore. This vampire thing, I mean. It really isn't."

"He did, Felicia." He raised his hand like a Boy Scout. "On my love for you, I swear it. One second, he was in my rearview and then he just disappeared. Vanished. The only people who can do that are vampires."

A certain pity had come into her eyes now. "Sam, would you take me out to the mansion—and would you do me a favor?"

"Anything. You know that."

"Just don't talk about this anymore, please. Because I am starting to get scared—but not for myself—for you. I hope you're just saying all this because you love me and want to start seeing me. I hope you're not saying it because—" And here, for the first time, she looked uncomfortable. "Because you truly believe it, because then—"

"Then what?"

"Then I'd say you needed to see a shrink or something."

FOUR

Gates of black iron covered the entrance to the mansion. Ground fog shone silver in the light of a half-moon. Beyond the massive stone walls light from mullioned windows spread yellow across the snow.

"I guess I should go in now."

They'd been sitting in his cab for twenty minutes now—the radio tuned low to an FM station playing some soft Stanley Clarke songs—and really not talking much at all.

It was just that every time she started to put her hand on the door handle, he turned around and said, "Please, Felicia, please don't go."

He's said it four times now and four times she had complied.

But he knew this time—hand on the door, a kind of pity in her eyes—that she would go.

"Felicia, I—"

"I really do have to go.

"He's a vampire, Felicia. Honest and truly."

"You're sweet, Sam. You really are. You care about me so much and—"

Then she startled him by leaning forward and kissing him gently on the lips.

His mind literally spun; his heart was a wild animal.

"Felicia, please—"

But then the back door opened and the dome light went on, exposing the shabby insides of the cab, the battered dash and the smudged seat covers and the big red, white, and blue thermos he carried coffee in. This was his life—the life of a shabby hack in a shabby cab. He guessed he couldn't blame her (his eyes rising to see the imposing mansion against the gray night sky) for wanting the type of life Karl Richards offered.

Except Karl Richards was a vampire.

"Felicia—"

This time she touched a finger to her lips and then touched that same finger to his lips and then she was gone, lost in fog, the gates opening automatically now that she'd inserted the access card Richards provided all his women.

Debbie.

Janice.

Stacey.

Gone.

"Felicia!" he cried but already the gates were creaking open and then creaking closed and she was lost to him forever.

FIVE

His were the particular pleasures of the lonely. He could eat what he wanted (Snickers, Fritos, Good & Plentys) and watch what he wanted. (Tonight, unable to sleep, thinking of what was happening to Felicia, he started watching *Twins of Evil* but switched channels as soon as the vampire theme started getting oppressive, and then tuned into the Home

Shoppers Channel, a subculture even more fascinating than professional wrestling or professional religion. Who wanted to buy a George Washington clock that recited the names of the first thirteen colonies over and over again? Apparently thousands of people did, and at $48.31 apiece. He had purchased only one thing from the Shoppers Channel, a genuine longbow with quiver and arrows. Over the past six months the bow had become his sole hobby. He was reasonably good with it.) Finally, fitfully, he slept on the couch of his drab efficiency apartment.

Then it was morning, the sky a light shade of gray. He shaved, showered, ate his bran, did his sit-ups, and then said an Our Father and three Hail Marys for Felicia. This was around 7:30. Around 8:30 he called the modeling agency where she worked, and said he was her brother (did she even have a brother?) and asked if he could find out where she was working today and, after only a teensy bit of hesitation, the woman gave him the address and even the phone number where Felicia could be found so her brother (in from Egypt; what the hell—if you lie, lie big) could surprise her.

So he promptly called the photography studio where she was on location today and was surprised to learn that she was there.

She hadn't called in sick.

She hadn't just mysteriously vanished.

She was there.

Working.

Could he possibly speak to her?

"Afraid not. We're in the middle of a bitch of a production problem here and she's really tied up. If you'd care to leave your number, though, we could have her call you back."

Baffled, Sam said, "No thanks. Thank you." And hung up.

The rest of the morning, before he had to start hacking (you had to average seventy hours a week behind the wheel if you wanted to reach even the official poverty level of income), he went to the laundromat and to the

supermarket and to the video rental store and then to the submarine place where he got this salami hogie that could have fed a Third World nation.

Somewhere in the middle of all this, he had started to whistle and the rest of the day he whistled his ass off because she'd proved him wrong and there was nothing he'd wanted more than to be proved wrong.

Karl Richards might be a jerk-off but he wasn't a vampire.

And eventually he'd dump her and then she'd go through a period of heartbreak and then she'd entrust the rest of her life to Sam.

At least, that was the notion that got Sam to whistling and kept him whistling all day.

Around two he went down to the cab company, to the underground garage that always stank of wet concrete, and said a few words to the man without a voice box and then got in his cab and started his workday.

The first two hours went slowly. There was a chatty plump woman going to the hospital to see her herniated husband. There was a somber priest who made a magnificent sign of the cross whenever they passed a Catholic church. And there was a very tiny woman who smoked those 100 mm cigarettes and coughed so hard she jumped around on the backseat.

Then came February dusk, lights up in stores, people slanting into the bitter wind running to garages and bus stops, and then he thought of a wonderful idea.

He knew just where Felicia was.

Knew roughly what time she'd get off.

Why not go wait for her there?

Which is what he did, still whistling all the time, shaping the words of his apology, getting ready to laugh a lot about his stupid notion that Karl Richards was a vampire.

The studio was on the northwest part of town, in a forlorn section of the city. He was parked at the curb for nearly an hour before he began to think that maybe the session had ended early and she'd gone home.

Ten minutes later he sat up and was all ready to go when he saw her in the rearview coming out of the door.

Behind him, suddenly a yellow cab pulled up.

She'd phoned for somebody else.

He jumped from the car and over the roof and yelled, "Felicia! Tell him to go on and let me give you a ride!"

She saw him, of course, and recognized him. But she started to get into the yellow cab anyway.

He ran over to her, grabbed her slender wrist before she could close the door.

"I'll take her," Sam said to the angry-looking cabbie. Sam flung a ten-dollar bill at the man. Then he tugged on Felicia's arm and said, "Come on. Please. All right?"

She sighed, looked embarrassed that the cabman was watching them, and then said softly, "All right."

So she got out of one cab and got in another, and then Sam ran around and got behind the wheel and had them in traffic in moments.

"You going home or to the mansion tonight?"

"The mansion."

He shook his head and said, laughing at himself, "I don't want you to hold it against me."

"Hold what against you?"

"Come on, Felicia. You know—my theory about Karl Richards being a vampire."

"That's the trouble," Felicia said and began suddenly and madly to sob. "You were right. He *is* a vampire."

SIX

For the next two hours they drove through every part of the city imaginable. Past glum slums and palaces; through shopping districts

and industrial zones; and along the river where ice shone like glass
in moonlight.

Sometimes she talked, though little of it made sense, but mostly she
alternated between sniffling and sobbing and staring out the window.

Then she slept.

The radio off, the cab gliding along two-lane asphalt, the only
manmade object in sight a radio tower with a single red warning line at
its top—in this silence her snoring was reassuring because he thought,
She can't be a vampire: vampires don't sleep at night.

Karl Richards might have hypnotized her, or voodoo'd her, or drugged
her, but he hadn't turned her into a vampire.

He drove and was hungry suddenly and thought of how good a big
slice of double cheese pizza would taste along with a cold mug of beer.

"Have you looked in your rearview mirror yet?" she asked, sounding
muzzy with sleep.

"Huh?"

"Your mirror. You still don't believe me, do you, Sam? So look back at
me and then look in your mirror."

So he did. Turned around and saw her looking beautiful if slightly
mussed in the backseat. Then turned around and looked for her image
in the rearview.

And saw nothing.

"My God."

"Pretty crazy, huh?"

"My God," he said again.

"Imagine how I feel," she said, and started sniffling again. "Then he
really did bite you on the—"

"On the arm."

"The arm?"

"It's harder to see the puncture wound on the arm. He laughed
about it afterwards. He said the whole world would know there were

vampires if all these women walked around with big blue holes in their necks. Here."

She pushed her lovely right arm over the front seat and then pulled up her sleeve and, after pulling up a Band-Aid, showed it to him. By now the teeth marks had scabbed over into what appeared to be a very bad infection of some kind.

"So that," she said, "was my very special Valentine's gift."

"Why does he do it on Valentine's Day?"

"Because that's when he became a vampire. Four hundred years ago. In London. He's sentimental about the day." She sighed. "I have to admit that part was fascinating."

"What part?"

"Hearing about London four hundred years ago."

"He talked to you?"

"Oh, sure. I mean, after I woke up from the bite—it put me out an hour or so—and after he got me calmed down, we had a pretty regular night. He made dinner—we had shrimp with black bean sauce; he's a great cook—and then we listened to his big band records and then we talked. Except now he was free to tell the truth about himself, including what London was like in those days." Then suddenly she broke into sobs again.

"Why are you crying? Except for getting turned into a vampire, it sounds like a pretty wonderful night." He heard jealousy in his voice.

"Because I haven't told you everything."

"What's everything?"

"That I'm part of his entourage now. Forever."

"His entourage?"

She had to stop crying to tell him. He took a small box of Kleenex from the front seat and handed it back to her. He looked in the rearview again just in case the first time had been a fluke.

It hadn't been.

"He has more than thirty women living there at the mansion. They're pretty regular women, for the most part—everything considered, I mean. He keeps them healthy and beautiful and he uses them for sustenance and he uses them for sex and everything's fine as long as he gradually replenishes the supply by adding a new one every Valentine's Day. It's really not a bad life if you like total security—but I hate it, Sam. Already I hate it."

"He has a harem."

"Yes," she said, "that's exactly what it is, Sam, a harem. He's the ultimate male chauvinist. He calls us vampirettes."

"But I thought vampires—"

"Skulked around alleys? Preyed on young women in the fog? Perched on window ledges disguised as bats?"

"But the night I saw him disappear—"

"It's because you looked in your rearview mirror. The thing about turning yourself into a bat is strictly comic-book stuff. Anyway, he's very squeamish about bugs and rodents and such. Unnaturally so." She paused and stared out the window at the silver hills again.

"I'm going to help you," he said.

"Sam, that's sweet, it really is. But you can't help me."

"There's got to be something—"

"What? Go to the authorities? Even if you did prove to their satisfaction he was a vampire, you'd be dooming me the rest of my life—and it's going to be a long one, Sam, it really is—to being kept in a prison somewhere by the authorities. No, Sam." She leaned up and touched his shoulder. "Please don't do anything. You'd probably only make it worse." She paused. "Do you know what time it is?"

"Eight thirty-five."

"Gosh, you'd better get me back to the mansion."

"I thought maybe we could have something to eat. A pizza or something."

"I'd like to but he's very strict about hours."

"Hours?"

"He runs the place like a dorm. We all keep our jobs—sleeping all day is another myth—but we have to be back at the mansion by nine or we get demerits."

"You're kidding."

"No, he's got this big chart in his den. He puts stars by your name—gold if you've been great, blue if you've been good, black if you've been bad."

"What happens if you get black?"

"I don't know and I'm afraid to find out."

So, not wanting her to get a black star, he broke speed limits getting back to the mansion.

It was 8:57 when he pulled up in front of the iron gates.

He said, "God, Felicia, I've got to see you again. I do."

"Even though I'm a vampire?"

"Felicia, you could be a werewolf and I wouldn't care. I really wouldn't."

"Oh, Sam," she said, and brought her face to his and kissed him tenderly on the cheek. She felt a few degrees cooler than most human beings, but that was about the only difference.

She looked up at the mansion's spires against the gold disc of moon. "Gosh," she said, "I wish we could go back to my apartment. We could order in a pizza and snuggle up on the couch and—" She started crying again. "If only I'd listened to you, Sam."

"You'd better hurry, Felicia," he said. "I don't want you to get a black star."

Miserably, she nodded. "You're right."

As she got out of the car and the dome light came on, he took her arm and said, "I love you, Felicia."

And she said what he'd waited so long to hear in return. "The weird thing is, as soon as I came to last night, the first person I thought about was you, Sam. Even before I thought about my parents or my, cats or my

lovebirds." She smiled sadly. "I guess that must mean I love you, too."
Then she was gone.

SEVEN

The next day he called the modeling agency to find out where she
was working this time, but the woman on the other end said, "Is this
her brother, again?"

"Uh, yes."

"I checked her files. She doesn't have a brother."

"Oh."

She hung up.

He spent the two hours before work at the library riffling through
books on vampires—they had a surprising number of such volumes—but
soon discovered that most of them did little more than promote myths.
In books, vampires skulked in alleys, preyed on fog-enshrouded young
women, turned themselves into bats. They didn't—unlike the only
vampire Sam knew—cook gourmet meals, play Tommy Dorsey records
and give his thirty girl friends black stars for bad behavior.

He left the library and raced to a pay phone. He got the modeling
agency on the phone again—the same woman. As she answered, he slid
a handkerchief across the receiver and said, "This is Lieutenant Carstairs
from the Fourth Precinct. We need to get in touch with one of your
models. A Miss—" He paused, pretending to be looking at a notepad.
"A Miss—"

"It's you again, isn't it?"

"Huh?"

"You. The so-called brother. The pest. We've got enough creeps
bothering our girls. We don't need any more."

She slammed down the receiver.

EIGHT

That night he sat in front of the mansion, watching the ground fog wrap itself around the turrets and spires of the great stone house, hoping she'd try to make some kind of escape and would come rushing out to the gate.

She didn't and Sam just sat there drinking Diet Pepsis, and then getting out of the cab and taking a pee in thick mulberry bushes where the occupants of passing cars couldn't see him, and then getting back inside the cab for more of his lonely vigil.

Two hours later he ended up on his couch eating Ding-Dongs with skim milk and watching *The Tall T* with Randolph Scott. He fell asleep with a box of Cracker Jacks on his stomach.

In the morning, exhausted, he put on the only tie he owned and went up to the modeling agency where Felicia worked. He also brought a small spiral tablet. A 35 mm camera was slung over his tan corduroy jacket.

The woman was about what he'd expected—short, overly made-up, with a dark-eyed gaze that could melt diamonds. "Yes?" she snapped when he went to take his place at the reception counter.

"I'm Bryant from the *Times.* I'm supposed to interview one of your models: Felicia Ames."

"The *Times?* The *New York Times?*"

He smiled. "I wish my paper was that important. No, I'm afraid I'm with *Modeling Times.*" He hoped that his self-effacing smile would convince her he was telling the truth.

"Never heard of it."

"That's because we haven't published our first issue yet."

Then the woman did something odd. She sat back in her chair, closed her eyes, and put her fingertips to her temples. "Say something."

"What?"

"Say something."

"What do you want me to—"

"It's you!" she said. "The fake brother. The phony cop. Now, you get out of here!"

She stood up and pointed to the door, and he had no choice but to comply.

The rest of the day he drove his cab, taking every chance to cruise by the three studios where she normally worked, but finding no sign of her.

That night he took up his vigil at the mansion again. Around midnight he thought he heard a scream, faint behind the fog, but he couldn't be sure if it was only his imagination and his exhaustion.

On the couch he watched *This Island Earth* with Jeff Morrow and a woman who'd been a real babe named Faith Domergue, and fell asleep with a box of Screaming Yellow Zonkers on his chest.

He didn't wake till nearly noon and was therefore in a hurry, shaving while he peed, ironing a shirt while he ate his bran.

He was fifteen minutes late starting his shift. The man without the voice box laid some very angry sci-fi effects on him.

There were skinny people, black people, white people, pudgy people, straight people, gay people, nice-looking people, repellent people, pleasant people, surly people—it was one of those inexplicably busy days. He didn't really get an opportunity to buzz past the studios where she generally worked and it was nearly eleven o'clock before he got to the mansion where he sat for twenty minutes and dozed off.

The stress of the past three days, plus the late hours, had drained him.

He went home and lay on the couch again, the movie tonight being one of his favorites, *D.O.A.* with Edmond O'Brien, who'd been the chunkiest leading man Sam had ever seen, but he was asleep even before the doomed Edmond realized he'd been fatally poisoned. A sack of chip-dip–flavored Lay's potato chips next to his head.

The pounding started around 4:00 A.M. At first he thought it was part of a nightmare he couldn't wake up from.

Pounding.

Finally, still thinking he was acting out a role in a nightmare, he got up and stumbled to the door, clumsily taking off the three security locks, and at last seeing who stood there.

Felicia.

Tears streaming down her face.

A small overnight bag in her left hand.

"Sam," she sobbed. "Sam, may I move in with you?"

NINE

Two hours later, over a pepperoni pizza delivered steaming hot, she said, "I don't blame you if you're scared of me."

"Why would I be scared of you?"

"Well . . ." she said, and stopped eating.

"Felicia—" he began, and put his hand out to her.

But she stopped him. "There's a very good possibility I'm a vampire."

"But you look fine. You look wonderful, in fact."

"I'm pale."

"Sure you're pale. But you've also been under a great strain."

"And this pizza is the first thing I've eaten in two days."

"It's just the stress really. I read a magazine article on stress and—"

"I don't want to—"

He stared at her. "To what?"

"To get you involved in this any more than you are already."

"But, Felicia, I love you and you love me."

She started sniffling again. "But maybe it's not enough."

He sprang to the couch and sat next to her. "I know this isn't much." His hand swept the drab apartment, the dated posters from the seventies, the collection of sci-fi and horror paperbacks in orange crates, and the longbow and its attendant paraphernalia. "But we'll move. Arizona.

New Mexico. Oregon. Someplace, Felicia—someplace where we can get started on a new life. And—"

She put her head on his shoulder and drew him into her. "But I'm a vampire."

"Everybody's got things wrong with them, Felicia. Everybody."

"But being a vampire is more than just something wrong."

So he kissed her because it was the only way to keep her quiet. In the course of the kiss, he realized how much he loved her. It was frightening—far more than vampires could ever be.

"I'll go to the bank tomorrow and draw out my savings and then we'll go to the bus depot and we'll leave for New Mexico. He'll never find us there."

She sighed. "That's what scares me."

"What?"

"I don't think he'll give up so easily."

"Felicia, I promise. He won't even remember you."

"Oh, Sam," she said, drawing closer to him for another kiss, "I sure hope you're right."

"I am right, Felicia, I promise." Then he paused and gulped and said, "Felicia, I—"

She smiled at him. "I know. Me too." Then she said, "Do you really think we're going to be together, Sam?"

"Always."

"You're not just saying that?"

"I promise you, Felicia. I promise you."

* * *

For purposes of lovemaking and sleep, Sam decided to give her the royal treatment. He turned the sofa into a bed and dug out his only set of clean sheets from a cardboard box filled with a reasonably complete collection of Jonah Hex comic books.

The lovemaking was tender, and immediately afterward, she fell asleep in his embrace, there in the long shadows of the tiny apartment, the nimbus of streetlight like faded gold against the cracked west window, traffic sounds faint in the night.

Sam wondered: Could it really end this happily? This easily? Karl Richards just handing her over to him?

But eventually, no matter how compelling his doubts, he fell asleep, too, as crazy in love as he'd ever been, the woman in his arms all the things a woman was capable of being—lover, friend, sister, partner, conspirator.

His last waking thought was of how wonderful life could be.

He was asleep maybe twenty minutes before a sound woke him. Through one groggily opened eye, he saw Felicia in silhouette at the window. She was putting her clothes on.

"Felicia—what's wrong?"

Nothing. She said nothing. Just continued to dress.

"Felicia?"

He threw the covers back and went over to her. He wore nothing but jockey shorts.

He got around in front of her and put both his hands on her shoulders and started shaking her. He forced her face up so he could see her expression in the deep night shadows.

Her eyes were dark vacuums. All he could think of was some kind of hypnosis or mind control or—

Then he moved over to the window rimed with silver frost around the edges and looked down into the street. A long black limousine sat beneath the streetlight. A tall, slender man dressed in a black topcoat stood outside the limo. He stared directly up at Sam's apartment.

The man was Karl Richards.

"No, Felicia!" Sam screamed. "Don't go with him! Don't go with him!" He dashed to the sink, soaked a towel in cold water, came back to her, and pressed the icy cloth against her face.

177

Dimly, he saw recognition in her eyes.

"Felicia?"

"Yes." She sounded robotic.

"If you go with him, you'll never be free again. Do you understand, Felicia?"

"Yes."

"Then fight back. Resist the thoughts he's sending out." He shook her hard. "Fight back, Felicia. You want to stay here with me. We'll leave for New Mexico in just a few hours. You'll be safe and happy and loved and—"

And then she let out an animal roar that paralyzed him.

He could not imagine such a sound coming from this beautiful woman.

Nor could he imagine a woman—or a man, for that matter—possessing the sheer physical strength she displayed: she took him by the shoulder and flung him across the room, slamming him into the wall where the longbow hung.

The back of his head cracked against the plaster hard enough that a darkness even deeper than the night began to spread before his eyes and . . .

Just before tumbling into unconsciousness, he heard the terrible animal roar she'd made earlier . . . and then he heard his apartment door flung back . . . footsteps down the creaking wooden steps and . . .

And then, despite every effort, he felt himself pulled inevitably down into the waiting gloom that was not unlike death.

* * *

When he woke, his teeth were chattering from the cold. His head hurt him worse than the worst hangover he'd ever had.

The window was purple-gold with dawn glowing through the frost. The room, always a mess, was now a shambles, evidence of the strength she'd suddenly shown.

He needed clothes and he needed coffee and he needed to very
carefully think through—

If he hadn't been right next to the fallen longbow, maybe the idea
would never have come to him. But as he started to push himself to
his feet, his fingers touched the sleek wood, the curving bow, and right
then—right there in his jockey shorts and needing very badly to pee—he
got the idea.

And it was a wonderful idea, and he knew it was a wonderful idea as
soon as he had it.

It was the idea that was going to win him Felicia back once and for all.

TEN

"Peace," Albert Carney said when Sam entered his carpentry shop three
hours later. Albert, a fat and unkempt man with wild hair and beard turning
gray these days, wiped pudgy fingers on his bib overalls and flashed Sam
the V sign for peace, the way people used to greet others back in the sixties.
He looked as if he hadn't shaved, bathed, or slept for several months.

Sam always thought of Albert as the last of the hippies, the one person
he knew who would never give up the flower-power era. For instance,
now the air was being stirred by the slashing sounds of Jefferson Airplane
singing "White Rabbit" on the cassette deck. The shop, which was really
a large, converted garage that smelled sweetly of wood shavings, was
decorated with posters of people such as Ken Kesey, Allen Ginsberg, and
Jerry Rubin. Nobody could ever accuse Albert Carney of giving up the faith.

Albert picked up a tiny marijuana roach, lit it, toked deep and true,
then offered the clip to Sam.

Sam shook his head. "How's business?"

Albert nodded to various pieces of cabinetry in various stages of
carpentering or staining. "Enough to last me a couple lifetimes." He
smiled with teeth that would have required two dentists to get clean and

then said, "Say—you're goin' to be haulin' me around Saturday night. Big sixties festival down at the Freak."

The Freak was a beer and wine bar near the railroad depot, where once a month they had a sixties night. Albert, who didn't want to get busted for drunk driving, always had Sam haul him back and forth in the cab. That's how they'd met.

"Be glad to, Albert."

Albert had another toke. "So what brings you here, man? Especially with that bow. That mother looks fierce!"

"It is fierce, Albert. Very fierce. And that's why I need to talk to you. I need to make it even fiercer."

"How you gonna do that?"

"With your help, I'm going to make a very special kind of arrow."

"What kind would that be, Sam?"

"It's got to be a wooden stake that I can notch in my bow and shoot."

"A wooden stake?" Albert laughed, taking the final toke. "What you gonna hunt—vampires?"

Sam laughed right along with him. "You think you can do it?" Albert shrugged. "Probably."

"It would have to be able to pierce—armor."

"That's why the English invented the longbow. So it could do just that." He took the bow, examined it. "That shouldn't be any problem."

"How long?"

"How long?"

"Yeah, how long will it take?"

"Well, I'd have to use the lathe and then fire-harden it and—"

"Albert, I need this arrow by six o'clock tonight."

"You're kidding."

"I'm not, Albert."

"God."

"Albert, it's life and death."

180

Albert looked him over. "You look real strung out, man."

"I wish I could tell you."

Albert looked at him and said, "OK, man. The number of times you've kept me out of the drunk tank, I guess this is the least I can do for you." He nodded to the lathe. "You come back here at six tonight and I'll have it ready for you."

Sam put his hand on Albert's shoulder. "I wish there was some way I could repay you."

"There is, man "

"What's that?"

"Tell me the truth about why you want this arrow."

Sam laughed again, though the sound was obviously strained. "Like you said, I'm going to go hunting vampires."

But this time Albert didn't laugh. "You know, man, I'm beginning to wonder if you're not serious."

ELEVEN

Sam spent the afternoon taking care of passengers. It seemed important to him to stay calm. What lay before him tonight required not only skill and luck but steady nerves.

Whether talking to the rich dowager who always told him about her son-in-law the songwriter ("Kenny Rogers calls him all the time just to talk") or taking Mr. Gunderson to his doctor's appointment ("I'm eighty-two and they want to know why I don't feel so good—and that's why I don't feel so good, because I'm eighty-two that's why, the stupid bastids")—whatever he did, his mind remained on the plan, or, as his mind thought of it. The Plan.

Last night, summoned to the waiting limo by Karl Richards, Felicia had forgotten her purse in which resided the electronic access card that would let whoever possessed it inside the walled estate.

The card now rested in Sam's shirt pocket.

Four dragged by; five to six crawled: it was time to go to Albert's.

This time the cassette machine played Neil Young singing "My Old Man" and Albert had himself a much more formidable joint than the little roach he'd sported before.

This one was fat enough to last for a couple hours of watching a light show.

"Here you go," Albert said, toking up.

What he handed Sam looked like a small tree that had been shaved down to the size of a baseball bat.

"Sure hope that bow of yours can handle this," Albert said.

"No problem," Sam said, holding the huge arrow. The feathers near the end of the nock were bright yellow.

"Thought I'd kind of dress it up," Albert said. "What do you think of the point?"

Pure wood, the point pricked Sam's finger at the slightest touch. A drop of blood appeared.

"Kind of heavy duty, wouldn't you say?"

"Sam, if I was into kissing guys, I'd plant a big one on your cheek." He dug into his back pocket for his wallet. "What do I owe you?"

"I already told you."

"The cab ride?"

"Right."

"You got it."

Now so intent on his mission that he even forgot to say good-bye, Sam took the arrow and started to leave the garage.

"Hey," Albert said.

Sam turned around. "Oh, yeah. sorry. Shoulda said good-bye."

"No, not that," Albert said.

"What then?"

"Put the tip of it up by your nose."

Sam angled the long, pointed shaft of fire-hardened wood to his nose. Immediately, he pulled the arrow away from his nostrils. "Whew. What'd you dip it in, anyway? Sheep dung?"

Albert looked very proud of himself. "What else? Garlic."

TWELVE

There was an electronic buzz and then the black grillwork of the gates parted and Sam went inside.

In the silver fog that lay across the land so heavily all he could see of the mansion was a single spire silhouetted against the round yellow disc of moon, Sam moved cautiously to the house.

Now that the gates had been opened, Karl Richards would be expecting somebody. Probably one of the women, done with her day's work.

Sam had to move quickly, and did, his feet making sucking sounds in the damp grass, the sound of his heart huge in his ears.

After ten minutes, he reached what appeared to be a large screened-in veranda. He tried the door—locked.

From his pocket he took a switchblade, clicked it open. He tore a four-foot gash in the screen and then went inside, carrying his longbow carefully in one hand, the arrow carefully in the other.

He crossed a flagstone walkway filled with summer furniture that looked dirty and cold on this winter's night. He went up three steps to a door that would take him inside. He put his hand on the knob and then whispered a prayer before turning it. If it was only open—

Locked.

Glancing wildly around, he saw a window three feet off the veranda floor. He went over to it, pulling a deck chair with him. Standing on the tarpaulin seat, he peeked through the window. What he saw was a shadowy hallway at the far end of which appeared to be a vast living room filled with Victorian antiques.

He said the same prayer he'd said before. This time his luck was better. The window eased open and he dropped inside the mansion.

He lay in the shadows, smelling furniture polish and floor wax and the remnants of a dinner that had included some kind of spaghetti sauce. Only after ten minutes did he make his move.

The living room—vast with a vaulted ceiling and huge fireplace— proved empty, as did an adjacent room which was filled with what looked like original oils by Degas and Chagall.

Carefully, he made his way through the first floor: dining room; kitchen; sewing room; den. Nothing.

Then from upstairs he heard the scream.

Racing to the bottom of a staircase that fanned wider as it stretched in carpeted splendor to the second level, Sam gulped and prepared himself for the confrontation that had been inevitable since the first time he'd dropped Felicia off at the mansion.

He crept up the stairs, the sound of an angry male voice growing louder the higher he went.

A wide corridor with walls of flocked red wallpaper; a large flattering portrait of Karl Richards himself decked out in a black suit and high white collar (eyes glistening as blackly as his hair); a partially opened door through which the man's voice came—these were the first things Sam saw.

Hefting the wooden crossbow, he got up on tiptoe and edged to the door.

Inside he saw a large group of women, dressed in everything from baby doll pajamas to diaphanous negligees, gathered in a circle in the center of a huge room appointed, as the living room was, with Victorian furnishings.

Pacing back and forth before the women was a tall man in a red silk dinner jacket and black slacks. He was flawlessly handsome and flawlessly angry.

"I want obedience!" he snapped. "Not mere compliance!" He paused and said in a lower yet curiously more menacing tone, "None of you can escape me—so why not obey me!"

"We're people, too," a strawberry blond with wonderful breasts said. "We have rights."

"You are *not* people," Karl Richards said. "You are vampires."

"So you're not even going to listen to our petition about forming a committee to change some of the rules?"

"I am the absolute master!" Richards screamed. "Not only the master of darkness—but the master of this house."

It was then that Sam saw Felicia. She sat near the back. She wore a modest blue cotton nightgown that made her look little-girlish and all the more beautiful.

She chose that moment to look up and when she did so, she saw Sam. He held up the bow and arrow for her to see and then touched a finger to his lips, shushing her.

"There will be no more talk about committees or changing the rules or anything!" Karl Richards said. "And to prove it, I want all of you girls in bed within fifteen minutes—with the lights out."

Sam gulped.

The moment was here.

He notched the arrow, gulped, said another silent prayer, kicked the door open, and pulled back on the bowstring.

Karl Richards did just what Sam had hoped he would. Startled by the door's flying open, the vampire turned around to face Sam.

And Sam let go the stake that had been shaved into an arrow.

Richards, seeing what was about to happen, grabbed a nearly naked woman who had been standing a few inches from him—and pushed her into the path of the arrow.

She twisted as the stake went deep into her heart. The noise she made was nearly intolerable to Sam.

Then Karl Richards went crazy.

Teeth the size of wolf fangs appeared in the corners of his mouth, and his lips began to drip silver saliva.

"Oh gosh, Sam, now he'll get you for sure!" he heard Felicia shout. The idea had occurred to Sam.

As Richards moved forward, hands turning into talons now, Sam backed up against the staircase until there was no place he could go unless he jumped the considerable distance to the first floor.

"You have enraged me long enough!" shouted Richards, his face distorted by rage and spittle.

Behind Richards, Sam could see the fallen woman, the arrow sticking up out of her bloody chest like a lance.

He shouted to Felicia: "Pull the arrow out and bring it to me!"

It was then that Richards's talons shredded through Sam's cheeks.

Sam spent the next two minutes dodging the taller and more athletic man, running down the hallway, only to be tripped—then pinned down, only to squirm free at the last moment.

He did not notice Felicia until Richards had backed him up against a corner.

"Here, Sam!" she called and threw him the arrow.

It fell two feet short of Sam's grasp.

Richards, cursing, bent to pick up the arrow. "I'll break it in half and then I'll do the same to you!"

But as he stooped, Sam sprang from the corner and kicked him hard on the side of the face, sending Richards awkwardly to his knees.

Sam snatched up the arrow and notched it for the second time in the bowstring. It was sticky with the woman's blood.

Then Sam let go the giant arrow. It ripped through the vampire's heart with such force that it emerged from the beast's back, dripping blood and entrails.

The master of darkness was dead as hell.

THIRTEEN

"Good-bye," said the brunette, embracing Felicia in the vestibule downstairs.

The brunette wore a gabardine business suit and carried a large gray piece of American Tourister luggage and had a tan London Fog draped over her arm. She sure didn't look like a vampire.

"Where will you go?" Felicia asked.

"My uncle owns a travel agency in Cleveland. I'll probably give that a try first."

"We should have a get-together once a year."

"Yes, a picnic or something," the brunet said. Then she put out her hand to Sam. "I owe you a lot more than I can say." He looked at Felicia and smiled.

"I had selfish reasons."

Quite seriously, the brunette said, "I'll always be a vampire, but at least now I'm my own person."

An airport limo pulled up and honked.

"Well," the brunette said, "good-bye."

Then she walked outside to the sunlight that was almost white. The grass was brilliant green. As usual in the Midwest, spring had simply shown up one morning, like a lover one had almost forgotten.

Sam said, "Well, that's the last of them."

"Yes," Felicia said, smiling. "Every one of the women packed and away from this place." She leaned over and kissed him on the cheek. "Oh, Sam. We all owe you so much."

"You know I don't want gratitude, Felicia. I did it because I love you." He nodded upstairs. "Now why don't you go upstairs and pack? Then we can get out of here, too."

She kissed him again. "It won't take long."

She went up the broad stairs. He entertained himself by walking through the room with the Chagall and Degas oils. It was warm in here

The furnace in the basement was roaring. He had put Karl Richards's corpse in it.

She was back, an overnight bag in her hand, a few minutes later.

"Ready?" he asked.

"Oh, Sam, if you could only know how ready I am."

"Good. Then let's lock this place up and never think about it again."

She giggled. "Let's."

So they went outside to the brilliant day and he put the key in the lock and started to turn it and that was when a rough piece of wood scraped the knuckle of his left thumb.

And several small bubbles of blood appeared.

He laughed. "Mr. Graceful strikes again," he said.

He finished locking the door and then turned around to look at her.

The fangs didn't alter her face all that much. And she wasn't spitting all over the place. And her eyes weren't psychotic and crazed.

She was a vampire, OK, but at least she was a very pretty and feminine one.

She started sobbing instantly and fell into his arms.

* * *

An hour later they had completed their second lap around the huge estate. They had seen dogs, they had seen horses, they had seen deer; they had seen oak, they had seen maple, they had seen elm; they had seen rock and grass and lake.

And they had faced a terrible truth.

Now, sitting on a porch swing in the park pavilion: "We can't be together, Sam."

"Don't say that anymore. Please."

"It's true. The mere sight of blood—I'm a vampire. My teeth—"

"You didn't bite me. You're not some terrible beast. You're—"

"As vampires go, I'm probably pretty OK," Felicia said, watching the course of a jay as it flew up to a tree limb. "I mean, I was a decent human being, so I'll probably be a decent vampire. But that still doesn't mean we can be together."

"Oh please, Felicia. Please don't say that anymore."

She stood up, then bent down to take his hands and pull him up, too. Her eyes were wet with her tears. "I love you more than I've ever loved anybody, Sam. But it won't work and you know it and I know it."

"But it's no different from my marrying a Polynesian woman. There'll be some cultural differences at first but—"

"Yes. I don't cast a reflection, my whole body surges when I see blood, and I'm probably going to live to be a few thousand years old. But other than that I'll just be a typical suburban housewife, right, Sam?"

"I—"

She put her lips to his. Their kiss was long and tender and halfway through, Sam recognized the kiss for what it was:

Good-bye.

She entwined her hand in his and together they walked out of the estate, the grillwork gates closing behind them.

They stood on the curb and Sam said, "What will you do?"

She tried a smile but it was mostly sad. "Right now I'm not thinking very clearly, Sam. I guess I don't have any idea at all what I'll do. Just whatever comes along, I guess."

Then she waved good-bye to him and started walking away, a beautiful, retreating figure, until she rounded a corner and was out of sight. Gone.

Forever.

FOURTEEN

During the next year he saw a shrink who tried to convince him that none of it had ever happened, a priest who accused him of being a satanist, a minister who wanted him to come on his TV talk show and discuss how even vampires could become good Christians.

He also tried singles bars, dating services, and old girlfriends.

But no matter what he tried, there were still the lasting memories of Felicia, and of their plans, and of how much he'd loved her and loved her still.

Spring became summer became autumn became winter. A new cable channel appeared, one that played a lot of Monogram films, including the best of the Charlie Chans and Bowery Boys, and that helped some, and scores of new types of junk food came along, and that helped a little bit, too.

But mostly there was just driving the cab and lying on the couch thinking about Felicia. Thinking uselessly about Felicia. He had tried all the agencies and all the studios, but there was no word of her. Obviously she had moved away.

He contented himself with cable and food that only a chemist could love.

He had only a vague idea of what day it was, that overcast February Tuesday.

He'd had his usual afternoon-load of people he liked and people he disliked.

Now it was dusk and the dispatcher had just sent him to an address near the downtown area.

He pulled up and waited in front of an aged brick building.

A woman in a fashionable felt hat, one whose rim obscured her face, walked gracefully from the building and got in the car. She smelled wonderfully of perfume and womanness.

He was halfway down the block before he said, "I forgot to ask, where would you like to go?"

All she said was, "Why don't you look in your mirror, Sam?" He didn't have to look in the mirror. He knew the voice.

"My God," he said.

"It's Valentine's Day," she said.

"My God," he said.

"It's selfish of me, Sam, but I just had to see you—"

"My God," he said.

"I've missed you so much and—" She whipped off her felt hat and let her lovely blond hair tumble free.

Finally, he was able to speak coherently. "I've looked everywhere or you. For a year."

"That's so sweet—"

"To tell you something."

"Tell me what?"

"That I have a plan."

"What plan?"

"There's a park up ahead."

"All right."

"And I'm going to pull into that park."

"All right."

"And then I'm going to ask you to sit up in the front seat with me."

For the first time she sounded a bit hesitant, suspicious. "All right." He pulled into the park. At night the only illumination was the nimbus of electric light off dirty snow.

They parked next to a pavilion. "OK," he said. "Get up front."

"What's going to happen, Sam?"

"You'll see. Please, Felicia. Just get up front."

So she got up front.

As soon as she was in the front seat, he did it: grabbed the church key he kept on the dash and cut a deep gash on his hand.

In the shadows, he saw her entire body begin to tremble, saw the

fangs begin to form in the corners of her mouth.

"I should have thought of this that day we walked around the mansion," Sam said, holding out his hand. "I can't turn you back into a human but you can turn me into a vampire."

"Sam, are you sure you want to—"

Sam laughed. "Make me your valentine, Felicia. Make me your valentine right now."

DANIEL

C. T. ADAMS AND CATHY CLAMP

ONE

*J*enna! Jenna! Ohmigod, Jenna Cooper! Is that you?" I made my voice a girlish squeal. Inwardly I was wincing, but I played the role to perfection, running up to the mark like a long-lost acquaintance, making sure everybody in the restaurant would be watching so that there'd be witnesses later if she tried to deny what was about to happen.

A gorgeous woman in a lavender silk suit and pearls the size of gumballs leaned back from her salad plate and eyed me suspiciously. But she didn't bolt or try to deny it, so I plowed on.

"I'm not surprised you don't remember me. Nobody ever does. But it's you, isn't it? You *are* Jenna Cooper?"

She blinked a few times, and I could see her trying to match my face with a memory and failing. I mean, let's be honest, the Jennas of the world are beautiful, and popular enough that from the day they're born there are hangers-on and wannabes enough that they really don't remember. Was I that girl from high school or college? The quiet mousy one? Maybe from that office she worked in briefly before marrying well? The other woman at the table gave her a sympathetic look. It's always so embarrassing to be caught flat-footed.

"Yes. I'm Jenna, but it's Jenna Ross now. I'm sorry, I really don't seem to remember you."

"That's all right," I assured her as I pulled a stack of folded papers from my fashionably large purse. "You wouldn't. We've never met." I dropped the pages onto the napkin in her lap. "My name is Karen James, and you've just been served."

I turned and walked away, my high heels clicking on the hardwood floor. All eyes were on me as I made my way through the restaurant. Not because I looked good—I did, but I will never be in the same league as the Jennas of the world. I'm short and stocky, rather than tall and elegant, my suit was black polyester, my necklace tiny seed pearls. But I'd done my job, and done it well. Mrs. Ross had been served her divorce papers very, very publicly, just the way her husband wanted.

Nobody bothered me on my way out. Since I hadn't bothered with the valet, I waved him away when he started to approach, walking to the farthest end of the lot where the employees park. I'd left my car there, because my battered, twelve-year-old subcompact would've stuck out like a sore thumb among the shiny new BMWs and Mercedes.

I walked confidently up to my car, keys in hand. I'd parked directly under the street light. I could see every detail in that flat, orange light. He didn't step out of the shadows. There were no shadows. He simply appeared. Like smoke, in thin air.

I didn't scream. I've seen the show before. Only this wasn't Daniel. Which meant I was in trouble.

"That was cleverly done. A brilliant piece of acting work you pulled off in the restaurant, if I do say so myself." He was tall and slender, but well built. His hair was a natural silver-blond that looked perfectly in keeping with his marble-white skin. The voice was cultured too, as smooth as that same marble. Soothing. It was all part of the package. I didn't dare look into his eyes, but I had no doubt they were gorgeous—and utterly mesmerizing.

The stranger stood in quiet amusement as I took in every bit of his appearance.

"Thank you. I'm actually very good at my job."

"As am I."

I didn't doubt it. With those looks and attitude he probably had to beat off the prey with a stick. Sex is a powerful lure, and by God he was sexy. His whole body breathed pheromones. I felt my body tighten, and it wasn't from fear. Dammit.

"Look at me," he ordered.

"No." I fought the compulsion. It wasn't easy. But I'm as stubborn as hell and I've had lots of practice, so I managed.

"Look at me." There was a hint of a growl in the voice:, and I felt my body give an involuntary jerk. But I closed my eyes and fought for all I was worth.

"You know our ways, how is that possible?" Hands like steel bands dug into my shoulders as he grabbed me, intending to drag me towards him. "I smell . . . Daniel."

He pulled harder, and the pain was blinding. I fought long enough for him to put some strength into it then surprised him by going utterly limp. When he bent over to catch me, I punched upwards as hard as I could, driving my car keys deep into his throat, my fist slamming against his windpipe.

He reared back, blood pouring from his neck in a wide spray. I'd caught an artery. His teeth bared, and I caught a glimpse of vicious fangs.

I started screaming bloody murder. The valet turned, as did the customers he was serving. They moved slowly, as if coming out of a trance. But they did move. Apparently I'd injured him badly enough that he couldn't heal and use his mojo. The men ran towards us. The woman pulled out a cell phone and began dialing 911.

"You'll pay for that, bitch." He spit the words out with a spray of blood, and vanished, like a puff of smoke.

"Are you all right? You're covered in blood! What happened? Where did he go?"

"I'm fine, I'm fine." I stood up and tried to brush the dirt and leaves from my torn stockings, which just smeared the blood around worse. My hands were covered in it. In fact, there was enough blood that if he'd been human I'd have worried about him bleeding to death. But he wasn't. Which meant that I'd just pissed him off. Of course, I couldn't tell my rescuers that. After all, vampires don't exist.

Yeah, right.

The police came, and there was an ambulance. It took hours to deal with all of the official crap. Other than bone-deep bruising on my shoulders, I didn't have any injuries, but the doctors were worried that I was going into shock. So I had to call my boss. His irritation at my being off duty for the rest of the night was only slightly mollified by the fact I'd gotten Mrs. Ross. Knowing my luck, he'd dock me for the extra hours. Between the statements for the police and the emergency room rigmarole, it was 3 A.M. by the time I climbed out of the cab that dropped me off at my apartment door.

My eyes burned with exhaustion, my clothes and keys had been impounded for evidence, and I was out the cab fare home. If a particularly kindly ER nurse hadn't loaned me a spare set of scrubs, I don't know what I would have done. As it was, the thin cotton did nothing to cut the chill breeze blowing. I shuddered, shivering as I scrounged the last of the change from the bottom of my purse to come up with enough to pay the cabbie. No tip. But there you go.

A blast of cold wind plastered the thin green cotton of the borrowed scrubs against my skin. Swearing, I hurried across the short stretch of gravel that led to the back door of my apartment building.

Twitchy with nerves, I kept looking over my shoulder, my fingers trembling as I tried to punch in the access code for the door. "What's happened to you?"

I screamed, not a full-throated shriek, but one of those sort of half-screams you give off when you're startled. I knew that voice. It was Daniel.

"Easy, easy." He started to reach for me, to pat my shoulder, but I flinched away in fear and pain.

"Karen, what happened?" He stood utterly still, perfect body outlined in the harsh shadows cast by the stark white light of the security bulb overhead. He sniffed, and a shudder ran through him. Even his eyes reacted, pupils expanding, moving more like the slitted eyes of a cat than a human.

"You smell of blood, and it isn't yours."

Another, longer, sniff, and he stepped closer, invading my personal space, but there was no threat to the motion. Nor was there any of the heat and sexual tension I'd come to expect.

He stepped back, his expression horrified. "Dear God, Karen. What have you done?"

I was shivering from the combination of cold and shock. My teeth weren't quite chattering, but that would probably be next.

"Let's get you inside."

"What do you think I'm trying to do?" I reached around his bulk to try to enter the numbers onto the keypad again, but he made a disgusted sound in the back of his throat. He placed a hand gently on my arm. I felt a rush of warmth, and I was suddenly standing in the middle of my living room.

"Lie down on the couch under the blankets. I'll run you a bath. You need to keep warm."

I didn't even bother converting the futon into the bed position, just curled up on it as it was. I wrapped myself up in the quilt my sister had made for me (as well as in every other blanket that I owned) and still I was shivering. Daniel moved with brisk efficiency, but none of his usual smooth elegance. He started a hot bath running before crossing the few steps into the kitchen to set a kettle on to boil.

I watched him because I couldn't not. Whenever he was near me, he had my full attention. He was so damned beautiful. His skin was the colour of caramel, smooth and creamy. The hair a mass of soft dark curls. Saying it was dark brown didn't do it justice. Every strand seemed a separate shade of brown, some with glossy highlights, others so dark they were almost black. Every time I looked at his hair I had a wild urge to run my fingers through it.

Tonight he was wearing new jeans in that deep shade of indigo that seems to fade after the first few washings. The collar of his navy silk shirt was unbuttoned, exposing his throat and giving just a glimpse of his smoothly muscled chest. I saw the pulse jumping in his throat and realized something completely unexpected.

"You're afraid."

He stopped, turning to face me. The movement was . . . odd, inhuman.

"You smell of blood and of Alexander. You haven't been bitten. I'd know if you had. Which means that you have somehow managed to hurt one of the most powerful of my kind. He won't let that stand. He *can't*. Yes, I'm afraid. And so should you be."

The phrasing struck me, as it sometimes did: "So should you be," not "You should be, too." How old was Daniel, I had no idea. He'd never say, just smile and change the subjiect.

"What do I do?"

The kettle began to whistle, and he moved into the kitchen. I heard him rummaging in the cabinets for a mug, heard him rip open one of the little metal packets of instant cocoa I drink. A few clinks of the spoon against china, and he reappeared, mug in hand. "Drink this, and tell me what happened."

I did as he said. It didn't take long. There wasn't much to it really, and I'd had lots of practice repeating the story to the police and the doctors.

He didn't interrupt. He just perched on the edge of my wooden rocking chair, sitting unnaturally still, barely seeming even to breathe

until I finished. The stillness was odd, foreign. It wasn't like him. Normally he was animated, more alive than most of the people I know. Not tonight.

I was the one who got up and shambled into the kitchen to refill my cup, then into the bathroom to turn off the taps and strip for my bath. Daniel just sat. "Why me?" I muttered. It was meant to be a rhetorical question, but he answered.

"Because you were clever. It caught his attention. Alexander always says 'You are who you eat.'" He paused, his voice gaining a hint of dry sarcasm. "Of course, it didn't help that you parked in the farthest, most deserted part of the lot."

"There were people. It was well lit."

He let out a soft snort, but didn't argue.

I didn't hear him go—not that I would. But I'd been in the tub just long enough for the water to start to cool when he appeared in the bathroom doorway. In his hand he held what looked like a necklace of three charms strung on a black satin ribbon.

The warmth of the cocoa and the bath had helped. I felt better— good enough that I risked something I'd never done before.

I'd always been cautious around Daniel: kept my distance, carefully avoided looking him in the eye and never, ever, coming close enough to touch. It had become a game between us. We'd tease, play up the sexual tension, but we never stepped over the line. He'd moved slowly, allowing the friendship to develop. It had occurred to me more than once that he wanted—needed—that more than sex, more than blood.

I rose slowly and stepped out of the tub. I watched with satisfaction as his eyes followed the water that trailed down every curve of my body. His eyes darkened until they were almost black, and a bulge began to show beneath the tight denim of his jeans.

"Hunters are always alone."

"Always?" I put a teasing note in my voice and stepped up to him. Only a fraction of an inch separated us. Such a tiny distance. I could smell the hint of soap on his skin, feel actual heat radiating from his body.

"Karen . . ."

"Shush." I reached up and placed a finger against his lips. "We've known each other for months. If you were going to bite me, you would've done it by now."

"You don't know that." His whisper was as rough as the stubble that decorated his cheeks.

"Yes, I do."

He held his body stiff, motionless. He didn't move forward, but he didn't resist as I moved my hand against his chest for balance and went up on tiptoe to kiss him.

It started as a gentle touch of the lips, my body barely brushing his. It didn't stay that way. He had me in his arms so suddenly it was startling, his hands sliding down my body until they reached my thighs. He grabbed me then, lifting me from the ground, pulling me tight against him, so that the rough denim ground against the most intimate parts of me as his tongue plunged into my mouth.

I whimpered, my hands tearing at the cloth of his shirt. I wanted, needed, to feel the warmth of his skin; needed to touch him, to have him touch me.

He groaned, pulling back from the kiss, but not putting me down or letting me go. Burying his face in my throat he spoke in a whisper that was hoarse with need. "We can't do this."

"Yes, we can."

I felt him gathering himself together, preparing to pull back. I couldn't stand it. Pride went out the window in the face of pure need. "Daniel, please."

"You don't understand." He lifted his face and for the first time ever, I looked him straight in the eye.

"I don't care. I want you. Want this." I ground my body against his hardness.

He blinked, and I was caught in the magic of his gaze, a swirl of gold and copper, bronze and the rich brown of dark chocolate. I heard myself gasp, felt myself being carried into the living room.

He took his time, licking the water from every part of me, using teeth and tongue to tease as his hands explored. His shirt was gone. I writhed against him, shouting myself hoarse.

When we were done, he collapsed beside me, both of us sated and spent, the weight of his body pinning me to the futon mattress.

"When we can move, you need to put on the charm I made you. It'll make you harder to find and more difficult for Alexander to connect us. It'll let me know if you're in trouble."

"Harder to find?" I shifted my weight, rolling towards him, the fingers of my right hand tracing delicately over his sleekly muscled chest and six-pack abs.

"Alexander will be looking for you. He's going to want to kill you, as slowly and painfully as he can. I'm not going to let him."

"Can you stop him?"

"I have to."

TWO

I rolled over and slapped my hand in the general direction of the alarm clock, hoping to hit the snooze button. The movement sent a wave of pain shooting through my shoulder and down my arm. The pain was a far more effective wake-up call than the buzzing of the clock. I gasped, my eyes going wide.

It took a second for my mind to click into gear, to remember last night. It hadn't been a dream. I had the bruises, and the charm necklace, to prove it. But Daniel was gone, and I had things to do before I went into work this evening.

I was sore and stiff, both from my injuries and from my amazing night with Daniel, so I set the shower massage on high, and turned the temperature up as hot as I could stand. By the time I had spent a few minutes under the spray, I was able to raise my arms above my head. Not without pain, mind you. The bruises were too deep for that. But at least I had full range of motion and was able to brush my teeth without screaming in agony.

I dressed simply: black jeans and a loose polo shirt. The bra straps hurt against the bruises, but I'm too busty to feel completely comfortable braless, so I wore it anyway. Dark socks and running shoes completed my outfit.

When I was dressed, I called in to the office. If anyone hadn't shown up there might be work available, and since I'd lost half of my shift to the hospital visit, I could use the money.

"Anderson Investigations and Process Service. This is Amber, may I help you?"

"Hey Amber, it's me."

"Karen! Ohmigod. Are you all right? I heard you were mugged and had to go to the ER last night."

"I'm a little banged up, but I'll be OK." Maybe. I hoped. Assuming Daniel and I could handle Alexander.

"Oh thank God. Well, look, there's nothing for you here until you come on shift, so take it easy and rest up. Good job on the Ross service by the way. The boss is pleased."

"Thanks." Glad he was pleased, but too bad there was no extra work. Oh well.

"See you when you come on shift."

"Right."

I hung up the phone feeling a little depressed. I needed to take my mind off of things, distract myself. So I flipped on the television and hooked up the game console. In minutes my mind was off in la-la land, chasing through dangerous mazes collecting weapons and killing aliens.

The more the day wore on, the more tense I became. I'd gotten lucky yesterday. Alexander had been expecting an easy kill and had been careless. Next time he'd be prepared.

I knew that Daniel wanted me to let him take care of it. Fine. I mean, let's face it, the "creatures of the night" have all sorts of advantages over the rest of us. First, nobody believes they exist; if I asked anyone but Daniel for help, they'd lock me up in the loony bin and throw away the key. Then they have that whole hypnotic-stare, super-strength, gotta-stake-me-and-cut-off-my-head-to-kill-me thing going.

Could I drive a stake through somebody's chest to save my own life?

Probably. But it wouldn't be easy. It takes a lot of strength, both of body and will to do that sort of thing.

Cut off the head?

Ewww. Um . . . maybe. But how do you explain it to the police after? "Gee, officer. I'm pretty sure the victim was a vampire . . ." Not so much. See previous comment re rubber room with padded walls.

But I'm not the type to just let the man take care of things. I'm not. So I needed to be prepared. I just wasn't sure how. Last night I hadn't taken the time to ask Daniel which of the myths about vampires were true and which were, well, myth. We hadn't spent much time talking.

Not that I regretted any of the not talking. That had been spectacularly wonderful, wonderfully spectacular, and I wanted more just as soon as I could get it, thank you very much. In fact, it had lived up to every single fantasy I'd had about him since our first meeting. But now I had a problem on my hands and I needed to figure out what to do about it.

I grabbed the spare set of keys from their hook and pulled on my jacket. It would take a little time to ride the bus out to the restaurant and pick up my car, but if I left now, I should still be able to get there before sundown. In fact, if I hurried, I might be able to run a few errands before it got dark and Alexander came a-calling.

I hurried.

* * *

"What is that smell?" The man changing the tire was short and bulky, with the beginnings of a gut hanging over the top of his belt. His name was Jack Baker, and I was serving him with a restraining order. He apparently had a habit of beating up on his wife, to which she'd taken exception. I'd serve the papers. It's what I do. But I'd be careful doing it. Because, while Mr. Baker looked innocuous enough, he was plenty dangerous.

I felt bad for his wife, and hoped she didn't believe that a simple piece of paper was going to keep him away from her. In my experience, most restraining orders didn't work. But if you're lucky—very, very lucky—they might result in the asshole going to jail long enough to give you a head start.

"Garlic," I answered him, because I was going to try to keep this friendly. It probably wouldn't work, but I was going to try. "I'm planning on making spaghetti when I get home."

"You cook? You don't look like the type." He raised his beady eyes from what he was doing to check me out, his hand clenching and unclenching on the tire iron.

"I cook," I answered. "By the way, my name's Karen. Karen James. What's yours?" He was busy tightening the lug nuts, and didn't look up when he answered me.

"Jack Baker," he answered. Grunting, he finished tightening the last lug nut. "But make the check out to Baker Towing."

"Right." I dug in my purse, pulling out a stack of papers and setting them, along with my checkbook, onto the hood of the car. I made out the check, tearing it out and dropping the book back into the bag. Turning to Mr. Baker, I thrust both the check and paperwork into his hand.

"What the *hell?*" He tried to shove the paperwork back at me, but I backed away.

"Mr. Baker, you've been served."

I climbed into the car, slamming and locking the door before he could react. It was just as well that I did, because when he actually got a glance at the papers I'd handed him, he lost it completely. He swung the tire iron in a wicked arc, smashing it into the car window, which cracked in a spiderweb pattern. Meanwhile I'd started the vehicle and threw it in gear. I was taking off, gravel spitting from my tires when the second blow fell with the clang of metal on metal.

Crap. That had been close. Damn it anyway! My poor car. The clients were definitely getting the bill for this one.

I drove west, towards the last rays of the setting sun that were nearly blinding me, checking my rearview mirror every few seconds to make sure Mr. Baker hadn't decided to follow. He might. He didn't seem like the type to let things go. But luck was with me; there was no sign of a tow truck.

My eyes were on the mirror when Daniel materialized on the seat beside me. I shrieked, and jerked, swerving across two lanes before I got the car back under control.

"Don't do that. Cripes! You scared me half to death."

"I scared you? What the hell are you doing out of your apartment? Damn it! Don't you realize how much danger you're in?" His handsome features twisted into a snarl. "And what is that smell?" He rolled down the window, letting fresh air into the car. I couldn't say I blamed him. In an enclosed space the smell was a little overpowering.

"Fresh cloves of garlic."

He sighed. "If you're thinking it will hurt him, it won't. Although the smell might just drive him off." He leaned towards the window, breathing deeply. "Tell me you're not wearing it in a necklace."

"No, but I've got some in my jacket pockets. The holy water is in a gun on the back seat."

He twisted around and peered over the top of the seat. I saw his eyebrows rise at the sight that greeted him. I'd gone to a toy store and

bought *the* top-of-the-line squirt gun. It was made of neon plastic with no less than five tanks of assorted sizes, all of which I'd filled with holy water from the baptismal font at the Catholic cathedral, before having the gun itself blessed, along with a smaller one that was tucked in the inside pocket of my jacket. I was pretty sure the priest thought I was nuts. But he did as I asked.

"Does holy water work?"

"As a matter of fact, it does. So make sure you aim that thing carefully. Assuming, of course, you get a shot off." Shifting his weight, he pulled the briefcase I'd had on the seat out from beneath him. "I don't suppose I can talk you into staying home where you're relatively safe while I deal with this."

"No. Not really. I've got a job, bills to pay—a *life*. I refuse to cower in the corner."

Actually I'd thought about doing just that, but decided that the stress of worrying would probably do me in just as effectively as the monster hunting me. And then there was the worrying about Daniel. Because I did. Yes, he was a big, strong vampire, perfectly capable of taking care of himself. But I'd seen his expression in that fleeting instant when he'd realized I was up against Alexander. He'd been afraid.

"You do realize how stupid that is." He said it softly.

"Yes. But it doesn't matter." I took the 120th Street exit, heading for my next assignment. This should be an easy one: little suburban housewife getting divorce papers. She was even expecting them.

"I could make you go home."

I thought about that for a moment. Maybe he could. I'd looked in his eyes last night, had felt the magic pulling me like an undertow. Could he use that same magic to bend me to his will? Probably. I just hoped he wouldn't.

"If you do, it's over. I won't be anybody's meat puppet. Not yours, not anyone's."

"Maybe I don't care. Maybe having you alive matters more than whether or not you hate me."

I wasn't sure how to answer that. So I didn't. The silence stretched uncomfortably. I pretended to concentrate on driving, turning left and slowing, my eyes scanning the row of split-level houses for the correct address. When I found it, I pulled the car to the curb and shut off the engine. I grabbed my briefcase and climbed out of the car. Daniel did the same, following a few steps behind as I strode up the sidewalk to the front porch.

I rang the bell and Mrs. West came to the door. She was pretty; a petite brunette that looked harried. In the background I could hear the sound of children fighting. She took the papers, thanked me and quickly closed the door.

It was only when I turned to go back to the car that I noticed.

Daniel wasn't behind me. Instead, he was standing in the middle of the Wests' manicured lawn. In front of him was the most striking woman I'd ever seen. She was tall, taller even than Daniel, with a muscular build and harsh features. I didn't know who she was, but I could guess what she was. And while she was distracting Daniel, Alexander was moving in from behind.

"I cannot *believe* you are sleeping with a *sheep*. God, Daniel. How can you?"

"Hey, you! Who are you calling a sheep?" I shouted the words as I reached into my jacket, my hand closing around the handle of the squirt gun.

I had expected her to react, to attack me. She did turn, and would've charged, if Alexander's magic hadn't struck out at her like a lash.

"The sheep is mine." His voice was a harsh caw. His throat might've looked whole, but either it hadn't healed completely, or there was permanent damage.

I didn't know what he was doing, but he somehow froze both the woman and Daniel in mid-motion. They stood, like statues, only their

eyes moving. Those eyes followed Alexander's gliding steps as his stalked me across the grass. I kept my head down, and began edging towards the car.

"Stop right there."

I felt his power wash over me, felt him willing me to do as he said. But when the power hit the necklace Daniel had given me it scattered, leaving me in possession of my own mind, my own will.

It was then that I had a flash of insight. Daniel hadn't made the charm for me. There'd been no time. No, he'd given me his charm—the one thing that had protected him from Alexander's power. He'd left himself completely vulnerable to protect me. I knew, too, that if I didn't stop Alexander somehow, we'd both die.

Time seemed to slow. Everything was preternaturally clear. I would have to let Alexander get close enough to use the squirt gun. But if he got that close, with his speed and strength, I'd have almost no chance of survival. I might just be able to wound him, maybe even badly enough for Daniel to finish him off.

There'd still be the woman to deal with, but there was nothing I could do about that.

I stayed utterly motionless, barely daring to breathe. He was close now. So close that I could see the glint of moonlight off the buttons of his shirt, smell the scent of old blood on his breath. "Look at me," he ordered.

I turned, stepping forwards, lifting my head as though to comply, giving him exactly what he expected, right up until the last instant. When I pulled the gun from its hiding place, I aimed for the place where his heart should be, spraying holy water directly into his chest.

He screamed, an unearthly, high-pitched, keening wail that was nearly deafening. His body jerked back and flames erupted from a spreading hole the size of my fist, burning through his ribcage. I could see his lungs move as he tried to draw breath, then saw him raise his fist.

I knew that if that blow landed, I would be dead. But it didn't land. A last squeeze of the trigger took out what was left of his heart, and he collapsed. Flames leaped up from his corpse as though it had been doused in gasoline. The heat was horrendous, and I fell back from it, my arm thrown up to protect my eyes. The stench of burning flesh filled the night, gagging me. Dropping the empty squirt gun, I staggered back, horrified.

By the light of the flickering flames I saw a battle raging. Magic and blows fell like rain, too many, too fast for me to follow.

They were evenly matched—the perfect offence meeting an equally perfect defense. Neither had the upper hand.

In the distance I heard sirens. We were running out of time. I stumbled towards the car, intending to go for the large water pistol in the back seat.

The movement distracted her for barely an instant—just long enough for her to turn her head to make sure I wasn't a threat.

It was enough. Daniel used that moment to lunge forwards, claws extended. I heard the wet tearing of flesh, followed by her scream of rage and despair. She struggled, fought, as he tore the still-beating heart from her chest. She collapsed, like a puppet whose strings had been cut. With a roar of triumph, he threw it onto the still-burning thing that had been Alexander

Bathed in blood, lit by firelight, the creature that stood before me was completely inhuman. It couldn't be Daniel. And yet, it was.

He turned to me then, slowly, his movements those of a predator that spots easy prey. He took that first step forwards, and a second, and I felt my pulse speed—primal fear making the blood thunder through my veins. I couldn't fight. I had no weapons. I couldn't flee either. All I could do was stand my ground, face the inevitable.

He stopped. I watched him swallow, saw him struggle against the beast that was so much a part of him. It wasn't easy. But slowly, the beast retreated and Daniel returned. When he was fully himself, he disappeared.

THREE

I doused the woman's body with the holy water in the gun from the back seat. By the time the cops arrived, all that was left of the vampires was a pair of black burned spots on the grass. Normal human bodies do not burn that completely, nor that fast. But that didn't keep the police from investigating.

Eventually, I was cleared. But it took time: days and weeks. Long nights spent alone.

Daniel was gone. Vanished.

The sensible part of me knew it was for the best. The rest of me mourned his loss, hoped for him to return, if only to retrieve the charm necklace. I told myself I could go on without him—I didn't need him. But I did.

Nearly two months had passed. It was late: I was awake, staring out the window at the moonlight, unable to sleep. My mind was on the night I first met Daniel as I traced my hand absently over the charm I continued to wear around my neck.

"I came to say goodbye. It will never work." His voice was soft. "You're human. I feed on humans. I'm immortal. You're so terribly fragile. Anything could take you, at any time. If any of my kind find out, they'll kill us both. Alexander isn't the only hunter out there. I want you to live."

I turned slowly, letting him see the tears that coursed down my cheeks. "There's existing, and there's living. Without you I'll exist, but it won't be living."

He looked at me then, and I took a chance, met his gaze full on. If the eyes are the windows of the soul, I let him see mine, without any hiding or pretence. "I'd rather have a day with you, than a lifetime without. If time is so precious, do we even dare waste a second?"

It was a long time before he answered. Taking me into his arms, he pulled me close enough that his whisper was a breath of air against my hair. "No, we don't."

*T*HERE'S NO SU*C*H THING

CHARLES DE LINT

"*K*en Parry," Apples said.

Cassie nodded.

"Is a vampire."

Cassie nodded again.

Apples had heard that Ken needled the kids he baby-sat, but this was the first she'd heard about his claiming to be a vampire.

"But, there's no such thing," she said.

"Samantha said she saw him turn into a bat one night—right in front of her house when he didn't think she was looking. He was baby-sitting her, and instead of walking home when her parents got back, he *flew.*"

"Flew?"

Cassie nodded solemnly.

Apples tapped her hairbrush against her hand, then set it down on her dresser.

Their mother had been heavily into mythology when she got out of the university, which was how, though they had a nice normal surname like Smith, the two girls got saddled with their given names

of Appoline and Cassandra. Apples had looked them both up at the public library one day, hoping to find something she could use to stop the incessant teasing that they got, but Appoline just meant having something to do with Apollo—the Greek god of music, poetry, archery, prophecy, and healing. That sounded nice on paper, but came out sucky when you tried to explain it to someone. Cassandra had been a prophetess who Apollo was all hot and heavy over—and that would really be fuel for some bad-news ribbing if it ever got out.

Apples wasn't much good with music or poetry. She was lucky to get a C in either at school. She couldn't read the future, and about the most she could do along the healing line was put on a Band-Aid. But hunting milkweed seedpods in the field behind her house as a kid, she'd learned to shoot a mean arrow. Trouble was, that didn't mean much when you were sixteen—not unless you were planning to go in for the Olympics or something, which wasn't exactly an ambition that Apples had set her sights upon.

Cassie couldn't read the future either. She was a sweet eight-year-old with curly blond hair and a smile that just wouldn't quit. She should have had a great life laid out in front of her, except she had severe asthma so she couldn't go anywhere without her bronchodilator. Then there was her right leg, which was half the size of her left and a good three inches shorter. The only way she could walk around was by wearing a leg brace that gained her sympathy, or weird stares, but wasn't exactly endearing.

Except to Apples. She'd do anything for Cassie.

But give up her first date with Rob D'Lima, considering that she'd been mooning over him for three months before he finally asked her out?

"You know there's really no such thing as vampires," she said.

Cassie only regarded her with all the gravity that an eight year old can muster when they know they're right but can't prove it.

Apples sighed.

"I've seen him in the middle of the day," she said. "I thought they couldn't go out in the sunlight."

"That's just part of their legend," Cassie explained. "They've made up all kinds of things about themselves so that people will think they're safe from them. You know, like the bit with the mirror . . . and crosses and garlic. The only thing that's real is that they have to be invited into your house, and Mom and Dad have *done* that."

Apples picked up her hairbrush again.

"You're really scared, aren't you?" she said.

"Wouldn't you be?"

Apples smiled. "I guess I would. Okay. I'll stay home with you tonight."

"It won't do any good."

Apples thought Cassie was talking about her date with Rob.

"If Rob's half as nice as I think he is, he'll understand," she said. "Maybe he'll even come over, and the three of us can . . ."

Her voice trailed off as Cassie started shaking her head.

"I already asked Mom," Cassie said. "and she said no way."

"You told her Ken was a vampire?"

"I had to . . ."

Apples sighed again. While Cassie hadn't been gifted with the ability to see into the future, she *had* been gifted with an overactive imagination. Their parents had long since lost patience with her stories.

"You should have come to see me first," she said.

"You were late coming back from volleyball practice, and I didn't know if you'd be back in time for me to tell you about it."

"I'm sorry."

"It's okay."

"So what can we do about this?" Apples asked.

"Could you, maybe, come home early . . . ?"

Apples smiled and tousled her sister's hair. "You bet. I'll be back as soon as the movie's over. We'll send Ken packing, and then pig out on popcorn and watch some music videos."

"It'll be past my bedtime."

Apples laughed. "Like that's ever stopped you."

* * *

Rob was really nice about it. After the show was over, they went back to Apples's house. Ken seemed surprised to see them, but that was about it. No fangs. No big black cape. Apples paid him from the house money her mom kept in a jar in the pantry cupboard and closed the front door behind him.

"Just let me go check on the Munchkin," Apples said as Rob settled down on the couch. "Won't take a moment. You . . ." She hesitated. "If she wants to sit up with us for a little while, you won't mind, will you?"

Rob shook his head. "That's one of the things I like about you, Apples: the way you take care of Cassie. Most kids hate their little brothers and sisters. Me, I just wish I had one."

"Well you can share mine tonight," Apples said. "I'll hold you to that."

Be still, my heart, Apples thought as she headed upstairs to Cassie's room.

She was thinking about how it would feel to have Rob kiss her when she stepped into the room and her heartbeat jumped into double time. Cassie was huddled on her bed, hunched over and making wheezing sounds.

Oh, jeez, Apples thought, *she's having an attack and that bloody fool Ken never checked on her.*

But when she got to Cassie's bed, she found that her sister was crying, not struggling for breath. Apples sat down on the bed, the bedsprings dipping under her weight. Before she could reach out a hand, Cassie had turned and buried her face against Apples's shoulder.

"It's okay, it's okay," Apples murmured, stroking Cassie's short hair.

She was going to kill Ken Parry.

"What happened?" she asked.

"He . . . he . . ."

Apples had an awful thought.

"Did he . . . touch you, Cassie?"

Cassie nodded and started to sob louder. Apples held her until her crying had subsided; then she brushed the damp hair away from Cassie's brow and had a good look at her little sister. There were questions she knew she should ask, but somehow she felt the best thing to do right now was to get Cassie over the immediate trauma. The poor kid looked miserable. Her face was all puffed up and her eyes were red. She sniveled, then blew her nose when Apples handed her a tissue.

"He said," Cassie began. She hesitated, then started over. "I . . . I woke up and he . . . he was sitting on the bed and he'd pulled my nightie up, but then . . . then you came home . . ."

"Oh, Cassie."

"He . . . he said if I told anyone, he'd come back in the night and he'd . . . he'd hurt me. . ."

"No one's going to come and no one's going to hurt you," Apples told her. promise you."

"Everything all right in here?"

Apples looked up to find Rob standing in the doorway. She nodded.

"Ken just scared her, that's all," she said.

She felt inordinately pleased when she saw his hands clench into fists at his sides and anger flare up in his eyes.

"Sounds like this guy needs a lesson in—"

Apples cut him off.

"There's not much we can do—not without getting into trouble ourselves. This is the kind of thing my parents are going to have to handle."

"But . . ."

Apples gave a meaningful nod to her sister—it said, *Not in front of Cassie, please*—and was grateful to see that he caught its meaning without her having to actually say the words aloud.

He took a breath, then let it out slowly and put a smile on his face.

"You promised me some popcorn," he said. "I hope you're not going back on the deal now."

Apples gave him a grateful look. "Not a chance. How about you, Cassie? Do you feel like having some with us, or are you going to make us eat it all on our own? You know me, I eat like a bird. Maybe I should put mine in a bird feeder."

The smile she got back was small, but it was there, and by the time the popcorn was popping in the microwave and a Richard Marx video was booming from the television set, Cassie was almost back to her old self again. All except for the hurt look in the back of her eyes that Apples was afraid might never go away.

Rob left before her parents got back.

"You're going to talk to them about this guy?" he asked when they were standing out on the stoop.

"I'll get it all worked out," Apples said. "I promise."

"But if you need some help . . ."

"You'll be the first I'll call."

The kiss was everything she'd hoped it would be—multiplied maybe a hundred times more. She felt a little breathless as she watched him go down the walk, and the tingle he'd called up from deep inside her didn't go away for hours.

She was in bed when her parents got home and didn't say anything to them except for a sleepy good night that was half muffled by her pillow. She waited until she was sure they were asleep before she got up again.

She couldn't get Ken Parry out of her mind. Not even thinking of Rob helped. Her mind just kept coming back to Ken and what he'd tried to do to Cassie.

Mr. Vampire. Right.

She had to talk to him, and talk to him now. But first she had to get his attention. With a guy like Ken, there was only one way to do that.

She went to her closet and rummaged around in it until she came up with a black leather miniskirt and a scoop-necked blouse. She brushed her hair and tied it back, put on a slash of red lipstick, then tiptoed down the stairs and out of the house. She put her high heels on when she was outside and click-clacked her way along the sidewalk, two blocks north, one block west, another north, until she was standing in front of Ken Parry's house.

The streetlight cast enough light for her to make out the Batman poster in the left front bedroom on the second floor. There was only one kid living here, so it had to be his room.

Stooping awkwardly in the short skirt, she picked up some small bits of gravel from the Parry driveway and tossed them up at the window. It took three tries before a very sleepy-looking Ken Parry slid up the window and peered down at her.

He woke up quickly when he saw who it was. "What do you want?" he called down in a loud whisper.

"I thought we could make a trade," she whispered back. "I'll give you something you'll like and you leave my little sister alone."

"You're kidding."

Apples put a hand on her waist and thrust out a hip. "Do I look like I'm kidding?"

He made a soft noise in the back of his throat. "I . . . I'll be right down."

When he opened the door, she was standing on the porch.

"Aren't you going to invite me in?" she purred.

"I . . . my parents . . ."

"Are sleeping, I'll bet."

"Uh, sure. You, uh, come on in."

He stood aside to let her pass by.

Apples gave him a considering look as she stepped into his house—just to be sure. One look at him was all it took to confirm it. Ken Parry wasn't a vampire. She should know. Her only regret as she let him lead her downstairs to the rec room was that his dumb stunt had forced her to tell Cassie:

There's no such thing as vampires.

Because it was the first time she'd ever lied to her little sister.

* * *

Ken Parry never came back to school. Rumor in the halls had it that he'd come down with a kind of anemia that the doctors simply couldn't diagnose. It left him too weak for normal teenage pursuits; so weak that he ended up staying in the hospital until his family finally moved away just before midterm exams.

Apples didn't miss him. She only needed to feed once a month, and there were always other people around, just like him, who got their kicks out of tormenting some little kid.

She didn't give Ken or any of them the Gift itself—not the way that the woman had given her the Gift in the parking lot behind the Civic Center after a Bryan Adams concert this past summer. She never did find out why the woman chose her. All she knew was that vampires lived forever, and she didn't want any of those guys around for that long.

No, she was saving the Gift. Vampires never got sick, and if there was something wrong with them when they got that special bite, then the Gift cured them. So she was waiting for Cassie to turn sixteen.

Until then she had to figure out a way to deal with her parents' always remarking on how she just never seemed to get any older. And she had to decide if Rob really was someone she'd want to be with forever.

Because forever took on a whole different meaning for those with the Gift.

TUMBLING DOWN THE NIGHTTIME

DEAN WESLEY SMITH

*N*ightly routine:

Between one and one-fifteen, the nurse, an overbusted, overthighed woman with bottle-thick glasses, would rudely flip on the overhead light, pull back his covers, and check to see if the sheets were wet.

They usually were. A source of continued embarrassment. More so with the presence of the almost always-young, almost-always-pretty aide.

The routine went on.

Without a smile, the nurse would say, "Ed, I'm going to change your bed now and clean you up. All right?" With the help of the aide she'd grab him under the arm and butt and roll him to one side. God, that hurt. Their rough, always-clean hands were sandpaper against his thin, aged skin.

They never asked him to help. He always groaned. What more was there for him to say? Some nights he would try to remember being young, being with Rebecca, running and playing baseball. Anything but the routine. But it very seldom took him from the reality. So he just groaned.

In answer to his groan, the nurse would say, "Ed, I've got to change your sheets. It will just take a minute. All right?"

As if he had a choice.

The routine went on.

They'd pull up the sheets from the hall side of the bed while he lay with his back to them, bare ass exposed to God and anyone who chose to walk down the hall at that moment. Then she'd take a wet cloth, always cold, and clean him. He wished some night the nurse would use a warm cloth.

She never did.

The routine went on.

The two of them would grab him again, roll him back over on the clean sheet side, pull up the rest of the old sheet, and finish putting down the new one. Then, with their sandpaper hands, they'd roll him onto his back, pull the sheet loosely over him and flip off the light on the way out, leaving him bruised, battered, and exhausted from the battle.

End of routine.

He glanced at his glow-in-the-dark clock: 1:00 A.M. The nurse and the aide would be in any moment. He focused his mind on Rebecca, her dark eyes and jet-black hair. They had been lovers for years until finally she had left him, without warning or reason. But those years with her had been his best, and they were now the years he focused on when trying to escape the routine.

An intense white flash brought the room into sharp focus before he could snap his eyes shut. It surprised him and he jumped. For a brief moment he thought it might have been the nurse and the overhead fluorescent bulb had just exploded.

But instead of the nurse's voice or footsteps, a loud crash filled the room. The building groaned. His bed shook. The picture of Maggie, his dead wife, rattled on the nightstand. He could hear glass shattering from somewhere down the hall.

Then it ended.

Another new sound. He opened his eyes as shouting came from down the hall. It sounded like he was suddenly in a hospital and someone was trying to die.

The hall lights flickered, then went out. A dull engine sound came from the back of the building and the lights came back on, not quite as bright. Probably the standby generator. He wondered what could have happened to cause the power to go out.

Next he heard doors slam, a woman sob, "Oh, no," and footsteps running. It all ended with one final door slam.

Buzzers exploded in the nurse's station like horses from a starting gate as residents, disturbed by the noise, rang for the hired help. That was a sound he always tried, and failed, to put to the back of his mind. The buzzing sound was a part of nursing home routine that he heard every day. Every hour. A sound that annoyed him, grated at his nerves, and made him angry. He never understood why, since he was here to die, he couldn't do it without the metallic sound of others doing the same thing.

He quickly checked the darkened room. His roommate, Mel, still slept, snoring like he always did. Mel could sleep through anything. Everything else seemed to be in its place. The clock said 1:03. He strained to listen for any sound as the clock's ticking got louder and louder until it fought to cover the sounds of the buzzers.

Mel's snoring kept time with the clock. He always slept soundly, dreaming dreams of the war he'd fought in years earlier. His dreams continued through his waking hours and he talked of nothing else. WWII . . . the Big One. Mel yearned for the time when dying seemed glorious and purposeful instead of boring and without pride. Someday, in a dream, Mel would catch a bullet while leading his platoon and die in his sleep. For him it would then be worthwhile.

The nurse and the aide would change Mel's sheets and roll in a new roommate so Ed would have company. Then he and his new roommate would race to see who would die first.

It had happened twice before. Ed had lost the race both times.

But tonight they were racing on a new track. Over the buzzers, the ticking of the clock and Mel's battle snores, Ed could hear Mrs. Reeges, two doors down, ring for the nurse. He could tell her buzz because it sounded higher, as if something was slightly broken with it. She always rang around one in the morning. She needed her fix of pills. Sometimes she rang before the nurse attacked him. Sometimes during. Once in a while after. She stayed in her routine now and rang for the nurse, mixing her useless annoyance with that of others.

Mel continued his snoring, successfully dodging bullets, the clock kept its ticking, and a moment later, Mrs. Reeges rang again. No one answered any of the rings. No movement in the halls at all.

Mrs. Reeges rang again.

Then again.

Where the hell was the damn nurse?

Ed thought about the large woman who changed his bed five nights a week. He knew through the grapevine that she had two kids and a husband who worked swing shift at the plywood plant. She didn't much give a shit about any of the residents. To her they were just like the rough lumber her husband tossed around. The two aides who were the only other employees who worked the night shift were both students and both newly married. They cared even less. It had been lucky nothing much ever happened on graveyard shift. Except people dying. The nurse and the aides never had any trouble with that.

Mrs. Reeges let out a yell.

"Nurse!"

Ed knew she would yell eventually. Others were starting to. Mrs. Reeges would panic and follow their lead.

"Nurse!" Her voice, weak and raspy, barely carried over the rhythmic duo of Mel and the clock.

"Nurse . . . please?"

All the yelling and buzzing was becoming damn annoying. He could imagine the nurse's station echoing, empty, its colored metal folders in stacked slots with name tags below each. Last week he had noticed that every name tag had a small white tab on the right side to ease in the tag's removal when the owner died. That's how it was around here.

Tonight no workers answered the grating sound of the buzzers. No one rushed in to change his sheets. No one would remove his tag when he died. Not even the white tab would help at the moment. Something major had happened out in the street, or against the side of the building, to make all three employees leave.

Mrs. Reeges rang again, then yelled, "Nurse!"

She had now combined the ring and the yell. She sounded desperate. His sheets felt cold and downright uncomfortable.

Damn it all. "Nurse!" he yelled. His voice sounded weak and hollow. Mel snorted in time with the clock.

Mrs. Reeges rang again. She didn't yell. Maybe she figured that he would do all the yelling. She would do the ringing and he the yelling. Now they were a team of sorts.

"Nurse!" he yelled again, this time his voice carrying more authority. He waited, breathing shallowly, to hear the answer. He could almost hear Mrs. Reeges waiting, breathing shallowly.

She rang again. He yelled with authority. They waited. He could hear over the buzzing some movement from other residents. No help.

No amount of authority in his yell would bring help. The workers weren't coming back for a while. He was sure of that. He could feel it in the silence over the buzzing and the snoring and the ticking.

Mrs. Reeges rang. She expected him to yell. There was no point.

A minute later, she rang again and yelled, taking up his part of the team. He turned his head from the door toward the curtain over the patio door and the faint light coming from outside.

"Hello, Ed," a soft voice said and a shadowy shape stepped toward the bed. "Do you need something I can get for you?"

He jerked on the wet sheet like a fish out of water and for a moment he thought his heart was going to pound right out of his chest. The shadow outlined against the curtains moved closer to the bed as he fought to catch his breath.

"I'm sorry," a woman's voice said. "I didn't mean to startle you."

"But you sure as hell did," Ed managed to choke out, taking deep breaths. "How'd you get in here?"

She laughed softly, and Ed's stomach twisted. He knew that laugh. But it couldn't be.

"How about turning on a light so I can see who's giving me a heart attack?" He pointed to the lamp on the nightstand beside the bed. The shadow moved to the lamp and with a click lit the room with soft yellow light.

Down the hall the buzzers and the yelling for the nurses continued. Mel kept snoring and life beyond the circle of the lamplight kept on. Ed blinked a few times and then looked up into a face he hadn't seen in forty years, a face that every night he dreamed about, a face that couldn't be. "Rebecca . . . ?"

"Hi, Ed," she said, putting her hand on his arm. Her cool touch sent shivers through him. "It's good to see you again."

All he could do was stare. She was still just as young as he remembered her. Her black eyes sparkled in the lamplight and her long black hair shined. She had on a short black leather coat and Levis. And she was more beautiful than he remembered.

He wanted to run, but his body wouldn't move. He wanted to scream, but he knew it would do no good mixed with the calls and buzzers of the others. He wanted to reach out and hug her as he had done forty years ago, but fear held him back.

"Can I sit for a moment?" She pointed to his wheelchair, and he somehow managed to nod.

He watched her, trying desperately to clear his mind, as she pulled the chair over beside the bed and sat in it, again putting her cool hand on his arm. He shook his head and laughed. "I'm dreaming, aren't I? Or I'm dead and you've come to take me to heaven. That's it. I'm dead." Somehow that thought comforted him and he managed a deep breath. If he was dead, why couldn't he move? Why couldn't he climb out of bed and go down to the nurse's station and pull his white tag, so everyone would know?

She laughed and again the memories of all those wonderful nights of laughter with her flooded over him as if they had happened yesterday.

"You're not dreaming and you're still very much alive."

Ed sighed. "A guy can always hope."

She squeezed his arm and laughed at his poor joke, but this time he could tell her laugh was not sincere.

"So," he said, rolling the best he could to face her, "after all these years, why are you here? Better yet, why did you leave me in the first place?" And as he talked he noticed that there were absolutely no wrinkles at all in her face or around her eyes. She looked twenty-five years old. "And an even more important question, what's the name of your plastic surgeon?'"

She smiled. "To answer your questions one at a time, first I'm here because I wanted to see an old friend and maybe see if I can help you a little."

He didn't say anything. There was no way this could be his Rebecca. She was too young. The real Rebecca would have been eighty-one, two years younger than he was. This must be her granddaughter. But why would her granddaughter pretend to be Rebecca?

"Second," she said, "I left you because I had to. If I had stayed you would have noticed that I wasn't aging and you were."

She held up her hand to stop his comment. "Remember how, that last year we were together, people were commenting on how young I looked? Remember how old Charlie the bartender even said I looked like your

daughter? I never changed, did I? In all the years we were together, did I age at all?"

He fought his memory, but he knew she was right. It just hadn't seemed important at the time. It had seemed more like a bonus to him. Not important enough for her to leave him. So what if she looked younger than he did? "Go on," he said. "Not that I believe any of this, but do please tell me how you stayed so young." He swept his arm in the general direction of the room around them and then at his almost useless body. "I would love to know your secret."

She held his arm firmly and looked him directly in the eye. "I'm what you would call a vampire. I was over three hundred years old when we met. My four hundredth birthday was two months ago."

He stared into her dark eyes, wanting to believe her, and almost, for a short second, he did. Then he realized fully what she had said, and the laughter overcame him, slowly building in his stomach and finally erupting in such force that it hurt. Tears filled his eyes, and he could feel that he was wetting himself again, the familiar warm feeling mixing with the cold, damp sheets.

She sat up straight in the wheelchair, and it rolled an inch or so back from the bed, but she never let go of his arm, and the serious expression on her face never changed. After a minute or so he finally stopped laughing and worked at catching his breath.

Mel snorted and rolled over. Down the hall the buzzers and the yelling continued.

"I suppose," he said, between gulps of air, "that you are responsible for the nurse and aides leaving."

She nodded. "It was necessary. I just helped a car go out of control. It hit a power pole and plowed into the side of the building. The driver and three passengers were all drunk, but no one was seriously hurt. The nurse should be returning shortly, as soon as the police arrive, so we don't have much time."

He almost started to laugh again, but the cold sheets under his butt and her stern expression stopped him. "You're serious, aren't you?"

She nodded.

"Okay," he said, lifting himself as best he could with his arms and turning so that he could completely face her. "Assuming that I believe you are a vampire, which I don't, why would you come here to see me now after all these years? You want my thin old blood?"

She looked almost hurt at his sick joke. "Think back," she said. "Did you ever see me in the full light of a summer day?"

"You worked days," he said, but that sounded weak even to him.

"No, I usually slept days. Not that the old myth about sunlight killing us is right. It's not. But direct sunlight is very uncomfortable to me, so I have always preferred nights: All vampires do, thus come the myths. And we haven't killed for blood for centuries."

"That's good to know," he said. "Okay, Rebecca was always a night owl, I will grant you that. But that doesn't make you her. Tell me something about her that only I would know." He smiled at her, figuring he had her. But she smiled back, let go of his arm, and stood. In a flash she had unzipped her Levis and pulled them down enough to expose white lace panties. Facing the lamp she pulled the panties down to the top of her black pubic hair, and there was the birthmark.

Rebecca's birthmark.

He glanced up into her serious eyes and then back at the apple-shaped birthmark. An apple with what looked to be a bite taken out of it. A very distinctive, one-of-a-kind birthmark.

"You always used to call it the 'apple of your eye' because you liked to look at it so much." She laughed, again a sincere, deep laugh. "In fact, the last few years you called it an appetizer because it always came right before the main course."

The room was spinning, and he closed his eyes to force it to stop. The clock kept ticking and Mel kept snoring. Down the hall the buzzers were

still going strong. He must be having a nightmare. He would wake up, open his eyes, and the nightly routine would be about to start. It would only be 1:00 A.M. and the nurse would be coming to change his sheets.

He would laugh at the nightmare and tell Mel about it tomorrow morning, birthmark and all. Rebecca was a vampire who had come back to visit him. That would get old Mel laughing for sure.

He opened his eyes. The buzzing continued and the clock said fifteen minutes after one. Rebecca was again sitting in his wheelchair, her cold hand on his arm.

For the longest time he did nothing but stare into her eyes. The clock ticked. Mel snored. Buzzers buzzed. And he looked into her eyes.

Finally he said, "It really is you, isn't it?"

She had the grace to only nod.

He nodded with her, suddenly more tired than he had felt in years. "So why come back to me now, after forty years?"

She looked away, her gaze moving in jerks around the room. Finally her gaze stopped on the picture of his wife, Maggie, that rested on his nightstand. Maggie had been dead for seven years. They had met and married three years after Rebecca had left him. It had been a good marriage, but nothing more.

"I think I would have liked her," she said, nodding at the picture.

"You can tell that from a picture? Another special power?"

She half-laughed. "No, I'm afraid not. I don't think you ever realized how much I loved you. For most of the past forty years I have kept track of you, watched your life, always from a distance."

"You did?" He stared at her while she continued to stare at the picture of Maggie.

She nodded. "I even managed to meet and talk to Maggie a number of times when you weren't around. Twice, as a matter of fact, in the grocery store line. She seemed to be a very nice person and I was happy for you. It made me very sad when she died."

He glanced at the picture of Maggie and then back at Rebecca, his first and only true love. "I loved her, but never as much as I loved you."

Rebecca turned to face him. "I know," she said. Her grip was firm on his arm, and he placed his other hand over hers.

They stayed that way, in silence, as Mel snored, buzzers called for attention, and the clock ticked the night away.

After a short time a door slammed down the hall, and the sounds of talking drifted over the commotion.

"I don't have much time," she said. "The nurse will be coming soon."

"So come back tomorrow night. We can talk about old times."

She shook her head. "I'm moving on. I have a husband and he was transferred back east to Chicago. We're leaving tomorrow."

"Is he a vampire, too?"

"No," she said softly.

"So you will one day leave him too?"

She looked away, back at Maggie's picture. "Everyone leaves someone sometimes. It's the way of the world."

He glanced at the picture of Maggie and then back at Rebecca. "I knew why Maggie left me. She even said good-bye. I always wondered why you did."

"I know. That's one of the reasons I'm here tonight."

"What's his name?"

"Craig. His name is Craig."

"And you love him?"

She nodded. "Yes, I think I do. But I also still love you." She looked him directly in the eyes and he knew, without a doubt, that she was telling the truth.

They continued to stare at each other. She was still so beautiful, so young and he was so old, so crippled. It didn't seem fair to him that it had turned out this way.

When the buzzers all shut off at once he knew the time was short. He could feel Rebecca starting to pull away. "You said you might be able to help me? What did you mean by that?"

Rebecca glanced at Maggie's picture again and then back into his eyes.

"Can you make me young again? Make me into someone like you? A vampire?"

She shook her head no. "It doesn't work that way. But I can help you out of this."

She nodded at the room, and it took him a moment staring into her serious expression to completely understand. "You could do that?"

She nodded. "If it's what you want."

He laughed a light, halfhearted laugh. "It's been what I have wanted since my legs quit working and I ended up in this damn room. Every night I hope, and even pray, that I will die so I won't have to wake up in a wet bed, or have some nurse's aide lift me onto the toilet in the morning. Getting out of here has been my strongest wish for five years."

She didn't say a word, and again, after a short moment of looking at her, he asked, "You're serious, aren't you?"

She nodded.

He closed his eyes and listened to the sounds of the night. The sirens outside, the police coming to the wreck, the muffled talking from the nurse and aides drifting down the hall, Mel's snoring, and the continuous ticking of the clock.

How many nights had he wished for this very thing?

How many thousand nights had he wished he could see Rebecca again?

How many thousand nights had he wished he would just die so he could escape this old, useless body he found himself trapped in?

How many nights?

And now he had both of his wishes all wrapped up together like a sick joke.

He opened his eyes and gazed into her concerned face. "You know, you are as beautiful as ever."

She half-smiled and squeezed his arm as the nurse and aides went into the room across the hall. He would be next on their rounds.

"Thanks for the offer. But I think I will pass. I'd just like to remember you like this."

This time her smile filled her face, and the relief was obvious. "I still love you," she said as she leaned forward and kissed his cheek.

"And I love you."

She stood and looked at him for a short moment. Then she moved toward the window.

"Wait!"

She turned, one hand on the drapes.

"Say good-bye this time."

She nodded. "Good-bye, Ed."

"Now that wasn't so hard, was it? And when the time comes, promise me you will say that to Craig."

She stared at him for what seemed like a long, long time. Then she smiled. "I promise."

"Good," he said.

"I love you." She pulled the curtains back and disappeared into the black night.

"I love you, too," he said to the swaying curtains.

A moment later the fluorescent overhead light snapped on and the nurse, an overbusted, overthighed woman with bottle-thick glasses stepped into the room. "Sorry we're late, Ed," she said. "There was an accident outside, so it's been a long night."

"No, actually," he said, still staring at the curtains, "it's been a short life."

The nurse looked at him oddly for a moment, then said, "Let's check to see if these sheets are wet."

And the routine started again.

BROTHER'S KEEPER

LILITH SAINTCROW

ONE

A shrill scream jerked her out of the deep well of sleep.

Selene fumbled for the phone, pushed her hair back, pressed the talk button. "Mrph." She managed the trick of rolling over and blinking at the alarm clock. *Oh, God, what now?* "This had better be good."

"Lena?" A familiar voice wheezed into the other end of the phone. He gasped again. "Lena, it's me."

Oh no. Not another panic attack. "Danny?" Selene sat straight up, her heart pounding. "Danny, what's wrong? Are you okay?" Sweat began to prickle under her arms, the covers turned to strangling fingers before she realized she was awake.

"Cold," he whispered, breath coming in staccato gasps. "Selene. Help. Help me. The book—the *book*—"

Another panic attack, it sounds like another one, oh God. They're getting worse. Selene swung her feet to the cold floor, switching the phone to her right ear, trapping it on her shoulder. "Where are you? Danny? Are you at home?" She grabbed her canvas bag the moment her

232

feet hit the floor, craning her neck to read the Caller ID display. *Daniel Thompson*, his familiar number. He was at home.

Where else would he be? Danny hadn't left his apartment for nearly five years. "Keep breathing. Deep breaths, down into your tummy. I'll be right there."

"No," Danny pleaded. His asthmatic wheeze was getting worse. "Cold . . . *Lena*. Don't. Don't. Danger—" The line went dead.

Selene slammed the phone back into the cradle, her breath hissing in. Her fingers tingled—a sure sign of something awful. *What was I dreaming? Something about the sea, again.* She raced for the bathroom, grabbing a handful of clothes from the dirty-laundry hamper by the bathroom door. *Just keep breathing, Danny. Don't let the panic get too big for you. I'm on my way.* She tripped, nearly fell face-first, banging her forehead on the door. "Shit!"

She yanked her jeans up with one hand and turned on the faucet with the other, splashed her face with cold water. She fastened her thick blonde mane with an elastic band and raced for the door, ripping her sweater at the neck as she forced it over her head. She had to hop on one foot to yank her socks on, she jammed her feet into her boots and flung her bag over her head, catching the strap in her hair. *Just keep him calm enough to remember not to hurt himself, God. Please.*

She slowed down at the end of her block, searching for a cab. *One down, nine to go.* She sprinted across the street. Rain kissed her cheeks and made the sidewalk slick and slightly gritty under the orange wash of city light. Deep heaving gasps of chill air made her lungs burn. Her forehead smarted, making her eyes water.

She crossed Cliff Street, slowing down, pacing herself. *Can't run myself out on the first blocks or I'll be useless before I get halfway there. If this is another one of his practical jokes I am just going to kill him.*

Three down, seven to go. Selene's boots pounded into the sidewalk. Rain whispered on the deserted streets and along the length of her

messy ponytail, dripped down her neck as she crossed Martin Street and cut across the intersection. There were more streetlamps here, she checked her watch as she ran.

Two-thirty. Santiago City held its breath under the mantle of chill night.

The back of Selene's neck prickled, uneasiness rippling just under her skin.

Why can't these things happen in the daylight? Or when I don't have lecture in the morning? This had better be something good, Danny, I swear to God if you're just throwing another snit-fit I will never *forgive you. Never, ever, ever.*

Something chill and panicked began to revolve under her breastbone. The back of Selene's neck crawled. *I'm getting a premonition.* Her breath came in miserable harsh sobs of effort. *Either that or I'm just spooked. Who wouldn't be at 2 A.M. in this busted-down part of town?* She set her teeth, grimly ignoring the stitch in her side. *Danny. Just breathe, please God, let him remember to breathe. Don't let him be in the kitchen, there's knives in there. This sounds like a doozy, he hasn't had a bad panic attack in at least six months, Christ don't let him hurt himself.*

"Hey, Selene."

Selene whirled. "Bruce!" she choked, her hand leaping instinctively to her throat. The silver medallion was still under her sweater, warm against her skin. She hadn't taken it off. "Good God, don't *do* that!" She clenched her hands at her side. *If only he was human, I could punch him.*

Bruce grinned down at her, canines glittering in the pallid orange light, his eyes glowing just like a small nocturnal animal's. Beneath his loud polyester sport jacket and eye-searing yellow tie, his narrow spotted chest was pale and hairless. "Don't worry so much, Lena. I wouldn't *dream* of taking a taste. His Highness wouldn't like that one little bit." His lips curled back even more, exposing more gleaming teeth.

Selene's heart slammed once against her ribs. Taking a long deep breath, she willed her pulse to slow. *Focus, goddammit! Danny needs you, you can't fight anyone or anything if you're busy screaming.*

"I don't have time, Bruce," she gasped. "Danny's in trouble."

"I'll go with you." Bruce shrugged and peeled his lanky frame away from the streetlamp. He had just been Turned, and still looked almost human.

Almost. The feral glow in his eyes and the quick jerking of his movements screamed "not-quite-normal."

Not quite human.

Still, for a Nichtvren, Bruce was as close to human as possible. He'd just been Turned, so he didn't have the scary immobility of older suckheads. Small blessing, but she'd take it. "That's not neces—" she began.

Bruce folded his arms, the smile gone. "Danny's under Nikolai's protection too, Selene. If I let you go over there and get hurt, His Highness will peel off my skin in strips and salt me down." Bruce shivered, his long pink tongue wetting his lips. "Trust me. I'll go with you."

"Oh, for Christ's sweet sake." Selene wasn't about to argue with a dead lounge lizard. He fell into step beside her, long legs easily keeping pace as she trotted up the sidewalk. She glanced down. Black loafers and no socks. *All you're missing is a clutch of gold chains and chest hair.* She tried to keep her breathing quiet, pushing down a lunatic desire to giggle nervously. *Danny, Danny, I'm on my way. Don't hurt yourself.*

"I don't . . . know what . . . he's thinking," she gasped, speeding up. "I'm . . . perfectly . . . safe."

Bruce managed a high thin giggle. "Oh, no you're not, chickadee. You should be glad His Highness took an interest in you." He didn't even sound winded.

I don't need Nikolai's protection. I did just fine on my own.

Okay, so she didn't *want* Nikolai's protection. She'd rather tap dance naked through a minefield singing *Petticoat Junction*. Just because Nikolai was the prime paranormal Power in the city, responsible for

keeping the peace among all the other factions of paranormal citizenry, didn't mean *she* would ever kowtow to him. His Highness Nikolai indeed. Just another suckhead come out from the shadows under the protection of the Paranormal Species Act.

Only this one had an interest in her.

Don't think about things like that. Danny, please be okay. Don't bite your tongue or cut yourself.

Her bag shifted, clinking when it banged against her shoulder. Steel and salt, the tools she needed to banish anything evil or unwanted; it didn't pay as well as teaching but God knew there was a need for her talents. She'd been so tired when she got home she hadn't unpacked, poltergeist infestations were like that. Not very difficult, but messy and draining. She pushed the strap higher. "I don't need his . . . protection or . . . yours, suckhead."

"That's what *you* think." Bruce grinned down at her, his words soft and even. "Want me to carry your bag?"

"Of . . . course . . . not." Selene sped up. *To hell with pacing myself. Danny needs me.*

Selene's medallion warmed against her skin, reacting to Bruce's presence—at least, she *hoped* that was what it was reacting to. By the time they reached Danny's building, the metal thrummed with Power. Gooseflesh raced down her body; she choked back a final gasp as she rounded the final corner and saw the slim, tall black shape on the steps.

Bruce smirked, letting out a soft little snort of laughter. Selene curled her hands into fists, resisting the urge to claw the smile from his face. *Jumping the Nichtvren won't get you anywhere, Selene. Just ignore him, and concentrate on what matters. Danny, my God, please be okay. Remember the visualizations I taught you.*

The tall black-clad shape rose from the shadows lying over the concrete steps. *Oh, no. Could this possibly get any worse?*

Of course not. Of course Nikolai would show up now. He always seemed to know when there was trouble.

Bruce dropped back behind Selene. *At least I won't have to see that fucking smirk on his face. Danny, please be okay, don't be banging your head on the wall again. I'm on my way, I'm coming.*

Her heart slammed once against the cage of her ribs and her fingers curled into fists. Fire flamed in her cheeks, spread down her neck, and merged with the growing heat of the medallion between her breasts. She fought for control, ribs flaring as she struggled against hyperventilation.

Hands in his coat pockets, chin tilted toward her, Nikolai's dark eyes catalogued her tangled blonde hair, camel coat, scuffed boots. Her fingers itched to straighten her clothes, brush back her hair, check for loose threads. As usual, he was so contained she longed to see him roughed up a little.

I suppose you learn a little self-control when you're a Master powerful enough to rule Saint City. He's the Prime, after all. We all live our little lives in his long dark shadow.

A few strands of crow-black hair fell over his eyes as Selene, impelled by the medallion's growing heat and the pull of Nikolai's eyes, skidded to a stop inches from him. Her ponytail swung heavily, but he didn't reach out to grab her arm and "protect" her from falling headlong on the steps. Her heart actually *leapt*, to see him again.

Stop that. He's not human, you know that, stop STARING at him!

Nikolai said nothing, the light stroking his high cheekbones. His mouth, usually curled into a half-smile, was compressed into a thin line. His dark, electric eyes flicked over Bruce, who cringed another three steps back.

Selene suppressed a burst of nasty satisfaction. *Serves you right.* She started up the stairs, pressing her left hand against the sudden stitch gripping her side. Her toe caught on the second step.

She fetched up short when Nikolai closed his hand around her left arm, steadied her before she could fall over, and let her go, all in the space of

a moment. "Selene." The chill rain-soaked air shivered under the word, his voice soft and irresistible. At least he didn't have the scary gold-green sheen on his eyes tonight, Selene hated that. "Stirling."

"I was on watch." Bruce didn't sound half so smug now. Of course, he was an accident, Turned as a joke or mistake; Nichtvren didn't Turn ugly humans. It was an unwritten rule: only the pretty or the ruthless were given the gift of immortality, and Bruce was neither. Why Nikolai kept him around was anyone's guess, and Selene didn't want to ask. Bruce's doglike attachment and gratefulness for any crumb Nikolai threw his way was telling enough.

Besides, if she asked she had a sneaking suspicion Bruce might answer, and she wouldn't like the answer at all. Not to mention what she might have to pay for it.

Selene brushed past Nikolai. Her boots smacked against the cold, wet concrete of the steps. She reached the glassed-in front door and stopped short, digging in her coat pocket for her keys. *So Nikolai's having me watched.* She filed the information away.

Her fingers rooted fruitlessly around in her pocket and found nothing but an empty gum wrapper. "Oh, no." Her keys were on the table by the door at her apartment, she had *not* scooped them up on her way out. Just run right past them in her frantic dash. "Bloody *fucking* hell on a cheese-coated *stick*."

"You need to go in?" Nikolai's breath brushed her cheek, the faint smell of aftershave and male closing around her. He was *right* behind her, so far into her personal space it wasn't even funny.

A violent start nearly toppled her into the firmly-shut door. She hadn't heard or *sensed* him behind her, he just appeared out of thin air. *Dammit, does he have to do that all the time?* The only place she could go to escape him was through the glass. She stared at the door, taking in deep harsh breaths and willing it to open. There was a quick, light patter of footsteps—Bruce, making off into the night. "I left my keys at

home. Danny called. I think it's a panic attack, and when he gets them he sometimes hurts himself. There's an intercom—"

Nikolai reached around her, his body molded to hers, and touched the lock. The gold and carnelian signet ring gleamed wetly in the uncertain light as his pale fingers brushed the metal. He went absolutely still. The medallion's metal cooled abruptly between Selene's breasts, responding to the controlled flare of energy Nikolai was using. She could almost see what he was doing, despite the stealthy camouflage of a Master Nichtvren's aura. The only thing scarier than their power was their creepy invisibility.

I really wish he'd quit crowding me. Her worry returned, sharp and acrid. Her lungs burned, the stitch knotting her left side again. *Please, Danny. Please be okay. I don't even care anymore if it's one of your midnight games, I hope you're all right.*

The lock clicked open with a muffled *thunk* and Selene grabbed the handle before it could close again. Nikolai's hand brushed hers, slid over the handle, he stepped aside and pulled the door open. She yanked her hand away, her skin burning from the brief touch. *He didn't have to touch me. He did that on purpose.*

"Thanks," she managed around the dry lump in her throat. *Stop it,* she thought desperately, biting the inside of her cheek. The pain helped her focus. *It's only Nikolai. You know what he is, and why he's doing this. You're here for Danny, remember?*

"My pleasure." His eyes dropped down to the medallion safely hidden under her sweater. The metal flushed with icy heat now.

He's looking at my chest like he sees dinner there. Heat sizzled along Selene's nerves. "Oh, stop that." She stepped through the door, sliding past him, suddenly grateful for someone else's presence. Her heart hammered thinly, the taste of burning in her mouth. *Danny. Just remember to breathe, kiddo. Little sister's almost there to take care of you.* "I suppose you want to come up."

"Of course." His voice stroked her cheek, slid down her neck. He leaned back against the open door, his dark eyes now fixed on her face. Selene gulped down another breath, her heartbeat evening out. The familiar bank of mailbox doors was on her right, and the peeling linoleum floor glared back at the dirty ceiling. "It is pleasant to see you, Selene."

Nikolai cat-stepped into the foyer, gracefully avoiding the closing door. Little droplets of rain glittered in his hair, sparked by the fluorescent lights. Under his coat, he wore a dark-blue silk T-shirt and a pair of designer jeans. The shirt moved slightly as muscle flickered in his chest.

Selene dropped her eyes, turned away from him. Oddly enough, he wore a high-end pair of black Nikes. *Vampire fashion just ain't what it used to be.* Selene had to stifle another mad giggle. *Where's the fangs and the black cape, not to mention the evening wear?* Her heart sped up, thundered in her ears. *God love me, I'm going to have a fucking cardiac arrest right here in the foyer.*

"Well, come on, then." She started up the orange-carpeted stairs, sidling away from him. Nikolai followed closely behind, but not too close, letting Selene take the lead. For once.

Given how he's always going on about how I need "protecting", it's a wonder he's letting me in the building at all. But dammit, if he showed up at the door he'd just scare Danny more. He's being tactful for once. Lucky me.

Her legs trembled and she rubbed at her eyes as she trooped up the stairs. Nikolai made no sound. "Would you make a little noise?" She immediately regretted asking. The silence behind her intensified. "Danny sometimes has panic attacks so he calls me. I just hope he's okay. He hasn't left the apartment for years." *Shut up, Selene, Nikolai knows. Danny'll be okay, it's probably nothing. He just stayed out of his body for too long and had trouble when he came back, another panic attack and the numbness. He's okay. Be okay, Danny, please?*

Nikolai's footsteps echoed hers as he climbed behind her. That was a relief, but Selene still felt the weight of his black eyes as they reached the fourth floor. Her thighs and ass burned. Climbing stairs after almost-running ten blocks without rest was a workout she could do without.

Nikolai's arm came over her shoulder again and held the heavy fire door open. The hall was dingy, most of the light fixtures missing bulbs, and a drift of fast food wrappers curled up from the far end. Selene's nose dripped from the chill. She rubbed at it with the back of her hand, tried not to sniff too loudly. Threadbare orange carpet whispered under her boots. The entire hall was so familiar she barely paid any attention. Down the hall a wedge of light speared through the gloom.

Danny's door was open.

TWO

Long jagged splinters popped out from the frame, the door splintered and loosely hanging from its hinges. Lighter, unpainted wood peered through ragged vertical cracks. *Oh, Jesus. Oh no.*

"*Danny!*" Selene leapt forward just as Nikolai's hand closed around her arm and pulled her back, jerking her arm almost out of its socket. "Let *go* of me!"

"No," he said, quietly. "Let me."

"He's *my* brother." She struggled frantically, achieved exactly nothing.

Nikolai's fingers tightened, digging into her softer, human flesh. He pushed her back against the wall. "Stay here." He looked down at her, his lips a thin line and his dark eyes fathomless. No cat-shine in them now, either. *He must be worried.*

Selene's lungs labored to catch even a small breath. Her back and arms prickled. "Nikolai—" she began, but he laid a finger on her lips. The contact was electric. Her entire body went liquid, a moan starting in her

chest. Selene strangled it before it reached her lips, making a thin dry sound instead. *Stop it, stop it, no time for this, stop it, God, what kind of a talent did you give me if it makes me feel like this? Goddammit, please, help me.*

Nikolai's skin was fever-warm. He must have fed, he was metabolizing whatever he'd taken that night—blood, or death, or pain, or sex. Was it wrong to be grateful it hadn't been her? Though God knew she'd done her share of feeding him. Being *fed* by him.

Danny. Selene tried to slip along the wall away from Nikolai, but he pinned her in place without even trying. He was being gentle, he could have broken her arm or put her *through* the wall if he'd wanted to. With hardly any effort.

He wasn't human, after all.

"Move again and I will force your compliance." Nikolai leaned closer, his lips a breath away from Selene's, inhaling. Tasting her breath.

Well, the dead do breathe, when they want to, she thought in a lunatic singsong. *Just like the first night I met him.* She hastily shoved the thought away, freezing in place. It was a mark of *possession*, smelling her breath like that; a Nichtvren didn't get that close unless he or she intended to feed or mark you. If she struggled, his predatory instinct might come into play and he might well decide to sink his fangs in her throat right here.

So instead of looking at him, she stared over his shoulder. There was a spot of discolored, peeling paint on the opposite wall. Selene looked intently at it, her eyes hot and dry. She felt his eyes on her, waiting for her to speak, argue, something, Selene bit the inside of her cheek. *I'm not going to give you the fucking satisfaction. Something hacked his door down, oh God, oh God. Oh, Danny.*

The weight of Nikolai's gaze slowly lessened when she didn't struggle. It took everything Selene had not to move, to stay still and passive. *I will not give you the excuse. Danny, please be okay. Come on, Nikolai,*

you're so blasted interested in both of us, help *him!* "Danny." The whisper escaped despite her. Nikolai took another long breath, leaning close, inhaling her scent deeply. Her knees went weak.

"Stay here." He disappeared. Selene felt the shimmer of Power in the close still air of the hallway. To a human it would feel like a chill walking up the spine, a tightness under the lungs, if they were sensitive. Someone without psychic sensitivity might feel a momentary breeze, a cold draft, a sudden flash of fear that would quickly be disregarded.

The shimmer slipped through the space between the door and the shattered frame. *God, please,* she prayed. *Please, God. Please.*

Always begging. They called witches like her—*tantraiiken*—the "beggers." Always moaning and pleading. It was hard not to, when you had a talent that made your body betray you over and over again.

Stop it. Think about something useful. Why was Nikolai here? Or Bruce? Bruce's hunting ground wasn't around Selene's apartment building, at least, it hadn't been three weeks ago, when he'd turned up . . . well, Turned.

Nikolai must have set Bruce to watch her. Why *now* when she'd known Nikolai for all this time?

Known might be too strong a word. You can't know a Nichtvren. They're not human, no matter how charming they can occasionally be. You're food to them. That's all.

Selene's back prickled, her breath coming in shallow adrenaline-laden sips. *Danny, be okay. God, please, let him just be panicked. Let him just be upset but okay. Or even just a little hurt. Let him be alive.*

Caught between fear and excitement, Selene let out a slow sharp gasp. Her knees shook slightly, the outer edges of her shields thickening reflexively. The jeans she'd thrown on were damp at the ankles from the rain, and would be damp between her legs soon.

Oh, God. It was her cursed talent. A sexwitch didn't feel fear the way other people did. No, being afraid just turned into a different sensation

entirely. One below the belt, thick and warm enough to make her heartbeat pound in her ears, a trickle of heat beginning way down low.

The agonized dread spiraled, kick-started a wave of desire that tipped her head back against the wall, forced her breath into another jagged half-gasp. Any more of this and she'd be a quivering ball of need and nerves by the time Nikolai reappeared.

Goddammit, Selene, focus! She shook out her trembling hands; if she had to throw Power she would need her fingers. Her heartbeat thundered in her ears. She repeated the mantra, as if it would help. *Please, God. Please let my brother be safe.*

Begging, again. Loathing crawled up her spine, mixed with the desire, and turned her stomach into a sudsing, bubbling washing machine.

The shimmer returned. Nikolai solidified right in front of her, a faint breeze blowing stray strands of hair back, her forehead cold as the moisture evaporated. Wisps of hair stirred at her nape. Her ponytail was loose.

He looked absolutely solid, *real.* Did his victims ever see him coming? It was like swimming with a shark and suddenly wondering if you'd cut yourself shaving that morning.

Selene met his eyes, tipping her head back. Nothing. She blinked, and then looked at the shattered door again.

Nikolai caught her shoulders, pushed her back against the wall. "We will call the police."

Her body, traitor that it was, understood before she did. Her heart plummeted into her belly with a splash, and the stew of desire and horror faded under a wave of stark chemical adrenaline. "What's this *we*? What's wrong with Danny? What's *happened*?"

He smiled, and Selene backed up—or tried to, her shoulders hit the wall again. There were few things worse than Nikolai's lazy, genuinely good-humored grin. Especially his eyeteeth—*fangs,* she corrected herself, *the word is fangs, let's call it what it is, you're old enough to call*

things what they are. She could all too well imagine what those teeth could do to her jugular.

It's not his teeth, though. It's the rest of him I have trouble with.

"You will disturb the evidence. We can't have that, can we? The police prefer to observe the formalities." Nikolai was calm, too calm, and that grin . . .

Danny, she thought, but it was merely a despairing moan.

Nikolai continued, softly and pitilessly. "We will go downstairs and call the police. *Verscht za?*"

She slid away toward the door, blindly. Nikolai pinned her to the wall, his body curving into hers. Heat slammed through her; she tasted copper adrenaline. Selene drew in a sharp breath and kicked, missing him somehow. He smiled, caught her wrists. He could hold her all night and struggling would only excite him—and her. *Stop it.* Then she said it out loud. "Stop it." Her voice broke, helplessly.

"You are being unwise." His tone was a mere murmur, so reasonable. "Do as I say, Selene. Help me."

Help you? Help *you?* "You bastard." The steel vise of his fingers strangled her wrists. A twisting wire of pain lanced up both arms. Jerking backward, she smacked her head against the wall, brief starry pain twinkling in front of her eyes. "Tell me what happened."

"Your brother is dead, Selene. Now we must call the police. Will you come with me or shall I drag you?" Nikolai smiled, his eyes twinkling. "I would enjoy carrying you. Particularly if you struggle."

"Let go of me. I'll go downstairs and call the police." *Like a good little girl.* Her teeth clenched together, her jaw aching. She'd have a goose-egg on the back of her head for sure. *Danny . . .*

"Very good," he breathed, and released her, finger by finger. Selene stared up into the lightless pools of his eyes. A kind of stunned calm slipped down over her body. Nikolai's eyes were so *dark.* So endlessly dark.

When he spoke next, it was in something approximating a normal voice. "I am sorry, Selene. I will help you, however I can."

Christ, does he have to sound like he means it? Any help from you is help I can do without, Nikolai. "Leave me alone." Her lips were too numb to work properly. "If you won't let me see, just leave me alone."

"You do not want to see. It is . . . disturbing. Now come."

* * *

The metal box of the pay phone gleamed dully under the fluorescents. A phone book, four years out of date and scarred with permanent marker, dangled from a rust-pitted chain. Someone had tagged the plastic hood at the top of the box—an out-of-date gang sign, a phone number, a caricature of a donkey, other symbols much less pleasant. Selene picked up the receiver in nerveless fingers, staring at the graffiti-covered plastic.

"I suspect you will want to call your police friend first." Nikolai produced two quarters with a flick of his fingers, dropped them in. Selene's eyes burned dryly, the numbers on the square silver buttons blurring. Nikolai even dialed the number, his signet ring flashing dully, blood on gold. Somewhere in the numbness a thought surfaced. *How does Nikolai know Jack's number?*

The phone rang four times. "Urmph."

Selene couldn't get the words past the dust in her throat. Nikolai bumped against her, sending a rush of fire through her veins, kick-starting her brain. "Maureen?" she whispered, her voice coming from a deep screaming well of panic. "It's Selene Thompson. I need to talk to Jack. Now."

"What the . . ." Maureen's tone changed suddenly. Mother to the world, that was Maureen. She'd cooked Selene dinner more than once, during the cases Jack needed paranormal help on. "Sweetheart, are you okay? Jack, wake up."

Selene's knees nearly buckled, a moan bubbling up. The vision of the hacked and shattered door rose up in front of her. *Dear God what happened to his door . . . Danny . . .*

Nikolai's fingers slid under her ponytail, fever-hot. Fire spread from her nape, a deluge of sensation pooling in her belly. She hated the feeling, hated *him*, but the Power would help her. She was going into shock. Years of training kicked in, turning the desire into Power, shocking her back in control, her mind adding, subtracting, calculating. *What happened? He hasn't left here in five years. What went wrong?*

Danny was a Journeyman, an adept at etheric and astral travel. He didn't need to leave his apartment, and anyway couldn't bear to be away from the safety of the wards and defenses Selene erected around his three-room world. Nothing touched him inside his magickal cocoon, no thoughts or emotions that might compromise his body when he projected. Time had strengthened Danny's gifts, making him more sensitive to random buffetings, but also more sensitive to Selene's defenses and powers. He couldn't be with her all the time, so an apartment of his own with heavy shielding was the best—

She stiffened. *The wards!* They were a part of Danny now; he had taken over maintaining them since Selene had other problems. But they were originally *her* wards and would answer her call.

And they would have recorded what went on inside Danny's walls.

"Jack here." Detective Jack Pepper's cigarette-rough voice came over the line. "What the *hell*?"

Her voice almost refused to work. "It's Selene. Something's killed Danny. Jack, Nikolai's here." *I sound like I'm twelve years old again. And scared. I sound so scared.*

Selene heard Jack breathing. "Jesus, why is he there? Forget it; I don't want to know. Hang up and call 911. You got it?" The sound of cloth against cloth filtered through the phone. Jack was sitting up. Maureen's whispered questions, then . . . silence.

"I . . . He c-c-called me. Said he was c-c-cold and something about danger." Autopilot pushed the words out, she listened to her own ragged gasping breath. *Danny, oh God. Danny. Jesus Christ . . .*

"Selene, put Nikolai on the phone, honey. Now." Jack was fully awake. A click and a flare of a lighter, deep indrawn breath. *It must be bad if he's smoking in bed, Maureen won't like that.*

She handed the phone to Nikolai. He slid closer, pressing her into the phone booth, his fingers kneading heat into her neck.

I wonder what a gun would do to him? The thought surfaced, she pushed it hastily away. She wasn't sure if he could hear it; Nichtvren were psychic as well as physical predators. If he heard her, what would he do?

"Yes?" Nikolai paused. "Bad enough . . . No, not human . . . I did not. Nor did she. The door is shattered. She will of course not enter the apartment." Selene strained to listen. "Of course. I will stay out of sight. I would not want to cause trouble for my Selene."

Her neck muscles burned. *"My Selene"? Oh, boy. We're going to have to have a talk about that, suckhead.*

Selene's mind skittered sideways. *Danny. The door. What happened?* Nikolai brushed his thumb over her nape. Lightning shot down her spine and burst in the pit of her stomach. *Oh, God.*

"I will." Nikolai reached over her shoulder again, hung up. His hands slipped down over her shoulders. He gently turned her to face him, Selene didn't resist. Her head was full of a rushing, roaring noise, his voice came from very far away. "You must call the emergency services, Selene. You received a call from your brother. It was interrupted and you came to see if he was well. You noticed the door had been forced and decided to call 911. Do you understand?"

She stared up at him, his face suddenly oddly foreign. He looked more like a stranger than ever. Selene took a deep shuddering breath, fury crystallizing under the surface of her mind. "Why are you doing this, Nikolai? One dead human, more or less."

His fingers tightened. "One dead human under *my* protection, dear one. Whatever killed him is very dangerous. Now you will call the emergency services and you will be a very good girl for me." He touched his lips to her forehead, a gentle kiss that made her body burn, fire spilling through her veins. *How can I even think about that when Danny's upstairs?*

Hot acid guilt rose in the back of her throat. *I should have gone in there, I should have seen.*

Her eyes filled with tears. "I hate you," she whispered, looking up into Nikolai's dark eyes. "I *hate* you."

"Call them." The corner of his mouth quirked up, as if he found her amusing.

She turned back to the phone and blindly picked up the receiver. Punched the nine, the one, the one. A deep breath. Nikolai moved away suddenly, and she swayed, grabbing the metal edge of the booth to steady herself. One ring. Two. Three. Four. Five.

"911, what are you reporting?" A passionless, professional voice, possibly female.

For one awful moment Selene couldn't remember who she was or what she was doing. The metal bit into her fingers. Blood pounded in her ears and the hallway swirled beneath her. "My-my brother. He c-c-called me. I c-c-came to his apartment and the d-d-door is b-b-roken and I'm afraid t-t-to go inside."

How strange, she thought from inside the glass ball of hysterical calm descending upon her. *I sound like I'm scared to death.* It was her voice giving information, stammering out the story to the operator. Danny never left his apartment. The door was broken. She was afraid. Tiny diamond mice fleeing the huge black wolf running around in her brain made her voice jittery, made her hands tremble.

She glanced over her shoulder. The empty foyer glared under the fluorescents. There was no sign of Bruce or of Nikolai, though the

medallion throbbed a heated beat between her breasts. A heartbeat. His heartbeat?

The urge to tear it off and throw it away made her shake. *Danny. Oh, Danny, please. Please, God.*

She slumped, trembling, against the phone box. Her nails drove into her palm. The terrified mice spun round and round inside her brain.

"Miss, please try to be calm. We have dispatched a unit to your location."

Try to be calm? Danny. Oh, God. How can I be calm if you're dead?

THREE

The fourth time the operator told her to be calm, Selene jammed the phone back down. She looked across the mailboxes to the stairs, and the medallion tingled harshly against her skin. A warning. Her throat was full of something hard and slick, she swallowed several times, resting her forehead against cool cheap metal.

Don't go back, the operator had said. *Stay outside the building. Stay and wait for the police. It's safest to wait for the police, ma'am.*

Selene's hoarse inarticulate moan bounced off the stairwell walls. The stairs squeaked under her slow feet. Her legs burned numbly.

She only got halfway up to the first floor before Nikolai's hand closed over her elbow. She gave a startled, wounded little cry and found herself facing him, looking at his chest. He was somehow on the step above her, and his mouth moved, fangs flashing in something less than a good-natured grin. It was more like a smirk, or a warning.

"No," he said. Selene stared at him, and he gave her a little shake. Her head wobbled, the entire stairwell reeling. "Outside. This is not for you."

"He's my—" Her mouth was so dry the words were a croak.

"Your brother. Yes." He used his grip on her arm to pull her down the stairs. Selene went limp, resisting him, but he slid his arm around her

shoulders and simply dragged her as if she weighed nothing. Her boots dropped from stair to stair as if they weren't attached to the rest of her. "You cannot help him now. And I would not have you see this, *milaya*."

"I hate you." The fluorescents seared her wet eyes. "I wish I'd never met you."

He gave a gracious nod, as if she'd complimented him. "Thank you." They reached the bottom of the stairs. He half-carried her across the peeling linoleum. He shouldered the door to the building open, dragged her out and let the door go. The lock engaged.

Selene looked up at him. He set her down on the cold, wet sidewalk and brushed her hair back, settled her camel coat on her shoulders, stroked her sore damp forehead, she'd be lucky to escape a bruise from cracking her head against the wall.

His fingers were still warm. Too warm to be human, feverish, but oddly soothing.

She hated that comfort.

Distant sirens cracked the still air. *Breathe,* she repeated. *In through the nose, out through the mouth. Breathe.*

The mantra didn't help. "I mean it. I hate you." Her voice shook. "I *hate* you."

"And yet you need me." He smiled, an almost-tender expression that made her entire body go cold. Selene would have fallen over backward, but his fingers closed around her wrist, a loose bracelet. Sirens hammered at the roof of the night. "Selene, you do not wish to see what lies in that room. Remember your brother the way he was."

"I don't *need* you." Selene tore her wrist away. His fingers tightened slightly, just to let her know he could hold her, before he let her go and she stumbled. There was something hard and small and spiny in her hand, cold metal.

A police cruiser materialized around the corner, whooping and braying. She opened her hand to find her key ring. *He must have had Bruce*

*sneak into my house and get my keys. The little thief. Always creeping
around, peeping in windows and doing Nikolai's bidding. No wonder
His Highness keeps him around.*

She looked up. Except for the police car—siren, flashing lights—the
street was deserted. Nikolai had vanished. She saw the blurring in the air,
the shimmer that might have been him or just the tears filling her eyes.
She fumbled on the ring for the key to the front of Danny's building.

Numb, her cheeks wet with rain and tears, she raised her hand to flag
the cops down. Thankfully, they cut the siren as soon as they pulled to
a stop. Selene waved, her bag bumping at her hip. *No poltergeist here,
no curse to be broken, no client looking down their nose at me. No, this
time the person needing help is me.*

Two cops, a rookie and a graying veteran who looked at her as if he
recognized her. Selene hoped he didn't. If he recognized her, he might ask
questions. *Hey, aren't you that freak who hangs around with Jack Pepper?*

"My brother." Her teeth chattered. "He's a shut-in. He doesn't leave
the apartment. He called me—his doorjamb's all busted up—it's not
normal—"

They barked questions at her, who was her brother, what apartment,
who was she, was anyone armed, what did she see? The mice scurrying
in Selene's head supplied answers. "4C, apartment 4C, Danny Thompson,
I'm Selene, I'm his sister—no, nothing, just the door, that's all I saw, it's
busted all to hell—"

Before she unlocked the building door for them, the medallion
scorched against her skin. Warning her.

Fuck you, Nikolai.

She followed the cops up the stairs, sliding the medallion's chain up
over her head. She pulled it out of her sweater. Light flared sharply from
the silver disc before she tossed it into a dark corner of the second-floor
landing. The cops didn't notice—they were too busy looking up the
stairs and speaking back and forth in cryptic cop-talk. Both had their

guns out. "Fourth floor. Apartment 4C," she repeated, and took a deep breath, choking on tears.

"Go back downstairs," the older cop told her. "Go back downstairs!"

Fourth floor. They saw the shattered door, the wedge of light slicing through the dim hall. The older cop radioed for backup.

They edged forward and cautiously pushed the splintered door open. Told her again to go downstairs. Selene told them she would and stood where she was, hot tears spilling down her cheeks.

Now that she wasn't standing next to Nikolai, the wards vibrated with Selene's nearness, lines of light bleeding out from the hole torn where the door used to be. Something had blasted right through the careful layers of defense she'd painstakingly applied to the walls. What could do that?

She took two steps, and the rookie backed up out of the apartment. He was paper-white and trembling, freckles standing out on his fair face, his blond mustache quivering.

After glancing past him once, Selene could see why.

She clamped her right hand over her mouth, staring past the rookie, who stumbled to the side and vomited onto the hall rug. Selene didn't blame him. She could only see a short distance down the entry hall and into the studio room. The kitchen was to the left, bathroom to the right, and she had a clear view almost to the night-dark window, with the orange streetlamps glowing outside.

A moment later her eyes tracked a shimmer up over the streetlamp, a shimmer that resolved into a dark shape balancing atop the streetlamp's arm. A tall shape, crouched down, hands wrapped around the bar, eyes reflecting the light with the green-gold sheen of a cat's eyes at night.

I wish he wouldn't do that, perch up there like some kind of vulture.

Selene looked down again, and her hand tightened over her mouth. Her throat burned with bile. The shapes she was seeing refused to snap into a coherent picture. Blood painted the white-painted walls, soaked into the thin beige carpeting, and the . . . the *pieces* . . .

Footsteps echoed in the hall, shouts, radios squawking. Four more cops. Selene stepped back against the wall, her hand still clamped over her mouth, fingernails digging into her cheek. She struggled to swallow the hot acid bile instead of puking like the rookie.

Detective Jack Pepper, his graying buzz-cut and familiar rumpled gray wool coat steaming in the hall's heat, came striding from the other end. She stumbled back, hitting her head against the wall. Jack gave her a look that could have peeled paint. "Aw, Christ. Get her downstairs," he said as one of the cops took a look past Selene and into the apartment, swearing viciously.

Selene couldn't help herself. She began to giggle into her hand, her eyes streaming. The shrill sound echoed under the crackle of radio talk and more sirens outside.

After wiping his mouth, the blond rookie was finally delegated to take her downstairs. Selene had to steady him, her fingers against the creaking leather of his jacket. The queasy flickers of fear coming off the young man were enough to make her flush, her stomach tightening. Her mental shields were as transparent and brittle as crystal, he was hyped enough to broadcast all over the mental spectrum.

Lawrence, his name is Lawrence. He's an open door right now, and I don't have enough control to shut him out. Knowledge burned through her, the fear turning into a wash of heat that made her nipples peak and her entire body tighten. Her jeans were definitely damp between her legs.

I wish I'd stopped to put my panties on. The sanity of that thought saved her, slapped her back into herself. *Focus, Selene. In through the nose, out through the mouth. Breathe.*

She filled her lungs and tapped in, the rush of Power sparking along her nerves. *I hope he puts me in a car, I can use this and yank the wards off the apartment. A killing like that leaves a mark on the air, the wards will be vibrating with it. I'll be able to track whoever did this to him.* Selene made a slight crooning noise, patted the rookie's shoulder when

they reached the foyer. He was looking a little green again, his cheeks pooching out and his lips wet. Selene smelled fear, the sharp tang of human vomit, and her own smell, rich floral musk. *Tantraiiken* musk, the smell of a sexwitch.

Put me in a police car. She patted the rookie's back as he heaved near the stairs. A loose ring of cop cars sat in the wet street. More sirens cut the distant darkness. *I don't want to work magick right here on the street. God alone knows what sort of notice it will attract if I pass out, too.*

"It's okay, Lawrence." She looked up in time to see another cop come flying out of the door—some thoughtful soul had braced it open with a chunk of pavement. This man—tall, stocky, brown hair combed over a bald head Selene could see because he'd lost his hat—made it to the bottom of the stairs before he puked, too, vomit spraying out onto the street.

Selene's gorge rose. She swallowed against it. "Nice boy," she said softly, stroking Lawrence's back. "It's okay. You okay?" *Quit retching and put me somewhere quiet where I can Work, you waste.* The coldness of the thought almost surprised her. He was just the type of ordinary civilian to come running to Selene for her help in dealing with something extraordinary—and then decide she was less than a used Kleenex when everything was said and done.

They were all alike, every one of them. Except Danny, and Danny was gone. Selene's jaw clenched, her teeth grinding together.

Come on. Quit puking so I can work.

* * *

He did put her in a police car, mumbling something about her safety and a report, and she closed her eyes, settling back into the cracked vinyl seat. *Finally. What did you eat for dinner, anyway, it certainly stank . . . oh, God, what am I going to do now? Danny.*

255

Tears pricked behind Selene's eyes. *Quit it! Focus!* She pictured the hallway leading into Danny's living space, the foldout bed and salvaged wooden shelves of books and curios and the bloody pieces of—

Her concentration guttered, came back; her ability to visualize under stress had plenty of practice. *Don't fail me now,* she thought, and dropped through the floor of her own consciousness, into the place where she truly lived. Her breathing stilled, her heartbeat paused. An onlooker would have thought she was sleeping, or just sitting with her eyes closed, head tilted back, mouth slackly open. In shock.

She dove into a black blood-warm sea, her concentration narrowing to a single point. Pulled on the threads of the Power she'd spent warding Danny's apartment. The defenses recognized her, left the place in the world where they had been bleeding free, and leapt for her.

Selene 'caught' the energy, folded it deftly. The resultant mass shrank, a small bright star to her mental vision, taking on more mass as she compressed it. Selene's body arched upward, gasping for air. The energy she'd taken from the hyped-up rookie drained away. Her skin was prickling and her lips wet, her hips rocking forward slightly, tensing, tighter, tighter, aching for release.

She couldn't afford to let it spend. She had to find something physical to hold the Power until she could take a closer look. Her fingers dipped into her black canvas shoulder-bag and found smooth wood.

My athame. Christ. Here I am in the back of a police car with an illegal-to-carry eight-inch ritual knife. Why did I have to be born a tantraiiken?

Training brought her focus back and the star of Power drained into the knife, leaving her sick and shaking, her entire body aching for completion. The pain was low between her legs, and it would torture her all night unless she found some way to bleed off the pressure.

The whole event had taken less than five minutes. The rookie was gesturing to an ambulance crew. Lurid light from the cop cars and stuttering flashes from the ambulance painted the street in gaudy

flickers. The entire street was now swarming with cops and emergency personnel. Selene slumped down against the cracked vinyl and peered out the window, her senses dilated, looking for a dark blot or a breath of anything that didn't belong. Nothing. Not even a shimmer in the air.

Was Nikolai gone? She couldn't be that lucky.

Danny. The numbness was still there. Whatever was locked inside her athame would give her a direction, somewhere to go . . . hopefully. At the very least, she would see how her brother died.

The *how* might tell her *who*, and once she knew she could start planning. There weren't many things she could take on as a *tantraiiken*, she was worse than useless in a fight since pain and fear turned to desire and swallowed her whole.

But she could give it a try, couldn't she? Nikolai wouldn't help, he would be too interested in getting leverage on her. One more dead human wouldn't matter, even if it was the brother of his semi-pet sexwitch.

I hate you, Nikolai. The hate was a bright red slash across the middle of her mind. She closed her eyes, set her jaw. Her fingers itched to unzip her jeans, slide down, touch the slick heat between her legs. *Hate you. Hate you.* She felt her face contort into a screaming mask, tears spilling down her cheeks.

The door creaked open, letting in a burst of chill rainy air. "Hi, princess," Jack said. "Get your ass out. We got a hot date with some paperwork."

Selene blinked, her fists curled at her sides. She let out the breath she'd been holding. Her cheeks hurt, so did her lower belly; her eyes were hot and dry.

Jack didn't mean to be cruel, he was just used to treating her like one of the boys. If she had been waiting to join another investigation, he would have acted the same way. Selene would have had an equally brisk response for him. She searched for something sharp and hard as a shield to say.

Instead, her throat swelled with grief. "Danny?" she whispered. It was stupid, she knew it, Nikolai would not have lied and her own eyes had told her the truth. But still, she had hoped. Hope, that great human drug.

Jack's face turned milk-pale. He was thin and stooped, except for his potbelly straining at his dingy white shirt. His lean hound-dog face under its gray buzzcut was almost always mournful, now it was actively sad. "Lena . . . Jesus, I'm sorry. Nikolai was supposed to keep you from seeing . . . any of that."

I have a right to see what happened to my brother, Jack. Selene slid her legs out of the car. She had to catch her breath as the material of her jeans rasped against swollen tissues. She *needed*, and there was no way to fill that need tonight.

"Nikolai can go to hell," she rasped around the obstruction in her throat. That helped—it sounded like the old Selene, the tough Selene. "I'm sure it's where he's bound sooner or later."

She twisted her hands together. Her palms slid against each other, damp with sweat. The image of Danny's apartment, framed by a shattered blood-painted doorway, rose up again. Numb disbelief rose with it.

Her jeans were uncomfortably wet, and she was starting to sweat under her arms. Her neck prickled, and she was suddenly aware of empty hunger. She was starving.

How can I think of food at a time like this? Jesus.

"I'll do your report up for you. Come by, sign it in the morning. Look, Selene—" He offered her his hand and she took it, nervous sweat slicking her palm. He pulled her to her feet. The car's windows were frosted with vapor. *How long was I in there?*

He also firmly took his hand away from her, tearing her fingers free.

Selene would have kept his hand, run her thumb along the crease on the inside of his wrist, wet her lips with her tongue. Her eyes met his. She *needed*, and he was male. Women were also good for what she needed, but there weren't any around.

God. Look at me. Look at what I almost did. I'm a whore, and my brother is dead.

"I'm sorry," Jack continued awkwardly. He was starting to sweat now, too, looking down until he realized he was looking at her chest, then staring up over her shoulder at the circus of lights and people in uniforms milling around. "Christ, I'm sorry. Lena . . . I'm so sorry."

Selene crossed her arms, cupped her elbows in her hands. Jack took her upper arm, kicked the cruiser's door shut, and steered her away from the hive of activity the street had become. People were starting to peek through their windows, lights were coming on. The cops were too busy to pay much attention to one lone woman being led away by Detective Pepper—especially when some of them recognized her as his tame spook, the woman that had broken the Bowan case last month. Just how she did it nobody knew—but then again, nobody wanted to know. The girl was just too weird. And Pepper was starting to look a little weird himself. The joke was that he'd apply for the new Spook Squad soon, just as soon as he could get his head out of a bottle and quit working hopeless freezer-cold homicide cases.

Selene shivered, hugging herself, their easy dismissal of her roaring through the open wound she was becoming. *I've got to get home before I start to scream. I'm in bad shape.*

"You're pretty worn out," Jack said, diffidently. "Look, go home. I'm sorry, Lena. I'm glad you called me. I wish you wouldn't have gone up there." He stopped near a pool of convenient shadow, and Selene looked up.

Of course.

Nikolai was there. Part of the darkness itself, his long black coat melding with the gloom that filled an alley's entrance.

Jack faced her. Here, numb and shocked, with her shields thin and the aftermath of the Power she'd jacked and the magick she'd worked pounding in her pulse with insistent need, she drowned in what *he* was feeling.

Agonizing pain. Nausea. Sick aching in his chest, the heartburn that wouldn't go away—*she shouldn't have to see this, shouldn't have seen it.*

Jack sighed, his shoulders slumping. "It's bad, Selene. Something I ain't never seen before. And Nikolai says it's not human. Which means . . ." His brown eyes were almost black in the uncertain light. "Christ," he finished, when she just stared at him, her mouth slightly open. Her breath rasped in the chill rainwashed air. "Just go home. Come by the station tomorrow to sign your statement. I'm sorry."

Selene shrugged. "Great. Just go home, he says." She heard the funny breathless tone in her own voice. She was close to the edge, so close—did Jack think she was numb and grieving? Or did he guess that she wouldn't be able to grieve until the need pounding in her blood was blotted out?

Grieve, hell. There was something sharp as a broken bone in her chest. *I'm going to get whoever did this.*

Nikolai stepped forward. His eyes were depthless. "I will take her, Jack. Thank you."

Jack nodded. "Go with—"

"Like a good little girl, right?" Her voice sounded shrill even to herself, it bounced off the alley's walls and came back to her through a layer of cotton wool. "What I'm hearing is that you're not going to work too hard, because it's a P-fucking-C. Right?"

Jack's shoulders hunched as if she'd hit him. "Paranormal cases are technically not the jurisdiction of the Saint City police force, until the new laws go into effect. They're the jurisdiction of—"

"Of the reigning prime paranormal Power in the city." She stepped away from Jack and his hand fell down to his side, releasing her. "Which means Nikolai. Which means I can kiss any hope of finding out who did this to my brother goodbye."

"Not necessarily." Nikolai's eyes never left her. He moved closer, not precisely crowding her, but stepping past Jack without so much as

glancing at the detective. "Cooperate with me, Selene, and I will see the killer brought to you, for your revenge. Will you take that bargain?"

Jack coughed, uncomfortably. "I've got to go. Sorry, Selene."

You son of a bitch. Both of you. "Are you really," she said, flatly, and turned on her heel. She put her head down, started to walk. At least she wasn't staggering. *Oh, God. Danny. What happened to you? Who did this to you?*

Nikolai murmured something behind her—no doubt talking to Jack, something along the lines of *women, irrational, what can you do, she'll see reason in the morning.*

It was too much. Rage and something like a sob made flesh drew tighter and tighter under her breastbone, and the tension snapped.

Selene ran.

FOUR

By the time she reached Cliff Street, she was stumbling. She'd fallen once, scraping her palms on pavement, and scrambled to her feet, looking up to see a shadow flitting over a rooftop above her. He didn't even have the decency to try and conceal himself.

Her hands jittered. Her keys jangled, her scraped palms singing in pain. Her heart threatened to burst out of her chest. Sweat rolled down her spine, soaked into the waistband of her jeans.

She checked the street behind her, deserted under the orange streetlamps. It took her three tries to unlock the door to her apartment building, her breath coming high and harsh and fast, expecting to feel a hand closing on her shoulder at any moment.

The run up her own stairs took on a nightmarish quality, moving too slowly while something chased her from behind. Those had been the worst dreams when she was little, running through syrup while the monster snarled behind, gaining on her.

Her own door. Her *own* door. She fumbled out her keys, tried to unlock it, made a short sound of agonized frustration when her fingers slipped.

Finally the key slid into the lock.

She twisted it, opened her door, yanked the key out, kicked the door shut with a resounding slam that shook the building. She threw the deadbolt, then turned around and hurled her keys down her dark hall.

Nikolai plucked the keyring out of the air, his signet ring glittering. One moment her pretty, spacious one-bedroom apartment was empty—the next moment, a slight breeze brushed Selene's cheek and she let out a strangled scream. The protections placed in the walls of her apartment and the whole building shuddered with a sound like a crystal wineglass ringing, stroked just right. *Don't worry, nobody will hear it, I'm the only Talent in the building. A merry little party, just Nikolai and me.*

And whatever he's going to do to me.

Selene whirled and started trying to unbolt the door. Her sweat-slick fingers slipped against cold metal. *Christ why can't he leave me ALONE?*

"Stop." He was suddenly *there*, laying the keys down on the small table by the front door. His fingers bit into her shoulder and he yanked her back, locked the second deadbolt with his other hand. The sound of the lock going home was the clang of a prison cell closing.

Selene heard her own harsh sobs, the low moaning sound of a strangled scream.

Nikolai slid the coat off her shoulders while he dragged her along. Tossed it over the back of the couch as he pulled her into the living room. Then he grabbed the canvas strap of her bag, wrapped it around his fist, and jerked it up over her head. Selene let out a short cry, cut off midway when he clamped his free hand over her mouth. He dropped the bag on the couch as well, and looked down at her.

Silence, except for the muffled sounds slipping past his fingers. Fire raced up her side, tearing through her ribs—the stitch in her side, getting

worse. Her calves were burning too. Her lower back ached, and her palms were scraped raw.

Worse than that was the miserable, hot, prickling need slamming through her. The low, relentless burn between her legs, spreading through her entire body. Now that she wasn't running, it returned. When would she start to beg?

He considered her, cocking his head to one side. A few soft strands of black hair fell over his forehead. "I told you not to look." There was no inflection to his voice, it was a passionless murmur. "But look you must. Are you happy? Are you *satisfied*?"

Selene's shoulders slumped. *I could bite him. What would he do if I bit him? Would he hold me down and . . .*

Nikolai let out a low pent breath. It was for effect—he didn't need to breathe, did he? He only did it when he *wanted* to.

He slid one hand around her waist, flattened it against the small of her back. His fingers scorched through her sweater. "I forgive you much." His hand exerted a little pressure, enough that she shifted back away from him, resisting. "I forgive you because you are young, and because you are unique, and because you amuse me." A ghost of a smile touched his lips. "Sometimes you even surprise me, which is rare. But sometimes, my Selene, I wonder if I forgive *too* much."

She tried to twist free, but he had her, one hand on the small of her back, the other over her mouth. Tears trickled down her cheeks. He pulled her close to him, closer, until she could feel something very definitely alive pressing against her belly, through his jeans and her sweater. *I could give a lecture on this,* she thought hysterically. *Vampire Anatomy: Dead or Alive? I never even knew a Nichtvren could get a hard-on—they didn't cover that in the textbooks.*

It was her effect on him—her effect on any man. Maybe it was pheromones, maybe it was only her cursed power making sure it could complete itself. Nikolai had known what she was the first time he smelled her.

Or so he said.

"Now," he said, leaning down just a little, whispering in her ear. "You disobeyed me. You tossed my last gift to you away like a piece of trash. You also acted as a complete fool, dropping your defenses and working the Art while you sat in the back of a police car. And I saw where you found the Power for that trick, my sweet." He was murmuring, and Selene shut her eyes. Her entire body shook now, straining against his, recognizing that here was something it *needed*. Something that could take the ache away. "I wonder how you're feeling."

He took a step, and let her move too, back toward the bedroom. Only the nightlight in the hall broke the darkness of her apartment, but that would present no difficulty to him. Not to a Nichtvren, who could see in complete dark.

"Well?" He moved, his legs bumping hers.

Selene's body betrayed her. Her hips jerked forward and her hands came up, sliding along his arms to find his shoulders and clenching, trying to pull him forward. Her lips parted, and she sobbed in a breath behind his hand. Two.

I hate myself. It was the only clear thought in the straining welter of sensation she'd become, her curse awake and alive under her skin. *I hate him and I hate myself.* She tasted salt, and kissed his palm, her lips softening, unable to help herself.

"I see," he continued, pitilessly. "The succubus needs her food."

That's not what I am! She wanted to scream, but his hand was still over her mouth.

"You are the only *tantraiiken* of adult age to walk the earth freely for five hundred years, and you do so because of my protection." He moved her back a step at a time, toward the bedroom. "If I were cruel, dear one, sweet Selene, I'd chain you in a stone cell and let you suffer. Let you burn for a little while, until you better appreciated me and the

liberty I allow you." Then he gave a bitter little laugh, and Selene went liquid against him, relieved. She knew that sound.

He would give her what she needed. He would make it *stop.*

Then she could do what she had to do. Find out who had done . . . *that* . . . to Danny.

"Please," she mouthed against his palm, before she could stop herself. "Nikolai."

I am such a whore. Loathing filled her mouth like spilled wine, added another complex layer to the straining need pounding in her blood.

"Hush." He pushed her through the bedroom door, kicked it shut. She flinched, shaking so hard she couldn't walk, and he pushed her down on the bed. She landed hard, her head flung back, her back arching. The covers were still thrown back from when she'd leapt out of bed.

Danny, the part of her that wasn't crazed with need sobbed. *Danny. Oh, my God. My brother is dead, and what am I doing? God help me.*

He stood there, watching her shake against the cotton sheets. Selene bit her lower lip. That was a mistake—the pain now fed the loop of sensation, fear and pain and lust driving in a circle that wrung shuddering little sounds from her.

Finally, he shed his coat, draping it over the chair set by the closet. Selene closed her eyes, twisting, her hips rising, falling back down. Her clothes were impossibly hot, confining, scraping against suddenly sensitive skin.

He knelt down, and worked her damp boots off, and her socks. Touched the inside of her ankle with a fingertip, under the damp cuff of her jeans. The touch sent a spark racing up her leg, through her entire body. "Selene." Why did he have to sound so *human,* so soft and reasonable? "I wanted to save you that sight."

"My *brother,*" she whispered, and then moaned as the bed accepted Nikolai's weight next to her. He propped himself up on one elbow and used the other hand to pop the button on her waistband. *I'm going to*

kill whoever did that to him. Just get this over with so I can go on. She drew in a sobbing breath, her hips lifting helplessly.

"I would rather have you remember him alive." Nikolai slowly unzipped her jeans. The sound of the zipper was loud in the dark stillness of her bedroom. Tears leaked out between Selene's eyelids, and her sweater was drenched with sweat.

Addicted to this, but I have no choice. I never have a choice. The need would get worse and worse, a *tantraiiken*'s curse burning through her bones, until she was little more than an animal. She'd gone that far sometimes, when she was young and thought she could rule her own body, at least.

Before she'd learned how to use the curse for her own benefit. And before she'd met *him*. Since she'd come to Nikolai's notice, she hadn't needed to feed her curse in alleys or cheap hotel rooms. Even if she *could* forget it, he reminded her often enough. She owed him.

Owed, and was owned by. There wasn't much of a difference where Nichtvren were concerned.

"Nikolai . . ." It was a long despairing moan. It wouldn't take long before she started to beg. She'd drained her batteries and worked herself into a frenzy.

He slid his hand into her jeans, settling the heel of his palm against her mound. His fingers slipped down, and made a slight beckoning motion. Selene arched, her breath hissing in. But then, torture of tortures, he stopped.

"Why disobey me?" His breath was warm against her cheek. "Why, Selene? You leave me no choice."

"Nikolai—" It was all she had left, the pleading. He would give her what she needed, and then she could think again, ponder, consider, plan. But how much would he make her suffer, first, and how much of the suffering would she enjoy because of her traitorous body?

He took pity on her then, and made another little beckoning motion with his fingers, and another. He knew exactly what to do. It was all Selene needed, and she cried out, arching, her head tipped back and her entire body shuddering. It was like being dipped in fire, and the relief was instant.

Relief—and fresh need. She would need more. Much more. But now she could think, the first edge of her curse was blunted.

"Nikolai," she said, when she could speak again. "You were in there, what did you see?" *Give me something, you fucking suckhead. Get it, Selene? Fucking suckhead? You're such a whore.*

The image of Danny's apartment rose in front of her eyes again, and she struggled away from Nikolai's hand, curling into a ball, pulling her knees up while she hugged herself, making small sobbing sounds like an animal in a trap. Her wet clothes rasped uncomfortably against her skin.

Nikolai sighed again. He sounded frustrated. Good for him.

"Later, dear one. Right now you are in pain." He sliced her sweater up the back—his claws, extended delicately, not even brushing her skin beneath the wool. Chill air met her wet skin. Then his fingers, skating down the muscles on either side of her spine. His claws were retracted, but she could still feel the strength in his hands. He pushed her hair aside—the elastic band holding her ponytail snapped—and his mouth met her nape. She shivered, curling even more tightly into herself. He stroked her shoulder, touched the two dimples down low at the small of her back.

The first edge of pain was gone, and the burning settled back into a low dull agony. Her Talent wasn't like others, she *had* to fuel it with sex. It was the only thing that worked.

But Christ, do I have to let him touch me like this? He's not human. Can't he just fuck me and get it over with, leave me alone so I can do what I need to do?

The rest of her ruined sweater was discarded over the side of the bed. He worked her jeans free and tossed them away too, then took her in his

arms. His own clothes were gone—how he did that she couldn't guess, but it probably had something to do with his claws, and the fact the she was too busy trying to gulp down air and fight her body's need to really pay attention to him.

She was paying for the magick she'd done earlier. No preparation, no patterning—she'd simply dropped her defenses and gone for it, performed a major Work without any thought of the consequences. No wonder she was shaking with need.

Everything has to be paid for. She realized she'd said it out loud. "Everything has to be paid for in magick, Nikolai, *everything*."

"Do you think I do not know?" He pushed her onto her back, slid his hand between her legs. She was slick and feverish, damp with need. "Hush. Lie still."

It took a massive effort to do what he said. It would be quicker if she just let him—if she submitted, if she gave in.

Selene erupted into wild motion, trying to fight him off. He caught her wrists, stretching them above her head, and pinned her to the mattress. She would have been screaming, but his mouth was on hers, catching the scream, killing it. She tried to kick him, straining, but he slid a knee between hers. Then all of his weight, and Selene felt the edges of his hips against the soft insides of her thighs. He was much warmer now, his skin almost scorching hers.

The energetic discharge of sex would feed him, too. That was why a *tantraiiken* was such a valuable paranormal pet.

Pet? *Slave.* It was frowned upon, of course, but paranormals and Talents weren't that tightly policed, even though the laws were almost in effect to give them some protection and codify them. The higher echelons of the human world—the powerbrokers and politicians—knew about the slavery, of course, it was an open secret in some circles. But no newspaper would ever report on it, and no television anchor would ever talk about the things that went on under the blanket of normality.

How sometimes, people born with certain Talents were lost to the night side of life.

He found the entrance to her body, thrust in, and his hands tightened around her wrists, the small bones grinding together. Selene gulped back another useless scream, relief spilling through her. His fingers gentled, threaded through hers. He murmured something—maybe it was Russian, she didn't know, didn't care, the only thing she cared about was that the agony had stopped. He was in her to the hilt, stretching her, her hips slamming up, silently begging.

He moved, again, and Selene closed her eyes. Pleasure tore through her, a dark screaming pleasure wrapped in barbed wire and dragging hot velvet laceration through tender flesh. Soon enough she would be able to think about grieving.

"Get . . . it . . . over . . . with." She set her teeth together, even as her hips rocked and her ankles linked together at the small of his back. Her body betrayed her over and over again, that was the worst. Her body was an enemy, a traitor, it didn't care who he was as long as he had what she needed.

"Oh, no," he whispered into her ear, then caught her earlobe in his teeth, gently, delicately. A slight nip of razor teeth, and she sucked in a breath. He laughed, a low harsh breath against her cheek. "There are a few hours until morning."

"I hate you," she whispered back, even as her body shook and the blind fire took her again. And again.

FIVE

In the end, exhausted, she lay limp against the bed, hugging a pillow rescued from the floor. Nikolai curled against her back, sweat slicking his skin so it slid against hers. Her entire body sparked pleasantly, and her shields were back up, thick enough to protect her again.

If Danny had been able to shield himself, would he have died? If he'd been able to run away from whatever had battered his door down, maybe he would have survived.

Don't worry, Danny. Little sister's on the job. I'll get whoever did this to you. I promise. The words were a lump behind her breastbone, steel closing around her beating heart. *I swear to you, Danny. I'm going to find who did this to you. I'll do whatever I have to do.*

That was one thing being a whore was good for. It let her contemplate doing just about anything to get what she wanted. What she needed.

Nikolai's hand polished the curve of her hip, something cool and metallic sliding against her skin. He drew it up over her ribs, under her breast, until the medallion lay where it used to, half the chain spilling down to pool on the sheet. He fastened it at the back of her neck, one-handed, and flattened his other palm against the silver lying between her breasts. "There. This is important, Selene. Without it, you're at risk. This gives you *protection*. You cannot throw it away. Understood?"

Shut up, suckhead. "Someone killed my brother." Her throat rasped from choking back screams. "What happened? What was it?"

"If I tell you what I know, it would be nothing. If I tell you what I suspect, it will be confusing, because I suspect many things." He yawned, burying his face in her hair, then spread one hand against her belly. He was warm enough to pass for a feverish human, metabolizing the jolt of sex into fuel. "If I tell you what I expect, we will be here for many hours, since I have learned to expect everything. It is too soon to tell."

"My brother," she said, tonelessly. His knees were behind hers, one arm under her head, the other holding her to him. A huge exhausted yawn took her unaware, threatened to crack her jaw. "Someone killed my *brother*, Nikolai." *If you won't help me . . .*

"Cooperate with me, and I will find whatever killed your brother," He sighed again, relaxing against her back the way a cat might. A very big, very warm cat. "Dawn is approaching. Will you come with me?"

She should have known. The same offer as always, delivered as if she should be grateful for it. Leave it to Nikolai to use even her brother's murder to try and get what he wanted out of her. "I have work tomorrow." She watched the edge of her pillowcase, breathing shallowly. *Leave me alone. You got what you wanted, now go away.*

"Already attended to. You are not expected there for another two weeks."

Jesus. "I can't afford—"

"With pay."

"I don't want your money." *I don't want to fuck you, either. See how well that works out?*

"Mh. It is not mine; it is from the college. You may call it a gift. For my Selene."

She closed her eyes. *If he was human, what would I do? I'd ask him to help me and he might even do it without turning it into a power play.* "Don't call me that. I'm not yours."

"You must belong somewhere," he said softly.

"I belonged with my brother." Poor Danny. Locked in his apartment except for those times he slipped the chain of his own body and went Journeying. How many times had Selene climbed the steps to his apartment to ask his help for the cases Jack Pepper brought her? How many times had she brought him meals, or little things he needed because he couldn't stand to leave the wards Selene had made for him?

Danny had been immune to her pheromones, immune to her curse. He had been the only man capable of seeing her without her goddamn body complicating things.

I belonged with him plenty, you undead jerk. Now he's gone, and you wouldn't have even let me look at his body.

I hate you.

And he was so easy to hate, wasn't he? A Nichtvren. Inhuman, for all that he'd been mortal once, however long ago. How old *was* he, anyway?

"He was under my protection too," Nikolai said. "Come with me, Selene. You will be safer."

Like hell I will. "No."

"One day you will." He didn't push the issue, for once. "Jorge will come to offer you use of a car."

"And to keep an eye on me? No thanks, Nikolai." Selene bit her lower lip. It was bruised already. She tasted blood. She would ache tomorrow. It had been too long, she'd built up a heavy debt, and her body had exacted its toll with a vengeance. Not only had she cleared a poltergeist infestation and pulled the wards from Danny's apartment, but there had also been the work for that witch over on Seventeenth Street.

She'd needed the money. She always needed the money. Lecturing didn't pay nearly enough for both her rent and Danny's. And by God, Selene never wanted to be poor again. She agreed with Scarlett O'Hara on *that* count, thank you very much.

Nikolai paused, and his hand tensed against her belly. She held her breath, but he didn't move, just tightened his arm around her.

"This is not a request. Jorge will come, and if you leave this place it will be with him. If you do anything foolish I will be vexed." Even his breath was warm against her hair. *Does he breathe because he knows it makes me a little more comfortable? I suppose he has to breathe to talk, doesn't he? I should ask.*

Exhaustion crept in. If she fell asleep now she might be able to get a few hours of rest before . . . no. The fatigue blurred everything, made it difficult to think.

"Vex all you want, Nik," she said, and his fingers tapped against her belly once, twice. Then he stopped. "I'm not your servant. I don't take your orders."

Yeah, Selene. If you lie often enough, you might even be able to halfway believe it.

He made a low sound against her hair, and Selene's entire body leapt. The medallion gave one scorching burst of heat. "Of course, if Jorge is incompetent enough to lose you, I suppose he will need punishment."

You bastard. I should have known. "You wouldn't."

"I would, Selene. I would also make you watch." He sounded calm as if he was discussing a grocery list. "I dislike the thought of damage to you. I will take steps to avoid it."

Everyone knows I'm your little pet. Nobody messes with me anymore, you jerk. I might even be able to use that to find out who killed Danny. "Nothing's going to happen to me."

"Especially not with Jorge watching over you." He sounded pleased to have painted her into a logical corner.

"Fine," she said. "I'll wait for him. I'll be a good little girl. Now go away and leave me alone." *So I can cry in peace. Leave me that, at least. Just leave me alone so I can cry.*

Nikolai rolled away from her, his arm sliding out from beneath her head. She heard him moving, getting into his clothes. She could imagine him getting dressed, pulling his jeans up, pulling his T-shirt back over his head, running his fingers back through his hair to push it back out of his face. Then his coat. She heard the sound of the heavy wool moving.

Best of both worlds. He has to go home before dawn. Can't stay to make things sticky. And he's so fucking careful not to damage me. Though I can take it, can't I? It's hard to kill me. With sex, at least.

He leaned over the bed to pull the sheet and the blankets up, tucking her in gently and efficiently. Finally, when the covers were smoothed, he settled on the side of the bed and touched her hair. Ran his fingers through the heavy mass, lifting it slightly, and gathering it all up, pulling it back from her face. He stroked her cheek with his fingertips, delicately. His claws didn't prickle, but she knew they were there.

Go away. I have to cry first, then I have to figure out what to do first. Oh, God. Danny. Selene kept her eyes shut. Her breathing evened out.

273

She hugged the pillow. Her right hand was under the covers, and she made a fist, her nails biting into her palm. Squeezed. Tighter. *Tighter*.

Finally, Nikolai touched the corner of her mouth with a fingertip. Selene didn't open her eyes—but she did peek out through her lashes. Under the bedroom window shade, a faint grayness showed. Dawn was coming.

There was a slight sound—a breath of air. A cold breeze touched Selene's cheek.

Nikolai was gone.

Selene drove her fingernails into her palms and took in a shuddering breath.

Now, at last, she could cry.

*L*OVE-STARVED

CHARLES L. GRANT

*Y*ou really think I'm that different, do you?

Oh, I know you meant it as a compliment, don't worry, Bud seeing as how we've each other for so long now, I'll give you your due, and a warning at the same time that you won't believe a word of it. And I won't mind if you laugh, or raise an eyebrow or two. As a matter of fact, I'll be disappointed if you don't. I'm a fair man, I think, and you really should know what you're getting yourself into.

No, of course I'm not trying to break tomorrow's engagement. But as I said: I'm a fair man.

Can't you see it in my eyes?

So. Where should I begin? With a woman, I suppose, though I hope you won't be jealous. It's all very pertinent. Believe me, it is. What it comes down to, I think, is that I remember Alicia Chou, not because of the experience we shared, but because it was she who stopped me from even dreaming about marriage again. Or about love in the sense you would ordinarily consider it.

Unrequited passion? I hardly think so, though I've considered it that's true. That sounds too much like a line from a grade B, 1940s film; though, if I were pressed, I would have to admit that in a grotesquely

perverse way I may love her yet. Or part of me does, anyway. But that's the one thing I can't explain just now. I'm not even sure that I'll ever have the answer.

The attraction certainly wasn't her astonishing, almost exquisite beauty—I told you not to be jealous, be patient—though that too lingers, rather like an aftertaste uncommitted to being either sweet or sour. And if that sounds odd to say in this day and age, it's because she herself was a strange one, in a way only someone like myself can truly appreciate.

As of this moment, to be frank, I honestly cannot think of exactly what it was about her that affected me first, despite the apparent simplicity of the problem. But, then, perhaps I'm still too close to the situation after ten short years.

Tell you what. Let's turn this into a game of sorts. You order yourself another one of those pink things (none for me, thanks; perhaps later), and we'll pretend we're in one of those nineteenth-century country inns, whiling away the winter evenings scaring the hell out of each other with nonsensical ghost stories. I haven't much time, but I think I can give you a hint of what's happening—not that I expect that you'll take it. No one ever does. Which is odd, my dear, because it's not only happening to me.

* * *

If you'll remember, it was a remarkably short time before the photography studio I'd opened downtown was doing extremely well for its rather limited size. Over the first few months I'd been commissioned to shoot cover material for just about every men's and general circulation magazine going; there were even a few location trips to Europe thrown in to sweeten the lot. But when July came around, I felt myself going stale—my head was beginning to feel groggy in the same way you feel when you've just completed two or three final exams in a row. Every model was getting that same vapid, hurry-up-you-creep-

these-lights are-hot look. Every location was flat and uninviting.
I dreaded going to work, dreaded even waking up in the morning.
And naturally, all this eventually surfaced in the final product, I had
obviously been pushing too hard, too fast, trying to make a few
bucks and a name.

Finally, when the very thought of sticking my eye anywhere near a
lens made me want to gag, I said the hell with it, and I left. Oh, a few
clients squealed and wrung their hot little hands; a few editors growled
at me over the phone; but when I told them all in the plainest, non-
advertising language what they could do with their precious campaigns
and covers, all they did was purse their lips and shake their heads and
tell me I needed a vacation.

So I took one. As simple as that.

I packed a bag and fled the city without looking back. It had been
some time since I'd bothered driving with the top down, and the wind
cresting over the windshield felt absolutely great. Just cool enough
to take the sting out of the hot sun, and strong enough to make me
feel glad I still had all my hair. Everything, then, and every miserable
working day was blown so far away I had to think to remember what
I did for a living. Knowing me as you do, you're not going to believe
this, but I was even singing out loud at the top of my voice and thinking
I should have practiced for the Met.

Whim chose my direction, and I paid little attention to the odometer,
gladly patching a tire or two myself simply because there was no
appointment I had to make by two o'clock or we'll cancel the contract
and find someone else more reliable, thank you. God, but that was a
magnificent feeling! On the second morning out, in fact, I'd stuffed my
watch into the glove compartment and didn't put it on again for three
days. It's almost supernatural; the freedom one feels when you don't turn
your wrist every ten minutes to see that ten minutes have passed since
the last time you looked. Incredible. And wonderful.

But then, by hook, crook, or some other heavy-handed and cliché-scarred beck of Fate's temptation, I found myself missing a few familiar comforts and ended up back in the Cape Cod I'd bought over there on Hawthorne Street, right on the river above the bend. I guess I had it in the back of my mind all along, in spite of the fact that my conscious plan was just to keep driving until I'd refueled, you should pardon the pun. I'd picked it up already furnished, but I'd never had a chance to really enjoy the overstuffed chairs and the dusty bookcases, the stereo, the TV, and God knew what else; I'd seldom stayed there more than just to sleep, and sometimes not that, if you know what I mean. But now . . . Lord, I could roam through the cool and quiet, let that old place soak out of my system everything the drive in the Country hadn't banished. I turned myself into the absolute sloth, and I loved it, every minute, even fell in love with the shadows in the house.

And though I wasn't used to taking things easy, I had no problem at all falling into the slow, casual tempo of summer neighborhood life. Early evening walks really *seeing* the place where I'd chosen to live, scuffing leaves in the park and listening to bandstand music after a leisurely cooked dinner, once even stringing a hammock between two trees in the yard and humming in time to the river that marked the end of my lot.

It was . . . beautiful, because, for I don't know how many champagne days, I was actually seeing things through my own eyes instead of a camera's, and I was totally convinced I couldn't have been happier.

Then, one afternoon, I was baking in a sauce of suntan oil on a small section of riverbank set aside as a beach. I spent a lot of good time watching the kids splashing around, dunking each other and really getting frustrated learning to swim in the river's moderate currents. For a while there I really got involved rooting for one little guy who was experimenting holding his breath and trying not to drown at the same time. I was timing him by counting thousands and making bets with myself, when this indescribable pair of legs blocked my view.

Now I know that some men are devotees of the decolletage, and others are—as one of my girls once put it—admirers of ass; but I prefer those anatomical delights that carry the rest of the woman around. It has always been my solemn creed that bust or buttock, nose or navel, aren't anything at all without a fine pair of legs to support them. Not that this woman didn't have the appropriate accessories, mind you . . . but Lord, those legs! All the Troys in history would have gladly fallen for them, would have definitely been singed by the rest of her. Curiously, she was wearing a one-piece bathing suit that would have aroused attention on any beach simply because it was so out of place it was quaint. Black, too, her hair, curled inward slightly at the ends and cut to a point between her shoulders.

I lay there quietly, waiting for her to turn around, and paradoxically hoping that she would stay facing the water.

But she turned, abruptly, and looked straight into my eyes.

(As I do now, so I can see you're not jealous.)

Disconcerted though I was, her stare wasn't at all unfriendly. She was Eurasian: so temptingly French (perhaps), so tantalizingly Oriental (perhaps), that a dozen years' concentration couldn't have discovered where one began and the other left off.

When I sat up, she knelt directly in front of me and smiled, her deep tan looking darker in the shadow of her lips. I felt a bit fuzzy, as if I'd had too much sun and beer, but I managed a weak grin in return. Obviously, I wasn't at the top of my form.

"I'm sorry," I said, thinking all the while how brilliant that sounded and how stupidly seventeenish I was feeling.

"For what?" She laughed clear into eyes perfectly framed by black bangs.

"You got me. For staring at you, I guess. It's not exactly the most polite form of introduction."

She laughed again, tossing her head from side to side, and damned if I didn't feel shocked—at myself. Right at that moment I wanted to rape

that animal—there's no other word—kneeling so primly not a hand's breadth from my feet. I know you know me well enough to understand that I'm not one to get upset over an occasional erotic impulse; but the sheer force of that woman had to be felt to be believed.

And while I was smothering in this sense-overload trance, she covered her mouth with silver-painted nails and swung around on her heels until she was resting on the grass beside me. Which is how we spent the rest of the afternoon. Seduction without words.

Except . . . most of the time I tried to stay just a few inches behind her. To avoid her eyes.

Alicia Chou. Eyes brown-black, with a single gold fleck in each, just off-center.

And when I finally introduced myself, she said, "Carroll is an odd name for a man, isn't it?" Her voice was less a purr than a growl lurking beneath thin velvet. "Your father must have been a very handsome man."

The touch of her hand on my knee, thigh, shoulder—the gentle way she brushed my back was colder than the lotion she rubbed absently into my skin.

Cobra and mouse.

Once, she kissed the back of my neck, and I nearly grabbed a mirror from a passing woman to see if I'd been branded.

Everyone smiled at us. The adults at me, the children at her. What a handsome couple, I knew they were thinking.

It was only natural, then, that I asked her to dinner.

* * *

She wouldn't tell me where she was staying—a wise precaution for a woman alone—but promised to meet me at my place at seven. We parted and I ran—you're laughing, but I did—I ran home and stood in front of the bedroom mirror, thinking that all that had happened was far too

good to be even remotely true. I scowled at my reflection: too much hair for a smallish head, eyes too blue, nose too long and too sharp, ears too close to my head. No leading man, that was for certain, and thus no physical reason why Alicia should clasp me so suddenly to her not insubstantial bosom. I laughed aloud. By God, Carroll, I said to myself, you've been picked up. You've actually been picked up. By a raving nymphomaniac, a psychotic murderess . . . I couldn't have cared less. She was elegantly available and I was on vacation.

What I hadn't planned on, of course, was falling in love.

And that is the wrong place to laugh, my dear. It was marvelous, right out of Hollywood, magnificent . . . and terrifying.

If I'd listened to myself then, I wouldn't be telling you this now.

So she came, and we drove to a riverbank restaurant in a hotel in the next town. Dined and danced and stood on the balcony that faced the water. I kissed her cheek, felt giddy with the wine, kissed her lips . . . and when it was over I was drained, so drained that I had to lean against the marble railing to keep from collapsing.

For one second, hardly worth mentioning then, I hated her.

Then it was over and we headed back to my home. There had been no innuendo conversation. The slight turn of her mouth, the graceful flow of her hands spoke for her. She never asked about my job, family, income or tailor. I myself had been too stunned by what I had thought was instant love to mumble even a hello and you look wonderful and why don't we dance.

I never felt the pain that lanced my will.

Neither do I remember the drive back to the house, the opening of the door, the walk upstairs. I couldn't help but feel as if the world had wound down to slow motion, so languid her movements, so careful the display of her smile and her charm.

She sat on the edge of the bed and gestured toward the chair I kept by the nightstand. "Drink?"

Why not, I thought. Get bombed, Carroll, and let's get on with whoever is raping who.

"Of course," I said, mixed what she asked and finally, at last, she let me sit down.

We toasted each other, and I loved her again.

Then her gaze narrowed over the top of the champagne glass, and I realized with a start how I had spent most of the afternoon avoiding those eyes, all the evening losing myself in them. But when, as an experiment in masculine control, I tried to break away, I couldn't. And my palms became unaccountably moist.

"Carroll is a strange name," she said.

"You've already said that once, Alicia," I said, grinning stupidly. "It was my dear departed mother's idea, not knowing what she would have at the time and not feeling like coming up with two sets for the sexes."

"I love you, strange name," she whispered. Not a word out of place, not a change in tone. Something broke briefly through the sparkling cloud I felt over me, but I couldn't put a name to it and so shrugged it away.

Instead, I emptied the glass and set it on the floor beside me. Cleared my throat and said, "This is going to sound . . . well, it's going to sound ridiculous, under the circumstances, Alicia—but, damnit, I think I love you, too." It was all so bloody serious, so intolerably solemn that I wanted to laugh, But I couldn't; I was too nervous. Not of breaking the spell that nights and champagne and mysterious women weave, but of her and those eyes with their single flecks of gold.

"For how long, strange name?"

"Shouldn't that be obvious? Forever. How else?"

It was she who laughed then. Deeply. In her throat. And as she did, I became inexplicably angry. Didn't she know, I demanded of myself, that in thirty-four goddamned years on this road I had said that only once before when I'd meant it—to a cheerleader in high school. Who

had also laughed, but loudly and shrilly, with her head thrown back and her eyes rolled heavenward in total disbelief.

"Strange name, love me," Alicia said.

I hesitated. I stalled. Her request became a demand.

And I did and am now regrettably forced to resort to the old purple-prose lines of jungle passions and animal ferocity. But that, I'm afraid, is exactly the way it was. Stripped, perspiring even before we began, stalking each other without benefit of cinematic loveplay, manual directions of foreplay and stimulation. Sheets and blankets were literally torn, glasses were shattered, bottles smashed . . . again and again and again . . . and again.

"Love me," she hissed.

And I did. Bleeding, drawing blood, bruised and bruising . . . again and again.

"More," she crooned.

I did, God, I did.

Dawn, and I did not see it. Dusk, and I could not see it. Crying, laughing—a haze of cigarette smoke, a waste basket gushing uneaten meals one of us made downstairs in the kitchen.

It must have been her. I couldn't have moved.

We stood by the window in caftan robes and watched the river pass a beautifully bright day beneath us, beneath the willows. It was peaceful and wonderful; I held her gently against my chest and told her so, whispering in her ear all the idiot lovephrases that men think original when the loving is done.

"Then love me," she whispered back.

The radio played Brahma and Vaughan Williams. Nothing louder for this room, on this day, at this time.

"Love me," she sang.

I told her how, when I was in college up there in Hartford, I had exhausted myself during one summer vacation visiting ten European

cities in less than sixteen days: I must have been drunk when I said it,
I don't remember now, but I suddenly turned mawkish and sentimental,
muttering "Those were the good old days" over and over again and
praising their lack of tears and responsibility and extolling my love
for them in dreams and bursts of unbidden nostalgia. I told her about
an Irish setter I once had, how he could never go with us on vacation
because he always got carsick and had to stay at the vet's. About the
cheerleader. About the models. About the slices of my soul that went
into my work.

"Love me," she comforted.

Everything is relative, said the speeding turtle to the snail. There must
have been Time someplace, but two days were gone before I first began
to think that I was losing my mind.

Alicia was sleeping at my side, peacefully, evenly. My mouth was
burlap, my head cement, and God, dear God, how everything ached.
For one nauseating moment I thought of a morning a couple years back
when I'd eaten tainted food in a Boston fast-food joint and they used a
fool stomach pump while I was semi-conscious, I groaned and pushed
myself up on my elbows, looking for a mirror to see if in fact I was
really turning into an airless balloon; but a pain I knew instantly was
frighteningly abnormal flattened me like a hammer, and I had to gasp for
a breath. Beyond that, however, I felt nothing. I registered the room and
what I could see through the window, but there was nothing left inside
me to hang the pictures on.

That, I think, is when the terror began. As if I were suffering a malaria
attack, I simultaneously grew cold and soaked the sheets with a bath of
perspiration that made me tremble. And I grew still more terrified when
I tried to cry out with that slow-growing pain, and my mind said there
was no reason, and my mouth made no sound.

I fell asleep then, unwillingly, and I dreamt as I do now—in blacks
and greys and splashes of sterile white. And once, in that dream, I heard

someone mention food, and I heaved dryly for ten minutes before I could fall asleep again.

The last thing I recall seeing was a floating, broken camera.

I woke once more. I think it was daylight. I really don't know because Alicia was bending over me, her lips parted and smiling.

"Can you love me, strange name?" she asked, carelessly tracing a meaningless pattern from my chest to my stomach to my groin and back.

"My God, Alicia!"

"Can you love?" she insisted.

"My God, no!"

She pouted through a smile that told me she knew better.

"Alicia, please,"

"You don't love me anymore,"

A fleeting array of artfully shadowed images: of Alicia in her gown, the swimsuit, the robe, her nakedness atavistic in the arousal it produced, all made me smile lazily until I turned my head . . . and saw the look in her eyes.

And in that final moment before she smiled again, I knew at last what I'd been trying to avoid: Alicia was still hungry, and she kissed me, hard, before I finally passed out.

* * *

So then. Before you tell me what you think, my dear, let me tell you what I think you've already decided. Let's see: maybe I'm simply crazy, right? Ah, too easy. Perhaps then it's a fantasy, cleverly manipulated to hide a disastrous affair. Or, better yet, perhaps I had become so drunk at dinner that I was physically incapable of playing the Don Juan in anything more than high-sounding words, thus striking myself low with assorted simple trauma.

I was right, wasn't I.

Well, it all sounds very intelligent, I admit; all very up-to-date and properly sophisticated. In fact, if I didn't have to hurry along right now, you might even have convinced me, given enough time.

But I really must run, as. I warned you at the start. And, for heaven's sakes, stop worrying about my health. I'll promise you now, if you like, that I'll dine without fail later this evening.

Ah, my darling, you are jealous, aren't you?

But you know me, first things first; so please don't worry, I won't forget. You see, there's this wonderfully attractive brunette named Claire who's dying to see the river from my bedroom. Look, why don't you have another drink on me, and I'll see you tomorrow. I've worked up a marvelous appetite talking with you, and Claire is waiting for me right this moment.

I think you'd like her. She's a wonderful girl. A great girl. She thinks the gold in my eyes is sexy.

She loves me. She really does.

But just so you'll know that I will keep my promise lean over here and I'll give you a kiss.

One kiss.

That's all

One kiss.

I'm hungry.

KISS AT MIDNIGHT

RUSSELL DAVIS

(FOR MISTI)

"On Sunday mornings I remember the first girl I loved,
red hair so dark it looked like a bonfire."

—Waltzing with the Dead

I imagine her this way:

She wakes to red velvet and lace. Though there is not the tiniest sliver of light in the darkness, her green eyes can make out the tiny swirls in the fabric of the cloth canopy above her with ease. She licks her dry, red lips, and her delicate, pale hands move over the white silk sheets of her bed. She rises, her long, red hair a pillow-cloud around her shoulders, and she greets the night once again—a beautiful angel of love and lust and death. She wakes in this manner every night, as she has every night before . . .

I fell in love with her in a single night. I answered her ad, expecting nothing more than an evening of enjoyable, commitment-free sex.

I didn't get what I expected—nor, I suppose, did she. For long months, I have been thinking only of her. Trying to find her once again so I can tell her that now I understand that true love does not care about the murky boundary waters between life and death, good and evil, or right and wrong. Love is the desire to consume oneself in the flames of another person—the flesh, minds, and souls combine and grow into a fire that burns with star-like heat at its most passionate, or burns out into the cold oblivion of darkness when it fails . . .

I started browsing the personals a year after my wife, Anaka, was killed in a car accident. At first, I found them grimly amusing—the desperate acts of people who were unwilling or unable to meet others in the real world. I didn't realize then how desperate I myself would become; when the long days at work would become longer nights at home, sitting in a silence that no music or television program could breach. I became a recluse of sorts. I didn't go out, didn't meet people, and didn't start my life over as I'd planned when the shock and grief of losing my wife had passed. I was alone, and reading the personals—at first a joke to me—became a quest to connect somehow with someone else, to live again.

I was scared, of course. Who wouldn't be in this age of unreason? I read the ads in the paper, over and over, searching for the ones that would interest me enough to answer. I had a process of reading them in no time at all—ignore every ad that involved men, couples, or home videos, and read every ad that involved a single female. It shortened the list considerably.

Occasionally, I would find the courage to respond to an ad, only to find that the people who placed the ad had misrepresented themselves. The women would—in actuality—be men, or unattractive to me, or simply undesirable in some other fashion. I went on several unsuccessful first dates before I decided to approach it from the other direction.

The day finally came when I placed my own ad, to generally poor results. Usually it read something like:

> *SWM, 30-something, not hard on the eyes, seeking SWF*
> *for relationship, possible long-term commitment. He is*
> *secure, honest, and intelligent. She must demonstrate*
> *similar qualities. Reply to Box 9673-626.*

More often than not, a brief phone conversation ended any hope of meeting in person—the results from this direction were the same as they were from the other one. It didn't seem to matter whether I was the advertiser or the respondent, everyone seemed unreal to what they said they were. After one such phone call, I realized that I was being too particular. I also realized that I didn't really care. I was looking for someone who could replace my wife, my soul mate—and that didn't seem possible anymore. How do you go about replacing someone who is irreplaceable? I didn't want to risk love anymore, or face the pain of losing a loved one.

At night, I would lie awake and remember Anaka in vivid detail. The way her dark hair curled when it was wet, the color of her eyes in candlelight, the sound of her voice, husky and low after we'd made love. I didn't believe that anyone could measure up to her. The very idea of love began to seem a little sad to me, like finding out that your religion is based on a falsehood.

Yet there was no doubt in my mind that I still longed for the touch of a woman. I became more and more lonely, and as the days and nights passed, I found that almost more than anything else, I missed physical intimacy. I would walk along the pier, fascinated by the way a woman's hips looked inside her jeans, or the press of her breasts against the fabric of her shirt. The scent of women's perfume mixing with the smell of the ocean in an intoxicating blend, the fading light of the day turning

faces and forms into silhouettes that could—in my minds eye—be a replacement for my lost Anaka.

Finally, I decided to ignore my continuing quest for true love, and find a way to appease my physical desires. Perhaps by extinguishing my lust I could find a path back to a place where love was possible again. I felt my desires were perfectly normal, and at the very least I would be on the same page as the other lost souls who were investing their time in the personals. My temporary hold on finding true love again would, if nothing else, save me from continued disappointments.

And then I saw her ad for the first time:

> *Very attractive, SWF in search of passionate SWM for one*
> *night stand. Must understand the hungers of the flesh.*
> *Guaranteed unforgettable evening. Discretion a must.*
> *Send picture and bio to Box 8267-473.*

The hungers of the flesh. I liked the sound of that a great deal. That is what I was suffering from . . . a hunger for the touch of flesh. How I lusted for the sweet scent of a woman's skin, the taste of her lips on mine. I sent her my picture, and a one-page description of myself and my life—such as it was. And I waited, in a strange state of trepidation and excitement, hoping for the phone to ring.

* * * *

The call came an hour after sundown.

"Hello?" I asked.

"Good evening," the low voiced, female caller said, "Is this Jameson Servais?"

My heart pounded. Was it her? Telemarketers never pronounce my name correctly, and I had mentioned the correct pronunciation in my

letter to her. I swallowed hard, and my tongue clicked once, dryly.

"Hello?" she said. "Are you there?"

"Yes," I managed to croak. "This is Jameson."

"Hello," she said. "You answered my ad."

"I guess I did," I said, feeling nervous.

"I'm glad," she said. "I was impressed."

"Well, uh, then I guess I'm glad I answered," I said, then added when I caught up with myself long enough to remember my manners, "What's your name?"

"Alexa," she said. "Alexa McKnight."

"It's nice to meet you." I was beginning to feel embarrassed. Plagued by an out of control libido, perhaps I had gone too far.

"Would you like to meet sometime, Jameson?"

"You mean like at a hotel or something?" I asked, floundering.

She laughed. It was a warm, throaty sound that sent a tingle up my spine. "Actually, I thought dinner might be nice. We can proceed to other things if—and when—it suits us." Her voice was a low tenor, and brought to mind hundreds of movie maidens who speak in just the same way before succumbing to the charms of the hero. I didn't feel like a hero, but like a teenager, fumbling with my words and my proverbial zipper at the same time.

"Dinner would be great," I said. "When and where?"

"You pick," she said. "I like to get to know a man before inviting him for . . . other pleasures."

I hesitated, then, in a rush, "How about tomorrow," I asked, "Around seven?"

"That would be fine," she said. "Where?"

"There's a Greek café on the corner of 9th and Mitchell. They've got good food, and even better atmosphere. Do you like Greek?" I asked.

"Very much," she said. "Who doesn't like a good bite of Greek now and then?"

"It's called 'Sybil's Rock'. Do you know it?"

"I've never been there, but I'll find my way. I'm relatively new in town, but I'm starting to know my way around."

"That's great," I said, thinking that I was sounding more and more like a teenage boy whose dream date had just said yes to the prom *and* a midnight roll around in the backseat of his parent's car. "So I'll see you around seven?"

"Absolutely," she said.

"Good," I said. "I'm looking forward to it."

"So am I," she said.

"Wait!" I said, thinking she was about to hang up. "How will I know you? I don't have your picture."

"I have yours," she said. "And besides, I think you'll know me."

"Oh," I said. "Then I guess I'll see you then." Somehow, I could imagine her smiling, thinking I was a fool. "Good night, Alexa."

"Good night to you, Jameson."

As you might guess, I slept very little that night. I thought of Alexa, and the things we might do to—and for—one another the next evening. The short conversation replayed itself like a scratched record in my mind. I thought of Anaka—I had not physically been with anyone since her death—and I thought of betrayal. Would she approve of this strange, dark liaison? I didn't think so, and my separate thoughts of two women—one whom I loved, and the other I didn't know—stayed with me even in my dreams.

* * * *

The café was dimly lit and pleasant, though it was busy. I had arrived a full half hour early to assure that we would have a good table. I sat in the semi-darkness watching other couples talk and sip shots of ouzo. When she walked in, I realized she had been right. I knew her in an instant.

Her feet were clad in black leather ankle boots, and she wore black denim jeans that hugged her slender waistline. Her shirt was crème-colored raw silk, open at the neck, and underneath, between the swell of her breasts, I could make out the faint lines of a dark purple, or perhaps red, lace brassiere. An embroidered black vest accented the outfit, and she carried a small, black purse in her left hand. I noticed her long nails, perfectly kept, and how flawless her hands seemed. Her neck was encircled with a slender gold chain and a locket. Her face was pale, and unblemished except for a small, circular birthmark just above her right eye. Her eyes were green—not the green of a forest glen, or a meadow in springtime, but the green of kelp washing onto the beach. And her hair . . . it was a dark, luxurious mane of red. It was a cigarette ember in the dark of night. It curled softly about her shoulders, a bonfire.

Her eyes met mine for the briefest instant, and she smiled. She was not what I had imagined on the phone, or while tossing and turning during the night . . . she was much more. As she made her way through the crowd, her eyes never left mine, and I did my best to appear composed. She walked effortlessly, somewhere (or so it appeared to my admiring gaze) between a glide and actual flight. The crowd seemed to melt away for her, clearing a path.

When she reached the table, I rose, and held out my hand. "You must be Alexa," I said.

She nodded, and set down her purse. "And you are Jameson," she said, taking my proffered hand lightly in hers, and clasping it gently.

"I am, and I'm pleased to meet you," I said, feeling a wild urge to kiss her hand.

"And I am pleased to meet you," she said. Her voice still carried that warm quality I had noticed on the phone.

I suppressed my gallant urges, and as we were seated, I gestured vaguely around the restaurant. "Will this be okay?"

"Oh, yes," she said. "Perfectly fine." She glanced around the room. "You were right about the atmosphere."

"I'm glad you like it," I said. "My wife and I came here often."

"You mentioned in your letter that your wife passed away a few years ago."

"Yes," I said, still feeling the guilt and grief from my thoughts of the night before. Seeing Alexa, those feelings were more distant, but there nonetheless.

"I don't wish to cause you pain, but may I ask . . ." she trailed off.

"Car accident," I replied. "Drunk driver. His third offense if you can believe it."

"I believe it," she said. "I'm sorry for your loss. How long have you been alone?"

"A little over three years," I said.

Just then the waiter arrived, rattled off the evenings specials, and took our drink order. I chose a bottle of red zinfandel, and we waited in agreeable silence until he came back with it, and took our dinner order. Both of us selected the feature—a cucumber salad, lamb chops and pasta, with new potatoes. After he left, we continued our conversation.

"Has it been difficult for you?" she asked. "Being alone all this time?"

Fidgeting a little at the scrutiny, I said, "At first, I thought I would start over. Find love again, make the life-long commitment, but I've found that facing that prospect is asking too much of myself. It's been more difficult than I thought it would be."

"I find that hard to believe," she said. "You're the first person I've ever met through the personals who was honest about themselves and actually matched their picture. In the photo, you have dark brown hair, streaked with white, and lo and behold—in person you're the same. I suspected you were too good to be true."

I laughed. "So, you've had the experience of meeting someone through the personals who didn't quite match up to their description of themselves?"

"Oh yes," she said. "Quite a few times. I decided that it was pointless fooling around with the whole quest for true love thing. I hadn't really been getting anywhere."

"That sounds familiar," I said.

She smiled. "I understood how you felt when I was reading about you. I've been alone for a long time, too," she said, then added, "But isn't it interesting how our feelings about love or lust can change rapidly from one moment to the next?"

"Yes, it is," I said. "You have me at a disadvantage, you know," I added. "You've read all about me, and I know next to nothing about you."

She laughed, lightly. "Just the way I like it," she said, grinning. "It's good to have mystery in a relationship of any kind, don't you think?"

I nodded. "Mystery is fine," I said, "But that doesn't mean complete unfamiliarity. Tell me about yourself."

So she did. She said she had been born in London, but had moved to the United States with her parents when she was less than a year old. Her mother stayed at home, and her father was a professor of cultural anthropology at the University of Nebraska. There were no other children. She had grown up in a fairly normal environment, finished her Ph.D. in human biology, and then moved out to California for her work as a researcher.

While she talked, I watched her in growing fascination. Her voice, her gestures—they seemed uniquely understated, as though she were holding back a growing level of internal excitement. I couldn't seem to take my eyes off her hair, and I found myself wanting to reach out and touch it, to bury my face in its fiery softness and smell her perfume. When she finally wound down with her brief history, I felt disappointed as I enjoyed listening to her melodic voice.

"So," she concluded, "I guess that's enough about me for awhile. I haven't told anyone that much about myself in a long time." She shrugged. "Tell me something more about you. What do you do for a living?"

"Crosswords," I said, still distracted by the play of light in her hair.

"I beg your pardon?" she asked. "Did you say crosswords?"

"Oh yes," I said, then, seeing her confusion, I added, "I write crossword puzzles."

"I see," she said. "That's refreshing."

"How so?"

"Well, you just don't meet someone everyday who does that for a living. Write crosswords, I mean. Do you like it?"

"I suppose I do," I said. "I enjoy the challenge of constructing clues, and I've always liked word games."

When our dinner arrived, we paused our conversation long enough to get a good way into our lamb chops. Finally, she said, "So you enjoy word games? You must be well read then."

"Yes," I said, "Mostly personal ads."

And we laughed again. The rich warm sound of her voice cascaded around me, and I literally felt myself grow warm as I watched her. "You have a fine sense of humor," she said.

"Thank you," I said. "But in all seriousness, yes. I do read quite a lot."

This set off an entirely new discussion of different books and their merits. We ate, and talked, drinking the wine, and drinking in each other. By the time our coffee arrived, I somehow knew that I loved her. The poets speak of this phenomenon, but for me it was as real as any love I'd ever known. And though it seemed foolish, I found I was comfortable being a fool. It was senseless and fast, but she was, in every sense, a lady of intense qualities. It was also then that I realized I couldn't tell her my feelings. She actually deserved better than a one-night stand, and I suddenly knew that for all my recent cynicism about love and relationships, I had to respect her wishes about a relationship. She had been upfront about what she wanted, and it wasn't my place to try and make her change her mind. I felt a little like a child. I was a weak man who had fallen to his knees at the first sight of her qualities.

When dessert was over, the conversation slowed, and then stopped. I watched her, trapped between my desires for her physically, and the bitter knowledge that what I now knew I really wanted, I couldn't have. "Well," I said. "That was a fine meal, but your company was better."

"Thank you," she said. "You mentioned the excellent atmosphere, but I had no idea it would be this good," she added.

I smiled. "What happens now?" I asked.

"Now?" she said. "Would you like to take a lady for a walk along the pier?"

I nodded. "It would be a pleasure," I said, and I meant it. "Besides, I need to work off this baklava." I couldn't tell her no, and I knew I couldn't say yes to the implicit want in her eyes.

I paid our check, and we left. As we stepped out into the darkness, I took the liberty of taking her hand in mine, and in companionable silence, we made our way to the stone pier that borders the ocean.

* * * *

For a long time, nothing was said. We listened to the water lapping onto the shore, and the snap as it rolled over jetties of rock where people who couldn't afford real docks tied up their small boats. Occasionally, we would pass another couple walking along and enjoying the night. Orange colored arc sodium lamps provided the occasional island of light, but mostly there was darkness, and boat lights distant on the water that looked like stars. It was the most comfortable I'd been in years. Even though it was dishonest to continue on, I didn't want it to end.

Still, I was the first to break the silence. "Alexa, I've enjoyed tonight," I said. "Very much."

"As have I," she said. "More than I expected."

"Yes," I said, "Even more than expected. But . . ." I trailed off, looking for words.

"But?" she said.

"Well, I guess I've misjudged myself."

"How do you mean?" she asked.

"I thought I wanted a one-night stand. Something purely physical, and by extension, something simple. But being with you tonight reminded me of all the reasons I loved Anaka, and I realized that I still want love, even more than I do sex."

She nodded, "I understand."

I was startled. "How so?"

She shrugged. "I find that I'm in the same boat. You see, I, too, lost my soulmate, and even though he isn't dead, I can no longer be with him. Being with you reminded me of him, much as you being with me reminded you of your late wife. I was wrong about what I wanted, and the only thing I can say is how happy I am that we're both in agreement of a sort."

I laughed, and she turned on me, a little hurt and angry. "This is funny to you?"

"No, no," I said. "Not at all. It's just that here we are, two adults dancing around the idea of sex, and both of us are thinking about love, and lost loves."

She smiled then. "You're right. There is something strangely funny about that."

"Look," I said, "I like you, Alexa. A lot. But I can't sleep with you because you deserve better than a one nighter with no commitments. I thought I was ready for something like that, but I guess I'm not, at least not with you. Maybe I'm not as cynical about love as I thought."

She softened visibly. "That's really quite sweet, Jameson. And spending time with you has helped me change my mind, too. Love exists, even for someone like you," she said, "Or me."

"Don't get me wrong, though" I added. "Alexa, I was watching you tonight, how the light played in your hair, the little gestures you make

while you speak, and I hungered for the touch of a woman—but I want something more. Something permanent like I had before. I want to wake up every morning knowing that you're—excuse me—that someone's there."

"Someone?" she asked.

We were standing in a pool of that orange lamplight, and she turned towards me, her eyes upturned. "I want...well, that is, I think that . . ."

"Oh, shut up," she said. Then, with unexpected strength, she pulled my face down to hers, and kissed me. In the distance, the waves continued their rhythmic pounding of the shoreline, and somewhere in the city, church bells tolled the midnight hour.

* * * *

Was it the bells sounding the midnight hour? Was it the passion of the moment, the way we seemed to join together in that instant? I still do not know. As our kiss deepened, the bells tolled, and I felt her lips tracing a small crescent along the line of my jaw and down to my neck. Then, a sudden pain as her entire body tightened—every muscle locked rigid, and she clasped me so strongly I thought my ribs would shatter. She held me this way for a few moments, and I could sense her struggling with something. Her lips moved against my neck, as though she were praying or nuzzling me. Finally, as though she could stand no more, she pushed me away.

"I can't," she said, so quietly that it was hard to hear her.

"I don't get it," I said. "You can't what?"

"I can't be with you," she whispered. She was turned away from me, staring out into the dark ocean, her body visibly trembling.

"I don't understand, Alexa. It's obvious you want to be with me."

She shrugged. "You don't have to understand. Just accept it. I can't be with you."

"Be fair, damn it! I want to be with you—you at least owe me an explanation!"

"I can't give you that, either. I'm sorry, Jameson." The bells had faded to silence, and over the waves, the city sounds resumed. "I've got to go," she said.

"Wait a minute," I said, grasping her shoulder and turning her around.

"No, Jameson!" she cried, but it was too late. I had seen her face.

Her eyes were now the color of blood, even in the orange light I could see they were red. Her skin looked vaguely feverish, and pale, though she had appeared healthy enough earlier. But the worst was her teeth. They had grown! They were so long and pointed that her canines jutted down past her bottom lip.

"What the . . ." I said, before she quickly turned away.

"So," she said. "Now you know."

I was dazed. "What do I know?" I asked. "That you aren't who you appear to be?"

She laughed, and now it was a grim sound, full of old disappointments. "You like word games, Jameson. You've seen me, you saw my ad, what am I?"

Still reeling, I tried to piece it together. Her ad said she wanted a one-night stand. What was so significant about that? And then it hit me—all at once, and I was stunned I hadn't seen it before. Her box number . . . when you signed up for the personals service, you selected your own box number. Mine, 9673-626 spelled out "word-man" on any standard phone pad. Hers, 8267-473, spelled vampire! Her ad had said that the respondent must "understand the hungers of the flesh." I put a hand to my head, which was suddenly aching.

"You're a vampire?" I asked. "A vampire?"

"You really are good at word games, Jameson," she said. Then, "Yes, I am a vampire. And now you know why I can't be with you." She was still turned away.

"A vampire?" I asked again, still floundering.

"Yes!" she half-screamed. "A vampire! You know, a blood-sucker. Creature of the night. The whole thing."

Feeling like my head was buried in cotton, I tried again. "Why are you dating?" I asked.

She spun around, and I took a not-so-involuntary step backwards. "Do you think that being a vampire is proof against loneliness?" she hissed. "Do you have any idea how long forever is?"

Taken aback, I gestured vaguely around. "I . . . I guess not. How the hell would I know, anyway?" I asked, annoyed. "I'm standing here having a conversation with a vampire. Either that or I'm cracking up. It's not like you take a vampire to dinner every . . ." I trailed off as a thought struck me. Vampires don't eat dinner. "Wait a minute," I said. "Vampires don't eat, right? What'd you do with your food?"

"Simple illusion," she said. "One of the few benefits of being what I am."

"How did you . . . oh, never mind," I said. Then another thought struck me. "You weren't looking for a date, were you?"

She turned away again, but I could hear her response. "No," she mumbled. "Not really."

"You were going to *feed* on me, weren't you?" I asked, nearly shouting myself. "Jesus Christ! Do you do this often? Let guys take you out to dinner and then drink their blood?!"

She didn't answer, and that was answer enough.

"So, this wasn't a date, wasn't even cheap sex. It was how a vampire hunts in the modern age, right? Everything you told me was bullshit."

"It's not like that," she whispered. "Not really."

"Then what's it like," I snapped. "*Really.*"

"It's a little more death every day," she said softly. "Always aching to be alive again, to feel something besides the hunger—and always being denied. It's too late to lie to you, and I don't really want to anyway." She turned back to me, and for a moment, I saw *her* again. Not the monster

within her, but the real woman trying to escape. "You're right, of course," she said. "Everything I told you before about me, who I am, was a lie. A necessary lie, but a lie nonetheless. And usually, this is how I feed. I hate it, but that's a hunger that cannot be denied. Some desperate soul responds to an ad that appears to be for sex, he takes me out and then I feed on him. It's not pretty, but it gets the job done."

"Then why didn't you feed on me?" I asked. "I'm pretty desperate. In fact, you might say that death would be a blessing."

She nodded in understanding. "For many of them, it is. But for you . . . I couldn't do it. That's just it. When I read your letter, and then I met you in person, I thought that . . . well, I thought that you might be the one. And when we kissed, I knew for sure, and that's why I pushed you away—before it went too far."

"Before what went to far?" I asked.

She pointed at my neck. "Touch yourself," she said, "There on your neck where I kissed you."

I did, felt a small wound, and pulling my hand away, I saw blood. "You were sucking my blood?"

She nodded glumly. "Yes," she said. "But I stopped in time. You may feel a little weak for a short time, but that is all. I stopped because when I tasted you, the essence of you, I knew you were the one."

"The one what?" I asked.

"Even vampires can love," she said. "Isn't there a saying that there's someone for everyone? Well, it's essentially true, but in the case of a vampire it's more than basic. It's part of the deal."

"What do you mean?"

"I mean that all vampires have soul mates. We don't run around making other vampires. We only make other vampires out of our true soul mates—sometimes a good friend, more often, a lover. Some vampires find theirs right away, while others search for years before finding the right person."

"So you're lost love is a vampire, too?"

"Oh yes," she said, bitterly. "And that's why I have to go now. He's coming here, this night, and I can sense him drawing closer to me."

"But why would you leave?" I asked. "If he's your soul mate, why can't you be with him? I would give anything—anything at all—to have my Anaka back."

"Because he's not who he was then. He's become a true monster, feeding on those he chooses without regard. Two hundred years ago, he was nearly killed by a mob of peasants, would be vampire killers, outside of London. He was horribly scarred, physically and emotionally by the ordeal. He lost his love of the world, and those in it, and slowly, I lost my love for him."

Thinking on this, I felt a little bad for her. "What about you, Alexa? How long have you been alone, looking for another soul mate?"

"Most of the last two hundred years," she said. "But who's counting?"

"Will I become a vampire now?" I asked, a little frightened.

"No," she said. "It didn't go nearly far enough. I stopped in plenty of time."

"I'm flattered, I guess," I said. "It's not everyday that one meets a vampire who thinks you might be their soul mate." I paused, thinking, and added, "That is that what you meant when you said you thought I was the one, isn't it? That I am your soul mate?"

"I haven't changed my mind, Jameson," she said. "You *are* my soul mate."

"But I can't be a vampire!" I said.

"Not yet," she said.

"Not yet?" I echoed.

"I can tell you're not ready yet. Not ready to make a true commitment. This is a true commitment, Jameson. There's no turning back, no divorce. It's forever and ever, amen." Then she added, "I don't mean us per se, because even soul mates can lose their way in the darkness. Love can fade and people can change. I mean becoming a vampire. There's no turning back into a human."

"I think you're wrong, Alexa. I'm ready for a commitment, but not this fast and not this sudden. And I don't think I'll ever be ready to be a vampire."

"You will one day," she said. "I can see it when I look at you. I can taste it." She turned, scanning the pier with her eyes. "He's coming closer, now. You must go."

"I think you're wrong about me, Alexa. If you think I'm destined to be your soul mate—to be a vampire for God's sake—then fine. But I'm glad you didn't turn me into a vampire or kill me. This is just way too much, Alexa, and way too weird. Thanks for an interesting night." I turned, and began walking down the pier. For some distance, I was alone with my morbid thoughts.

"Jameson, wait!" she cried, running towards me.

I turned. "What is it?"

"It wasn't my choice, you know," she said. "To be a vampire."

"I didn't assume so," I said. "Who would choose that?"

"You'd be surprised," she said. "But the point is that the vampire who made me didn't ask, or give me a choice. He simply said, 'You are one of us' and made me what I am. He was a good person, but he had no sense of timing and certainly no subtlety. I'm giving you the choice I didn't have."

Looking at her then, with the city and ocean sounds surrounding us, I almost said yes. Part of me wanted to scream yes with all my strength. But I couldn't then, and I could sense her fear, too. Whatever her maker had become, it scared her. And if it scared a vampire, it must be quite horrible. Her observation of me had been correct. I wasn't ready for an eternal commitment, not really. And I certainly wasn't ready to face a scorned lover from her past, who happened to be an angry vampire. "I'm sorry, Alexa, or whatever your real name is. I can't. Not now, and probably not ever."

"I understand," she said. "But one day, you'll change your mind."

"Maybe," I said.

"Love is funny that way," she said. "Once you feel it for somebody, once the fire has begun to burn, there's no turning back, only turning away. Sooner or later, your heart leads you to find that person again, and to warm yourself next to whatever flame they will offer."

"Maybe," I repeated.

She tensed slightly, and I could see her fangs once more. "I have to go now," she said. "The hunger grows. It's long past time for my dinner. I will lead him away from here, and you. I can sense your fear." She began walking away, when she stopped and looked back at me. "We are connected now, Jameson. When you are ready, I will know it, and we will meet again."

And with that, she walked away. Her long red hair flashing like fire in the lights along the pier. I watched her until I couldn't see her anymore, thinking about what she'd said. Thinking how cold it was at home with no one there and nothing to comfort me but old memories of a wife three years in her grave. Thinking that she was probably right—sooner or later, I'd want to be warm again.

I returned home, alone, and wondering.

* * * *

Two weeks later I saw him for the first time. I was walking home from a late night walk to the corner store for ice cream, and I saw a man who had once been quite attractive, but now bore the scars of someone who had been in a horrible fire. He walked behind me for some distance, and I waited, trying to control my urge to run, certain that at any moment he would pounce on me, perhaps drain my body of blood and leave me lifeless on the pavement, a bizarre headline for the following day's newspaper. Finally, with my heart racing, I couldn't stand it any longer, and I turned to face him, only to find myself alone on the sidewalk. With my breath rasping in my throat, I made my way home.

That night, I wondered how long it would be before we actually met. His intention, no doubt, was to confront me, perhaps kill me, so that I could no longer be of interest to Alexa. Had he found her that night, I wondered? I didn't know for sure. I had long since realized that Alexa was right about one thing. I thought about her constantly, and was soon searching for her along the pier, and once, I accosted a red-haired woman who was perfectly human—and quite startled by the madman grabbing her and calling her Alexa.

Sometimes, during quiet moments alone, it seemed as though we were connected, that I could feel her inside of me. I wondered where she was, if she was safe from the machinations of the monster that now stalked me. I wanted to talk to her again. To watch the light play in her hair like little children made of fire. How had he found me? Was he watching us that night from some great distance? Could he feel her, as I seemed to?

For another month, I watched for him. Sometimes catching the merest glimpse of his shadowed form in the distance. Once, I thought I saw him staring through my window, but when I looked closer, I saw only my reflection. Seven weeks after Alexa had gone, her lost soul mate and I met, though not in the way I had expected.

Shortly after sundown, the doorbell rang. When I answered it, he was there. The scarred face I had seen earlier stared in at me, and I jumped backwards, holding up my hands to ward him off.

"Stop," he said. "If I meant to harm you, no force in the world could stop me." His voice carried a vague accent, and was quite deep.

My pulse was racing. "What do you want from me?" I asked.

"Nothing you will not freely give," he said. "You have already—in a sense—done what I desire. I merely wish confirmation."

"Why have you been following me?"

"To see what kind of man you were," he said, and then gestured into the house. "May I come in?" he asked, "So that we may speak as civilized beings?"

"I've done my homework, vampire," I said. "You cannot enter here unless you are invited."

He smiled, and stepped into the entryway. "Not everything you read is accurate, fool. A writer, even one such as yourself, should know that. I was being polite."

I nodded. "Okay," I said. "Come on in, as it seems I cannot stop you."

He stepped the rest of the way into the house, his long stride carrying him past me and into the living room. He was quite tall, and moved with easy grace. His hair was long and black, and tied into a ponytail with a length of dark silk. Turning back to me, I saw that his eyes were dark blue. "Why don't you sit down," he said, "and we can talk."

I sat in the wingback chair I preferred and gestured him into the other. "Alright, talk," I said.

"You are a direct man," he said. "That's good. I find it refreshing."

"I think we can dispense with the compliments and polite necessities for the most part," I said. "What do you want?"

"Your word," he said. "Your word that you will not pursue Alexa. She is mine, for now and eternity."

"I think you're mistaken," I said. "She is her own. You can't own somebody like that. Love doesn't work that way."

"I think your opinion of such matters is of little value. I made Alexa, when your long dead ancestors were still trying to fight off the natives of this land. I have loved her from the first, and she has loved me. She cannot deny that. She mustn't."

"For someone as old as you apparently are, you haven't garnered a lot of wisdom in those years. Love is something that cannot be permanent by its very nature—it takes work and sacrifice, it is built on those foundations, not on a flimsy foundation of want or desire. Like any fire, if you leave it untended long enough, it will go out."

"So, you're wise enough to instruct me in the ways of love between immortals? Bah! Alexa doesn't understand me. That is all. She thinks I

am some sort of monster, when all I am is a realist. Humans despise and fear us. Caring about them will only get us hurt or killed, because sooner or later, humans—who are no more than animals that walk upright—will strike out at that which they despise and fear."

I was frightened of him, then. Truly scared. Not because he could kill me, though that was scary enough in its own right, but because he saw us as animals. And when you see something as an animal, it usually has less value in your eyes than others of your own kind. I thought of Alexa, and I knew why she had left this . . . thing disguised as a man. "What is your name?" I asked.

"My name?" he said. "What does it matter? Give me your word, and I will leave you in peace. You will not see me—or her—ever again."

"Your name, please?" I said again. I was still thinking of Alexa, and then I could feel her. Somehow, I could feel her as though she were in my arms, and I felt safe.

"Don't be foolish, human," he said. "I do not like games."

"This is no game," I said. "Your name—what is it?"

"Very well," he said. "My name is Demetri Vasile."

"Okay then, Demetri Vasile, I'm Jameson Servais, and I cannot give you my word."

He looked at me then, and I watched in that slow moment as his eyes turned from their dark blue color to the icy blue of arctic frost. He hissed. "Do you wish to die, fool?" he asked.

"No," I said. "I don't. But I'm not a liar, and I won't append my name to a lie. I love her, which is more than you can truly say, having kept her away from everything she's wanted for two hundred years. She was right, you are a monster."

He leapt to his feet then, and I was certain that he would reach out and kill me with one blow. His fangs were bared, and I found that his eyes, which had changed again to become the color of blood, impaled me. "Then you've made your choice," he snarled, reaching towards me.

When Alexa spoke from the doorway, he froze in amazement. "Demetri! Stop!"

He turned to her. "Alexa!"

And then it happened, so fast that I barely saw it. Her arm whipped forward, and a long wooden spike flew across the room and buried itself in Demetri's chest. He howled, an animal sound of rage, and pain, and love finally broken and betrayed. I stood, stunned, as she crossed to his writhing form on the floor. He tried to pull the stake out, and couldn't seem to find the strength.

"I'm sorry, Demetri. You don't know how sorry. But now it's truly over, as it should have been years ago. The stake is barbed, and you cannot remove it. In a few more moments, all the years you have cheated death as a vampire will return for you, and you will be nothing but a withered husk that will blow away in the night wind."

He looked up at her then, and I could suddenly see the man he'd once been. "Alexa," he said. "Why?"

"Because you are no longer my soul mate," she said. "The bond is broken." I felt a strange internal snap, and the connection I felt with her grew even stronger.

"You cannot!" he said. "To be soul mates is to be together forever."

"You are not who you were," she said. "I'm sorry."

His struggles slowed, and age lines began to appear on his face, wrapping around the scars from that long ago bonfire. "I love you, Alexa," he whispered.

She shook her head. "No, Demetri, you don't. Or it never would have ended this way."

Suddenly, his whole form stiffened, and he howled in anguish one last time. Alexa and I stood silent, while the returning years took their terrible toll. Finally, he fell still, and his clothing collapsed in on itself. Nothing remained but the cloth, the stake, and a few pieces of bone.

She turned to me, then, tears the color of blood tracing paths down her face making a bizarre compliment to her hair. I wrapped her in my arms and held her, very glad to be alive and with her once again. "I loved him once," she said. "Long ago."

"I know," I said.

For nearly half an hour we stood just like that. Our arms around each other, knowing that the storm was over, and wondering how we'd managed to survive. Then, she gently pushed me away. "I have to go," she said.

"Why?" I asked. "I want you to stay. I was wrong before. I am ready."

She smiled at me then, and took her hand. "No, Jameson. You weren't wrong before. You're not ready for this yet. I didn't destroy Demetri for you, or even for us. I did it for me, and even for him."

"I love you, Alexa, but I guess you know that."

"I do, Jameson. And I love you, too. But you need more time to truly accept what becoming a vampire means. I'm giving you the time."

I didn't say anything, realizing she was right. For the first time since Anaka had died, I was truly glad to be alive. I nodded in acceptance, and said, "You won't forget about us, will you?"

"No," she said, softly. "I will be waiting for you, and when the time is right, I will come and we will be together." She reached down and gathered up what was left of Demetri. "I have to go now. It's getting late."

I nodded again. "When will I see you again?"

"When it's time, Jameson. When you are ready."

I kissed her then, once, softly, and I could see that this was not easy for her either. "You're right," I said, wanting to make this easier for her, maybe even easier for me. "I'm not ready yet. But I will be one day, and on that day, I want you to come for me. We can be warmth for each other."

"You are already my fire," she said. Then, quietly, she left.

And when I knew for certain she was gone, I sat down in the wingback chair, put my head in my shaking hands, and cried.

* * *

Many long months have passed since that night. And I think I'm almost ready now to face what being a vampire really means. Sometimes, I can feel Alexa nearby, so I know she is watching over me. Does she keep me safe from whatever other creatures hunt the night? I do not know.

Of course, I don't read the personals anymore—there is no real need, even for the grim amusement I might feel once again, now that I have found love. At night, I lie in my cold bed and wonder if this will be the night she comes. I wonder if she is not also waiting to be ready herself, if the wounds she must have felt when she destroyed her lost soul mate Demetri have begun to heal? Those wounds will heal, in time.

And we have a long time. I can wait for her, though I am impatient to hold her, wrap her long hair in my hands and taste her lips. When we are both ready, she will know it. She will come to me in my darkened bedroom, my angel of death, and love, and lust. When that night comes, whatever warmth she brings, I will welcome her. I will bear my throat to her gentle fangs. And we will consummate our relationship with a kiss at midnight, in blood the color of roses, the color of her hair, the color of fire.

THE TRUE BLOOD OF MARTYRS

RACHEL CAINE

*T*he invitation to Jinx's funeral came in the mail on Saturday before Halloween. It arrived in a gold-lined envelope the color of heavy cream, but the sheet of paper inside was black printed with silver ink.

> *You are invited to join*
> *Mr. Ivan Jenks*
> *for a celebration of his death*
> *beginning at Midnight, October 31*
> *in this Year of Our Lord 1997*
> *and ending promptly at dawn*
> *All Saint's Day.*

The address below was that of a very old graveyard, one so old it had long ago been abandoned by those who thought cemeteries should resemble suburban back yards. The Elysian was an overgrown tangle of leaning headstones, memory heavy as jasmine in the air.

I thought in sheer disgust, oh, not again. I picked up the telephone and dialed his number, listened to the hollow rings. After three of them the receiver lifted with a click, and Jinx's cool, faintly English voice said, "Helen, I've been expecting your call."

"It's not funny," I said. "I'm not coming."

"It's not meant to be funny, and of course you will. You always do, Helen. Don't feel obliged to bring anything. I can't take it with me."

And he hung up, a gentle, definite disconnection that left me standing in the middle of my kitchen with the telephone in my hand. I should have been angry with him, or at the very least annoyed. I was afraid.

I had known him for more than five hundred years.

The blurring growl of the engine soothed my anger. I drove out to one of the freeways, a marvelous wide stretch of blacktop where I could fly in peace.

Why? There was no answer to the question. The Jinx I knew was a creature of air and fire, full of impenetrable hungers. He was subject to bizarre fits of melancholia and spasms of drama, and his humor could only be called twisted.

Few, if any, of the others, understood that Jinx's little funerals were not jokes.

I left behind the glaring amusement-park brilliance of the city doing a smooth, purring ninety miles an hour. My mind emptied. The night closed around me, softened by the stars, and it seemed at this hour that I was indeed flying, through a space that held no other life.

I closed my eyes and allowed my flesh to begin to mist. I went weightless. I heard the growl of an oncoming engine and kept my eyes closed, squeezed them shut until tears leaked from under the lids and whipped back cool on my cheeks, driven by the wind through the open window.

A truck horn blared. I felt the hot wash of headlights and heard the indignant squeal of tires as the oncoming truck locked its brakes and swerved to avoid me.

Perhaps I would hit it. My eyelids trembled, my hands spasmed on the hot softness of the steering wheel, but I held my eyes tight shut.

I heard the trucker screaming curses as I floated away into the night, the smell of burning oil and rubber hot in my nose. I opened my eyes and saw an unbroken silent roadway ahead, the stark white stare of the moon, and I laughed.

I laughed until it frightened me.

I stopped at an all-night gas station. Spoiled child that I am, I long for the days of uniformed servants and smiling Texaco men wiping dust from my windshield. I bore the self-service pump in silence, presented my card to the teenaged clerk, and turned away to stare into the darkness. Moths fluttered like tattered leaves in the lights. I closed my eyes and listened to the whisper of their wings.

"Ma'am?" The boy interrupted the music with his harsh Texas drawl. "Here y'go. Sign ri' chere."

He pushed the slip across the counter toward me. I signed it and looked up at the video camera that jutted its arrogant chin from the wall.

It was a simple matter to erase it. They'd find nothing but black when they attempted to play it tomorrow, or the next day, when the county sheriffs finished their pitiful investigation and the boy was buried. I kept both copies of the gas receipt and put them in my purse.

"Ma'am? Ah need th' white copy—"

"No you don't," I soothed him, reached across the counter and put two fingers precisely at the pulse on his neck. He froze, staring at me; he'd be thinking wild thoughts of pornographic fantasies, Penthouse Letters come to life. "You don't need anything at all."

I pulled him across the counter and bit. His soul flowed over my tongue, hot and red and tasting of the oil under his fingernails. His name

was Clarence, and his brother had always called him Clare before his brother was hit by a train and his mother got so tired all the time, her fingers shaking as she sewed little pieces of needlepoint to sell and his friend Mary Ellen pregnant and crying on his shoulder asking him to marry her but he couldn't he wouldn't and Mary Ellen gone on a bus to California and no goodbyes, ever again.

He faded out of me like a whisper. I swallowed the last of Clarence and let his flesh slip out of my hands. His chin hit the counter hard enough to crack bone but it didn't matter and would never matter to Clarence again.

* * *

The night of October 31 dawned cloudy, the air icy as it whipped around corners to surprise. Children avoided the houses of strangers. A brave few skipped and giggled in darkness, trailed by cloaks made of folded sheets and comet-sprinkles of glitter.

I was determined that I wouldn't pander to Jinx's insanity this time. I would not be a witness. But as the hours slipped by, as the night grew quiet outside my door and hunger made me restless, I was seized by a need to see him. What if it was the last time? What if I failed him, after all these years?

I reached the Elysium Cemetery less than an hour from sunrise, shading my car under a huge oak tree from the fitful moonlight. As I walked the little distance to the creaking iron gates—padlocked still— I heard the sounds of a party in progress.

I misted through the bars with little thought, and shrugged off the inevitable discomfort as I joined the solid world again. I took the chalk-white, overgrown path under looming branches and past damp, empty-faced angels hovering over darkness. I hated cemeteries. How very like Jinx to find the one thing I could not abide.

There were about ten gathered in a small clearing toward the back
of the graveyard; they'd spread out blankets, like hungry picnickers at
midday. I knew them all, of course; there were not so many of us that
we were strangers. Charity McCollum gave me a quick glance and nod,
no more greeting than that; we had never been close. Luther rose from
where he sat at her side, came to me and took both hands to kiss. He
was an old-fashioned gentleman, was Luther, impeccable in Regency
dress and old world manners. I wondered where the devil he'd found
the costume he wore tonight—fantastic silver and blue.

There was blood smeared over his face and down the side of his coat.
They had, indeed, been dining, though not productively—no mortals
about. The more perverse among us—like Luther—fed upon other
vampires merely for the entertainment value. It had the same value as
a thirty mortal drinking seawater.

"Helen, my dearest love, where have you been? It's simply been ages."
Luther's forced cooing reminded me of bad melodramas put on in the
prisons in France, where aristos like Luther had waited for the kiss of
Madame la guillotine. "I wish you'd keep in touch. I never know what
you're doing."

"I've been busy," I said, kissed his cold, marble-blue cheek and tasted
the scent of his last kill rising like perfume from his skin. A boy, about
twelve. If I concentrated, I knew that I'd be able to unroll that life like a
carpet into the darkness. "Where is he?"

"Jinx?" Luther made an elaborate gesture with one lace-frothed hand.
"Over there. Preparing." He rolled his eyes, and I had to agree with him;
this was worse than a joke, it was pointless. There was no death for us.
No end.

There never had been. Jinx knew that better than anyone.

I saw that the picnickers, in the fashion of vampires who grew bored,
had begun to turn on each other. That was no doubt where the blood
on Luther's face came from. We danced this little dance, our kind, out

of the lazy cruelty of boredom; death was a party game, no more or less intriguing than charades. There was even an air of seduction to it—it was the only way we had to connect, as predator and prey.

One or two of those who'd come were young, far younger than I— they had the studied ennui of children who'd grown up knowing how a vampire should act. They were also far more solid than I, or any of the others; they were closer to mortality, their flesh heavy on them. One of them was frightened enough to tremble as Charity rose with ethereal grace and trailed ghostly fingers over her neck.

I dismissed the spectacle of the youngster's death, because someone was approaching out of the mists behind her.

Jinx.

He had come dressed for a funeral—a simple, elegant black suit, a white shirt, a tie. None of Luther's overdone fancy dress, though Jinx would have looked more at home in it. There was something essentially antique about him that even Luther could never hope to attain.

He was a small man, really, but he'd been born to a time when men did not grow so large. Slender, broader in the shoulders than was immediately apparent. His soft blonde hair feathered across his forehead a shade too long for neatness and too short to please current tastes.

I had always loved the lazy elegance of his eyes. The sad humor.

He came around the vampire-child and Charity, who were locked in a silent, desperate embrace of pain, and held out his hand to me. I took it, not knowing quite what to say; this was a different greeting from an old friend, almost formal.

"What do you want most in the world, Helen?" he asked me. Unexpected question. I struggled for the proper tone of sarcasm in my reply.

"Eternal peace at last? Do I get a prize?"

He smiled. Sadness in his pretty eyes.

"Perhaps you will," he said. "Come with me."

We walked off from the party a bit, into a white whisper of fog. Jinx perched on the elaborate marble arm of a cross, and I leaned on the shoulder of a blind angel. He looked up at the fitful sky and shook his head.

"It's never quiet anymore," he said. "That's what I miss most, I suppose. The quiet. When I was breathing you could lie in the fields and listen to the wind and be so alone in the world."

He was talking about the constant, grinding whisper of life; even here, in this tangled garden of the dead, we could hear the bustle of all those mortals moving. Hearts pounding. So many of them now. So few of us.

"There's no point in dwelling on it. You'll become like—" I didn't have to finish, he knew who, or what, I referred to. We had no name for them, officially, but Jinx and I called them the Frozen. They were so old they were worn smooth by the currents of time. Over time, though their features did not change, they acquired an eerie sameness, like eroded statues, and they were so faint in moonlight we saw shadows through them, as if they were made of milky glass.

They terrified all of us, because we knew they were our future.

"I spoke to one," Jinx said. He looked down at the ground, poked an idle toe into the dirt of the grave. "They do remember words, some of them. He didn't remember his name."

The thought of going up to one of the Frozen and striking up a conversation was so ludicrous, so unsettling, that I laughed. He glanced up at me, eyebrows up, and resumed his excavation of the final resting place of Charles Wallace Debbs.

"I'm sure it was a fascinating conversation," I said. "Once you get them started, I'm sure they just ramble on and on about the good old days. Jinx, for pity's sake, the Frozen don't talk. They stare. You're delusional."

"This one spoke." Jinx's voice was so soft I had difficulty separating it from the wind. "He's old, Helen, he knows things we've forgotten. He told me how to die."

I had heard him say it before, more times than I could safely remember. I'd been told before I'd ever met him that Jinx had died by his own hand in mortal life; what a cruel joke, to be resurrected into this existence for eternity. How very discerning of God. As if in retaliation for that cosmic jest, death had been Jinx's continuing passion ever since.

He had, before this same appreciative audience, had himself drowned, burned, dismembered, and on one extremely memorable occasion served himself as a funeral! He had been buried with his head removed and the Host inserted where his heart had been cut away. He had been staked through the chest, in the grand old Hammer Films tradition.

I did not think I could bear to watch it again, most especially to watch him rise again the next night, whole and untouched and tragically disappointed. And yet, with all of eternity stretching out in front of me, what choice did I have? One could only spend so much time with mortals before time began to drag like insistent hands, wearing you away, scouring you smooth. Within our demented ranks, we could pretend, for a time, to be alive yet—and pretend that a future among the Frozen did not loom ever closer.

"So what is it this time?" I forced sarcasm into my tone; he would expect it from me. We'd ever been flint and stone. "You know, I haven't seen a really good Crucifixion in a long time. You'd make such a lovely suffering Christ. Or how about acid? Very entertaining. And I'm sure you haven't tried drawing and quartering in a few hundred years, though I'm not sure where we'd get the horses—"

"I'm serious," he said. I shook my head and sighed.

"You always are, with me. You know they think you're a clown, don't you? All of them? They come here to laugh at you." And I can't bear that, I wanted to tell him, but that was a confession that went too deep. Jinx did not encourage that kind of intimacy, and for that matter, neither did I.

Jinx smiled that charming, slightly odd smile of his, eyes wickedly amused. "They come here because there's nothing else to do but think

about eternity. And kill. I don't mind it that they laugh; at least they still can. You don't laugh enough, Helen."

"Ha," I said, "ha. I have nothing to laugh about, now, do I?"

Jinx didn't reply. His eyes gestured behind me. I turned to see— nothing. Trees shifting uneasily in the wind. Dead leaves fluttering. Marble angels staring.

Not an angel.

A Frozen.

He was naked, the palest tinge of blue in the white of his skin, and there was no more sense of life from him than from the marble I leaned against. I shivered as I moved closer to Jinx. I hadn't sensed even a hint of the Frozen's approach.

There was no smell on him, either. No sense of a kill, either recent or fading. It was as if he had never lived at all.

"Want to laugh now?" Jinx asked. I shushed him with chilled fingers on his arm.

"What does he want?"

Jinx shrugged in reply. He seemed perfectly at ease. After what felt like a cobwebbed eternity, the Frozen's head might have moved a fraction. Or not. I never saw his eyes move, but by some slow process he began to look at me. It was the most uncomfortable stare I had ever endured, like the unblinking attention of a god.

He wasn't the only one who'd come. No sense of their arrival, no sound, but there were more Frozen in the shadows. One was a woman, her body thinly covered by a torn gauzy robe, her tangled hair fluttering in the wind. I almost recognized her, and was afraid to follow that train of thought. It was so hard to focus on their faces, eroded into sameness by time.

Jinx, looking on this chilling and remarkable sight, checked his wristwatch and said, "We still have a little while. I wonder if—"

He hesitated. Jinx, who never hesitated. The strangeness of it drew me even from my unnerved study of the Frozen.

He couldn't meet my eyes. "I wonder if you'd do me the honor of a dance?"

"A dance?" I blurted. "Here? Now?"

"We never did dance before," he said, and still without meeting my eyes, he pushed himself to his feet and held out his hand to me. "Please."

No music. No room to dance, and why in the hell did he think I'd want to dance at a moment like this? I was exasperated and off balance, and could think of nothing in the world I wanted less to do.

Until he raised his eyes and looked at me.

I was all elbows and angles, unused to this kind of closeness; I felt it in Jinx too, a different stiffness of his body where it touched mine. His hands around my waist held me at a precise, almost religious distance. I rested my arms awkwardly on his shoulders as we began to slowly move, no rhythm at all, both painfully aware of the ridiculous truth.

Jinx began to move more confidently, drawing me with him; his hands relaxed on me and pulled me just a shade closer. I didn't remember the last time I'd danced—surely never danced like this—but all the same he led me into a slow, delicate waltz around tombstones. Around us the world turned like an unwinding clock, the faces of the Frozen reflecting moonlight and emptiness. I closed my eyes to them and, without any conscious thought, rested my head on Jinx's shoulder.

He was humming, music so faint I felt it rather than heard it; a tune I remembered from centuries ago. I smiled and turned my face into the hollow of his neck. Our bodies melted together, and we danced slower now, slower, until we were standing still, clasped together like lovers under the moonlight.

I raised my head. Jinx's lips met mine in one gentle, sweet, empty kiss. I tasted memories on his tongue, but they weren't his own. He had fed on a woman, and for a blinding instant I hated her enough to kill her again.

"It's nearly dawn," he said.

"No." I held on to him when he tried to let me go. "Jinx, tell me what you're doing. Tell me."

His eyes met mine, and centuries passed between us. Thousands of deaths. Blood flowing in rivers. What were we? Devils? Damned? We'd never found an answer to the question. But Jinx had continued to ask. His courage, at least, had never failed.

"I'm going to sit down," he said slowly, "and I'm going to wait for dawn. It's that simple."

I laughed. Threw his hands away from me with contempt. The fool. I should have stayed home.

"Wait for dawn?" I repeated. "Jinx, you're madder than Luther. It isn't possible. We've all tried it. If it was as simple as that, there'd be nothing but ashes left of any of us!"

We were not able to abide the sun, that much was true. Either we sought out shelter and darkness, or we suffered an intense, maddening agony for the instant of the sun's touch, and then we misted away.

And at sunset, we misted back. Whole. Untouched.

Jinx knew that.

"Have you tried?" he asked. Jinx, who never raised his voice, was almost sharp with me. "No, Helen, have you tried? Because I have. For the last two years, I have tried and I have failed, but I've been burned. You simply have to refuse to mist. You have to will yourself to burn, and you have to do it until you are gone."

"It's impossible."

"No. I've stayed in the sun for as much as three hours, but it wasn't enough. But this time—this time I will do it. I will stay in the sun the full turning of the earth, until the sun goes down, and I will die." Jinx searched my face. "You believe me?"

No one could do it. No one ever had.

"Yes," I said in a whisper. There was something in his eyes that forced

me to believe it. "You don't have to do this. Wait a little. One more dance. What's another year or two?"

He regarded me quite seriously. Touched my cheek with fingers that were too gentle for someone who'd spent centuries killing.

"I lose time, Helen. Hours. Sometimes days. I realize suddenly that the world has moved on and left me behind, and I know that one time I will sink into that sleep and I'll be like them. If I don't die, I will be Frozen." Jinx raised my fingers to his lips. "Help me."

The party was ending. Some of the picnickers had already misted away, bored with deathplay; a few lay tumbled in various stages of disarray on the lawn. Luther was still there; his laughter guided us through the tangled trees, into the clearing already taking on the colors of the day world. Dawn was coming.

"Charming party," Luther said. He checked the drape of the lace at his cuffs, flicked drops of blood from his fingers. Charity lay still embraced with the vampire child at his feet. They were both dead, their throats torn. "Really must be going, my dears—places to go, people to eat. Do let me know if you manage to die, won't you? Rap on a table. Send me a spirit message."

From behind me, Jinx said, "Luther." He received Luther's complete attention, the pale blue eyes suddenly very serious.

"Have you ever thought," Luther said, "that this is God's will? What did you do to deserve this, Jinx? You, Helen? I know what I did, and I can tell you, I'm not so very eager to face a God who made me."

His seriousness dropped away like a shed cloak, and he made a kissing sound toward me. "Helen, dearest, do keep in touch. My door is always open, et cetera, et cetera. We might have quite a lot of fun, you and I. Like the old days."

He misted away in a showman's puff of fog before the words were even complete, a ghost among ghosts, and when I closed my eyes I felt his chill pass through me.

Good bye, Luther. I was done with him. With all of them. Was this how Jinx had survived for the past five hundred years, with this curious aching emptiness? No wonder he was peculiar.

They were all gone. The sun was coming, like a pressure against my chest, pushing me away. One by one, the bodies of the dead faded like smoke, some into the ground, some into the air.

But not the Frozen. There were five I could see, more I half-glimpsed in the trees. They waited silently, growing ever fainter as the light rose, but never quite gone. They had found shelter, and they were waiting.

Jinx took my hand and sat down on a headstone big enough for two; we perched there together, companionably silent, as birds began to wake and sing, the air to grow warm on our faces.

"Helen," he said as the first crescent of the sun appeared in the distance. "I don't believe I ever said that I love you."

Fire. Fire poured through my veins, into my flesh, eating me alive from within—a pain beyond any mortal pain, beyond death, a pain that had no ending.

I endured it for as long as I could, holding Jinx's trembling hand. Our skin was blackening, crisping away from us. Tears boiled unshed in my eyes. I felt myself being stripped away, layer by layer, a cruelty that was beyond anything I had ever known.

I do not know how long it was before I let go. Not so long. Perhaps ten minutes. I heard Jinx cry out in despair as he felt me slip away—he reached for me with burning arms but I couldn't stay, I spread myself wide on the air and felt, if not peace, then at least an end to pain.

My last sight, before I faded entirely, was of Jinx, a burning torch, his eyes the only thing of him still recognizable. And around him, bearing silent witness, the milky shadows of the Frozen.

* * *

I misted back at nightfall, within touching distance of where I had vanished. Cool moonlight. Silence. Around me, the unmoving white glimmer of the Frozen. None of the others had bothered to come back.

He'd failed, of course. No one could bear that agony, no matter how pure their desire. I saw him sitting exactly where I'd left him, on top of a weathered old tombstone large enough for two.

"Jinx," I said. He looked whole again, though the experience had left him looking oddly—

I took a step forward as he turned his head toward me, and smiled. Really smiled. The joy in his eyes was heartbreaking.

"Jinx," I whispered. I closed my eyes and tasted him on my tongue, ripe with life, heavy with blood.

Not dead.

Mortal.

I almost fainted when he touched me; the ecstasy of that was more than I could stand. He was every need I'd ever had fulfilled, every desire consummated. I wanted him in ways I could not begin to comprehend.

I wanted to drink him down like a flood. I knew how his life would taste, so rich and delicate; the rarest of wines. The food of God.

His warm, warm hands brushed my cold face. I turned blindly into his touch, breathed deep of his pulse point, heard his heart laboring in my ears. Oh, Jinx. You magnificent fool.

"You see?" he said. "I waited for you. I knew you'd come back."

I couldn't answer. He guided my lips to his wrist, and as I kissed the thin skin I felt him shudder against me, as transported as I. We were one, Jinx and I. We had always been one.

"Drink," he whispered.

I did.

The blur of his life gathered me in its embrace, whirled me into the blaze that was Jinx, brilliance and compassion and hunger and need, the cold fire of a love he could neither have or forget. My face was the only

light in his darkness. And at this moment, when our souls merged and flowed together, we were at peace.

His heart fluttered. I would have pulled away, but his warm hand held me in place, and I couldn't stop myself, drawing him into me further and further, consuming him whole.

Dead weight in my hands. I cried out, but it was only a shadow of the anguish I felt; I had not meant to—

—to kill him—

Oh, Jinx. I had been a knife aimed at his heart by his own hand.

I held him in my arms, rocked his limp body through the long, long night as cold stars watched.

Just before dawn, a cold hand brushed my cheek, and I looked up to see the moonstruck face of a Frozen. With slow, deliberate care, he reached down for Jinx.

"No," I said. His face was completely unmoving, but I thought I saw a flicker of compassion in those dead eyes. "Not yet."

I cradled the body close. He had cooled during the night, as flesh does, but under my own skin I still knew warmth, and sunlight, and joy. In my veins, I was Jinx.

"The sun's coming," I said to Jinx. He was so heavy. So very real to me, more real than anything had been in the world for hundreds of years. "You didn't tell me how long it would take."

His blood told me it would be a long death. I was prepared for it this time. Jinx had endured. How could I do less?

As the sun's corrosive light touched me, I kissed Jinx's cool lips one last time, and gave myself up. I braced myself for the fire, but instead—

—instead, my skin tingled with the touch of clean warmth. Pale skin shading to palest pink.

In the utter silence, I heard my heart begin to beat. The clock of life, counting down.

Jinx's gift of blood and life. I was mortal.

I kissed Jinx again in silent gratitude, tears streaming down my cheeks to glitter on his cheeks. I closed my eyes to the brilliant dazzle of morning and listened, rapt, to the beating of my heart.

Forgiven.

And now I know my path. I will sit here, like Jinx before me, in the full warm embrace of the sun. With nightfall the Frozen will return, and I will offer my blood, and with my blood, the gift Jinx brought us at such great cost.

Death.

As I listen to the beating of my heart whisper his name, I know, without any shadow of doubt, that he is waiting for me beyond the sun.

$\mathcal{T}$HE BEAUTIFUL, $\mathcal{T}$HE DAMNED

KRISTINE KATHRYN RUSCH

ONE

I come from the Middle West, an unforgiving land with little or no
tolerance for imagination. The wind blows harsh across the prairies,
and the snows fall thick. Even with the conveniences of the modern
age, life is dangerous there. To lose sight of reality, even for one short
romantic moment, is to risk death.

I didn't belong in that country, and my grandfather knew it. I was his
namesake, and somehow, being the second Nick Carraway in a family
where the name had a certain mystique had forced that mystique upon
me. He had lived in the East during the twenties, and had had grand
adventures, most of which he would not talk about. When he returned to
St. Paul in 1928, he met a woman—my grandmother Nell—and with her
solid, common sense had shed himself of the romance and imagination
that had led to his adventures in the first place.

Although not entirely. For when I announced, fifty years later, that I
intended to pursue my education in the East, he paid four years of Ivy
League tuition. And, when I told him, in the early eighties, that, despite

my literary background and romantic nature, I planned a career in the securities business, he regaled me with stories of being a bond man in New York City in the years before the crash.

He died while I was still learning the art of the cold call, stuck on the sixteenth floor of a windowless high-rise, in a tiny cubicle that matched a hundred other tiny cubicles, distinguished only by my handprint on the phone set and the snapshots of my family thumbtacked to the indoor-outdoor carpeting covering the small barrier that separated my cubicle from all the others. He never saw the house in Connecticut which, although it was not grand, was respectable, and he never saw my rise from a cubicle employee to a man with an office. He never saw the heady Reagan years, although he would have warned me about the awful Black Monday well before it appeared. For despite the computers, jets, and televised communications, the years of my youth were not all that different from the years of his.

He never saw Fitz either, although I knew, years later, when my mother mailed me my grandfather's diaries, that my grandfather would have understood my mysterious neighbor, too.

* * *

My house sat at the bottom of a hill, surrounded by trees whose russet leaves are—in my mind—in a state of perpetual autumn. I think the autumn melancholy comes from the overlay of hindsight upon what was, I think, the strangest summer of my life, a summer which, like my grandfather's summer of 1925, I do not discuss, even when asked. In that tiny valley, the air always had a damp chill and rich smell of loam. The scent grew stronger upon that winding dirt path that led to Fitz's house on the hill's crest—not a house really, but more of a mansion in the conservative New England style, white walls hidden by trees, with only the wide walk and the entry visible from the gate. Once behind, the

walls and windows seemed to go on forever, and the manicured lawn with its neatly mowed grass and carefully arranged marble fountains seemed like a throwback from a simpler time.

The house had little life in the daytime, but at night the windows were thrown open and cars filled the driveway. The cars were all sleek and dark—blue Saabs and midnight BMWs, black Jaguars, and ebony Carreras. Occasionally a white stretch limo or a silver DeLorean would mar the darkness, but those guests rarely returned for a second visit, as if someone had asked them to take their ostentation elsewhere. Music trickled down the hill with the light, usually music of a vanished era, waltzes and marches and Dixieland jazz, music both romantic and danceable, played to such perfection that I envied Fitz his sound system until I saw several of the better known New York Philharmonic members round the corner near my house early on a particular Saturday evening.

Laughter, conversation and the tinkle of ice against fine crystal filled the gaps during the musicians' break, and in those early days, as I sat on my porch swing and stared up at the light, I imagined parties like those I had only seen on film—slender, beautiful women in glittery gowns, and athletic men who wore tuxedos like a second skin, exchanging witty and wry conversation under a dying moon.

I never trudged up the hill, although later I learned I could have, and dropped into a perpetual party that never seemed to have a guest list; but I still had enough of my Midwestern politeness to wait for an invitation and enough of my practical Midwestern heritage to know that such an invitation would never come.

* * *

Air conditioners have done little to change Manhattan in the summer. If anything, the heat from their exhausts adds to the oppression in the air, the stench of garbage rotting on the sidewalks and the smell

of sweaty human bodies pressed too close. Had my cousin Arielle not discovered me, I might have spent the summer in the cool loam of my Connecticut home, monitoring the markets through my personal computer, and watching Fitz's parties with a phone wedged between my shoulder and ear.

Arielle always had an ethereal, otherworldly quality. My sensible aunt, with her thick ankles and dishwater-blonde hair, must have recognized that quality in the newborn she had given birth to in New Orleans, and committed the only romantic act of her life by deciding that Arielle was not a Mary or a Louise, family names that had suited Carraways until then.

I had never known Arielle well. At family reunions held on the shores of Lake Superior, she was always a beautiful, unattainable ghost, dressed in white gauze with silver-blonde hair that fell to her waist, wide blue eyes, and skin so pale it seemed as fragile as my mother's bone china. We had exchanged perhaps five words over all those reunions, held each July, and always I had bowed my head and stammered in the presence of such royalty. Her voice was sultry and musical, lacking the long "a"s and soft "d"s that made my other relations sound like all their years of education had made no impression at all.

Why she called me when she and her husband Tom discovered that I had bought a house in a village only a mile from theirs I will never know. Perhaps she was lonely for a bit of family, or perhaps the otherworldliness had absorbed her, even them.

TWO

I drove to Arielle's and Tom's house in my own car, a BMW, navy blue and spit-polished, bought used because all of my savings had gone into the house. They lived on a knoll in a mock-Tudor style house with young saplings that had obviously been transplanted. The lack of tall trees gave the house a vulnerable air, as if the neighbors who lived on higher hills could

look down upon it and find it flawed. The house itself was twice the size of mine, with a central living area flanked by a master bedroom wing and a guest wing, the wings more of an architect's affectation than anything else.

Tom met me at the door. He was a beefy man in his late twenties whose athletic build was beginning to show signs of softening into fat. He still had the thick neck, square jaw, and massive shoulders of an offensive lineman which, of course, he had been. After one season with the Green Bay Packers—in a year unremarkable for its lackluster performance—he was permanently sidelined by a knee injury. Not wanting to open a car dealership that would forever capitalize on his one season of glory, he took his wife and his inheritance and moved east. When he saw me, he clapped his hand on my back as if we were old friends when, in fact, we had only met once, at the last and least of the family reunions.

"Ari's been waiting to see you," he said, and the broad, flat, uneducated vowels of the Midwest brought with them the sense of the stifling summer afternoons of the reunions, children's laughter echoing over the waves of the lake as if their joy would last forever.

He led me through a dark foyer and into a room filled with light. Nothing in the front of the house had prepared me for this room, with its floor to ceiling windows and their view of an English garden beyond the patio. Arielle sat on a loveseat beneath the large windows, the sunlight reflecting off her hair and white dress, giving her a radiance that was almost angelic. She held out her hand, and as I took it, she pulled me close and kissed me on the cheek.

"Nicky," she murmured. "I missed you."

The softness with which she spoke, the utter sincerity in her gaze made me believe her and, as on those, summer days of old, I blushed.

"Not much to do in Connecticut." Tom's booming voice made me draw back. "We've been counting the nails on the walls."

"Now, Tom," Ari said without taking her hand from mine, "we belong here."

I placed my other hand over hers, capturing the fragile fingers for a moment before releasing her. "I rather like the quiet," I said.

"You would," Tom said. He spun on the toe of a well-polished shoe and strode across the hardwood floor, always in shadow despite the light pouring in from the windows.

His abruptness took me aback, and I glanced at Ari. She shrugged. "I think we'll eat on the terrace. The garden is cool this time of day."

"Will Tom join us?"

She frowned in a girlish way, furrowing her brow, and making her appear, for a moment, as if she were about to cry. "He will when he gets off the phone."

I hadn't heard a phone ring, but I had no chance to ask her any more because she placed her slippered feet on the floor and stood. I had forgotten how tiny she was, nearly half my height, but each feature perfectly proportioned. She took my arm and I caught the fresh scent of lemons rising from her warm skin.

"You must tell me everything that's happened to you," she said, and I did. Under her intense gaze my life felt important, my smallest accomplishments a pinnacle of achievement. When I had finished, we had reached the terrace. A glass table, already set for three, stood in the shade of a maple tree. The garden spread before us, lush and green. Each plant had felt the touch of a pruning shears and all were trimmed back so severely that nothing was left to chance.

I pulled out a chair for Ari and she sat daintily, her movements precise. I took the chair across from her, feeling cloddish, afraid that my very size would cause me to break something. I wondered how Tom, with his linebacker's build, felt as he moved through his wife's delicate house.

She shook out a linen napkin and placed it on her lap. A man appeared beside her dressed as a waiter—he had moved so silently that I hadn't noticed him—and poured water into our crystal glasses. He filled Tom's as well, and Ari stared at the empty place.

"I wish he wouldn't call her before lunch," she said. "It disturbs my digestion."

I didn't want to ask what Ari was referring to. I didn't want to get trapped in their private lives.

She sighed and brushed a strand of hair out of her face. "But I don't want to talk about Tom's awful woman. I understand you live next door to the man they call Fitz."

I nodded as the waiter appeared again, bringing fresh bread in a ceramic basket.

"I would love," she said, leaning forward just enough to let me know this was the real reason behind my invitation, "to see the inside of his home."

Tom never joined us. We finished our lunch, walked through the garden, and had mint juleps in the late afternoon, after which everything seemed a bit funnier than it had before. As I left in the approaching-twilight, it felt as if Ari and I had been friends instead of acquaintances linked by a happenstance of birth.

By the time I got home, it was dark. The house retained the heat of the day, and so I went into the backyard and stared at the path that led up to Fitz's mansion. The lights blazed on the hillside, and the sound of laughter washed down to me like the blessing of a god. Perhaps Ari's casual suggestion put something in my mind, or perhaps I was still feeling the effects of the mint juleps, but whatever the cause, I walked up the path feeling drawn to the house like a moth to light.

My shoes crunched against the hardpacked earth, and my legs, unused to such strenuous exercise, began to ache.

Midway up, the coolness of the valley had disappeared, and perspiration made my shirt cling to my chest. The laughter grew closer, and with it, snatches of conversation—women's voices rising with passion, men speaking in low tones, pretending that they couldn't be overheard.

I stopped at a small rock formation just before the final rise to Fitz's house. The rocks extended over the valley below like a platform, and from them, I could see the winding road I had driven that afternoon to Ari's house. A car passed below, and I followed the trail of its headlights until they disappeared into the trees.

As I turned to leave the platform, my desire to reach the party gone, I caught a glimpse of a figure moving against the edge of the path. A man stood on the top of the rise, staring down at the road, as I had. He wore dark evening dress with a white shirt and a matching white scarf draped casually around his neck. The light against his back caused his features to be in shadow—only when he cupped his hands around a burning match to light a cigarette already in his mouth did I get a sense of his face.

He had an older beauty—clean-shaven, almost womanish, with a long nose, high cheekbones, and wide, dark eyes. A kind of beauty that had been fashionable in men when my grandfather was young—the Rudolph Valentino, Leslie Howard look that seemed almost effete by the standards of today.

As he tossed the match away, a waltz started playing behind him, and it gave him context. He stared down at the only other visible point of light—Ari's knoll—and his posture suggested such longing that I half expected the music to swell, to add too much violin in the suggestion of a world half-forgotten.

I knew, without being told, that this was my neighbor. I almost called to him, but felt that to do so would ruin the perfection of the moment. He stared until he finished his cigarette, then dropped it, ground it with his shoe, and slipping his hands in his pockets, wandered back to the party—alone.

THREE

The next afternoon I was lounging on my sofa with the air conditioning off, lingering over the book review section of the Sunday _Times,_ when the crunch of gravel through the open window alerted me to a car in my driveway. I stood up in time to see a black Rolls Royce stop outside my garage. The driver's door opened, and a chauffeur got out, wearing, unbelievably, a uniform complete with driving cap. He walked up to the door, and I watched him as though he were a ghost. He clasped one hand behind his back and, with the other, rang the bell.

The chimes pulled me from my stupor. I opened the door, feeling ridiculously informal in my polo shirt and my stocking feet. The chauffeur didn't seem to notice. He handed me a white invitation embossed in gold and said, "Mr. Fitzgerald would like the pleasure of your company at his festivities this evening."

I stammered something to the effect that I would be honored. The chauffeur nodded and returned to the Rolls, backing it out of the driveway with an ease that suggested years of familiarity. I watched until he disappeared up the hill. Then I took the invitation inside and stared at it, thinking that for once, my Midwestern instincts had proven incorrect.

The parties began at sundown. In the late afternoon, I would watch automobiles with words painted on their sides climb the winding road to Fitz's mansion. _Apple Valley Caterers. Signal Wood Decorators._ Musicians of all stripes, and extra service personnel, preparing for an evening of work that would last long past dawn. By the time I walked up the hill, the sun had set and the lights strung on the trees and around the frame of the house sent a glow bright as daylight down the walk to greet me.

Cars still drove past—the sleek models this time—drivers often visible, but the passengers hidden by shaded windows. As I trudged, my face heated. I looked like a schoolboy, prowling the edges of an adult gathering at which he did not belong.

By the time I arrived, people flowed in and out of the house like moths chasing the biggest light. The women wore their hair short or up, showing off cleavage and dresses so thin that they appeared to be gauze. Most of the men wore evening clothes, some of other eras, long-waisted jackets complete with tails and spats. One man stood under the fake gaslight beside the door, his skin so pale it looked bloodless, his hair slicked back like a thirties gangster, his eyes hollow dark points in his empty face. He supervised the attendants parking the cars, giving directions with the flick of a bejeweled right hand. When he saw me, he nodded, as if I were expected, and inclined his head toward the door.

I became a moth and flitted through. A blonde woman, her hair in a marcel, gripped my arm as if we had come together, her bow-shaped lips painted a dark wine red. The crowd parted for us, and she said nothing, just squeezed my arm, and then disappeared up a flight of stairs to the right.

It was impossible to judge the house's size or decor. People littered its hallways, sprawled along its stairs. Waiters, carrying trays of champagne aloft, slipped through the crowd. Tables heaped in ice and covered in food lined the walls. The orchestra played on the patio, and couples waltzed around the pool. I recognized a few faces from the jumble of Wall Street, others from the occasional evening at the Met, but saw no one I knew well enough to speak to, no one with whom to have even a casual conversation.

When I arrived, I made an attempt to find my host, but the two or three people of whom I asked his whereabouts stared at me in such an amazed way, and denied so vehemently any knowledge of his movements that I slunk off in the direction of the open bar—the only place on the patio where a single man could linger without looking purposeless and alone.

I ordered a vodka martini although I rarely drank hard liquor—it seemed appropriate to the mood—and watched the crowd's mood switch

as the orchestra slid from the waltz to a jitterbug. Women dressed like flappers, wearing no-waisted fringed dresses and pearls down to their thighs danced with an abandon I had only seen in movies. Men matched their movements, sweat marring the perfection of their tailored suits.

A hand gripped my shoulder, the feeling tight but friendly, unlike Tom's clap of the week before. As I looked up, I realized that the crowd of single men around the bar had eased, and I was standing alone, except for the bartender and the man behind me.

Up close, he was taller and more slender than he had looked in the moonlight. His cheekbones were high, his lips thin, his eyes hooded. "Your face looks familiar," he said. "Perhaps you're related to the Carraways of St. Paul, Minnesota."

"Yes," I said. The drink had left an unpleasant tang on my tongue. "I grew up there."

"And Nick Carraway, the bondsman, would be your—grandfather? great-grandfather?"

That he knew my grandfather startled me. Fitz looked younger than that, more of an age with me. Perhaps there were family ties I did not know about. "Grandfather," I said.

"Odd," he murmured. "How odd, the way things grow beyond you."

He had kept his hand on my shoulder, making it impossible to see more than half of his face. "I wanted to thank you for inviting me," I said.

"It would be churlish not to," he said. "Perhaps, in the future, we'll actually be able to talk."

He let go of my shoulder. I could still feel the imprint of his hand as he walked away. He had an air of invisibleness to him, a way of moving unnoticed through a crowd. When he reached the edge of the dancers, he stopped and looked at me with a gaze piercing in its intensity.

"Next time, old sport," he said, the old-fashioned endearment tripping off his tongue like a new and original phrase, "bring your cousin. I think she might like the light."

At least, that was what I thought he said. Later, when I had time to reflect, I wondered if he hadn't said, "I think she might like the night."

FOUR

Men with little imagination often have a clarity of vision that startles the mind. For all their inability to imagine beauty, they seem able to see the ugliness that lies below any surface. They have a willingness to believe in the baser, cruder side of life.

On the following Wednesday afternoon, I found myself in a bar at the edge of the financial district, a place where men in suits rarely showed their faces, where the average clientele had muscles thick as cue balls and just as hard. Tom had corralled me as I left the office, claiming he wanted to play pool and that he knew a place, but as we walked in, it became clear that we were not there for a game, but for an alibi.

The woman he met was the antithesis of Ari. She was tall, big-chested with thick ankles, more a child of my aunt than Ari ever could be. The woman—Rita—wore her clothes like an ill-fitting bathrobe, slipping to one side to reveal a mound of flesh and a bit of nipple. Lipstick stained the side of her mouth and the edges of her teeth. She laughed loud and hard, like a man, and her eyes were bright with too much drink.

I stuck my tie in my pocket, pulled off my suit jacket and draped it over a chair, rolling up my sleeves before I challenged one of the large men in a ripped T-shirt to a game of eight-ball. I lost fifty dollars to him before he decided there was no challenge in it; by then Tom and Rita had reappeared, her clothing straight and her lipstick neatly applied.

Tom clapped my back before I could step away, and the odors of sweat, musk, and newly applied cologne swept over me. "Thanks, man," he said, as if my accompanying him on this trip had deepened our friendship.

I could not let the moment slide without exacting my price. "My neighbor asked that Ari come to one of his parties this week."

Rita slunk back as if Ari's name lessened Rita's power. Tom stepped away from me.

"Fitzgerald's a ghoul," he said. "They say people go to his house and never come back."

"I was there on Sunday."

"You're lucky to get out with your life."

"Hundreds of people go each night." I unrolled my sleeves, buttoned them, and then slipped into my suit coat. "I plan to take Ari."

Tom stared at me for a moment, the male camaraderie gone. Finally he nodded, the acknowledgment of a price paid.

"Next time you go," Rita said, the only words she would ever say to me, "take a good look at his guests."

I drove Ari up in my car. Even though I had spent the afternoon washing and polishing it, the car's age showed against the sleek new models, something in the lack of shine of the bumpers, the crude design of a model year now done. The attendant was polite as he took my place, but lacked the enthusiasm he had shown over a Rolls just moments before.

Ari stared at the house, her tiny mouth agape, her eyes wide. The lights reflected in her pupils like a hundred dancing stars. She left my side immediately and ran up the stairs as if I were not even there.

I tipped the attendant and strode in, remembering Rita's admonishment. The faces that looked familiar had a photographic edge to them—the patina of images I had seen a thousand times in books, in magazines, on film. But as I scanned, I could not see Ari. It was as if she had come into the mammoth house and vanished.

I grabbed a flute of champagne from a passing waiter and wandered onto the patio. The orchestra was playing "Alexander's Ragtime Band" and the woman with the marcel danced in the center, alone, as if she were the only one who understood the music.

Beside me, a burly man with dark hair and a mustache that absorbed his upper lip spoke of marlin fishing as if it were a combat sport. A lanky and lean man who spoke with a Mississippi accent told a familiar story about a barn-burning to a crowd of women who gazed adoringly at his face. Behind him, a tiny woman with an acid tongue talked in disparaging terms of the Algonquin, and another man with white hair, a face crinkled from too much drink, and a body so thin it appeared dapper, studied the edges of the conversation as if the words were written in front of him.

They all had skin as pale as Fitz's, and a life force that seemed to have more energy than substance.

There were others scattered among the crowd: a man with an unruly shock of white hair who spoke of his boyhood in Illinois, his cats, and the workings of riverboats powered by steam; the demure brown-haired woman wearing a long white dress, standing in a corner, refusing to meet anyone's gaze. "She's a poet," a young girl beside me whispered, and I nodded, recognizing the heart-shaped face, the quiet, steady eyes.

In that house, on that night, I never questioned their presence, as if being in the company of people long-dead were as natural as speaking to myself. I avoided them: They had nothing to do with me. I was drawn to none of them, except, perhaps, Fitz himself.

He was as invisible as Ari. I wandered through the manse three times, pushing past bodies flushed from dancing, bright with too much drink, letting the conversation flow over me like water over a stone. Most of my colleagues spoke of Fitz himself, how he had favored them in one way or another, with a commission or, in the case of the women, with time alone. They spoke with a sigh, their eyes a bit glazed, as if the memory were more of a dream, and as they spoke, they touched their throats, or played with pearl chokers around their necks. A shudder ran through me and I wondered what I had brought Arielle into.

I found her at 3 A.M., waltzing in the empty grand ballroom with Fitz. He wore an ice cream suit, perfectly tailored, his hair combed back, and

she wore a white gown that rippled around her like her hair. She gazed at him like a lover, her lips parted and moist, her body pressed against his, and as they whirled to the imaginary music. I caught glimpses of his face, his brows brought together in concentration, his eyes sparkling and moist. He looked like a man caught in a dream from which he could not wake, a dream which had gone bad, a dream which, when he remembered it, he would term a nightmare.

Then she saw me, and her expression changed. "Nick," she said. "Nick Carraway." And she laughed. The voice was not hers. It had more music than before, but beneath it, a rasp older women gained from too many cigarettes, too much drink. "He will never leave us alone, Scott."

Fitz looked at me. If anything, he appeared paler than he had before. The sparkle in his eyes was not tears, but the hard glare of a man who could not cry. "Thanks for all your help, old man," he said, and with that I knew I had been dismissed.

FIVE

About a week before, an ambitious young reporter appeared on Fitz's doorstep as one of the parties began. He managed to find Fitz at the edge of the pool and asked him if he had anything to say.

"About what?" Fitz asked.

"About anything."

It transpired after a few minutes that the young man had heard Fitz's name around the office in a connection he wouldn't or couldn't reveal and, it being his day off, had hurried out to Connecticut "to see."

It was a random shot and yet the reporter's instinct had been right. Fitz's reputation, as spread by the people who saw him, the people who came to his gatherings, had that summer fallen just short of news. Stories of his mysterious past persisted, and yet none came close to the truth.

You see, he did not die of a heart attack in 1940. Instead he fell in, as he later said, with the ghouls of the Hollywood crowd. Obsessed with immortality, glamour, and youth, they convinced him to meet a friend, a person whose name remains forever elusive. He succumbed to the temptation, as he had so often before, and discovered only after he had changed that in giving up life he had given up living and that the needs which drove his fiction disappeared with his need for food and strong drink.

He watched his daughter from afar and occasionally brought others into the fold, as the loneliness ate at him. He began throwing large parties and in them found sustenance, and others like him who had managed to move from human fame into a sort of shadowed, mythical existence. But the loneliness did not abate, and over time he learned that he had only one more chance, another opportunity to make things right. And so he monitored the baby wards in the South, allowing his own brush with the supernatural to let him see when her soul returned. For his love affair with her was more haunting and tragic than those he wrote about, and he hoped, with his new understanding, that he could make amends.

Some of this I learned, and some of this he told me. I put it down here as a way of noting that the rumors about him weren't even close to the truth, that the truth was, in fact, as strange as fiction, and I would not believe it if I had not seen it with my own eyes. What he did tell me, he said at a time of great confusion, and I might not have believed him, even then, if later that year, I hadn't found the books, the novels, the biographies, that somehow even with my literary education, I had managed to overlook.

That night, I did not sleep. The phone rang three times, and all three times, the machine picked up. Tom's coarse accent echoed in the darkness of my bedroom, demanding to know why Ari had not

returned home. Finally I slipped on a faded pair of jeans and loafers, and padded up the hill to see if I could convince her to leave before Tom created trouble.

Only the light in the ballroom remained on, casting a thin glow across the yard. The cars were gone as were their occupants. Discarded cigarette butts, broken champagne glasses, and one woman's shoe with the heel missing were the only evidence of the gaiety that had marked the evening. Inside, I heard Ari sobbing hysterically, and as I walked up the steps, a hand pushed against my chest.

I hadn't seen him in the dark. He had been sitting on the steps, staring at the detritus in the driveway, an unlit cigarette in his hands. "You can't help her," he said, and in his voice, I heard the weariness of a man whose dreams were lost.

Still, I pushed past him and went inside. Ari sat on the floor, her bare feet splayed in front of her, her dress still the white of pure snow. When she saw me, the crying stopped. "Nicky," she said in that raspy, not-her voice, and then the laughter started, as uncontrolled as the crying. I went to her, put my arm around her shoulder, and tried to lift her up. She shook her head and pulled out of my grasp. For a moment, the horrible laughter stopped and she gazed up at me, her eyes as clear as the sky on a summer morning. "You don't understand, do you?" she asked. "When I'm here, this is where I belong."

Then the laughter began again, a harsh, almost childish sound too close to tears. Fitz glided past me, still wearing the white suit he had worn earlier. He picked her up and shushed her, and she buried her face against his shoulder as if he gave her strength.

Her thin, fragile neck was clear and unmarked. God help me, I checked. But he had not touched her, at least in that way.

He carried her to the plush sofa pushed back to the wall beneath the windows. Then he pushed the hair off her face, wiped the tears from her cheeks, and whispered to her, hauntingly: "*Sleep.*" Her eyes closed and

her breathing evened, and once again she was the Arielle I had always known, pink-cheeked and delicate.

He looked at me, and said, "This is why Daisy had to leave Gatsby, because he was wrong for her. The better part of me knew that being with me shattered her spirit. But I could not let her go. You knew that, didn't you, old man? That I could not let her go?"

But I didn't know, and I didn't understand until much later. So I remained quiet. Wisely, as it turned out.

"Ah, Nick," he said, his fingers brushing her brow. "Your arrival surprised me. I never thought—I never realized—how the characters live on, even when the story's over. I could believe in my own transformation but not your existence. And I never understood the past, so here I am repeating it."

He smiled then, a self-deprecating smile that made all his words seem like the foolish ravings of a man who had had little sleep.

"Go home, old sport," he said. "Everything will look different in the light of day."

I must have glanced at Arielle with concern, for he cupped her cheek possessively. "Don't worry," he said. "I'll take a good care of her."

Something in the throb of his voice made me trust him, made me turn on my heel even though I knew it was wrong, and leave him there with her. Some warble, some imperative, as if he were the creator and I the created. I wandered down the hill in the dark, and didn't return until the light of day.

SIX

I had slept maybe twenty minutes when I woke to the sound of tires peeling on the road outside my house. An engine raced, powering a fast-moving car up the hill. As I sat up, brakes squealed and a voice raised in a shout that echoed down the valley. The shouts continued

until they ended abruptly—mid-sentence—followed by a moment of silence and a woman's high-pitched scream.

It was still dark, although the darkness had that gray edge that meant dawn wasn't far away. I picked up the phone and called the police which, in my compulsion-fogged mind, felt like an act of defiance. Then I rose from my bed a second time, dressed, and ran out of the house.

I didn't think to take the car until I was halfway up the path. By then to run back and get it would have taken twice as long as continuing. The sun rose, casting orange and gold tendrils across the sky. The silence in Fitz's house unnerved me and I was shaking by the time I reached the driveway.

I had never seen the car before—a light gray sedan that lacked pretension—but the Wisconsin vanity plate made its ownership clear. It had parked on the shattered glass. A woman's black glove lay beneath one of the tires. In the early morning glow, Fitz's manse seemed ancient and old: the lawn filled with bottles and cans from the night before; the shutters closed and unpainted; the steps cracked and littered with ashes and gum. The door stood open and I slipped inside, careful to touch nothing.

A great gout of blood rose in an arch along one wall and dripped to the tile below. Drops led me to the open French doors. Through them, I saw the pool.

Tiny waves still rippled the water. The laden air mattress moved irregularly along the surface, the man's dark suit already telling me this was not whom I had expected. His eyes were open and appeared to frown in confusion, his skin chalk-white, and his neck a gaping hole that had been licked clean of blood.

* * *

Of Ari and Fitz we never found a trace. A man who had lived on the fringes as long as he had knew how to disappear. I had half hoped for an acknowledgment—a postcard, a fax, a phone message—something that recognized the dilemma he had put me in. But, as he said, an author never realizes that the characters live beyond the story, and I suspect he never gave me a second thought.

Although I thought of him as I read the articles, the biographies, the essays and dissertations based on his life—his true life. I saved his novels for last and his most famous for last of all. And in it, I heard my grandfather's voice, and understood why he never spoke of his life before he returned from the East all those years ago. For that life had not been his but a fiction created by a man my grandfather had never met. My grandfather's life began in 1925 and he lived it fully until the day he died.

I sold the house at the bottom of the hill, and moved back to the Middle West. I found that I prefer the land harsh and the winds of reality cold against my face. It reminds me that I am alive. And, although I bear my grandfather's name in a family where that name has a certain mystique, that mystique does not belong to me. Nor must I hold it hallowed against my breast. The current my grandfather saw drawing him into the past pushes me toward the future, and I shall follow it with an understanding of what has come before.

For, although we are all created by someone, that someone does not own us. We pick our own paths. To do anything else condemns us to a glittering world of all-night parties hosted by Fitz and his friends, the beautiful and the damned.

VAMPIRE HOURS

ELAINE VIETS

*I*t's three o'clock in the morning, Katherine. Go to sleep."

My husband, the surgeon. Eric barked orders even in the middle of the night.

"I can't sleep," I said.

"I have to be at the hospital in three hours. Turn off the light. And go see a doctor, will you? You're a pain in the ass."

Eric rolled away from me and pulled the pillow over his face.

I turned off the light. I felt like a disobedient child in my own home, as I listened to my husband of twenty-five years snore into his pillow. Eric could fall asleep anywhere, any time. Especially when he was in bed with me.

If I pushed his face into the pillow, could I smother him?

Probably not. Years of late-night emergency calls had given Eric an instant, unnatural alertness.

I lay alone on my side of the vast bed, stiff as a corpse in a coffin. My white negligee seemed more like a shroud than sexy sleep wear. My marriage to Eric was dead, and I knew it. I wanted him to love me, and hated myself for wanting a man so cold.

He wasn't like that when we were first married. Then he'd ripped off so many of my nightgowns, he'd bought me a thousand-dollar gift

certificate at Victoria's Secret. I'd model the latest addition and he'd rip it off again. Back then, he didn't care if he had early surgery. We'd had wild, all-night sex.

A tear slipped down my cheek, and I cursed it. Tears came too easily these days, ever since menopause. "The change," my mother had called it. Once, before I knew what those changes were, I'd looked forward to menopause. I wanted the monthly flow of blood to stop. I was tired of the bloat, the cramps, and the pain.

But the change was infinitely worse. Oh, the blood stopped, as promised. But nobody told me what would start: the weight gain, no matter how hard I dieted. How could I get fat on rice cakes and lettuce?

The change brought other changes. My skin started to sag along the jaw. The lines from my nose to my lips deepened into trenches. My neck looked like it belonged on a stewing hen.

And my husband, the old rooster, was chasing young chicks. I knew it, but I didn't dare confront him. I'd seen what happened to my friends when they'd faced down their rich, powerful husbands. Elizabeth, courageous, I-won't-stand-for-this Elizabeth, had been destroyed. She'd caught Zack, her husband of thirty years, groping some not-so-sweet young thing in the dim lights of the local bar. Elizabeth had fearlessly confronted Zack on the spot. She'd embarrassed him in front of his backslapping cronies.

Good old Zack hired a pinstriped shark—one of his bar buddies. Now the elegant Elizabeth lived in a cramped hot box of an apartment, with a cat and a rattling air conditioner. She worked as a checker at the supermarket and barely made the rent. Elizabeth was on her feet all day and had the varicose veins to prove it.

I'd taken her out to a dreary lunch last month. I'd wanted to do something nice. We went to the club, where we'd always lunched in the old days, when she was still a member. Some of our friends didn't recognize her. Poor Elizabeth, with her home-permed hair and unwaxed

eyebrows, looked older than her mother. She was so exhausted, she could hardly keep up a conversation.

That same fate awaited me. I had to stall as long as I could, until I could figure out what to do with my life. If Eric dumped me now, I'd be at the supermarket asking my former friends, "Would you like paper or plastic?"

I'd be one more useless, used-up middle-aged woman.

I was already. In seven days, I'll be fifty-five years old. My future had never looked bleaker. I had no money and no job skills. My husband didn't love me anymore. Happy birthday, Katherine.

"Lie still," Eric snarled. "Quit twitching."

I didn't think I'd moved. Maybe Eric felt my inner restlessness. Maybe we were still connected enough for that.

But I couldn't lie there another moment. Not even to save myself. I slid out of bed.

"Now what? Where are you going at this hour?" Eric demanded.

"I thought I'd get some fresh air. I'm going for a walk."

Eric sat straight up, his gray hair wild, his long surgeon's hands clutching the sheet to his hairy chest. "Are you crazy? You want to go outside in the middle of the night? After that woman was murdered two streets away?"

"People get murdered all the time in Fort Lauderdale," I said.

"Not like that. Some freak drained her blood. They didn't put that little detail in the papers. The city commission wants to avoid scaring the tourists. Dave at the medical examiner's office told me. That woman hardly had a drop of blood left in her. She went for a walk at three in the morning and turned up drained dry. For Chrissakes, use your head."

"All right," I said. "I'll sit on the balcony. I didn't want to wake you."

I put on my peignoir and padded into the living room. I never tired of the view from our condo. To the east was the dark, endless expanse of the Atlantic Ocean, lit by ancient stars. Straight down were the black waters of the Intracoastal. Across the little canal that ran alongside our building were the Dark Harbor condos. Those places started at three

million dollars. But it wasn't the money that fascinated me. Florida had lots of expensive condos. There was something about Dark Harbor. Something mysterious. Exciting. Exotic. Even at three in the morning.

I slid open the glass doors, careful not to make a sound. The warm night air caressed my cheek. I loved the night. Always had. Moon glow was kinder than the harsh Florida sun. I could hear the water softly lapping at the pilings on the dock, seven stories below.

Laughter drifted across the water, and the faint sounds of a chanteuse singing something in French. It was an old Edith Piaf song of love and loss.

There was a party in the Dark Harbor penthouse. Such a glamorous party. The men wore black tie. The women wore sleek black. They looked like me, only better, smoother, thinner. These were people in charge of their futures. They didn't have my half-life as the soon-to-be-shed wife. They were more alive than I would ever be.

I sighed and turned away from my beautiful neighbors. I drifted back into our bedroom like a lost soul, crawled in next to my unloving husband, and fell into a fitful sleep.

Eric woke me up at five-thirty when he left for the hospital.

"Good-bye," I said.

His only answer was a slammed door.

That night, while getting ready for bed, I looked in my dressing room mirror and panicked. I'd always had a cute figure, but now it had thickened. I had love handles. Where did those come from? I swear I didn't have them two days ago. I burst into tears. I couldn't help it.

I ran into the bathroom to stifle the sobs I knew would irritate Eric. But it was too late. "Now what?" he snarled. "I can't take these mood swings. Get hormone replacement therapy or something."

He was definitely getting something. I'd found the Viagra bottle in his drawer when I put away his socks. It was half empty. He wasn't popping those pills for me. We hadn't made love in months.

No pill would cure my problem. Not unless I took a whole bunch at once and drifted into the long sleep. That prospect was looking more attractive every day. Didn't someone say, "The idea is to die young as late as possible"? Time was running out for me.

I spent another restless night, haunting the balcony like a ghost, watching another party across the way at Dark Harbor. Once again, I drifted off to sleep as Eric was getting ready for work.

Tuesday was a brilliant, sunlit day. Even I couldn't feel gloomy. I was living in paradise. I put on my new Escada outfit—tight black jeans and a white jacket so soft, it was pettable. I smiled into the mirror. I looked good, thanks to topnotch tailoring and a body shaper that nearly strangled my middle.

I didn't care. It nipped in my waist, lifted my behind and thrust out my boobs. I sashayed out to the condo garage like a model on a catwalk. A sexy, young model.

I had a charity lunch at the Aldritch Hotel. I was eating—or rather, not eating—lunch to support the Drexal School. I didn't have any children, but everyone in our circle supported the Drex. As a Drexal Angel, I paid one hundred dollars for a limp chicken Caesar salad and stale rolls.

My silver Jaguar roared up under the hotel portico. A hunky valet raced out to take my keys. The muscular valet ogled my long legs and sensational spike heels, and I felt that little frisson a woman gets when a handsome man thinks she's hot.

Then his eyes reached my face and I saw his disappointment. The valet didn't bother to hide it. I was old.

I handed him my keys. The valet tore off my ticket without another glance at me. I felt like he'd ripped my heart in half. I used to be a beauty. Heads would turn when I strutted into a room. Now if anyone stared at me, it was because I had a soup stain on my suit or toilet paper stuck on my shoe. I was becoming invisible.

I caught a glimpse of myself in the hotel's automatic doors. Who was I kidding in my overpriced, overdressed outfit? I was losing my looks—and my husband.

I stopped in the ladies room to check my makeup. My lipstick had a nasty habit of creeping into the cracks at the lip line. I used my liner pencil, then stopped in a stall, grateful it had a floor-to-ceiling louvered door. I needed extra privacy to wriggle out of the body shaper.

I heard the restroom door open. Two women were talking. One sounded like my best friend, Margaret. The other was my neighbor, Patricia. I'd known them for years. I nearly called out, but they were deep in conversation and I didn't want to interrupt.

". . . such a cliché," Margaret said, in her rich-girl drawl.

"I can't believe it," Patricia said. Her voice was a New York honk. "Eric is boinking his secretary?"

Eric. My husband, Eric? Panic squeezed me tighter than any body shaper. There were lots of Erics.

"Office manager," Margaret said. "But it's the same thing. She's twenty-five, blonde, and desperate to catch a doctor. It looks like Eric will let himself get caught."

"Can you blame him?" Patricia honked. "Katherine's let herself go."

Katherine. No, there weren't many Erics with Katherines. I felt sick. I sat down on the toilet seat and listened.

"She won't even get an eye job," Patricia said. "And her own husband is a plastic surgeon. How rejecting is that? Eric did my eyes. Then he did the rest of me." Her words filled the room. I couldn't escape them.

"You slept with him?" Margaret sounded mildly shocked.

"Everyone does," Patricia said.

I could almost hear her shrug. I wanted to rush out and strangle her. I wanted to blacken her stretched eyelids. But I was half-dressed, and my jiggly middle would prove she was right.

"It's part of the package," Patricia said. "My skin never looked better than when I was getting Dr. Eric's special injections."

"You're awful," Margaret said. Then my best friend laughed.

"It's part of my charm," Patricia said. "But someone better clue in Katherine, so she can line up a good divorce lawyer before it's too late."

"It's already too late," Margaret said. "Eric's already seen the best lawyer in Lauderdale, Jack Kellern."

"And you didn't tell Katherine that Eric hired Jack the Ripper?"

"How could I? He's my husband."

And you, Margaret, are my best friend. Or rather, you were. Margaret had also had her eyes done by Jack. Did she get the full package, too?

I waited until my faithless friends shut the restroom door. I rocked back and forth on the toilet in stunned misery. It was one thing to suspect your husband was playing around. It was another to learn of his betrayal—and your best friend's. I was a joke, a laughingstock. I had even less time than I thought.

I pulled my clothes together, pasted on a smile, and found my table. A waitress set my salad in front of me. I studied the woman. She was about my age, with a weary face, limp brown hair and thick, sensible shoes. This time next year, would I be serving salads to the ladies who lunched?

Only if I was lucky. I didn't even have the skills to be a waitress. I picked at my salad, but couldn't eat a bite. No one noticed. Well-bred women didn't have appetites.

A polite clink of silverware on glasses signaled that the headmaster was at the podium. He was a lean man with a good suit and a sycophantic smile.

"You're heard that Drexal has one of the finest academic records . . ." he began. My thoughts soon drifted away.

Menopause had killed my marriage, but it had been dying for a long time. I knew exactly when it had received the fatal wound: the day my husband asked to cut on me.

I was thirty-five, but looked ten years younger. Eric was itching to get out his scalpel and work on my face.

"Just let me do your eyes," he said, "and take a few tucks. If you start early, you'll look younger longer."

"I look fine," I said.

"You don't trust me," he said.

"Of course I do," I said. "You're the most successful plastic surgeon in Broward County."

But not the most skilled. Eric was right. I didn't trust him. He'd never killed anyone, unlike some Florida face sculptors. But I saw his work everywhere. I could recognize his patients: Caucasian women of a certain age with the telltale Chinese eyes and stretched skin.

Eric gave them facelifts when no other doctor would. He'd give them as many as seven or eight, until their skin was so tight they could bikini wax their upper lip.

I pleaded fear of anesthesia. I invented an aunt who died from minor surgery when I was a child. But Eric knew the truth: I was afraid to let him touch me. I was his in every way, except one. I would not surrender to his knife.

For ten years, he never stopped trying. He nagged me for a full facelift at forty. At forty-five, I knew I could probably use one, but still I wouldn't submit.

"Nothing can make me twenty-five again," I said. "I'll take my chances with wrinkles."

It was the worst rejection a plastic surgeon could have. I made him look bad. Everyone could see my lines and wrinkles. These normal signs of aging became an accusation. They said every woman but his wife believed Eric was a fine surgeon.

When I turned fifty, Eric quit asking. That's when our hot nights together cooled. I suspected there were other women, but knew the affairs weren't serious. Now, things had changed. Eric was going to

marry a twenty-five-year-old blonde. In another five years, she'd submit to his knife.

Suddenly, I was back in the hotel ballroom. The headmaster's speech had reached its crescendo. "We have almost everything we need to make the Drexal School the finest educational institution in Broward County. Only one thing is missing. After today, we'll have it all. I'm pleased to announce the creation of the Drexal Panthers—our own football team. Your donations have made it possible."

The lunching mothers cheered wildly.

I looked down at my plate and realized I'd eaten an entire slice of chocolate cheesecake with raspberry sauce.

Worse, I hadn't tasted one bite.

No wonder I was fat.

On the way home, I picked up some college catalogues. I made myself a stiff drink and settled into my favorite chair in the great room to study the glossy catalogues. I looked at careers for legal aides, dental assistants and licensed practical nurses. One choice seemed more depressing than the other.

What had I wanted to be before I met Eric?

An English teacher. Back then, I saw myself teaching poetry to eager young minds, watching them open like flowers with the beauty of the written word. Now, I knew I couldn't cope with the young ruffians at the public schools. Would the Drexal School hire an Angel down on her luck? Would the headmaster remember how often I'd lunched to make his dream team possible?

If I went back to college, how many years would I need to complete my degree? Would my life experience count for anything? What had I done in fifty-five years?

I fell asleep on the pile of catalogues. I woke up at midnight when I heard Eric unlock the door. I hid the catalogues with my arms, but he

never noticed them. Or me. He went straight to bed without even saying good night.

I woke up at three. I couldn't sleep through the night any more. I kept vampire hours now. I drifted into the living room and watched the condo across the way. There was another party tonight. This time, the music seemed livelier, the guests more keyed up, more dramatically dressed, as if they were at some special ceremony.

Our condo walls seemed to close in on me. I slipped on my jeans and a cotton shirt. I was going for a walk along the water, even if it killed me. I'd rather risk death than suffocate inside.

The night air was delicious, cool but not cold. I was drawn to the lights of the Dark Harbor party, and picked my way along the docks until I was almost underneath its windows. I couldn't see anything, but I could feel the contained excitement inside. The walls seemed to pulse with life.

"Wish you were here?"

I jumped at the voice—very rich, very male.

The man who came out of the shadows wore evening dress. His skin looked luminous in the moonlight. His hair was black with a slight curl. There was strength in his face, and a hint of cruelty. I couldn't tell his age. He seemed beyond such ordinary measures.

"I'm sorry. I didn't mean to trespass," I said.

"You aren't trespassing, Katherine," he said. "You spend a lot of time watching us, don't you?"

"Am I that obvious?" I said.

"No," he said. "But I feel your yearning. It makes you very beautiful— and very vulnerable."

Inside the condo, there was a shriek of triumph, followed by polite tennis-match applause.

"Excuse me," he said. "I must return to my guests. My name is Michael, by the way."

"Will I see you again?" I said.

"If you want to," he said.

He was gone. Only then did I wonder how he knew my name.

I floated back to my condo wrapped in soft, warm clouds of fantasy. How long had it been since any man had called me beautiful?

I was beautiful. Michael made me feel that way. I crawled into bed beside my husband, and dreamed of another man.

In the morning, I woke up smiling and refreshed. For the first time in months, I didn't check my mirror for more ravages. I didn't need to. I was beautiful. Michael had said so. I was dreamy as a lovesick teenager, until the phone shattered the sweet silence at eleven a.m.

"Katherine, it's Patricia." Of course it was. She'd slept with my husband, and confessed it in a public restroom. I'd know her honking voice anywhere. Except today it had a different note. She sounded subdued, even frightened. "Have you heard about Jack?"

"Jack who?" I said.

"Margaret's Jack. They found his body in the parking lot of his law offices early this morning."

"What happened?" I said. "Was he mugged?"

"They don't think so," Patricia said. "The police say the murder didn't take place there. They think he was abducted."

"Kidnapped and murdered? But why?" Which wife killed him, I wondered. How many deserted women wished him dead?

"No one knows. But it gets worse. Jack's body was drained of blood. Completely dry."

"That's awful," I said. "I'll go see Margaret immediately."

I hung up the phone quickly, hoping to hide my elation. Jack the Ripper was dead—horribly dead. My husband no longer had a divorce lawyer. I felt a brief stab of shame for my selfish thoughts, but Jack's death was poetic justice. Someone had sucked the blood out of the city's biggest bloodsucker. Someone had given me more time.

I put on a navy pantsuit and a long face, and stopped by a smart specialty shop for a cheese tray and a bottle of wine. My long-dead mother would be proud. She'd taught me to bring food to a house of mourning.

There were other cars in Margaret's driveway, including what looked like unmarked police cars and three silver Lexuses. Lawyers' cars.

Margaret was a wreck. Her eyes were deeply bagged and swollen. Her jaw line sagged nearly as badly as mine. All my husband's fine work was undone. I felt petty for noticing. She's a new widow, I told myself. Show some pity.

"Katherine!" Margaret ran weeping into my arms, smearing my jacket with makeup.

"I'm sorry," I said, patting her nearly fleshless back. I could feel her thin bones. It wasn't a lie. I was sorry for so many things, including the death of our friendship. Women need the sympathy of our own kind. Margaret had destroyed even that small comfort for me.

"Come into the garden where we can talk," she said. "The police are searching Jack's home office. Three lawyers from his firm and a court-appointed guardian are arguing over what papers they can take."

We sat at an umbrella table near a bubbling fountain. Palms rustled overhead. Impatiens bloomed at our feet. It looked like every other garden in Florida. A Hispanic maid brought iced tea, lemon slices and two kinds of artificial sweetener.

"May I have sugar, please?" I asked.

"Sugar?" the maid said, as if she'd never heard the word.

"You use sugar?" Margaret might be dazed with grief, but she was still surprised by my request. In our crowd, sleeping with a friend's husband was a faux pas. Taking sugar in your tea was a serious sin.

"Doctor's orders," I said. "Sweeteners are out. Cancer in the family."

Actually, I liked real sugar. And it was only eighteen calories a spoonful.

"How are you?" I asked.

"I don't know," Margaret said. Two more tears escaped her swollen eyelids. "I thought Jack was seeing someone, and that's why he worked late so often these last few weeks. I was furious, but I couldn't say anything. I was too afraid."

"I understand," I said.

She flushed with guilt.

"My husband went to see Jack," I said. "So I know how you feel."

Margaret had the grace to say nothing. I appreciated that.

"Do you think Jack's lover killed him?" I said.

"I don't know. I don't even know now if he had a lover. One of the firm's associates found Jack in the parking lot when she came to work at six this morning. Maybe he really had been working late. I had to identify him. Jack didn't look dead so much as . . . empty. Someone took all his blood. It wasn't some slashing attack. Just two holes in the side of his neck. There were bruises, too. Terrible bruises on his wrists, legs and shoulders."

"Was he beaten?" I said.

"No. They think someone—or maybe more than one person—held him down while he was—while they—" Margaret couldn't go on.

"Do the police think it was a serial killer?" I asked.

"They won't say. But the way they're acting, I know it's strange. There were other attacks like this in Lauderdale. Jack wasn't the only person to die like this."

"No," I said. "Eric told me that the woman found off of Bayview had been drained dry, too. He heard that from the medical examiner's office. The police kept it out of the papers."

"It's like some nightmare," Margaret said, "except I can't wake up. Mindy is flying home this afternoon from college. This will be so hard for our daughter. Mindy idolized her father." Margaret started weeping again.

I wasn't sure what to do. If we'd still been friends, I would have folded Margaret in my arms. But she had betrayed me. I knew it, and she knew it.

I was saved by a homicide detective and a lawyer.

"Margaret," the lawyer said, "I'm sorry to disturb you, but we have some more questions about your husband."

"I'd better go," I said. "I'll let myself out." I air-kissed her cheek. It took all my self-control to keep from running for my car.

Once, I would have called my husband and told him the awful news. Now I didn't. What could I say? *You know that lawyer you hired to strip me of my last dime? The son of a bitch was murdered. Couldn't happen to a nicer guy.*

I suspected Eric already knew about Jack's death. He was probably looking for a new blood sucker.

I spent the afternoon taking calls from Margaret's shocked friends, pretending to be sad and concerned and hating myself because I couldn't feel any of it. Instead, I felt oddly excited. I broiled a skinless chicken breast, steamed some broccoli, and waited for my husband to come home.

At eleven o'clock, there was still no sign of Eric. He didn't bother to phone me. I didn't humiliate myself by calling around asking for him.

What if he turned up dead, like Jack? I wondered. Then my troubles would be over. I felt guilty even thinking that. But it was true.

At three in the morning, I woke up alone and drenched in sweat. Night sweats, another menopausal delight. I punched my soggy pillow and tried to settle back to sleep. At three-thirty, I gave up. I reached for my jeans, then abandoned that idea. Instead, I pulled out a long, nearly sheer hostess gown that looked glamorous in the soft moonlight.

I wasn't going for a walk. I was going hunting. For Michael.

There was no party tonight. His condo was dark except for flickering candles in the living room and the opalescent light of a television. Michael was alone, like me. He couldn't sleep, either.

He was waiting for me down by the Dark Harbor docks. At first, I heard nothing but the gentle slap of the water and the clinking of the halyards as the boats rocked back and forth. It was a peaceful sound. A light breeze ruffled my hair and pressed my gown against my body.

"You dressed for me, didn't you?" he said.

Michael seemed to appear from nowhere. His white shirt, open at the throat and rolled at the sleeves, glowed in the moonlight. His hair was black as onyx, but so soft. I longed to run my fingers through it

"Yes," I said.

His hand touched my hair and traced the line of my neck. I stepped back. It wouldn't do to seem too eager too soon.

Michael smiled, as if he could read my mind. "You don't have to play games," he said.

"I'm not playing games," I said. "I'm being cautious. I don't know anything about you. Are you married?"

"My wife has been dead for many years. I live alone."

"You have such lovely parties." I couldn't keep the wistful note out of my voice.

"I have many friends. We enjoy the night."

"I do, too," I said. "I'm tired of the Florida sun. It burns the life out of everything."

"You may be one of us," Michael said. "I'd like to see more of you, before I go."

"Go?" The word clutched at my heart. "Where are you going?"

"I'm selling the condo. Nobody stays long in Florida. You know that. Will you be here tomorrow night? May I see you again?"

"Three o'clock," I said. "Same time, same place."

There. I'd done it. I'd made a date with another man. My marriage was over, except for the legalities. It was time to face the future. Maybe, if I was lucky, I'd have Michael in my life. If not, I'd find someone else. He'd shown me that I was still attractive. I was grateful for that. I'd let Eric destroy my confidence.

I turned around for one last look, but Michael was gone. Only then did I realize he didn't ask if I was married. I wondered if he knew. Or cared.

Eric was waiting for me when I returned, tapping his foot like an impatient parent.

"Where were you?" he said.

"I could ask you the same question," I said.

"I was with a patient," he said.

"Administering more special injections?" I said. "Patricia says they're wonderful for the complexion. I wouldn't know. It's been so long I've forgotten."

"You're certifiable." Eric turned the attack back on me. He was good at that. "Jack is dead. Murdered! Some freak drank his blood. And you're roaming the streets at night like an Alzheimer's patient. I should hire a keeper."

I should hire a hit man, I thought. But I held in my harsh words. I didn't need Eric now. I had Michael.

"Good night," I said. "I'm sleeping in the guest room."

"You can't—"

I didn't stop to hear what I couldn't do. I locked the guest room door and put fresh sheets on the bed. What I am doing? I wondered. I have a 3 A.M. rendezvous with a man I don't know. There's a murderer running loose in my neighborhood. Yet I'd never felt safer or more at peace. I slept blissfully until ten in the morning. I woke up with just enough time to get ready for my literacy board meeting.

As I walked into the dark paneled board room, I caught snatches of conversation: "he was drained dry . . . don't know when they'll have a funeral . . . Margaret is devastated."

All anyone could talk about was Jack's murder, at least until the board meeting started. Then we had to listen to Nancy blather on about bylaws changes. She'd kept the board tied up with this pointless minutia for the last eight months.

Once I saw myself as a philanthropist, dispensing our money to improve the lives of the disadvantaged. But I'd sat on too many charity boards. Now, I knew how little was possible. Here I was in another endless meeting, listening to a debate about whether the

organization's president should remain a figurehead or have a vote on the board.

How did this debate help one poor child learn to read? I wondered.

"Katherine?"

I looked up. The entire board was staring at me.

"How do you vote on the motion: yes or no?" Nancy asked.

"Yes." I wasn't saying yes to the motion, whatever it was. I was saying yes to a new life.

Mercifully, the board meeting was over at noon. I dodged any offers of lunch and went straight home. I spent three hours on the Internet, looking at my career options. Work couldn't be any worse than board meetings. Then I'd get ready for my date with Michael.

By four that afternoon, I'd decided to become a librarian. It would only take another three years of college. The pay was decent. The benefits were not bad. The job prospects were good. I'd be a useful member of society, which was more than I could say for myself now.

I pushed away the memory of Elizabeth's dreary apartment and made an appointment with a feminist lawyer. Tomorrow, we would discuss my divorce. Today, I wanted to think about my date with Michael.

I washed my hair, so it would have a soft curl. I applied a mango-honey face mask and swiped Eric's razor to de-fuzz my legs. Eric hated when I did that. I hoped the dull razor would rip his face off tomorrow morning. I sprayed his shaving cream on my long legs. I was now covered with goo from head to toe. Naturally, the doorbell rang.

Who was that?

I looked out the peephole. A young woman with a cheap blond dye job was on my doorstep. Her skirt was some bright, shiny material, and her tight halter top barely covered her massive breasts. I'd seen her before, at Eric's office.

"Just a minute," I called, and quickly wiped off the shaving cream and the mango mask.

When I opened the door, I was hit by a gust of perfume.

"Yes?" I said. "You're from Eric's office. Is there a problem?"

"There is." She boldly walked into my home and sat down on my couch. "My name is Dawn. I'm Eric's office manager."

And his lover. The recognition was a punch in the face. Eric was leaving me for this big-titted cliché. I stood there in silence, hoping to make this husband-stealing tramp squirm. She'd have to do the talking.

Dawn came right out with her request. "We want to get married," she said.

"We?"

"Eric and I."

"He's married to me," I said.

"That's the problem, isn't it?" Dawn smiled. She had small, feral teeth and smooth skin. Eric would revel in that flawless skin. How my husband would love to put a knife into it. He had the gall to try to improve perfection.

"If you make it easy for me, I'll make it easy for you," Dawn said. "I'll make sure you get a nice allowance. You drag us through the courts, and I'll fight you every step of the way."

"You're threatening me in my own living room?" I said.

"It won't be yours for long," Dawn said. She looked around at my carefully decorated room. "No wonder Eric doesn't like to hang here. It's like a funeral parlor. White couches in Florida. Hello? Can you say corny? This place needs some life.

"Oh, dear, you've got some gunk on your forehead. Those do-it-yourself beauty treatments don't work. Should have gone to your husband for help. You might still have him. But maybe not. He can only do so much."

I sat there, speechless, while the little slut sauntered past me. I picked up the first thing I could find, a delicate gold-trimmed Limoges dish—a wedding present—and threw it at her. Too late. She'd already shut the door.

The dish shattered with a satisfying sound. Plates, glasses, candy dishes, even a soup tureen followed, until the hall's marble floor was crunchy with smashed crockery and broken glass. It took me an hour to sweep it up and drop it down the trash chute. I knew Eric wouldn't miss any of it. He wouldn't even notice anything was gone. These were the things I loved. I wondered if the slut would be dining off my best china and drinking from my remaining wedding crystal. Over my dead body. Better yet, over hers.

I cleaned off the remnants of the mango-honey mask and shaved my legs with a shaky hand. I had a date with a man at three o'clock in the morning. What kind of time was that? I nicked my leg and watched a small drop of blood well up. Blood.

Three A.M. was a good time for a vampire.

That's what Michael was, wasn't he? Who else had drained Jack dry but a vampire?

What else could Michael and his sleek, night-loving friends be?

I expected to feel shocked and horrified, but I didn't. Michael and his friends did me a favor by killing Jack. If they'd killed Eric, I would have been the center of a murder investigation. Instead, they gave me a little more time to arrange my life before it self-destructed.

Was Michael a danger to me? I didn't think so. If he'd wanted to kill me, he'd had many opportunities. No, Michael wanted more than a quick kill. But what, exactly? His conversation was full of innuendoes, invitations and explanations.

"I feel your yearning. It makes you very beautiful—and very vulnerable."

"My wife has been dead for many years. I live alone."

"I have many friends. We enjoy the night."

"You may be one of us."

Michael had told me what he was, if I listened carefully. Did I want to be one of his beautiful friends? Could I kill other people?

366

Depends, I thought. I could kill lawyers like Jack, doctors like my husband, and that little bitch who waltzed into my house and claimed my husband like a piece of lost luggage.

I wondered about the other woman who'd been drained dry. Who was she? Did she deserve to die? I didn't have her name, but I knew the date she'd died and the street where she was found—Forty-seventh, off of Bayview.

A quick Internet search found the story in the Fort Lauderdale *Sun-Sentinel*. The dead woman was forty-five, divorced, an IRS auditor. Another deserving victim. Another bloodsucker. Eric and I'd been audited one long, hot summer. The IRS found one small error, but the accountant and lawyer bills to defend ourselves were tremendous. We would have had more rights if we'd been accused of murder, instead of cheating on our income tax.

Yes, I could kill an IRS auditor. I could hand out justice to the unjust. In my new life, I would punish the wicked. I would be superwoman— invisible by day, fearless by night. That beat being a divorced librarian living in a garden apartment.

I hardly tasted my dinner, I was so excited by my new life. Not that my dinner had much flavor: four ounces of boneless, skinless joyless chicken and romaine with fat-free dressing.

For dessert, I treated myself to two ounces of dark chocolate and a delicious day dream of Michael. It had been a long time since any man had wanted me. And this man had so much to give me.

I watched the full moon rise, and paced my condo. Eric didn't come home that night. I didn't expect him to. I was glad. I was in no mood to confront him.

I dug out my favorite black Armani dress. It was specially designed to cover my flaws. The high neck hid the crepe under my chin. The short sleeves disguised the unsightly wings under my arms that no workouts could eliminate. The short hem showed my legs at their best. I put on

sexy high-heeled sandals. They were dangerous on the docks, but I was living dangerously these days.

Michael was waiting for me outside my condo. He'd come to me this time. His hair was black as a midnight ocean. His luminous skin was like moonlight on snow. He kissed me, and his lips were soft and surprisingly warm.

"You know who we are, don't you?" he said.

"Yes," I said. "I want to be like you."

"You must be sure. You must have no illusions before you adopt our way of life. You must ask me any questions tonight."

"Are you immortal?" I said.

"Almost," he said. "We can be killed by fire, by sunlight and by wooden stakes through the heart. All natural elements."

"What about crosses and holy water?"

He laughed. "There were vampires long before there were Christians."

"What will happen to me? How will I become one of you?"

"I will make you a vampire by giving you my blood. I will take yours. Don't be frightened. It's not painful. You'll find it quite exhilarating. Once the transference is complete, you must make your first kill."

"Will I change? Will I look different?"

"You'll look like yourself, only more beautiful. Any wrinkles will vanish. Any physical flaws will disappear. You'll quickly attain your ideal weight. Our people are never fat."

Vampirism—the ultimate low-fat diet. I wanted to smile. But suddenly, I couldn't joke. The changes were profound, and frightening. "I'll never be able to eat food again." I felt a sudden desperate pain at what I would have to give up.

"Do you eat now?" Michael said.

The question seemed ridiculous. "Of course," I said.

"But do you like what you eat? Do you actually hunger for carrot sticks? Do you long for steamed broccoli and romaine with diet

dressing?" He put his warm lips next to my ear and whispered, "When was the last time you had food you really wanted?"

I thought of the meals of my youth, when I could eat anything: fried chicken and cheeseburgers, crispy french fries lightly sprinkled with salt, hot fudge sundaes with warm whipped cream, crusty bread and butter.

"You haven't had any of those in years, have you?" Michael said.

He could read my mind. I knew that now.

"You'll never experience the pain of dieting again," he said. "You will have no need for ordinary food. You will drink the food of the gods. Blood is offered to them as a sacrifice. You will take it for your own pleasure. It is a thrill you cannot imagine. You will still hunger, but now you will be satisfied. You are hungry, aren't you? Even now, after your supper of skinless chicken."

"Yes." The pale, pathetic hunk of bird nearly turned my stomach. "I can do good, too," I said. "I can feed on those who deserve to die."

His eyes were suddenly darker, and I realized he was angry. "No! You must embrace the dark side like a lover. Any good you do will be accidental."

"But Jack—" I began.

"When Rosette killed that bloodsucking lawyer, she made a lot of scorned wives happy. But Jack will be mourned by his daughter. Randall killed the IRS agent because she'd been auditing his books. She nearly drove him crazy, and he was innocent. But she was the sole support of her elderly mother. And, irritating though she was, the agent was an honest woman.

"You cannot fool yourself into believing that you will only feed on serial killers or child molesters. That is romantic nonsense.

"You are evil and you must choose it. Your killing will not make the world a better place. We kill for revenge, for sport, for reasons that are impossibly petty. Marissa once killed a dress shop clerk on Las Olas because she wouldn't wait on her."

"So you've killed more people in Fort Lauderdale than Jack and the IRS agent?" I said.

"Many more," Michael said. "The details about the other bodies being exsanguinated did not make the papers. The police try to hide that information. When it becomes public, then it's time for us to leave. That's why we're going tomorrow night."

"What happened to the other bodies?"

Michael said nothing. He didn't have to. I realized we were looking at the wide black ocean.

"Where will you go when you leave?" I said.

"We'll summer in the south of France," he said. "I have a cottage by the sea. The air smells of lavender and the sound of the waves is wonderfully soothing."

A small sigh escaped me. He was offering me such a beautiful life.

"Why me?" I asked. "There are millions of women like me, a little past our prime, abandoned by our husbands."

"Do you define yourself only by your husband?" he asked. "I don't think so. Americans have such boring ideas about age. Older cultures celebrate all aspects of a woman's life. Americans only want youth, which can be the dullest time. I prefer a woman who has lived.

"And you are not like the others. You are strong. You have resisted the lemming-like urge for plastic surgery. It's became a national obsession, but you fought it, even though it cost you your marriage and your comfortable life. You knew it wasn't the right choice for you. That takes courage. You know who you are. Do you know what you are?"

For the first time, I knew I was someone special.

He took my hand. "I'd like you to join us," he said. "I want you. Now that you know, you have only two choices: join us or die."

"May I have twenty-four hours? I have some loose ends to tie up."

"Yes. But, remember, no one will believe you if you go to the police. And we will be gone before they can get a search warrant."

"I would never betray you," I said. "You've already helped me. Did you encourage Rosette to kill Jack? For my sake?"

"I wish I could take credit," Michael said. "But Jack was her idea. Still, I'm glad it helped you."

Then he kissed my hand. "You have much to think about," he said. "I hope you make the right decision."

I left him feeling oddly lighthearted for a woman whose only choice was death: my real death, the living death of middle age, or the death-in-life of a vampire.

I slept well that night, or what was left of it. Then, at five-thirty, I was awakened by Eric, slamming doors and opening drawers. He had four white shirts in plastic bags. I'd picked up those shirts for him from the best laundry in Lauderdale, prepared precisely the way he liked: hangers, no starch.

I sat up groggily in bed. "From now on," I said, "have your slut pick up your laundry. That's the last errand I'm running for you."

"Don't you dare call Dawn that," Eric said.

"Dawn! What kind of name is that? Has it dawned on you how trite you are?" My bitterness burst like a lanced boil, and I was screaming like a fishwife. My husband yelled right back.

Our argument was interrupted by a pounding on our front door. Marvin, our condo security guard, was standing on the doorstep. He looked embarrassed. "I'm sorry," he said. "But there have been complaints about the noise."

We both apologized to the guard. Now my humiliation was complete. Eric walked out a few minutes later, clutching his fresh shirts by the hangers. "You'll hear from my lawyer," he said.

That was it. That was how he ended our quarter-century marriage, the day before my birthday.

He'd forgotten that, of course. He couldn't even say, "I'm sorry, I've found someone else." Eric wasn't sorry, was he? But he would be.

I watched the sun rise on the last morning of my life. The new morning turned the air a pearlescent pink, and a shimmering fog drifted across the water. White birds skimmed along the Intracoastal.

I will never see this beauty again, I thought. But I didn't have time to wallow in regret. I had things to do. I stopped at a diner for a last, lavish breakfast. The young, busty waitress was too busy flirting with a table full of businessmen to pay any attention to me. I could hear the cook ringing the bell in the kitchen. When the waitress finally brought my breakfast, the eggs had congealed to rubber and the home fries were coated with grease.

"This food is cold," I said to the waitress.

"Huh?" she said, as if she'd just noticed me for the first time. Once again, I was the incredible, invisible middle-aged woman.

"I'll get the cook to warm it up," she said.

"Never mind," I said. "I'm not hungry after all."

I threw some money on the table and left. I'd lost my taste for food.

At ten o'clock, I was weeping in my lawyer's office. The tears came easily, and they weren't entirely false. Only the accusations were made up.

"Please help me," I sobbed. "My husband is divorcing me. He has a new girlfriend and he hates me. They're fighting about how soon they can get married. I'm in the way. I'm afraid Eric will harm me."

"Harm you how?" the lawyer said.

She would look perfect on the witness stand during Eric's murder trial, I thought. She was serious enough for the women to believe her, but sexy enough to get the men's attention. There was something about her tailored black suit, tightly pulled back hair and horn-rimmed glasses that made men wonder what she'd look like without them.

"K-kill me," I said. "Eric doesn't let anyone stand in his way."

"Have there been any threats?" the lawyer said.

"Nothing in front of witnesses," I said. "But we had a terrible fight this morning, and he said he'd kill me if I didn't give him a divorce and . . . I'm so embarrassed. Condo security had to knock on our door."

"That's good," the lawyer said. "I mean, it's not good, but it will help."

She made plans to get a restraining order, and told me to change the locks. Of course, I would tragically disappear before I could carry out her instructions.

It was after noon when I left the lawyer's office, my least favorite time of day in Florida. The parking lot was baking in the harsh sun. It showed all the cracks in the buildings and the sidewalks—and in my lips and skin. I won't miss this, I thought. Not one bit.

I wanted to treat myself to a special dress for this evening, my coming out. I strolled along Las Olas Boulevard, where all the smart shops were. The windows glowed with dresses in dramatic black and fabulous colors.

Black, I thought. Black was the right choice when you're going to the dark side.

I entered the cool shop. A young saleswoman, who looked like a thinner version of Dawn, was talking to another clerk. They didn't look up when I came in. They didn't notice me.

"Excuse me," I said. "May I have some help?"

The two young women smirked and rolled their eyes, and I understood why Marissa had killed her salesclerk. If I had more time in Lauderdale, I'd come back for this one.

But I didn't. I bought the first dress I tried on. It didn't fit quite right. I could see my drooping back in the mirror, the little rolls of fat at my waist. But they would be gone soon. In my new life, this dress would be spectacular.

As I left, I knew I'd made the right decision. Not about the dress. About my life. I would be invisible, but it would be my choice.

I would be powerful.

I would be beautiful forever.

I would get the blood back. It would flow again. It would flow into me, and I would feel the ecstasy. I would not be young, but I didn't want to

be young. The young were vulnerable, trusting, hurting. I never wanted to feel that way again.

I sat in my condo and thought about the rest of the night and the beginning of my new life.

When the sky began to bleed red, I walked once more through my condo, saying good-bye to all my things. It would be easy to give them up. I sat on the balcony until the sun set and the sky turned dark velvet. Then I dressed for my final night.

At midnight, I met Michael down by the docks. He was frighteningly beautiful.

"Have you made your choice?" he said.

"I choose you," I said.

He kissed me. "I'm so glad," he whispered. "Everyone is waiting for you. Who will be your first kill?"

"Dawn, Eric's office manager. The police will find her bloodless body outside his clinic."

"What about your husband?"

"I'll let him live. It will be fun to see how he explains his drained and dead girlfriend and his missing wife. I'll be gone, but I won't take anything with me—no money from our bank account, no stocks, not even my jewelry. I'll follow the trial on the Internet from the south of France."

Michael smiled. "I'm sure we'll all be entertained by the drama," he said. "Happy birthday, Katherine."

SCELERATUS

TANYA HUFF

*M*an, this whole church thing just freaks me right out." Tony came out of the shadows where the streetlights stopped short of Holy Rosary Cathedral and fell into step beside the short, blond man who'd just come out of the building. "I mean, you're a member of the blood-sucking undead for Christ's sa . . . Ow!" He rubbed the back of his head. "What was that for?"

"I just came from Confession. I'm in a mood."

"It's going to pass, right?" In the time it took him to maneuver around three elderly Chinese women, his companion had made it almost all the way to the parking lot and he had to run to catch up. "You know, we've been together what, almost two years, and you haven't been in church since last year around this time and . . ."

"Exactly this time."

"Okay. Is it like an anniversary or something?"

"Exactly like an anniversary." Henry Fitzroy, once Duke of Richmond and Summerset, bastard son of Henry VIII, fished out the keys to his BMW and unlocked the door.

Tony studied Henry's face as he got into his own seat, as he buckled his seat belt, as Henry pulled out onto Richards Street. "You want to tell me about it?" he asked at last.

They'd turned onto Smithe Street before Henry answered . . .

* * *

Even after three weeks of torment, her body burned and broken, she was still beautiful to him. He cut the rope and caught her as she dropped, allowing her weight to take him to his knees. Holding her against his heart, rocking back and forth in a sticky pool, he waited for grief.

She had been dead only a few hours when he'd found her, following a blood scent so thick it left a trail even a mortal could have used. Her wrists had been tightly bound behind her back, a coarse rope threaded through the lashing and used to hoist her into the air. Heavy iron weights hung from burned ankles. The Inquisitors had begun with flogging and added more painful persuasions over time. Time had killed her; pain layered on pain until finally life had fled.

They'd had a year together, a year of nights since he'd followed her home from the Square of San Marco. He'd waited until the servants were asleep then slipped unseen and unheard into her father's house, into her room. Her heartbeat had drawn him to the bed, and he'd gently pulled the covers back. Her name was Ginevra Treschi. Almost thirty, and three years a widow, she wasn't beautiful but she was so alive—even asleep— that he'd found himself staring. Only to find a few moments later that she was staring back at him.

"I don't want to hurry your decision," she'd said dryly, "but I'm getting chilled and I'd like to know if I should scream."

He'd intended to feed and then convince her that he was a dream, but he found he couldn't.

For the first time in a hundred years, for the first time since he had willingly pressed his mouth to the bleeding wound in his immortal lover's breast, Henry Fitzroy, allowed someone to see him as he was.

All he was.

Vampire. Prince. Man.

Allowed love.

Ginevra Treschi had brought light back into a life spent hiding from the sun.

Only one gray eye remained beneath a puckered lid and the Inquisitors had burned off what remained of the dark hair—the ebony curls first shorn in the convent that had been no protection from the Hounds of God. In Venice, in the year of our Lord, 1637, the Hounds hunted as they pleased among the powerless. First, it had been the Jews, and then the Moors, and then those suspected of Protestantism until finally the Inquisition, backed by the gold flowing into Spain from the New World, began to cast its net where it chose. Ginevra had been an intelligent woman who dared to think for herself. In this time, that was enough.

Dead flesh compacted under his hands as his grip tightened. He wanted to rage and weep and mourn his loss but he felt nothing. Her light, her love had been extinguished and darkness had filled its place.

His heart as cold as hers, Henry kissed her forehead and laid the body gently down. When he stood, his hands were covered in her blood.

There would be blood enough to wash it away.

* * *

He found the priests in a small study, sitting at ease in a pair of cushioned chairs on either side of a marble hearth, slippered feet stretched out toward the fire, gold rings glittering on pale fingers. Cleaned and fed, they still stank of her death.

" . . . confessed to having relations with the devil, was forgiven, and gave her soul up to God. Very satisfactory all around. Shall we return the body to the Sisters or to her family?"

The older Dominican shrugged. "I cannot see that it makes any difference, she . . . Who are you?"

Henry lifted his lip off his teeth in a parody of a smile. "I am vengeance," he said, closing and bolting the heavy oak door behind him. When he turned, he saw that the younger priest, secure in the power he wielded, blinded by that security, had moved toward him.

Their eyes met. The priest, who had stood calmly by while countless *heretics* found their way to redemption on paths of pain, visibly paled.

Henry stopped pretending to smile. "And I am the devil Ginevra Treschi had relations with."

He released the Hunger her blood had called.

They died begging for their lives as Ginevra had died.

It wasn't enough.

* * *

The Grand Inquisitor had sent five other Dominicans to serve on his Tribunal in Venice. Three died at prayer. One died in bed. One died as he dictated a letter to a novice who would remember nothing but darkness and blood . . .

* * *

The Doge, needing Spain's political and monetary support to retain power, had given the Inquisitors a wing of his palace. Had given them the room where the stone walls were damp and thick and the screams of those the Hounds brought down would not disturb his slumber.

Had killed Ginevra as surely as if he'd used the irons.

* * *

With a soft cry, Gracia la Valla sat bolt upright in the Doge's ornate bed clutching the covers in both hands. The canopy was open and a spill of moonlight patterned the room in shadows. She heard a sound beside her and, thinking she'd woken her lover, murmured, as she reached out for him, "Such a dark dream I had."

Her screams brought the household guard.

* * *

He killed the Inquisition's holy torturer quickly, like the animal he was, and left him lying beside the filthy pallet that was his bed.

It still wasn't enough.

* * *

In the hour before dawn, Henry carried the body of Ginevra Treschi to the chapel of the Benedictine Sisters who had tried to shelter her. He had washed her in the canal, wrapped her in linen, and laid her in front of their altar, her hands closed around the rosary she'd given him the night they'd parted.

Her lips when he kissed them were cold.

But so were his.

Although he had all but bathed in the blood of her murderers, it was her blood still staining his hands.

He met none of the Sisters and, as much as he could feel anything, he was glad of it. Her miraculous return to the cloister would grant her burial in their consecrated ground—but not if death returned with her.

* * *

Henry woke the next night in one of the vaults under San Marco, the smell of her blood all around him. It would take still more blood to wash it away. For all their combined power of Church and State, the Inquisition did not gather their victims randomly. Someone had born witness against her.

Giuseppe Lemmo.

Marriage to him had been the alternative to the convent.

He had a large head, and a powdered gray wig, and no time for denial. After Henry had drunk his fill, head and wig and the body they were more or less attached to, slid silently into the canal.

As Lemmo sank beneath the filthy water, the sound of two men approaching drove Henry into the shadows. His clothing stank of new death and old but it was unlikely anyone could smell it over the stink of the city.

"No, no, I say the Dominicans died at the hand of the Devil rising from Hell to protect one of His own."

Henry fell silently into step behind the pair of merchants, the Hunger barely leashed.

"And I say," the second merchant snorted, "that the Holy Fathers called it on themselves. They spend so much time worrying about the Devil in others, well, there's no smoke without fire. They enjoyed their work too much for my taste and you'll notice, if you look close, that most of their *heretics* had a hefty purse split between the Order and the Doge after their deaths."

"And more talk like that will give them *your* purse to split, you fool."

Actually, it had saved them both but they would never know it.

"Give who my purse? The Hounds of God in Venice have gone to their just reward." He turned his head and spat into the dark waters of the canal. "And I wish Old Nick the joy of them."

His companion hurriedly crossed himself. "Do you think they're the only dogs in the kennel? The Dominicans are powerful, their Tribunals

stretch all the way back to Spain and up into the north lands. They won't let this go unanswered. I think you will find before very long that Venice will be overrun by the Hounds of God."

"You think? Fool, the One Hundred will be too busy fighting over a new Doge to tell his Holiness that some of his dogs have been put down."

Before they could draw near the lights and crowds around the Grand Canal, Henry slipped into the deeper darkness between two buildings. The Dominican's Tribunals stretched all the way back to Spain. He looked down at Ginevra's blood on his hands.

* * *

"Drink, Signore?"

Without looking at either the bottle or the man who offered it, Henry shook his head and continued staring out over the moonlit water toward the lights of Sicily. Before him, although he could not tell which lights they were, were the buildings of the Inquisition's largest tribunal outside of Spain. They had their own courthouse, their own prison, their own chapel, their own apartments where half of every *heretic's* possessions ended up.

It was entirely possible, they knew he was coming or that *something* was coming. Rumor could travel by day and night while he could move only in darkness.

Behind him stretched a long line of the dead. He had killed both Dominicans and the secular authorities who sat with them on the Tribunals. He had killed the lawyers hired by the Inquisition. He had killed those who denounced their neighbors to the Inquisition and those who lent the Inquisition their support. He had killed those who thought to kill him.

He had never killed so often or been so strong. He could stand on a hill overlooking a village and know how many lives were scattered

beneath him. He could stand in shadow outside a shuttered building and count the number of hearts beating within. He could stare into the eyes of the doomed and be almost deafened by the song of blood running through their veins. It was becoming hard to tell where he ended and the Hunger began.

The terrified whispers that followed him named him demon so, when he fed, he hid the marks that would have shown what he truly was. There were too many who believed the old tales and he was far too vulnerable in the day.

"Too good to drink with me, Signore?" Stinking of wine, he staggered along the rail until the motion of the waves threw him into Henry's side. Stumbling back, he raised the jug belligerently. "Too good to . . ."

Henry caught the man's gaze with his and held it. Held it through the realization, held it through the terror, held it as the heart began to race with panic, held it as bowels voided. When he finally released it, he caught the jug that dropped from nerveless fingers and watched the man crawl whimpering away, his mind already refusing to admit what he had seen.

It had been easy to find a ship willing to cross the narrow strait at night. Henry had merely attached himself to a party of students negotiating their return to the university after spending the day in the brothels of Reggio and the exotic arms of mainland whores. Although the sky was clear, the moon full, and the winds from the north west, the Captain of the schooner had accepted their combined coin so quickly he'd probably been looking for an excuse to make the trip. No doubt his hold held some of the steady stream of goods from France, Genoa, and Florence that moved illegally down the western coast to the Spanish controlled Kingdom of Naples and then to Sicily.

The smugglers would use the students as Henry intended, as a diversion over their arrival in Messina.

They passed the outer arm of the sickle-shaped harbor, close enough that the night no longer hid the individual buildings crouched on the

skirts of Mount Etna. He could see the spire of the Cathedral, the Abbey of Santa Maria della Valle, the monastery of San Giorgio, but nothing that told him where the Dominicans murdered in the name of God.

No matter.

It would be easy enough to find what he was looking for.

They could lock themselves away, but Henry would find them. They could beg or plead or pray, but they would die. And they would keep dying until enough blood had poured over his hands to wash the stain of Ginevra's blood away.

* * *

Messina was a port city and had been in continuous use since before the days of the Roman Empire. Beneath its piers and warehouses, beneath broad avenues and narrow streets, beneath the lemon trees and the olive groves, were the ruins of an earlier city. Beneath its Necropolis, were Roman catacombs.

As the students followed their hired torch bearer from the docks to the university, Henry followed the scent of death through the streets until he came at last to the end of the Via Annunziata to the heavy iron gates that closed off the Piazza del Dominico from the rest of the city. The pair of stakes rising out of the low stone dais in the center of the square had been used within the last three or four days. The stink of burning flesh almost overwhelmed the stink of fear.

Almost.

"Hey! You! What are you doing?!"

The guard's sudden roar out of the shadows was intended to intimidate.

"Why the gates?" Henry asked without turning. The Hounds preferred an audience when they burned away heresy.

"You a stranger?"

"I am vengeance," Henry said quietly, touching the iron and rubbing the residue of greasy smoke between two fingers. As the guard reached for him, he turned and closed his hand about the burly wrist, tightening his grip until bones cracked and the man fell to his knees. "Why the gates?" he repeated.

"Friends. Oh God, please . . ." It wasn't the pain that made him beg but the darkness in the stranger's eyes. "Some of the heretics got friends!"

"Good." He had fed in Reggio so he snapped the guard's neck and let the body fall back into the shadows. Without the guard, the gates were no barrier.

* * *

"You said he was ready to confess." Habit held up out of the filth, the Dominican stared disapprovingly at the body on the rack. "He is unconscious!"

The thin man in the leather apron shrugged. "Wasn't when I sent for you."

"Get him off that thing and back into the cell with the others." Sandals sticking to the floor, he stepped back beside the second monk and shook his head. "I am exhausted and his attorney has gone home. Let God's work take a break until morning, for pity's . . ."

The irons had not been in the fire but they did what they'd been made to do. Even as the Hunger rose to answer the blood now turning the robe to black and white and red, Henry appreciated the irony of the monk's last word. A man who knew no pity had died with pity on his tongue. The second monk screamed and choked on a crimson flood as curved knives, taken from the table beside the rack, hooked in under his arms and met at his breast bone.

Henry killed the jailer as he'd killed the guard. Only those who gave the orders paid in blood.

Behind doors of solid oak, one large cell held half a dozen prisoners and two of the smaller cells held one prisoner each. Removing the bars, Henry opened the doors and stepped back out of sight. He had learned early that prisoners would rather remain to face the Inquisition than walk by him but he always watched them leave, some small foolish part of his heart hoping he'd see Ginevra among them, free and alive.

The prisoner from one of the small cells, surged out as the door was opened. Crouched low and ready for a fight, he squinted in the torch light searching for an enemy. When he saw the bodies, he straightened and his generous mouth curved up into a smile. Hair as red-gold as Henry's had begun to gray but in spite of approaching middle-age, his body was trim and well built. He was well-dressed and clearly used to being obeyed.

On his order, four men and two women shuffled out of the large cell, hands raised to block the light, bits of straw clinging to hair and clothing. On his order, they lead the way out of the prison.

He was using them to see if the way was clear, Henry realized. Clever. Ginevra had been clever too.

Murmured Latin drew his attention back to the bodies of the Dominicans. Kneeling between them, a hand on each brow, the elderly Franciscan who'd emerged from the other cell performed the Last Rites.

"In nomine Patris, et Filii, et Spiritus Sancti. Amen." One hand gripping the edge of the rack, he pulled himself painfully to his feet. "You can come out now. I know what you are."

"You have no idea, monk."

"You think not?" The old man shrugged and bent to release the ratchet that held the body on the rack taunt. "You are the death that haunts the Inquisition. You began in Venice, you finally found your way to us here in Messina."

"If I am death, you should fear me."

"I haven't feared death for some time." He turned and swept the shadows with a rheumy gaze. "Are you afraid to face *me*, then?"

Lips drawn back off his teeth, Henry moved into the light.

The Franciscan frowned. "Come closer."

Snarling, Henry stepped over one of the bodies, the blood scent wrapping around him. Prisoner of the Inquisition or not, the monk would learn fear. He caught the Franciscan's gaze with his but, to his astonishment, couldn't hold it. When he tried to look away, he could not.

After a long moment, the old monk sighed, and released him. "Not evil, although you have done evil. Not anger, nor joy in slaughter. I never knew your kind could feel such pain."

He staggered back, clutching for the Hunger as it fled. "I feel nothing!"

"So you keep telling yourself. What happened in Venice, Vampire? Who did the Inquisition kill that you try to wash away the blood with theirs?"

Over the roaring in his head, Henry heard himself say, "Ginevra Treschi."

"You loved her."

It wasn't a question. He answered it anyway. "Yes."

"You should kill me, you know. I have seen you. I know what you are. I know what is myth . . ." He touched two fingers to the wooden cross hanging against his chest. " . . . and I know how to destroy you. When you are helpless in the day, I could drag your body into sunlight; I could hammer a stake through your heart. For your own safety, you should kill me."

He was right.

What was one more death? Henry's fingers, sticky with blood already shed, closed around the old man's skinny neck. He would kill him quickly and return to the work he had come here to do. There were many, many more Dominicans in Messina.

The Franciscan's pulse beat slow and steady.

It beat Henry's hand back to his side. "No. I do not kill the innocent."

"I will not argue original sin with you, Vampire, but you're wrong. Parigi Carradori, the man from the cell next to mine, seeks power from the Lord of Hell by sacrificing children in dark rites."

Henry's lip curled. "Neither do I listen to the Inquisition's lies."

"No lie; Carradori admits it freely without persuasion. The demons hold full possession of his mind and you have sent him out to slaughter the closest thing to innocence in the city."

"That is none of my concern."

"If that is true, then you really should kill me."

"Do not push me, old man!" He reached for the Hunger but for the first time since Ginevra's death it was slow to answer.

"By God's Grace, you are being given a chance to save yourself. To find, if you will, redemption. You may, of course, chose to give yourself fully to the darkness you have had wrapped about you for so many months, allowing it, finally, into your heart. Or you may chose to begin making amends."

"Amends?" He stepped back slowly so it wouldn't look so much like a retreat and spat into the drying blood pooled out from the Dominicans' bodies. "You want me to feel sorrow for the deaths of these men?"

"Not yet. To feel sorrow, you must first feel. Begin by stopping Carradori. We will see what the Lord has in mind for you after that." He patted the air between them, an absentminded benediction, then turned and began to free the man on the rack, working the leather straps out of creases in the swollen arms.

Henry watched him for a moment then turned on one heel and strode out of the room.

He was not going after Carradori. His business was with the Inquisition, with those who had slowly murdered his Ginevra, not with a man who may or may not be dealing with the Dark One.

"*. . . you have sent him out to slaughter the closest thing to innocence in the city.*"

He was not responsible for what Carradori chose to do with his freedom. Stepping out into the square, he listened to the sound of Dominican hearts beating all around him. Enough blood to finally *be* enough.

" . . . *seeks power from the Lord of Hell by sacrificing children in dark rites.*"

Children died. Some years, more children died than lived. He could not save them all even were he willing to try.

"*You may choose to give yourself fully to the darkness. Or you may chose to begin making amends.*"

"Shut up, old man!"

Torch held high, head cocked to better peer beyond its circle of light, a young monk stepped out of one of the other buildings. "Who is there? Is that you Brother Pe . . . ?" He felt more than saw a shadow slip past him. When he moved the torch forward, he saw only the entrance to the prison. A bloody hand print glistened on the pale stone.

* * *

The prisoners had left the gate open. Most of them had taken the path of least resistance and stumbled down the Via Annunziata but one had turned left, gone along the wall heading up toward the mountain.

Carradori.

Out away from the stink of terror that filled the prison, Henry could smell the taint of the Dark One in his blood.

The old man hadn't lied about that, at least.

Behind him, a sudden cacophony of male voices suggested his visit had been discovered. It would be dangerous to deal further with the Inquisition tonight. He turned left.

He should have caught up to Carradori in minutes but he didn't and he found himself standing outside a row of tenements pressed up against the

outer wall of the Necropolis with no idea of where the man had gone. Lip drawn up off his teeth, he snarled softly and a scrawny dog, thrown out of sleep by the sound, began to howl. In a heartbeat, a dozen more were protesting the appearance of a new predator on their territory.

The noise the monks had made was nothing in comparison.

As voices rained curses down from a dozen windows, Henry ran for the quiet of the Necropolis.

The City of the Dead had tenements of its own; the dead had been stacked in this ground since the Greeks controlled the Strait. Before Venice, before Ginevra, Henry had spent very little time with the dead—his own grave had not exactly been a restful place. Of late, however, he had grown to appreciate the silence. No heartbeats, no bloodsong, nothing to call the Hunger, to remind him of vengeance not yet complete.

But not tonight.

Tonight he could hear two hearts and feel a life poised on the edge of eternity.

The houses of the dead often became temples for the dark arts.

* * *

Warning glyphs had been painted in blood on the outside of the mausoleum. Henry sneered and passed them by. Blood held a specific power over him, as specific as the power he held over it. The dark arts were a part of neither.

The black candles, one at either end of the skinny child laid out on the tomb, shed so little light Henry entered without fear of detection. To his surprise, Carradori looked directly at him with wild eyes.

"And so the agent of my Dark Lord comes to take his place by my side." Stripped to the waist, he had cut more glyphs into his own flesh, new wounds over old scars.

"I am no one's agent," Henry spat, stepping forward.

"You set me free, Vampire. You slaughtered those who had imprisoned me."

"You may chose to give yourself fully to the darkness."

"That had nothing to do with you."

Holding a long straight blade over the child, Carradori laughed. "Then why are you here?"

"Or you may chose to begin making amends."

"I was curious."

"Then let me satisfy your curiosity."

As he lifted the knife, the language he spoke was neither Latin nor Greek for Henry's father had seen that he was fluent in both. It had hard consonants that tore at the ears of the listener as much as at the throat of the speaker. The Hunger, pushed back by the Franciscan, rose in answer.

This would be one way to get enough blood.

Then the child turned her head.

Gray eyes stared at Henry past a fall of ebony curls. One small dirty hand stretched out toward him.

But the knife was already on its way down.

He caught the point on the back of his arm, felt it cut through him toward the child as his fist drove the bones of Carradori's face back into his brain. He was dead before he hit the floor.

The point of the blade had touched the skin over the child's heart but the only blood in the tomb was Henry's.

He dragged the knife free and threw it aside, catching the little girl up in his arms and sliding to his knees. The new wound in his arm was nothing to the old wound in his heart. It felt as though a glass case had been shattered and now the shards were slicing their way out. Rocking back and forth, he buried his face in the child's dark curls and sobbed over and over, "I'm sorry, I'm sorry, I'm sorry."

"... *confessed to having relations with the devil, was forgiven, and gave her soul up to God."*

"And I am the devil Ginevra Treschi had relations with."

Loving him had killed her.

* * *

When he woke the next evening, the old Franciscan was sitting against the wall, the shielded lantern at his feet making him a gray shadow in the darkness.

"I thought you'd bring a mob with stakes and torches."

"Not much of a hiding place, if that's what you thought."

Sitting up, Henry glanced around the alcove and shrugged. He had left the girl at the tenements, one grimy hand buried in the ruff of the scrawny dog he'd wakened and then, with dawn close on his heels, he'd gone into the first layer of catacombs and given himself to the day.

"Why didn't you?"

"Vengeance is mine, sayth the Lord. And besides . . ." Clutching the lantern, he heaved himself to his feet. " . . . I hate to lose a chance to redeem a soul."

"You know what I am. I have no soul."

"You said you loved this Ginevra Treschi. Love does not exist without a soul."

"My love killed her."

"Perhaps." Setting the lantern on the tomb, he took Henry's left hand in his and turned his palm to the light. The wound began to bleed sluggishly again, the blood running down the pale skin of Henry's forearm to pool in his palm. "Did she chose to love you in return?"

His voice less than a whisper. "Yes."

"Then don't take that choice away from her. She has lost enough else. You have blood on your hands, Vampire. But not hers."

He stared at the crimson stains. "Not hers."

"No. And you can see whose blood is needed to wash away the rest." He gently closed Henry's fingers.

"Mine . . ."

The smack on the back of the head took him by surprise. He hadn't even seen the old monk move.

"The Blood of the Lamb, Vampire. Your death will not bring my brother Dominicans back to life but your life will be long enough to atone."

"You are a very strange monk."

"I wasn't always a monk. I knew one of your kind in my youth and perhaps by redeeming you, I redeem myself for the mob and the stakes I brought to him."

Henry could see his own sorrow mirrored in the Franciscans eyes. He knew better than to attempt to look beyond it.

"Why were you a prisoner of the Inquisition?"

"I'm a Franciscan. The Dominicans don't appreciate our holding of the moral high ground."

"The moral high ground . . ."

"Christ was poor. We are poor. *They* are not. Which does not mean, however they need to die."

"I didn't . . ."

"I know." He laid a warm palm against Henry's hair. "How long has it been since your last confession . . . ?"

* * *

"The Tribunal's buildings were destroyed in an earthquake in 1783. They were never rebuilt. When I went back to Messina in the 1860's, even I couldn't find the place they'd been."

Tony stared out into the parking garage. They'd been home for a half an hour, just sitting in the car while Henry talked. "Did you really kill all those people?"

"Yes."

"But some of them were bad people, abusing their power and . . . that's not the point, is it?"

"No. They died because I felt guilty about what happened to Ginevra, not because the world would have been a better place without them in it, not because I had to kill to survive." His lips pulled back off his teeth. "I have good reasons when I kill people now."

"Speaking as people," Tony said softly, "I'm glad to hear that."

His tone drew Henry's gaze around. "You're not afraid?"

"Because you vamped out three hundred and fifty years ago?" He twisted in the seat and met Henry's eyes. "No. I know you *now*." When Henry looked away, he reached out and laid a hand on his arm. "Hey, I got a past too. Not like yours, but you can't live without having done things you need to make up for. Things you're sorry you did."

"Is being sorry enough?"

"I haven't been to Mass since I was a kid, but isn't it supposed to be? I mean, if you're *really* sorry? So what kind of penance did he give you?" he asked a few moments later when it became obvious Henry wasn't going to elaborate on how sorry he was.

"Today?"

"No, three hundred and fifty years ago. I mean, three Hail Mary's aren't gonna cut it after, well . . ."

"He made me promise to remember."

"That's all?" When it became clear Henry wasn't going to answer that either, he slid out of the car and leaned back in the open door. "Come on, TSN's got Australian rugger on tonight. You know you love it."

393

"You go, I'll be up in a few minutes."

"You okay?"

"Fine."

"I could . . ."

"Tony."

"Okay. I could go upstairs." He straightened, closed the car door, and headed across the parking garage to the elevator. When he reached it, he hit the call button and waited without turning. He didn't need to turn. He knew what he'd see.

Henry.

Still sitting in the car.

Staring at his hands.

ETERNITY EMBRACED

LARISSA IONE

ONE

*A*ndrea Cole had been hunting demons and vampires since she was eighteen, almost since the day she'd dropped out of college and returned home to witness both parents being torn apart by demons before her eyes. That was nine years, a hundred kills and two dozen broken bones ago. Killing evil creatures had never bothered her. Not once. But tonight was different.

Tonight she might have to kill the love of her life.

She gripped her stake so hard that she was surprised it didn't crack. Silently, she eased down the damp, narrow staircase that led to an underground chamber beneath the Oregon billionaire's mansion. The human scumbag was in league with demons who the Aegis, a society, of human warriors protecting the world from evil, had been watching for two years. Andrea's division, a special vampire investigative unit, had concentrated all its efforts on bringing this guy down, starting with the vampires he harbored on his property. Beneath it, anyway.

Recently, an Aegis Guardian had disappeared into the bowels of the mansion. Under the pretence of delivering a kitchen order from a local bakery, Kaden had snooped around and got lucky when he spotted the butler opening a secret panel in the pantry. He'd followed the butler down a staircase, speaking softly into his hidden microphone as he described everything he saw. At the bottom, he'd found himself in a giant chamber filled with torture devices, several cells, dozens of tunnels and, unfortunately, more vampires than he could combat.

Andrea had listened in horror as Kaden was overwhelmed. When the sound had cut off, something inside her had died, and she'd done nothing but live and breathe revenge ever since. And now, revenge was within her grasp, because at this very moment there were twenty Guardians swarming the mansion grounds, armed to the teeth and working on three separate missions.

One: Capture the billionaire scumbag, Blake Alden. Two: Kill as many vampires as possible. Three: Find Kaden.

Find Kaden so Andrea could kill him.

The thought rolled through her on a wave of nausea. Maybe he was OK. Maybe the vampires hadn't turned him. And maybe she was freaking delusional, because she knew damned good and well they'd done it. Vamps got off on torturing Guardians—or worse, turning them. Nothing amused bloodsuckers more than dropping an enemy head first into their worst nightmare.

Cautiously, she stepped out of the stairwell and into a huge, cavernous basement. From the stone walls hung wicked-looking implements of torture. The floor was dirt. It wasn't exactly basement, it was more of a cave, with cells carved into the walls. The doors were solid slabs of metal, with only a small, eye-level slotted window shot through with steel bars.

Ahead were tunnels she'd be willing to bet led to living spaces, and dozens of exits that would come out all over Portland. Behind her, six Guardians filed out of the stairwell.

"This is weird," Zach, a newer recruit, whispered. "There's no one here."

"They might have been tipped off and ran." Andrea moved towards the cells. "Or it's a trap and they're hiding. Be careful."

Zach and the others disappeared into the tunnels, leaving Andrea to clear the immediate area. The first cell was empty, the shackle on the walls hanging dejectedly from their chains. Some sort of spindly, man-sized demon occupied the second cell, cowering a corner and trembling. A colleague would dispatch the pathetic creature later.

She moved on, slowing when the small hairs on the back of he neck stood up as she sidestepped a dark stain on the ground. Her gaze tracked automatically to the ceiling. Above her, meat hooks swayed, grotesque even in the dim light from the wall sconces. And there, in the corner, were Kaden's weapons, boots and shirt.

Andrea's heart dropped into the pit of her stomach. Where was he? Forgetting caution, she checked the third cell. The fourth cell.

The fifth cell . . . *Dear God, the fifth cell.*

Inside, sitting with his back to the wall in nothing but jeans and a metal collar around his neck, was Kaden. Andrea's breath lodged in her throat, her pulse went double-time, and though she knew better than to hope, she did exactly that.

"Kaden?"

His head swung around, his grey eyes bright and wide with surprise. His dark blond hair was alternately grooved and spiky, as though he'd been thrusting his fingers through it, and his tan skin was marred by fading bruises and cuts.

If the vampires had had him for the full two weeks he'd been missing, she was surprised he hadn't been hurt more. Then again, maybe they *had* put him through hell, but he'd healed already, thanks to a vampire's rapid regeneration abilities.

But so far, she saw no signs of him being turned. Maybe, just maybe, everything would be OK. *God, please let it be OK.*

"Kaden, don't move. I'm going to get you out of there."

"No!" He lurched forwards, only to be drawn short by the chain linking his collar to the wall. Panic put a chilling, grim light in his gaze. "You can't."

Dread draped over her like a shroud, suffocating her last breath of hope. She knew what he was going to say. She didn't want to ask, but the question fell from her lips before she could stop it. "Why not?"

"Because," he said, opening his mouth to reveal two extra-long canines, "I might kill you."

* * *

Kaden Quinn braced himself for Andrea's reaction. The sight of the stake in her hand put ice cubes in his blood—but whether his reaction was an instinctive one brought about by his new vampire status, or whether it was because he was a Guardian who knew exactly what that pointed shard of wood would do to him, he didn't know.

What he did know was that he'd been here for two weeks, tortured for the first five days and then turned into a vampire on the sixth.

Oh, and he was *starving*.

Andrea's gorgeous brown eyes glistened with tears. "No," she rasped, shaking her head so hard her ebony hair slapped her pale cheeks. "No. Those bastards!"

Her curses echoed through the chamber as she worked the slide-lock on the cell door. She was going to kill him. The knowledge should have comforted him. Upon becoming a Guardian, every Aegi swore that they would never allow themselves to be turned into any kind of monster—not vampire, were-beast, or demon. If you had to take your own life in order to uphold that vow, you did it.

Kaden hadn't been able to make good on his promise—he'd been knocked unconscious during the battle—and by the time be came to,

it was too late. He'd awakened to find himself hanging from hooks outside this very cell. The physical torture hadn't been nearly as bad as the mental torture. The alpha vamp, an ugly bastard named Cedric, kept taunting that he was going to turn him. When Cedric finally latched onto Kaden's throat and began to drink, Kaden prayed for death. The alternative had been too horrible to imagine.

Then his nightmarish imaginings had warped into reality when Cedric opened a vein in his own wrist and, while another vamp held Kaden's mouth open, forced him to swallow his blood, activating the turn.

Kaden had drifted into blackness. When he'd come to the next night, his heart no longer beat.

He'd expected to feel different, as if getting dead and growing fangs would turn him into an insane, evil beast.

But nothing had changed. He still . . . felt. He still thought Andrea was the most beautiful woman he'd ever seen. He still hated vampires. Oh, sure, his senses were more acute and the sound of Andrea's blood rushing through her veins was making his mouth water, but he felt like he could handle being with her.

He'd warned her anyway. What if he was wrong? What if she got close and he jumped on her, ripped into her neck, and let that sweet lifeblood pour down his throat? Anticipation spiked, and lust stirred his sluggish body. While he drank, he'd take her and fist his hands in her thick black locks until she begged for mercy—

". . . uh, Kaden?"

He blinked, realizing he'd been caught up in his crazy fantasy. Shit. He was freaking *starving*. The vampires hadn't fed him, and he'd had to watch when they brought unwilling humans to the basement to feed. He'd been horrified, yet overtaken by cravings and fascinated in a way that filled him with disgust.

Andrea was inside the cell now, crouching, the stake at her side. He eyed it warily. "Sorry. I was just . . ." *Thinking about sinking my shiny*

new set of fangs into you. Cursing, he shoved his fingers through his hair. "Look, it's not safe for you here. Get your team out."

"The place is empty. I think they knew we were coming."

Adrenaline screamed through him in a stinging, hot rush that couldn't have jacked him up more if he'd shot it directly into his veins. "It's a trap." He leaped to his feet, startling Andrea to hers. "Get out."

"I can't just . . . leave you." Her voice broke, and his heart along with it. She'd faced an awful choice the day her parents died—stay, fight, and die . . . or flee, leaving them behind to perish. Her decision had been made when her father ordered her to save her sister, who had died anyway, leaving Andrea with a lifetime of regret.

She shouldn't have to make a similar choice now, but it was much too late for that.

His eyes latched onto the stake. He should tell her to kill him. He was a monster. An abomination.

But he didn't want to die.

"Andrea, you're a Guardian. You're tougher than this. You need to go."

She opened her mouth, but he didn't get to hear what she would have said, because suddenly the cell door slammed shut, trapping them both. On the other side was Cedric, grinning like a rabid coyote as he peered between the bars. He must have tripped a switch somewhere because the clamp around Kaden's neck snapped open with an ominous, metallic clang. He was free . . . in a manner of speaking.

Cedric's smile widened. "Now," he said, "let's party."

TWO

Disbelief and anger clawed at Andrea. How the hell had she let herself be trapped like this? "You are so dead!" she snarled at the bastard who'd shut the door.

Through the barred slot, the ugly, scarred piece-of-shit vampire smiled at her idle threat, his pallid, fishy lips peeling back off yellowed teeth.

"We've slaughtered most of your colleagues," he said, his harsh words hitting her like a punch to the gut, "but I'm holding on to a few. I'll have fun turning them, just like I did with your boy there." He smiled again, then walked away, leaving her alone with Kaden . . .

. . . who was now loose in the cell with her.

Evil unchained.

Except she couldn't see her lover as anything but the man whose touch had lit her on fire, who had been a gentle or urgent lover, depending on his mood.

Then again, on the job he was a ruthless warrior, capable of cutting down entire nests of viper ghouls by himself. Oh, yes, she'd stood by and admired the way he used his hands with lethal skill, the way he could gut a demon twice his size and shrug it off like it was nothing. Afterwards, the jacked-up burn of the fight had sent him into her arms, a male on a mission to claim her as his prize.

She couldn't count the number of times they'd won a battle and then attacked each other, unable to wait for a bedroom. They hadn't needed anything but a wall or a tree to support her back and shield them from prying eyes. Their passion had heated up snowy nights, steamed up rainy days, and drawn lightning during storms.

And now he was looking at Andrea with that same battle-lust in his eyes, the adrenaline high that gripped all Guardians when the victory, the kill, was close.

Heartbreak and fear collided, making her clumsy as she settled into a defensive position, stake ready. "I don't want to have to destroy you."

And she wasn't sure she would be able to. They'd always been evenly matched in skill, but with his strength and size he'd had the advantage when they sparred. And now, as a vampire, he'd be even stronger, and faster as well.

"The idea doesn't thrill me, either." He closed his eyes and clenched his hands into fists, the way he did when he was angry and trying to keep his temper contained—something he rarely had to do. Kaden had always been cool, calm and level, to the point where Andrea sometimes needled him just to get a reaction. Now, it appeared that no needling would be necessary. "Andrea . . . I don't . . . I don't know if I can control myself."

"You want to kill me?"

His eyes flew open, the grey depths turning steely. "No. Never," he swore. "But I'm . . . hungry." His gaze dropped to her throat. His lush lips parted and he drew closer. For some reason, she couldn't move, was anchored to the spot, mesmerized by the fierce hunger in his expression. Everything around her, from the damp, musty odour of the dungeon, to the skittering sounds of scavenging rodents, faded into the background. Everything but him.

Swallowing nervously, she found her voice. "Kaden?"

He uttered a rough noise of anguish and threw himself to the far side of the cell, shuddering so hard his teeth chattered.

Something inside her broke, and she reached for him, only to jerk back when he hissed.

This was bad. Very, very bad. She had to find a way out of the cell before Kaden lost control and she was forced into the fight of her life.

Whirling, she attacked the door. She shoved at it, rattled it, trying to fight the panic that had wrapped around her chest like a clamp.

She'd always believed she could take down any vampire without mercy, but Kaden didn't seem like a vamp. He seemed like . . . Kaden. With fangs. And maybe an extra scoop of menace. But other than that, he was the man she loved, and she couldn't stake him.

Thing was, she couldn't even be shocked by this knowledge. She'd failed at most everything she'd ever tried, from bowling, to cooking, to protecting her family. Never in her life had she stuck with anything when the going got rough or if she wasn't immediately good at it. Not until

she'd joined the Aegis, anyway. She'd stayed, because she was damned good at killing.

At least, she *was*. Until now.

"Let me try." His voice was guttural, warped, as though every word was being funnelled through a shrinking pipe. She stepped aside as he hit the door with his entire body. His weight left a dent, but on his fourth try it became clear that the cells had been built to handle creatures much stronger than any man.

Or any vampire.

She shivered. God, the very idea that Kaden was undead . . . it horrified her. And yet, as she watched him pound on the door with eye-blurring speed, the thick muscles in his chest and arms bunching and rippling, some secret, shameful part of her was fascinated—and maybe a little turned on by the raw power behind his every punch.

"Kaden?"

Slowly, he turned, braced his back against the door, and slid to his ass. Exhaustion put hollows in his cheeks, but his eyes were sharp as daggers. "Yeah?"

Maintaining a grip on the stake, she crouched and eased towards him. "What's it like?"

When he looked at the stake in her hand and growled, she set the stake on the floor and showed him her empty palms. She wasn't stupid though; she made sure the weapon was within reach. She also had an Aegis-modified squirt gun filled with holy water in her jacket pocket, as well as several blades stashed on her body. But he'd know that. His roving hands had long since learned the location of every one of her weapon hiding places. The memories made her body tingle and her mouth go dry.

"It's weird," he said gruffly, "I thought I'd feel like a beast. But I don't feel any different." He frowned. "No, that's not true. I feel stronger. And more . . . feral."

"Feral?"

He nodded. "It's like I'm a mass of instincts. Everything is magnified, from my senses to my desires. I don't know how to control them." He pegged her with a gaze so scorching she drew a harsh breath. "I've always tried to be gentle with you. But right now . . . " He threw his head back against the wall, and his throat worked on a hard swallow. "Damn. The things I want to do to you."

She didn't have to guess. His fangs had elongated into sharp, wicked daggers, and she could see his erection pressing against the fly of his jeans. Liquid heat flooded her body, a completely inappropriate response given what he was and where they were. But that dark part of her was enthralled with this new Kaden. Curious. Cautiously, she reached for him. The moment her fingers touched his knee, he went taut, his head snapped forwards, and once again she was in the cross hairs of his laser gaze.

Startled, she drew her hand away, but—lightning fast—he caught her wrist. For a breathless heartbeat, terror turned the air in her lungs to cement.

The stake was out of reach.

"I warned you," he growled. "I need . . . I *hunger* . . . " His fingers tightened, digging into her skin.

Common sense and self-preservation kicked in. He wasn't the only one with powerful instincts. Andrea threw a punch, nailing him in the jaw with her free hand. He didn't even flinch. She swung again, but this time he palmed her fist, stopping her throw as if she'd slammed her knuckles into a brick wall.

"Wow," she breathed. "You're really fast now."

"I wasn't exactly a slouch before." His voice was a husky purr that rumbled through every part of her body.

She snorted. "Becoming undead certainly hasn't done anything for your ego."

A slow, cocky smile turned up the corners of his mouth. Good Lord—were they really *bantering*? In this incredibly fucked-up situation? He seemed to realize the incongruity of it all and he sobered, releasing her as if she were a burning coal.

"Get away from me." He shoved at her, knocking her off balance and sending her sprawling. Instantly, he was on his knees beside her. "Oh, shit. Andy, I'm sorry."

She allowed him to help her sit up, but he didn't remove his hands from her shoulders. Neither of them moved a single muscle. Even the air went still with the uncertain tension hanging in the cell. Gradually, she became aware of the fact that Kaden's entire body was trembling, and, once more, his gaze was fixed on her throat.

Something touched her hand. The stake. He pressed it into her palm even as he lowered his head towards her neck. Her heart slammed into her ribcage and her stomach clenched, but she remained motionless. She focused all her energy on simply breathing, because that, at least, was still in her control.

"Don't let me do it," he rasped, but his lips were grazing her suddenly sensitive skin. He closed her fingers around the stake. His teeth scratched her throat—tiny, erotic pricks of pain.

His masculine need rolled off him in waves, and her traitorous body answered, going wet and molten hot. In the past, she'd always responded to him quickly, often after nothing more than his lustful look. But this was different. It was as though she was flame and he was fuel. There was nothing she could do but let it all burn out of control.

That's how they get you. Vampires are very sexual beings, they ooze sex appeal and are magnetic and irresistible to humans. They are spiders that capture careless flies.

The familiar words of Aegis leaders rang through her head, and though she knew she should fight, she couldn't.

"Please," he whispered brokenly. He lifted her hand, placing the point of the stake over his heart. "I can't hold on. Don't want to hurt you." His mouth was at her throat.

Andrea's entire body quivered, and a sob caught in her throat. What he was asking her to do . . . *oh, God.*

A shudder tore through Kaden's body. "Andrea . . . *fuck.*" Then his fangs pierced her skin. Her stake pierced his. They both gasped. Neither had gone deep, but there was no doubt that they both could kill.

They remained still, frozen in a twisted game of cat and mouse. He needed to feed, and she needed to kill him. But neither had the will power.

He squeezed her hand, putting pressure on the stake, driving it deeper into his flesh.

"No!" In one smooth move, she flung the stake away and grasped his head, pulling him firmly against her. His teeth penetrated her throat in a white-hot stab of pain that veered sharply to pleasure. His moan rattled through her, and she was lost to him.

THREE

She should have killed him.

But now it was too late. Kaden didn't think he'd ever be the same. He'd crossed a line—vaulted over it—and there was no going back. Sensation stabbed at him, shooting like mini-orgasms through his fangs, all the way to his groin. He should tear himself away from Andrea. Do the right thing.

But he was so cold and she was so warm. She smelled like leather and cherries—a strange combination, but one that had always excited both the lover and the warrior in him. And best of all, *worst* of all, she tasted like sweet, sweet sin. Silky, warm blood filled his mouth and cascaded down his throat, filling that empty, hurt hole inside him.

No, not filling . . . because his chest cavity was truly empty now. His ribs caged a useless heart and his lungs still breathed even though they didn't need air. Some sort of cell memory kept his lungs filling, he supposed. He wondered when that would end, when his lungs would collapse and shrivel.

Andrea's pulse tapped against his teeth, and he moaned at the ecstasy of it. He'd been guided by instinct when he'd bitten her, and even though guilt knotted his stomach, he couldn't fight the drive to suck harder.

He also couldn't fight the desire to ease her onto her back and settle himself between her legs. Only the knowledge that there was a camera mounted in the corner of the ceiling kept him from tearing off their clothes and plunging into her body. But still, some instincts were too powerful to deny, and he rocked against her, drawing a low, heady groan from her.

Beneath him, she writhed, arching up to plaster their bodies more solidly against each other. An erotic surge crashed through him in a hot tide. Andrea tightened her legs around his hips so he rubbed against her. With each thrusting motion, she gasped, her panting breaths coming faster and faster.

Damn, he loved the sounds she made when she was making love. Granted, they weren't exactly making love, not while they were fully clothed, but the motions were the same, the feelings were the same and—oh yeah—the way she drove him wild with her fingers digging into his back was the same.

"Kaden," she whispered, "yes, *yes*."

She was close, something he knew not from experience, but from his new senses. He could smell the delicious scent of her lust, could taste the zing of desire in her blood. It was like a drug he knew he couldn't kick. As a human, sex had been great. As a vampire, it felt out of this world, and he hadn't even gotten inside her.

Delicious agony.

He shuddered, sucked, rocked against her until the friction became nearly too hot to handle and a vibration sang through his veins. This was crazy, but his body had hijacked his thoughts, and nothing mattered but getting inside her. Impatient, he slid his palm down her body, but before he reached her zipper, she cried out, her orgasm hitting so hard and fast he could only hang on for the ride as she bucked beneath him.

She called out his name, over and over, her smoky, pleasure-soaked voice nearly sending him over the edge with her.

"I love you," she whispered. "God, I love you."

The words stopped him in his tracks like nothing else, not even his own will, had been able to do. She'd never said that to him, not in the entire year they'd been together. He'd suspected, but then, he'd suspected that he was in love with her, too. But it was something he'd never planned to admit, not when a Guardian's lifespan was as likely to be measured in months as in years.

Five years ago, he'd lost Gabrielle to this violent life just days after their engagement. She'd been bitten by a werewolf, had slaughtered several other Guardians, and Kaden had been forced to kill her.

He couldn't go through that again, and he'd guarded the words "I love you" with the ferocity of a lion protecting his pride. Andrea knew how he felt about love, and damn her for striking at him with weapon every bit as dangerous and painful as a stake.

Roaring in agony and fury, he broke away from Andrea, surprising himself at the speed with which he came to his feet. Wide, glazed eyes blinked in confusion even as she slapped a palm over her throat. Blood seeped from between her fingers, and shit, he was a dumb-ass. A newbie vampire dumb-ass, who must look utterly ridiculous, standing half-naked in a cell with a raging hard-on.

Quickly, he seized her upper arms, yanked her to her feet, and swiped his tongue over the punctures he'd made, another instinctive move. Then he stepped away, but the cell was far too small to allow enough distance

between them. An entire ocean of distance wouldn't be enough. Not when he still wanted her so badly it hurt, which was exactly what he'd been trying to avoid.

"Dammit, Andrea." He rammed his hands through his hair, needing to do something with them before he grabbed her again, and this time, refused to let go. "I told you—"

"Yeah, you told me." Her hands formed fists at her sides, and her face was flushed from her climax—and from anger. "Told me you never wanted to fall in love again, because it hurts too much when it ends. You told me when we first fell into my bed that our relationship could go nowhere except between the sheets. But it went a lot further than that, and you know it. It's time to stop skirting the issue and pretending that we only have *strong feelings* for each other."

Fuck. He flicked his tongue over one fang. It was a new habit he'd developed because he was now a vampire, a fact she seemed to have forgotten, even though two seconds ago he'd been at her throat and sucking her lifeblood out of her. How the hell could she be acting as though it hadn't happened? Acting as though she'd forgotten what he had become? For every second of every hour, until Gabrielle turned into a slavering beast, he'd been well aware of the fact that she had been bitten by a werewolf.

And yet, he'd been careless. Sloppy. Although it was Aegis policy to kill any human who had been bitten or scratched by a were-beast, he'd let his love for her cloud his judgment. He'd heard of humans who were immune to the infection, and on the off chance that Gabrielle was one of those rare people, he'd restrained her until night fell, bringing the Curse of the full moon with it. Worse, he'd not wanted to hurt her, so he'd kept her restraints loose. When she turned, she got free and killed three of their colleagues before Kaden put a silver killing-bolt through her chest.

The pain, the guilt, had mired him in misery until Andrea showed up in Portland a year ago, a transfer from the Phoenix cell. She'd been like

a whirlwind, sucking him into her life with her humor and fun-loving nature—exactly the opposite of the very serious Gabrielle. She was exactly what he needed after four years of loneliness and one-night stands.

"Well?" Andrea prompted, and he realized he'd been lost in his thoughts, which was not the place he wanted to be.

Not that their reality—locked in a dungeon—was much better.

Way to feel sorry for yourself. God, he was a moron. If growing up with two blind parents had taught him anything, it was that self-pity was a pathetic waste of time.

"Well, what?" he snapped, residual lust giving him the sharp edge he needed to do what he must. "You do realize that I'm a vampire, right? And you're a vampire slayer. Whatever *relationship* you think we had is over. The man you claim to love is gone, so you have two choices. You can stake me like a good little Guardian, or you can join forces with me to make an escape. But either way, there is no more *us.*"

Crimson splotches mottled Andrea's cheeks, but he didn't need to see her fury to know she was bubbling over with it. His enhanced senses picked up her anger as a scent that was so bitter he could taste it on his tongue.

"You son of a bitch." Like a well-trained warrior, she didn't give away her next move, which was to snap up the stake. He could have stopped her; his reflexes were twice as fast as they had been. But in truth, he was curious to see what she'd do.

And when she came at him, he had his answer.

* * *

Damn him! Crazed with hurt and anger, Andrea launched herself at Kaden, her stake aimed right at his cold heart. Effortlessly, as though she were nothing but a minor annoyance, he blocked her with one upraised arm. Humiliation aside, she was glad he'd done it. Oh, she wanted to

hurt him, but she'd planned to check herself at the last moment, not really wanting to kill him. And clearly, he didn't want to die. Or probably more accurately, he didn't want her to be the one to have to kill him. Not after the trauma he'd suffered when he'd had to put down his fiancée.

Yes, his words had put a fissure in her heart, but she wasn't stupid—he was trying to piss her off, to chase her away in order to save them both a lot of pain. She was sorry she'd told him she loved him, but she wasn't sorry for how she felt. She'd dated before meeting Kaden, but she'd never fallen in love. She hadn't known how good it could feel.

Or how bad.

Still smarting from his verbal smackdown, she struck out, slapping him across the face. His head snapped back and his eyes went wide as though he couldn't believe she'd just done that. In an instant, he recovered, red sparks turning his eyes to molten metal as he grasped her wrists and yanked her into him.

Just as she'd wanted him to do.

Still, her heart thundered in her chest. Angering a vampire, even one you loved, one that had just given you a world-class orgasm, wasn't the brightest move in the world. "There's a camera in the corner," she said, angling her face away from said camera in case whoever was watching could read lips. "We need to fight, and you need to pretend to kill me. It's the only way to fool that psycho vamp into thinking you've truly gone over to their side."

She struggled, feigning fury, though she did put some power behind her knee to his thigh. He totally deserved that, and she smiled, a little at his grunt.

"Good girl," he said through gritted teeth. "Didn't know you saw the camera." She didn't have time to bask in his praise, because suddenly, he spun her, put her back against the wall and his forearm across his throat. "So we fight." His teeth were bared and his eyes glinted, and if she didn't know any better she'd think he really was planning violence.

Then again, she *didn't* know any better. He'd changed. She shivered, but not with fear. No, once more, she was utterly turned on by the life or death game they were playing. And this was definitely life—heart-stopping, adrenaline-pumping life. Kaden had once said that you never felt more alive than when you were facing death, and if the way her skin tingled and heat blossomed between her thighs was any indication, he was *so* right.

"Fight me, damn you."

"Gladly," she snapped. Squaring her shoulders, she stomped on his foot and followed up with a swift kick to his shin and a hook of her boot to the back of his knee. His leg buckled, but before she could wrench free, he recovered.

"We've sparred for months," he said with an arrogant smile. "You think I don't know all your moves?"

She rocked her head forwards and caught him in the mouth. "You didn't know that one."

He grinned, flashing teeth smeared with blood. "Nice."

God, he was hot when he smiled like that and, again, the pseudo-battle stirred up something wicked in her. The puncture wounds on her throat began to throb in time with the pulsing between her legs, is if her body was preparing to take him inside her in any way he wanted. He was a very male animal, and her feminine instincts were answering without her brain's consent.

As though he sensed the change in her, his eyes darkened and his are dropped to her mouth.

"Kaden—"

He took her to the ground, twisting at the last second to absorb the brunt of the impact. In a smooth, easy motion, he rolled on top of her, pinning her with his superior strength and considerable weight.

Beneath him, she writhed, partly in a show of struggle for the camera, and partly because he felt so damned good pressed against her. She

schooled her expression into one of rage—using her anger at her situation, at Kaden's transformation, at a past that robbed her of a normal life—to make the emotion believable, when all she wanted to do was roll around with him on a soft bed instead of hard ground.

Kaden fisted her hair in one hand and wrenched her head to the side, exposing her throat the way he had before. A raw, purring rumble dredged up from deep in his chest. Her breath quickened as he lowered his mouth to her neck and struck like a snake, with no warning. Like before, pain pierced her, a sweet, erotic agony that drained her of any resistance. No wonder humans succumbed to vampires so easily. Pleasure streaked from where his teeth penetrated her to every pulse point in her body.

Moaning, she arched her pelvis into his, and he shuddered even as he shifted his weight to press her flat again. Right. She wasn't supposed to be getting off on this. This was a show for the camera, and she was ruining it by wanting to ride him like a horse.

Again.

It struck her that she might be a little stupid in trusting him not to kill her, but what choice did she have? Besides, despite what the Aegis had taught her, she knew Kaden. She knew it would take more than an exchange of vampire blood to make him turn evil.

Too soon, he disengaged his teeth, but the motion was subtle, and he repositioned his mouth over the bite and stroked his tongue along the wounds to seal them. But he never lifted his head, and she barely heard him whisper, "This is killing me. Later, we'll do this right, but for now, I need to pretend to be drinking from you until you're dead. In sixty seconds, go limp and play possum. With any luck, he'll have fed recently."

God, she hoped so. Apparently, a vampire's ability to hear a heart beating grew more acute the hungrier they were. If their ruse had any shot of working, she had to appear very, very dead.

She waited as he mouthed her throat, his tongue swirling and flicking on her hypersensitive skin. How was she supposed to play dead when every lick brought her body to shivering, vibrant awareness?

And wait. He'd said "later". Did he mean it? Could there be a "later"?

She'd have to find out—*later*—because he pushed away from her. With a vicious (but oddly careful) shove, he nudged her aside with his foot like a dead animal he'd found on the road. She lay motionless, trying to not even breathe, as he paced.

She wondered if this was how he'd been while he'd waited for Gabrielle to turn into a werewolf. A restless energy kept him prowling back and forth, grumbling to himself. Had he prayed for her life, as Andrea had prayed for Dee's?

Poor, brave Dee. She'd been only two years younger than Andrea, and she'd wanted to stay and fight the demons that had attacked their parents. Instead, she'd only fought when Andrea had dragged her screaming from the house. Six months later, it had been Dee who had been approached by the Aegis to join their cause. Apparently, her bitter and rather public insistence that demons were real had grabbed the organization's attention. They were always looking for new recruits— especially those who wanted vengeance.

Andrea had joined too, desperate to uphold her promise to keep Dee safe. But Dee had never forgiven Andrea for deserting their parents. Within six months of joining the Aegis, Dee's reckless pursuit of revenge had gotten her killed, when she'd slipped away from Andrea to hunt down a demon in an alley.

She didn't know how long they went on like that, with her playing dead and Kaden wearing a rut in the ground like a big cat in a cage. Finally, she heard the ominous thump of footsteps.

"Kaden." The psycho vamp's voice sent a chill slithering up her spine. "You are now one of us."

FOUR

You are now one of us.

The words rang through Kaden in a deafening clang. Yeah, he was one of them. No, he hadn't killed anyone. But he'd fed. He'd sunk his fangs into a human—a human *Guardian*—and had filled up on her lifeblood.

And he'd enjoyed it. God help him, he'd enjoyed it.

He allowed Cedric to see his pleasure and his misery before averting his gaze in a show of shame. Which wasn't much of an act. But he needed the other vampire to believe he had gone over to the dark side . . . reluctantly. Cedric wasn't stupid enough to think Kaden would convert without a fight. He'd have to play this smart if he wanted to get Andrea out of this alive.

"You've killed a slayer, *slayer*," Cedric said. "You are the worst kind of enemy to them. You know you can never go back. We can keep you alive."

"Go to hell."

Cedric didn't miss a beat. "The Aegis will hunt you to the ends of the earth. We can protect you. You know I'm right."

He was, but once he was free, Kaden would kill Cedric, which would draw the wrath of Cedric's entire clan. It was a trade-off Kaden was willing to live with. He'd survive as long as he could, inflicting damage and racking up vampire casualties until he could no longer fight. Until either Cedric's clan or the Aegis took him down.

Kaden swung his gaze around to Cedric, nailing him with every ounce of hatred he could muster. "The Aegis won't hunt me, specifically. They'll assume I'm dead."

Cedric laughed. "We allowed one of the captured slayers to witness you killing the girl. Then we released him. I doubt it will be long before the Aegis issues an order of execution with your name on it."

Fuck. Kaden's death would be a priority by sunrise. "You son of a bitch."

Through the narrow window, Kaden saw the light of victory in Cedric's pale eyes. "So. Are you willing to work with us? I've tenderized a few slayers, and now they're just waiting to be eaten."

That shouldn't have made Kaden's mouth water, and the fact that it did pissed him off even more.

"Yes," Cedric purred. "I can sense your hunger." The crisp clang of the sliding lock vibrated the air in a concussion wave.

Kaden tensed up so hard he was nearly shaking with the desire to leap through the doorway and tear the other vampire apart. *Stay calm, stay calm . . .* He kept himself in check as the door creaked open. Wisely, Cedric stood back, well away from Kaden as he stalked through the doorway without so much as glancing at Andrea.

His shirt and boots lay in a pile, where they'd been left after the vamps had stripped him to prepare for his torture, and he went to them without asking permission.

Cedric watched, a creepy, satisfied smile on his gaunt face, as Kaden tugged on his long-sleeved, black turtleneck and combat boots. Kaden's weapons had been taken away at some point, but his captors had missed the razor-thin obsidian blade Guardians lovingly called the "demon-biter" which was hidden, in his boot. The weapon was treated with holy water, which lost most of its effectiveness once dried, but the black stone reacted with the residue, leaving behind a caustic bite when activated by the blood of an evil entity.

Covertly palming the weapon, he swung around to Cedric. "Where are the humans?"

Cedric gestured to one of the tunnel entrances. "That way." Again, the guy wasn't stupid, and he waited until Kaden moved towards the tunnel before falling into step behind him.

They'd only gone twenty feet when Cedric ploughed into Kaden, struck from behind by Andrea. Kaden crunched into the wall, the impact bringing dust and stone down around him. Cedric wheeled around, Andrea's stake impaled in his shoulder. Roaring in fury, Cedric lunged at Andrea. Kaden's heart no longer beat, but it lurched with terror as Cedric's fingers closed, around her throat.

No! Two weeks of torture and five years of self-loathing fueled Kaden's strength, and he attacked, a whirlwind of unrestrained vengeance. A veil of red sliced down over his vision as he caught the other vampire with an arm looped around his neck.

In a smooth sweep, Kaden slashed Cedric's throat with the demon-biter, savoring the hiss of the holy water as it reacted with the vampire's blood. Andrea, in a coordinated move that reminded him what a great team they made, plucked the stake from Cedric's shoulder and plunged it into his chest.

A God-awful squeal rose from Cedric's body. The air around them heated and shimmered, and then the vampire flamed to ash. While the dust still swirled, Kaden swept Andrea into his arms.

"Thank God," she murmured against his chest.

"We're not done yet." He smoothed his hand down her spine, loving the way her muscles rippled under his palm. He wished they were anywhere but here so he could spend time touching her the way he wanted to. The way she deserved. "We've got to save the Guardians."

She nodded and pulled back, leaving him with an aching chest full of regret. Silently, they gathered what weapons they could from the dungeon and headed down the tunnel Cedric had indicated. It was dark, the walls seeping moisture from cracks in the rough stone, but his vampire vision allowed him to see as well as if it had been noon on a clear day.

Sounds drifted from the far end of the tunnel. Talking. Laughter. Some whimpers. The sound of flesh striking flesh.

Kaden crept into the shadows at the entrance to a large chamber. Inside, two vampires circled three Guardians who were bound and gagged, and sitting in the middle of the floor. Every once in a while, a vampire would kick or punch one of them and, while Kaden watched, the female vamp leaned over and licked the blood dripping down one of the Guardian's cheeks.

Kaden signaled to Andrea, and on the finger count of three, they went in. He took down the male vamp before the guy knew what had hit him. Even as his vampire flamed, Andrea's joined the fireworks show.

"That wasn't so bad," she said, as she holstered her stake with a sexy, confident shove home. Oh, yeah, he definitely appreciated a hot chick who knew how to handle wood. Pun intended.

But now wasn't the time to admire her warrior skills, or the way her full lips quirked in a satisfied smile, or the satin wisps of hair that curled around her flushed cheeks. Nope. Not the time.

"No, not bad," he acknowledged through clenched teeth. "But there are at least thirty vamps in Cedric's clan. They could show up at any moment." He knelt beside Zach, one of the newer Guardians in the North Portland Aegis cell, and sliced through his ropes as Andrea did the same for brothers Trey and Matthew.

The moment the three were released, they closed ranks, all glaring murder at Kaden. "Vampire," Trey spat. "You let yourself be turned."

Their weapons lay in a pile in the corner, and Matthew snagged a handful of stakes. Kaden didn't bother to stop him, but Andrea put herself between the Guardians and him.

"Stop it." She jammed her fists on her hips, looking all fierce and cute. "He just saved your lives."

Zach shot her an incredulous stare. "So? He's a vampire. He probably saved us from the others so he could eat us himself."

Kaden couldn't blame them for their skepticism. He'd have been singing the same tune just a week ago. "I don't want to eat you." He stepped away from them and the exit, because what he'd said wasn't entirely true. "You need to go before the rest of the clan gets here." He grasped Andrea's arm and turned her into him. "You too."

"No. We stay and fight."

"That'll be suicide," Matthew broke in. "It was a trap. Probably set by Kaden."

Again, he couldn't blame Matthew for his line of thinking, but at this point, Andrea's safety was his prime concern. He wasn't going to let these guys put her in jeopardy because they were too blinded by training to see the truth.

Kaden swung around, baring his teeth and giving them an up-close and personal reminder of why they shouldn't fuck with him. "Get. Out," he said, with a calm he didn't feel. "I could kick your asses before, and you can't even begin to imagine what I can do to you now."

Matthew turned crimson with fury, Trey went wide-eyed with surprise, and Zach paled so fast Kaden thought he'd pass out.

Once again, Andrea put herself between Kaden and the three Guardians. It was a sweet gesture, but unnecessary. Kaden hadn't been kidding about being able to kick their asses.

"Go," she said firmly. "Wait outside the chamber. Give me two minutes." She must have delivered her command with a side order of glare that dared them to argue, because they didn't. They filed out of the doorway, but not without muttering obscenities under their breath at Kaden.

When they were gone, she turned to him, but he didn't give her a chance to speak. "You need to go too, Andrea."

Hurt filled her expression. "Not without you."

"I can't go back, and you know it."

"You're going to get killed if you stay and fight."

"And I'm going to get killed if I go back to the Aegis. I'd rather go down swinging." He couldn't bear the sadness in her eyes or the sudden, cavernous emptiness in his chest. Without thinking, he palmed the back of her neck and brought her in close. He dipped his head, and the moment their lips touched, he poured everything he felt for her into his kiss.

He just hoped she didn't feel his regrets, especially the big one, the one that had foolishly kept him from committing himself fully to her.

Then there was the other regret, the one in which he'd told her there would be a "later".

* * *

The kiss was goodbye.

Andrea knew it to her very soul, and she felt it in a shiver over her entire body. Eyes stinging, she jerked away from Kaden, but she clung to his hand desperately, even when he tried to extricate himself from her death grip.

"I can't lose you," she said. Pleaded, really.

The resolve in his steel-cut eyes sliced through her like an arctic wind. "We can't be together."

"I don't care what you are. I'm tired of losing people I love. I can't do it again."

He laughed bitterly. "Really, Andrea? You don't care what I am? How can you ever trust me? How can you think I won't turn into a ravenous beast and kill you?"

"Because you aren't Gabrielle." The words made his head snap back as if she'd slapped him, but she pressed the advantage, going right for his jugular, because they didn't have time for a leisurely chat. She had to get through to him *now*. "Gabrielle became a creature that couldn't recognize the person she loved, and she couldn't control her nature. But you *can* control yourself, Kaden. You were starving in that cell, and you could have killed me. You didn't. If anything, you wanted me. You've been turned, but you aren't evil. I don't care what the Aegis say. They aren't always right."

Strain put lines at the corners of his made-to-please mouth. "Even if what I've become isn't an issue for us, it'll be a damned big issue for the Aegis. They aren't going to welcome me with open arms."

"There has to be a way." Her mind worked furiously, searching the darkest, dustiest corners of her brain for anything useful. She could leave

the Aegis, but that would be a last resort. Hunting demons was the one thing she was good at, and after an entire life spent quitting jobs, clubs and college, she didn't want to abandon this. Maybe she could transfer again. Someplace where having a vampire boyfriend wouldn't be a big deal. She almost laughed at that, because . . . wait . . . she sucked in a harsh breath at her sudden idea.

"I've got it." Andrea bounced on her toes, excited for the first time since all of this began. "We can move to New York. One of the cells there is rumoured to have a half-demon Regent. And remember how we heard that one of the Elders is married to a demon?" One of the twelve supreme Aegis leaders married to a demon? The story had spread like wildfire.

"Those are just rumours." Kaden's voice was tired, resigned.

Andrea's hope that they still had a shot at something began to wither. "I know, but—"

"Even if those things are true, life in the Aegis can't be easy for them. I won't subject you to that."

"I can handle it."

"I know you can," he rasped, "but I can't. I can't stand by and watch you be scorned."

"Then what are our options? Stay here and let yourself be killed? I don't freaking think so." She got right up in his face and poked him in the chest. "I've given up on everything in my life at some point. And I mean everything. If I attempt something new and I suck at it, I won't do it again. If I fail at something, I quit. The Aegis and you are the only things I've ever stuck with, and I will not go back to being a quitter. We will work this out."

Kaden stepped back, and the hardest thing she'd ever done was give him that foot of space. "And what am I supposed to do while you're out doing your job? Sit home and watch *Buffy* reruns?"

He had a point. Here she was thinking of her job, when he'd just lost his. He'd just lost everything, actually. Shaking his head, he looked up at

the ceiling. "There's no way the Aegis is even going to let me live. Unless . . . "

Her breath hitched, just a tiny catch of hope reawakening. "Unless what?"

One of the guys just outside the chamber whispered for them to hurry up, but Kaden ignored him and scrubbed one hand over his face. "Remember how Tony brought up that radical idea once? When he was drunk and half out of his mind?"

She rolled her eyes. "You'll have to be more specific. We're talking about *Tony*, the guy who thinks fairies enchant his weapons while he sleeps."

He snorted. "Good point. You know, his nutty idea about getting a Guardian to turn vampire and infiltrate clans as a spy?"

"That was crazy," she said. "I mean—" She cut off with a gasp, as what he was saying slapped her upside the head. "That's what you want to do?"

"Why not?"

"Well . . . " She trailed off, because actually . . . why not? He was right about how the Aegis wouldn't accept him as a regular member any more. But if they went for this, he could still work, still do the job, but from the other side. "So instead of fighting Cedric's clan . . . "

"I'd join them."

The idea filled her with terror, but at least it offered a shot at keeping him off the Aegis' most-wanted list—and alive.

So to speak.

"What if they refuse?"

He slid a covert glance at the Guardians, who were still watching him with murder in their eyes. He wouldn't get any other kind of reception at headquarters. "They'll try. But look what happened when you attacked this den. Vampire ops are dangerous. If I can help, they've got to give it a shot."

Her chest constricted with doubt. "It won't be easy to convince them."

"Then we consider your idea about moving to New York. Or I work anyway, and feed you the intel. Either way, this is what I have to do, just as you need to keep working for the Aegis."

That all sounded great, but the most important part of this discussion was still an elephant in the room. "OK, but what about us?"

In a blur of motion, Kaden caught her shoulders and tugged her against him. Her heart went crazy in her chest, skipping around like a lovesick idiot. "I was a fool before. But dying kicked me in the ass and made me see things a little more clearly." Tenderly, he cupped her cheek in one palm. "Everything is intensified now. All my emotions. Including love."

"W-what?"

He crushed her to him, holding on so tight she had trouble breathing. Not that she would change anything. "I love you," he said. "I've loved you for a long time but was afraid to say it." He pressed a kiss to the top of her head and then drew back, but his intense gaze drilled into hers. "I still don't know how to handle my new status, and I've got a lot to learn, but my parents taught me that everyone stumbles, and it's OK to feel your way around. Took me until now to remember that. Still, I can't promise it'll be easy for either of us."

She pressed a finger to his lips. "One day at a time. All I ask is that we try. No quitting without a fight."

His smile stole her breath. "No quitting." His expression was serious once again. "You need to go."

"I still don't want to leave you here."

"You have to. Before Cedric's clan catches me with you. Right now they don't know I was involved with his death."

Outside the chamber, one of the guys cleared his throat impatiently, and she checked her watch. "It's nearly dawn."

"I'll be fine. At sunset, I'll meet you at your place. And remember what I said we'd do later?"

Her body heated up, because *oh, boy,* did she remember. "Uh-huh."

The sharp little points of his fangs gleamed, matching a wicked light in his eyes. "Good, because *later* I'm going to see just how much more intense *everything* can be."

She couldn't wait. They definitely had a rough road ahead, but it seemed that, for the first time in her life, the road wasn't a dead end. This was one journey she would not fail.

ABOUT THE AUTHORS

C.T. Adams and **Cathy Clamp** began writing as a team in 1997 and quickly learned that their individual talents in writing created a dynamite combination in historical and paranormal fiction. Their novels include *Touch of Darkness, Cold Moon Rising,* and *Magic's Design*. Cathy resides in the Texas Hill Country with her husband, dogs, cats, and 24 Boer/Spanish cross goats. Cie lives in the Denver metro area with her dog and cats.

Kelley Armstrong is the author of the *New York Times* bestselling "Women of the Otherworld" paranormal suspense series, the "Darkest Powers" YA urban fantasy trilogy, and the Nadia Stafford crime series. She grew up in Ontario, Canada, where she lives with her family. A former computer programmer, she escaped her corporate cubicle and hopes never to return.

L. A. Banks (*a.k.a. Leslie Esdaile Banks*), a native of Philadelphia and a graduate of the University of Pennsylvania Wharton undergraduate program, holds a Masters in Fine Arts from Temple University's School of Film and Media Arts. After a ten-year career as a corporate marketing executive for several Fortune 100 high-tech firms, she changed careers in 1991 to pursue private consulting work—which ultimately led to fiction and film writing. Now, with over more than two-dozen novels and over a dozen anthology contributions in an extraordinary breadth of genres—plus many awards to her credit—Banks writes full time and resides in Philadelphia. Look for her "Vampire Huntress Legends" series and a full listing of her published works at: *www.vampire-huntress.com* or *www.LeslieEsdaileBanks.com*.

Roxanne Conrad has published more than 30 novels, including (as Rachel Caine) the *New York Times* and *USA Today* bestselling "Morganville Vampires" series, and the popular "Weather Warden" and "Outcast Season" series. She is also a contributor to several bestselling anthologies. She lives in Fort Worth, Texas with her husband, fantasy artist R. Cat Conrad.

Russell Davis has written numerous short stories and novels in a variety of genres under several different names. Some of his work appears in *Fellowship Fantastic, Man vs. Machine, Under Cover of Darkness,* and *Imaginary Friends*. He lives in Nevada, where he writes, rides horses and spends time with his family.

Charles de Lint is a full-time writer and musician who makes his home in Ottawa, Canada, with his wife MaryAnn Harris, an artist and musician. His books include the short story collection *Muse and Reverie* and the novels *The Mystery of Grace, Eyes Like Leaves,* and *Medicine Road*. For more information about his work, visit his website at *www.charlesdelint.com*.

Neil Gaiman, the worldwide bestselling author, has long been one of the top writers in modern comics, and has written books for readers of all ages. He is listed in the *Dictionary of Literary Biography* as one of the top ten living post-modern writers, and is a prolific creator of works of prose, poetry, film, journalism, comics, song lyrics, and drama. His *New York Times* bestselling 2001 novel for adults, *American Gods*, was awarded the Hugo, Nebula, Bram Stoker, SFX, and Locus awards, was nominated for many other awards including the World Fantasy Award and the Minnesota Book Award, and appeared on many best-of-year lists. His official website, *www.neilgaiman.com*, now has more than one million unique visitors each month, and his online journal is syndicated to thousands of blog readers every day. Born and raised in England, Gaiman now lives near

Minneapolis, Minnesota. He has somehow reached his forties and still tends to need a haircut. His children's book *The Graveyard Book* won several awards, including the Newbery Award, the Hugo, and the Locus award for best children's novel.

Ed Gorman was born in Minneapolis, Minnesota, and currently lives in Iowa with his wife Carol, who is also a writer. He spent twenty years in communications, working at various times as a political speech writer, a writer-director of television commercials, a copywriter for several advertising agencies, and owner of his own small agency. He has been a full-time fiction writer for almost a quarter century, working in suspense (his favorite genre) and Westerns, with a handful of horror short stories and novels. His fiction reflects his primary influences: Richard Matheson, Robert Bloch, and Cornell Woolrich. Among his best-known books are *The Autumn Dead* (mystery), *Cage of Night* (horror), and *Wolf Moon* (Western). He also collaborated with Dean Koontz on *City of Night*, the second novel in Koontz's modern "Frankenstein" series. He is a winner of the International Horror Guild Award, the Anthony, the Shamus, and the Spur. He has also published six collections of his short fiction, and has contributed to a wide variety of publications, including *The New York Times, Redbook, Penthouse, Ellery Queen's Mystery Magazine, The Magazine of Fantasy & Science Fiction, Poetry Today*, and *Interzone*. With Martin H. Greenberg, he has edited more than twenty anthologies.

Charles L. Grant (1942–2006) won three World Fantasy Awards, two Nebula Awards, and a Life Achievement Award from the British Fantasy Society, and was named a Grand Master of Horror, all for his contributions to the genres of horror and dark fantasy as both writer and editor. Editor of the award-winning Shadows anthology series and of the shared-world anthology series that began with *Greystone Bay*, he wrote several bestselling novels, including *The X-Files: Whirlwind, The X-Files: Goblins*, and *The Pet*. Other novels include *Jackals, Raven, The Nestling*, and volumes in the "Millennium Quartet," which begins with *Symphony*. Under various pseudonyms, including Timothy Boggs, Lionel Fenn, and Geoffrey Marsh, Grant also wrote humorous fantasy, action-adventure, and occasionally science fiction.

Nancy Holder is the *New York Times*-bestselling co-author of the dark fantasy series, *Wicked*, which has been picked up by DreamWorks. She also writes the "Possessions" young-adult horror series. She has received four Bram Stoker awards for her supernatural fiction, and has written many books set in the "Smallville," "Saving Grace," and "Buffy the Vampire Slayer" universes. A true Disney geek, she can frequently be seen in the Twilight Zone Tower of Terror gift shop, purchasing more bath towels for her Disney-themed house. She lives in San Diego with her daughter, Belle, two cats, and Panda, a psychic Cardigan Welsh Corgi.

Tanya Huff lives and writes in rural Ontario with her partner Fiona Patton and nine cats. (One more and they qualify as crazy cat ladies.) She is the author of numerous novels, including those in her "Victoria Nelson" series featuring vampire Henry Fitzroy, and her "Smoke" trilogy featuring wizard apprentice Tony Foster. Her novel *Enchantment Emporium* was published in 2009. Her short fiction has appeared in *Hotter Than Hell* and *Girl's Guide to Guns and Monsters*. When she isn't writing she practices her guitar and complains about the weather.

Larissa Ione, an Air Force veteran, has been a meteorologist, EMT, and professional dog trainer, but she never gave up on her dream of being published. In 2006 her dream came true, and she is now a *USA Today*- and *New York Times*-bestselling author. She is lucky

enough to write full time, which is a blessing, given her husband's very mobile military career. Though she considers the Pacific Northwest to be her home, she has lived all over the world and currently resides in Wisconsin.

Garry Kilworth writes: Born in York, 1941. Mish-mash education as a service brat raised partly in Aden. At 14 years sent to military school and thence served 12 years in the RAF, returning to Aden for the final withdrawal in 1967. Published his first story "Let's Go To Golgotha" in 1974 in the Sunday *Times*. Since then 80 novels and collections of short stories have followed in several genres: science fiction, fantasy, general fiction, young-adults' books and historical fiction. Latest young-adults' work is an sf novel *The Hundred-Towered City*. Latest novel is an historical war novel, *Kiwi Wars*, set in 1860's New Zealand. Latest story, a dark fantasy entitled "La Belle Dame Sans Grace" published in the British Fantasy Society's anthology.

Norman Partridge has written in the horror, suspense, and fantastic genres—"sometimes all in one story" says his friend, Joe Lansdale. Partridge's novels include the Jack Baddalach mysteries *Saguaro Riptide* and *The Ten-Ounce Siesta*. His novel *Lesser Demons* was published to rave reviews. Partridge's compact, thrill-a-minute style has been praised by Stephen King and Peter Straub, and his collections and stories have received both the Bram Stoker and IHG awards. A complete bibliography, free fiction and commentary, and news about upcoming projects can be found at *http://www.NormanPartridge.com*.

Anne Rice is known for weaving the visible and supernatural worlds together in epic stories that both entertain and challenge readers. Her books are rich tapestries of history, belief, philosophy, religion, and compelling characters that examine and extend our physical world beyond the limits we perceive. Rice's life experiences and intellectual inquisitiveness provide her with constant inspiration for her work. She wrote *Interview with the Vampire* in 1973 while living in Berkeley, California. The novel was published in 1976. She has written more than twenty-eight novels since. *Interview with the Vampire* was made into a motion picture, based on her screenplay, directed by Neil Jordan, and starring Brad Pitt, Kirsten Dunst, and Tom Cruise. Her novel *The Feast of All Saints* was made into a Showtime mini-series, scripted by John Wilder. A Broadway musical, *Lestat*, was also developed in 2004 by Elton John, Bernie Taupin, Linda Woolverton and Rob Roth. After her return to Christianity in 2005, she moved to California and embarked on a new direction in her writing. Rice's recent works include the novel *Christ the Lord, the Road to Cana*, and the spiritual memoir *Called Out of Darkness*. She currently lives and works in California.

Kristine Kathryn Rusch won the *Asimov's Reader's Choice Award*, and the *Ellery Queen Mystery Magazine Reader's Choice Award*. She has been nominated for the Anthony, the Shamus, and the Hugo awards. Her short stories have appeared in *The Best Science Fiction of the Year* and *America's Best Mystery Stories*. Her novel *Diving into the Wreck* is based on her internationally award-winning story of the same name.

Lilith Saintcrow is the author of the "Dante Valentine," "Jill Kismet," and "Strange Angels" series. She currently resides in Vancouver, Washington, with her children, cats, and assorted other strays.

Bradley H. Sinor recently ran into someone whom he hadn't seen for several years. The friend asked if Brad was still writing. Brad's wife, Sue, said "There's still a pulse. So he's still writing." He has written one novel *Highlander: The Eye of Dawn*. His short fiction has appeared in the *Merovingen Nights* series, *Time of the Vampires, On Crusade: More*

Tales of the Knights Templar, Lord of The Fantastic, Horrors: 365 Scary Stories, Merlin, Knight Fantastic, Such a Pretty Face, Single White Vampire Seeks Same, Gateways, All Hell Breaking Loose and *The Magic Shop*.

Susan Sizemore, the *USA Today*-bestselling author, writes epic and urban fantasy novels and fantasy short stories, as well as paranormal and historical romance. She lives in the Midwest, knits, collects art glass, and is a fanatical basketball fan. She can be reached at *http://www.susansizemore.com*.

Dean Wesley Smith has been an editor and publisher, and is the bestselling author of over eighty books and over a hundred short stories. For his work over the years he has won a World Fantasy Award, a Locus Award, and others award, and he has been nominated for every major award in science fiction and fantasy numerous times. He has handled comedy in two original *Men in Black* novels and suspense and action/adventure in many books, including the novelization of the movie *The Rundown*. Dean has also worked a great deal in the "Star Trek" universe, and still edits an annual anthology for Pocket Books entitled *Star Trek: Strange New Worlds* where he helps new writers and fans join into the fun of writing Star Trek. He has also written young adult novels and books based on comic book characters such as Spider-Man and the hit television show, *Smallville*. With his wife, Kristine Kathryn Rusch, he wrote the novelization of the first hit X-*Men* movie. He lives and works in the Pacific Northwest.

Elaine Viets writes two national bestselling mystery series. *Publishers Weekly* called her "Dead-End Job" series "wry social commentary." In book nine, *Half-Price Homicide*, Helen Hawthorne works at a designer consignment shop in south Florida. Her "Josie Marcus, Mystery Shopper" series is set in Elaine's hometown, St. Louis. Elaine has won the Agatha Award and Anthony Award, as well as the Lefty for the funniest mystery novel in 2008. Recent stories by her appeared in the MWA anthology *Crimes by Moonlight*, edited by Charlaine Harris.

ABOUT THE EDITORS

Rosalind M Greenberg is the President of Tekno Books, the world's leading book packager of commercial fiction, where she is in charge of the women's fiction and mystery lines for Five Star Publishing. She has had her own fiction published in *The Twilight Zone Magazine* and *The Magazine of Fantasy and Science Fiction*, and has co-edited eight anthologies of mystery, fantasy, and supernatural horror.

Martin H. Greenberg is the CEP of Tekno Books and its predecessor companies, now the largest book developer of commercial fiction and non-fiction in the world, with over 2,300 published books that have been translated into 33 languages. He is the recipient of an unprecedented four Lifetime Achievement Awards in the Science Fiction, Mystery, and Supernatural Horror genres—the Milford Award in Science Fiction, the Solstice Award in Science Fiction, the Bram Stoker Award in Horror, and the Ellery Queen Award in Mystery—the only person in publishing history to have received all four awards.

COPYRIGHTS